The Passion War

He had wrapped his arms about her, there was no escape. His mouth drank from hers, he rocked her in his arms, and pressed her closer to himself. She could feel the hard masculinity of his thighs, pressing to her soft rounded hips. Only their clothing kept him from taking her. His face grew more flushed, his black eyes blazed when he drew back a little from her, and gazed down into her dazed face.

"I want you," he said.

He did not say he loved her. He wanted her. She knew that! He had wanted her before, and had come very close to taking her.

"Well, you cannot have me!" she cried out.

Books by
Janet Louise Roberts

Golden Lotus
Silver Jasmine
Flamenco Rose
Forget-Me-Not
Scarlet Poppies

Published by
WARNER BOOKS

Janet Louise Roberts

SCARLET POPPIES

WARNER BOOKS

A Warner Communications Company

WARNER BOOKS EDITION

Copyright © 1983 by Janet Louise Roberts, Inc.
All rights reserved.

Cover art by Elaine Duillo

Warner Books, Inc.,
666 Fifth Avenue,
New York, N.Y. 10103

 A Warner Communications Company

Printed in the United States of America

First Printing: April, 1983

10 9 8 7 6 5 4 3 2 1

Chapter One

Iris Poppea Patakos draped the gold silk fabric carefully over the wooden model. If she set it so, it would fall in shimmering lines to the sandaled feet. She sat back on her heels, and surveyed the hem critically. What a marvelously soft fabric, how she loved the feel of it on her small, clever hands.

She had enjoyed the feel of fabrics since her earliest years, when she had painstakingly made little clothes for her first dolls. She enjoyed the crisp feel of linen, the rough nub of terrycloth, the sensuousness of satin, the kitten-fur of velvets, the warmth of wool.

She ran her hand slowly through the shimmering gold of the silk fabric. This did not look good enough. It was not the right shape. She sighed, stood up, and removed the fabric from the model, and began again.

Iris had a real flair for shapes and forms. By high school she had been making clothes for girls in the orphanage attached to the convent school where she was a live-in pupil. She made her own clothes, and clothes for many others, and the nuns had delightedly encouraged her talents.

After high school, she had gone two years to a fashion design school, then made the plunge to New York City— gaudy, vital, frightening, marvelous. Iris took a pin, and set it precisely in the fold, with care not to mar the fabric. She pinned another fold, and it began to come into shape. She worked rapidly now, the shape in her mind, and soon the folds hung beautifully from a simple bodice.

She stood back and looked at it from all sides, moving about it slowly on her stockinged feet. Her toes dug into the thick carpets. She loved working here. The gray carpets, silvery walls, the silence, were all conducive to inspiration. Against the quiet, the Egorova designs shone all the more.

"Iris, my child!"

Iris started at the voice, coming out of her absorption, and turned about to see her mentor, Nadia Egorova.

"Very nice," Nadia approved critically, gazing up and down the wooden model and gown. "Yes, yes. Work on it again tomorrow. I think a little more work on the skirt, yes?"

"Yes, Madame," said Iris, and unpinned the fabric carefully, to deliver it into the arms of one of the gray-clad maids who always seemed to appear just as they were wanted. Nadia had some half-dozen helpers in her studio, all silent, efficient, skilled at needlework, and devoted to the woman.

"Come into my office for a time, if you will, please," said Madame Egorova, and led the way up the low winding stairs to her attractive office on the mezzanine of the House of Nadia.

Iris followed obediently, admiring the trim tiny figure of the Russian-born fashion designer. She felt at her five feet three that she towered over Nadia, who was a birdlike slim four feet eleven. All of their tall models towered over them both.

The large office was a clue to the character of Nadia. A huge desk of rosewood had pride of place in the center of the large room. On the walls were sketches of her work, framed in gold. In one corner was an incongruous touch—a prayer stool of the seventeenth century, facing a languid Madonna in an icon, the large black eyes looking steadily at the viewer.

Chairs, small tables, stands, workbenches were all about the room, usually covered with swathes of cloth and sketches of various works in progress. Nadia cleared a chair near her desk by the simple method of sweeping all to the floor. Iris imitated her, and both sat down.

Nadia folded her long hands on the small desk. The rosewood table was for work. The desk was for thinking. She eyed Iris with a sort of benign heavy-lidded "Russian look," as Iris described it to her sister. She could seem to look right straight through you.

"My child!" she said. "You have been with me almost two years now."

"Two years in June," said Iris precisely. "I came in June, and this is April. Two wonderful years, Madame."

Nadia smiled on her, this was what she liked to hear. It was also the truth, and both knew it.

Iris was of the Greek Orthodox faith, and Nadia was of Russian Orthodox. The bond between them had grown from the first meeting. Their faith, their standards, their ideals, and most of all their pleasure in the work of designing fashions from beautiful fabrics—all had brought them close together.

"I am most pleased with you," said Madame Egorova. "I knew from early on that you had the fine talent that I looked for in a designer. But one must see first if you can work, and work hard, and that you have done. When genius is allied with hard work, it cannot lose, eh?"

"Oh, Madame!"

Iris breathed in half-protest and half-pleasure. The nuns had taught her not to accept flattery, to be wary of praise, to be humble and meek. But these words were so sweet!

"It is true, genius," said Nadia, and patted Iris's hand quickly, then withdrew it. She knew Iris did not like to be touched. The girl was sensitive and her upbringing was not what Nadia would have wished for a girl she cared about. To be discarded like a rag! When the girl was pure silk! "The nuns raised you well," she continued, with an absent half-frown. "The virtues of hard work and discipline are well instilled in you. Not like some of these girls today!" and she sniffed significantly. All they think about is being done with work and off to meet the lover-of-the-day!"

"Yes, Madame." Iris studied her small, clever hands. Her thoughts had flown to her half-sister, Charmian. She had not been raised by nuns; she was flighty, loved fun and her men friends. But she did work hard at the one job she adored, that of being a model. And her ambitions to be an actress kept her on track.

"However! You are not like them! You work hard! You are not afraid to try one idea and another! God has given you brains! God has given you talent! You should be grateful to God!"

Nadia paused to glare at Iris with her burning dark melancholy Russian eyes.

"I am grateful to God, I thank Him every day for my talent, and my good life."

"Hum. Hum! Well."

Sometimes Nadia, with her great oval eyes, her black hair in a severe style, her long hands, reminded Iris of the icon in the corner. Those great dark eyes with the thick black eyebrows, the black silky hair drawn back and into a coronet about her neat head, all could have been fit into a golden and silver frame and set with a candle to flare against her dark, intense face.

"So! You have worked for me almost two years, and you have learned quickly. I shall trust you! I wish you to take the next three months to make a line of your own! Eh? Design dresses, coats to match, jackets, suits. If you do well, and we can use them, you shall become my assistant! We shall make them up for the autumn lines!"

Nadia leaned back in her chair and beamed fondly on her stunned pupil.

"A line—of my own? Oh—Madame—oh—" It was her dream, but she had thought it would take years! And now Madame handed it to her grandly. In three months—a whole line! Her own dresses, gowns, suits . . .

"You will do it, eh?"

"Oh, yes, yes, I will work hard—"

"I know it," said Madame complacently. "But, more, you will stretch yourself. You will invent, you will lie awake to think! You will go to the museums, walk in parks, search for ideas—have you traveled?"

"No, Madame." Charmian had traveled, and Iris had envied her that, and prayed over her envy. Jealousy was such a sin! But Charmian had traveled in Mexico, in the Caribbean, in Europe, in the Orient—

"Ah, well. Someday I will take you to Paris, to the fashion shows. And to the gardens, such gardens! The French know gardens! And to the galleries, and to the fashion houses, of course. But—enough. You will work hard. You will sketch, and I will study your sketches, and you will think of a line. You know that a line must be built around one idea, it must be unified. You will think of some idea, and build your dresses and suits about that."

Iris had hundreds of sketches in her portfolios, but none of one unified idea. She nodded her neat head numbly.

"To become a fashion designer is a marvelous responsibility! One must not only know fabrics, designs, and be original! One must be a public relations person! After you become fashion conscious, dear Iris, and the first of your designs sell, then you must learn to promote fashion! You must forget to be shy! You must cater to publicity! You must be seen in great places, you must be in the media news! Design for yourself also, and always be in the height of fashion! We shall think of a style for you! Mine is the Russian style, as you know. For you, Iris—hum—we must think! To make the best of your tiny figure, your blue-black hair, your big blue eyes—that suit is nice, but not chic!''

Iris blanched. She wore today a suit of her own making, with a skirt of blue-and-white-checked wool, a simple pull-over of white, and a jacket of plain blue wool with an edging of blue and white braid. She had thought it quite nice.

"Perhaps gypsy outfits—with your hair long and loose—wild—we might see a hair stylist—that hair is prim with your coronet—it is for an old woman like me!''

Iris said automatically, "You are not old, Madame,'' as her own hand went to her coronet. "This keeps it out of my way while I work,'' she apologized, even as she thought—wild—gypsy—oh, no!

"Yes, you must be chic. Outstanding. Someone one notices at once. Well, we have three months to do this!'' added Madame cheerfully. "But as a fashion designer, you must be in the public eye and someone to be grabbing the headlines, eh? We shall see about parties—I have friends who will arrange some—they shall make the papers in some way—I must think about this!''

When Iris finally staggered from her presence, she felt dazed. She loved to make and create beautiful things, lovely dresses, sleek suits, marvelous coats. But for her to be on display—to court publicity—to look wild and eccentric—oh, heavens! Could she do it? She must—if she was to become famous.

But her first priority, she thought on the bus going home, her very first thoughts must be to create a line. And nothing else would matter if she could not accomplish that! Her head whirling with thoughts, she almost missed her stop.

She clutched her large pocketbook and the oversize sketch pad that accompanied her everywhere, as she fought her way through the crowd and dropped out on to the sidewalk with a gulp of relief. Sometimes she knew that her small size was a drawback. Charmian managed so well, she was five feet eight! And everyone stared at her and smiled, and helped her! But Iris got lost in crowds and got pushed about and buried behind big men and shoving plump women. It was always a relief to be headed for the quiet street of the apartment building on the East Side.

One block, and there was the huge old building. Many of the fine mansions of the nineteenth century and early twentieth had been turned into apartment buildings. When Iris had first come to New York, she had taken a single "efficiency" apartment, which meant a bed in one corner and a stove in the other.

When Charmian had left home rebelliously and fled to New York to pursue her ambitious dreams, their father had purchased a huge apartment and insisted the girls live together. Iris could keep an eye on Charmian, he had said. Iris's mouth twisted wryly as she remembered. Little Iris, looking after tall determined Charmian! But the apartment was marvelous, she did like that.

With six rooms on the upper floor of a mansion, they had room to spread out and not disturb each other. And the rooms were huge, lovely, with high ceilings and a plaster molding of cherubs and roses.

Her pocketbook under one arm and her large sketch pad

under the other, she fumbled for the heavy bunch of keys. Then she saw the man leaning against the wall near the door. As she glanced up, startled, he moved and came toward her.

Iris's eyes grew wide. Mugger? No. Too respectable. Tall, about six feet tall, with black piercing eyes, black eyebrows drawn together in a frown, black curly hair, dark-tanned skin, a gray silk suit with a darker shiny gray tie—he looked expensive, she thought. And now she realized there was an elaborate car at the curb, with a chauffeur sitting in the front seat—and the car was a silver Rolls-Royce. Charmian could have told her the year and model.

"Miss Patakos?" His voice was deep and gravely dark, a sort of growly masculine voice, British-clipped with a slight accent of some sort.

"Yes."

"I am Gregorios Venizelos. My cousin is Alex Venizelos— you know him well."

Her mind searched, found the clue. Alex had dated Charmian very heavily for several months, before disappearing by Christmastime. Charmian had complained, he had gone without giving her the expensive gift she had anticipated.

"Oh, yes, Alex, he—"

The man clipped her off, as though impatient of anyone else doing the talking. "I must speak to you—it is urgent."

Charmian should be home soon, it was after six. Iris nodded, inserted the key, and started to enter. The man came up behind her, pushed open the door, took the key, and padded after her to the stairs.

"No elevator?" he asked.

"No, the house is old, and the tenants prefer—"

"Good exercise," he said, following her closely up the marble stairs to the second-floor landing. She took the keys from him firmly, and opened the lovely door to their apartment.

He followed her inside, and she felt the hallway was not

large enough. His look seemed to take in everything, the rosewood hall table with the blue porcelain vase of pussy willows and yellow jonquils, the rich blue and rose carpet on the floor, the gracious arch to the living room.

"If you will be seated, my—"

"I must tell you about Alex," he insisted, and before she knew what he was doing he had taken her pocketbook and sketch pad from her, set them down on a table, and pushed her to a chair. "My time is limited. I have waited two hours for you!"

She opened her mouth to say, "I am not—" She was going to say she was not Charmian, he might as well keep his story for her sister, but again he interrupted.

"A housewife, I know," he said sardonically, and gave her a dark knowing look that went from her head to her low-heeled black shoes. "You are a model, very fashionable, very expensive to entertain! Have you stopped dyeing your hair?"

"I do not—"

"Well, that is better," he said, and sat down opposite her in the big armchair she had especially chosen for when the relatives came. Big Bill Roswell headed automatically for that chair on his visits to New York. So did Hilarion Patakos, her father, the few times he had come. Gregorios Venizelos settled happily into the leather arms.

"I must tell you," said Iris firmly, "that I am not—"

He waved his big tanned hand impatiently. "Will you listen to me?" he scowled. "I don't have much time. We must go to Greece tomorrow afternoon!"

She opened her mouth to explain again; he sighed like a gusty north wind.

"No, not a word!" he ordered. "Listen, you had an affair with Alex. Well, these are modern times, I don't condemn!" His glance slid over her again, insultingly this time. "I admire his taste," he said. "But Alex needs you now. You

15

must drop everything and come. I promised him I would bring you at once.''

Iris, a young virgin raised by nuns in a Roman Catholic convent, faithful to her Greek Orthodox faith, sat and burned with rage. His insults, his look over her, the way he refused to let her speak! Well, let him tell his story twice over when Charmian came! She folded her hands in her lap, and bent her head regally.

''You may speak,'' she said, sounding like her mother superior.

He gave her a sharp look, then nodded. ''Alex has been— hurt,'' he said.

She started. ''An accident?''

''No. But he has been injured. Seriously. He is calling for you. He was hurt just before Christmas—''

She stared. Christmas was months ago—it was April—

''He has been in a hospital in Athens. Finally his body has mended somewhat, though he is still in a wheelchair. We have taken him to our family villa on an island near Greece— the air is good, he is beginning to heal. But he broods—it is not good—''

''He has a good nurse?'' Charmian would have no patience for that, she shuddered at the thought of hospitals and sickness. She was herself healthy as a horse, so she said, and sick people usually brought it on themselves.

''He did, but she is now dismissed, no longer needed.'' Gregorios stood up and began to prowl the room restlessly, as though he hated to sit still. He was like a black panther prowling in a forest, she thought, admiring the fit of his gray suit, the sleek strength of his lean handsome body, the athletic stretch of his legs, the power in his shoulders. He was just about six feet tall, with wide shoulders, narrowing to slim waist and lean thighs. He turned, in time to see her assessing look, and gave her a narrow-eyed knowing smile.

She felt heat rise in her cheeks, and looked away from him hastily. She avoided men, she did not know how to act around men. Charmian had tried to fix her up with dates, and Charmian's men friends were often interested in shy little Iris. But she firmly refused their plans, hated to be pawed, and was most comfortable when she was alone in her rooms.

Her father had married three times; she had no belief in a man's faithfulness. At five, she had been placed in the convent; since then she had been raised by women. All her friends were girls. No one was close, she did not permit it. One got hurt when one let people come close. A talent that she had would lead to a fine, satisfying career—that was all Iris wanted. She sketched, painted, designed clothes, worked hard. In her spare time she watched some television, went to a few movies and more concerts and ballet. She adored ballet.

Gregorios had turned away again, as though uninterested. He paused to stare at the painting over the white marble mantel, a scene of a garden in France, that Bill Roswell had given them. He picked up a small statuette of a Chinese figure from the mantel, examined the porcelain carefully, then replaced it.

"Alex's problem is not his spine, that is healing," said his cousin, and his voice took on a rasp. "Alex—is blind." He whirled about abruptly and stared down at her, as though to judge her reaction.

"'Blind'!" gasped Iris, her hands flying to her mouth. "Blind? Oh—poor, poor Alex!"

She thought of him then, the memory coming back of a bright-eyed laughing Greek, slim-hipped and merry, with sparkling black eyes—

"Blind!" she whispered, and shook her head. "Oh, he cannot be—is it—lasting?"

"We hope to God that it will clear—there is some hope," said Greg, seeming satisfied with her reaction. Tears had come to her eyes, she reached for her pocketbook, found a handkerchief, and wiped her eyes. "But for now, Alex does not believe it. He is blind, he can see nothing—and he is in despair. The days drag—he is accustomed to sports, skiing, swimming, skydiving—he can do nothing."

"He must feel so miserable," said Iris, shaking her head again. "To be so vigorous, so active and now—nothing. How long—"

'No one knows. I want you to come to Greece with me tomorrow—we will fly overnight. I will pick you up about five, take you out to the airport with me. Pack all you want, there is plenty of room for your fripperies. Alex said you have a silver dress that makes you look like a goddess—" Gregorios gave her a puzzled look, then shrugged as though there was no accounting for tastes.

Iris knew the silver dress, it was one of the first gowns she had made for Charmian, and her sister raved about it. Charmian had naturally light brown hair, almost blond. As soon as she came to New York, she had experimented with hair coloring, and had finally settled on a stunning ash blond, almost silver. Iris had made the gown to set off her hair.

She was tired of trying to explain to this man that she was not Charmian, she was not a model, she did not have silver hair, she had not indulged in an affair with Alex. In fact, she firmly refused to think about Charmian and her affairs with the many men who swarmed about her. Charmian took pills, she worried about nothing, she enjoyed all the attentions she felt were due her. Iris tried to believe it was not her business what her sister did. But she did feel resentful at being saddled with her sister's reputation!

"Well, that settles it. I will pick you up about five, be ready on time, if you please! I cannot wait about, we have to set off on the hour of seven. You can dine on the plane—we will be in Athens by morning—"

Iris was musing about being in Athens by morning. Oh, to see the glories of Athens at sunrise, the Parthenon with the sunshine on it, the glorious glowing white buildings and those of golden marble. And the cypress trees, dark and flamelike against the blue sky, as in the pictures.

"Did you hear me?" he barked, and she jumped.

"Actually, I think you should know—"

"I know about your job!" he snarled. "It does not count, not against a man's life! ALEX IS EATEN AWAY—do you understand me? He cannot exist like this! He needs you, yes, you! He loves you, he wants you there—"

Charmian would not go, thought Iris. She had her work, her modeling engagements. Or would she? If she loved Alex enough, if that love had lasted—

She was musing about that, as Gregorios glared at her, when both heard the click of heels on the marble steps. Then a key was stuck in the lock, turned, and the door came open.

Iris jumped up and went to the hallway, as Gregorios snarled, "A live-in lover, I suppose? Well, he can just take himself away!"

In the hallway, Charmian was standing at the gilt-framed mirror, her silver hair windblown becomingly against her scarlet mandarin coat collar. Her hand flashed with a diamond and a sapphire Hilarion had given his daughter. She handed Iris her portfolio of model poses, her scarlet handbag, and the little mock leopard cap from the silver hair.

"Oh, darling, I am beaten! And I have such an important date tonight," she moaned. "What a shit of a day! A bastard photographer did a thousand poses of me tripping down the stairs until I could have kicked him—"

"Charmian, we have a guest," said Iris, urging her to the living room. She grinned a little impishly, as she made a dramatic gesture, a little copy of one of Charmian's, as the tall model entered the large room, and stared at the big Greek man waiting. "May I introduce Charmian Angelina Patakos, known as Charmian Angel? Charmian, this is Gregorios Venizelos."

She knew there could not be a greater contrast. Her sister was slim, five feet eight, her ash silver hair billowing about her stunning face, the large blue eyes set off with skillful blue makeup. And Iris, small, in the non-chic blue suit, weary and pallid and hair dark as a blackbird's wing—Gregorios had that stunned shaken look on his face that many men had on encountering Charmian for the first time.

Charmian loved it. She glided forward on her high heels, slipped her slim hand into the big hand of the Greek, and murmured, "Darling, what an intro! I love it, I love it. And what a pleasant surprise waiting for me—Gregorios—"

Her long lashes flirted at him. She was heavily made up for her sessions today. She looked everything that Iris was not, stunning, sensational, the way men loved it.

And the way she looked up at Gregorios told Iris that she liked what she saw—very much. And he was staring at her, unable to look away.

Gregorios was looking over Charmian from her head to her heels, in that sensual appraising look that men had when they gazed at her beautiful sister. A look of appreciation that grew into desire and hunger. Yes, he was a man who enjoyed beautiful women! He probably had his full share of them also, with his handsome looks, his money, his power.

Chapter Two

Iris stood aside, forgotten, she was quite sure. And she wondered why she felt a strong feeling of disappointment. The big male had stared at her up and down, she had resented that. Yet when his attention turned fully to Charmian, she felt—what? Outraged. Angry. Disappointed. Jealous.

Oh, well. She had expected it, anticipated it. It always happened. When Charmian came to the House of Nadia to meet her for an occasional dinner, all traffic stopped. She looked like a New York angel, smooth, silvery, so lovely, yet so knowing and smart. People could not help staring, heads turned, men stopped in their tracks, women envied.

Gregorios said, still holding the slim hand, "You are Miss Patakos? Charmian Patakos?"

He shot an accusing look at Iris, who murmured sweetly, "You did not allow me to get in a word. I am Iris."

He did not like that. He was embarrassed, in the wrong.

He gave her an angry black-eyebrowed stare, then looked back at Charmian. "You are—sisters? Cousins?"

"Half-sisters," said Charmian, with her slow model smile, that started in her eyes and went to her wide red mouth. "We each resemble our mothers. Only our voices are alike."

"Ah—yes, I noticed that. Low, melodic voices, womanly, sweet," said the man, and he sounded sardonic.

Charmian gave him a sharp look. She was no fool, and she had been manipulating men all her life. "Do sit down again. Did you come to see me?" She settled herself in the blue chair automatically—the blue silk set off her coloring.

Iris sat down in her chair, happy now to be an onlooker. Let the man flash his commands at her sister, and see what happened!

Gregorios Venizelos sat down again in the big brown leather chair, his arms going to the sides, his big hands folding over the leather, smoothing it. Iris watched those big hands in fascination. The nails were neatly kept, buffed. He wore a single signet ring on his left hand, no jewels. He would save them to hang on the neck and on the arms of his woman, though she did not know how she knew that. Diamonds—no; sapphires, and emeralds, and rubies—all the color and fire of the jewel colors . . .

He was looking at Iris again, and she blushed; she felt the heat rising in her cheeks. Charmian was speaking; both turned to listen.

"Your name—Venizelos—oh, you must be related to Alex!"

"Yes, he is my cousin, we are in business together—in hotels." The man had settled back, and was for once listening, instead of barking at Iris. Charmian had that power.

"How is dear Alex? I am angry with him, he disappeared about Christmas—I do miss him so!"

"He was injured, and lies seriously hurt—"

Charmian lost her smile, she looked alarmed. "No! Oh, no, not darling Alex! What happened?"

The black eyebrows drew quite together, in an alarming frown, his mouth seemed to snarl. Iris watched, fascinated. "He was struck on the head, knifed also."

Both girls gasped.

"Mugged?" asked Charmian. "In New York?"

"No, it was in Athens. I had sent for him, on business. Well—more of that another time. As I told your sister, Alex is now blind."

He watched, in a sort of cruel intensity, for Charmian's reaction. He was not disappointed. A slow tear gathered in her eye, was joined with another and another.

Iris pulled a paper tissue from the box near her, and handed it silently to her sister. A little dab, the eye makeup was not disturbed. "Oh, God," said Charmian. "How horrible! Alex— blinded! Oh, my God, that is awful!" She was biting her full red lips.

"Yes, awful—for him and for those around him," said Gregorios dryly. "He is calling for you—" He gave Iris a glance of dislike, recalling he had said those words to her. She met his look blandly, delighting in his discomfort. He hated to be wrong! "He wants you to come to him. I promised to bring you."

A narrowed glance, the tears dried. Charmian sat still, her fingers clenched about the tissue. "How—sweet—" she said slowly. "But poor, darling Alex—blinded—"

Iris said swiftly, "Mr. Venizelos thinks there is some hope it is not permanent."

Mr. Venizelos gave Iris another look from those black eyes that said he resented her interference. Iris got up. "I'll see to supper. Charmian, you said you had a date—"

"Oh, yes, but only yogurt for me, darling! Sammie is picking me up at seven-thirty—we're going to an opening, and the cast party afterward. The director is Fred Queen—I adore his work—the chance to meet him is—"

Gregorios interrupted her rapture. "The plane ride is long. Do you think you should be out late tonight? You will need your sleep!"

"'Plane ride'? Oh, to Athens? No, I cannot go," said Charmian simply. "I have modeling engagements for months ahead. I shall have to decline. But do give Alex my love!"

The strong mouth folded into hard lines. "You are going," he said sharply. "No career in—modeling—can match the need to give comfort to a man who has suffered as Alex has—"

"You said this happened at Christmas?" said Charmian. "And this is mid-April. It took him long enough to decide he could not live without me!"

Gregorios nodded slowly. "He was unconscious much of the time. And he was frantic about the blindness. But you must come now, he needs you."

Iris had been standing, a fascinated observer of the sharp battle of wills. She thought she knew who would win, Charmian was very experienced. But let them fight it out; she murmured something and went out to the kitchen.

As she chopped herbs and broke up the Bibb lettuce, she was smiling to herself. Mr. Venizelos was meeting his match! Charmian thought first and foremost of herself, and nobody would be allowed to interfere with her career, which was going so well. She wrapped men around her fingers, her father and stepfather, and every man she encountered, with the exception of an occasional brute of a photographer about whom Charmian would then complain bitterly.

She shook the bottle of her special dressing, and opened the oven door to peer at the bubbling *moussaká*, thankful for the timer that started the oven in her absence. She had made up several casseroles of the favorite dish last week, and had frozen them. Should she ask the big Greek man to stay, and continue the argument over dinner? It was past seven. She wondered how long they would quarrel.

There were some *dolmáthes* in the refrigerator: everybody liked her rice and meat in vine leaves. Cucumber slices, some green beans cooked in bacon and onion—she sighed. Hospitality was a fearsome thing.

She went back to the living room, paused in the doorway. There was silence, the two were glaring at each other. Charmian had red spots like coins in her cheeks, and it was not makeup.

"Mr. Venizelos, may I invite you to dinner? It is just *moussaká* and salad—and some wine—"

He frowned, then lifted his head and sniffed. An unmistakable look came on his face, the man in hunger. "*Moussaká?*" he asked. "You can cook?"

"Oh, Iris is a marvelous cook," said Charmian hastily. "And Bill brings us the best wine every time he comes—do stay and eat with Iris. I'll just have a bite, and run. I must not be late tonight!" And she rose swiftly, glad to end the argument.

"Who is Bill?" asked Mr. Venizelos, rising also, glancing to Iris.

Charmian replied, gathering up her red handbag and her precious portfolio. "He is my stepfather, Bill Roswell. In oil tankers, in Boston. Whenever he comes to New York City, he stops off to visit us, and brings us wine. He is a darling, really."

"A very nice man," echoed Iris. Bill had been very sweet to her, once he saw the situation there. He came often, bringing wines, advice, helping her buy things for the apartment, arranging furniture, making up for the coldness of his wife, Shelley, the mother of Charmian. "But, Charmian, do

eat some food with us. You cannot eat yogurt every meal of
the day! It is not healthy, you need minerals and vitamins—''

"I eat them by the pound, darling!" sighed Charmian.
"And I dare not gain an ounce, Sammie would scream,
really! My agent," she added to the man, smiling. "Now I
must change, really. It takes me half an hour to put on fresh
makeup. Darling Iris, please bring a container of strawberry
yogurt to me in the bedroom?" And she started down the hall
to her room.

"Miss Patakos!" the man yelled after her. "Do be ready
by five tomorrow afternoon! We must leave promptly. You
may take two suitcases!"

Charmian turned about, stared, then gave him her slow
smile. He did not know her, Iris did. "Of course, Mr.
Venizelos," she said sweetly. "I am never late!"

She disappeared in her bedroom, and the door closed
gently.

Iris hesitated. "Would you care—for dinner?" she asked
meekly, hoping he would go away.

He looked down his big long nose at her, and suddenly
smiled a sweet big smile like a boy, and she melted. "May I?
I haven't eaten since breakfast!" he confessed.

"Of course. Come on in the dining room," she said. She
had set the table for three; she seated him at one end, and
brought him the huge wooden bowl of salad and the serving
forks. "Please help yourself."

She whisked away Charmian's place setting, poured water,
took yogurt to Charmian's bedroom, and stuck the container
on the dressing table along with a spoon. Charmian was in
the bath, humming.

A brilliant scarlet dress was laid out, low-necked and
low-backed, and Charmian's diamonds. She meant to stun
them tonight. Iris sighed, and returned to the dining room.
The big man had finished one bowl of salad, and was starting

on another. Iris set the dish of *dolmáthes* before him, then returned to the kitchen. When she returned she had the huge casserole of hot steaming *moussaká* in her padded hands. She set it down near him. He was sniffing and beaming like a boy.

In the kitchen, the wine bottle defeated her. "Mr. Venizelos— would you mind—"

He was in the kitchen in an instant. Charmian was right, men always liked to be asked to help. He took the bottle, the wine bottle cork opener, and dealt with it efficiently. He studied the label. "I do not know this one—but I am not familiar with American wines," he said, not ungraciously, but as one curious.

"This is a New York State wine. Bill says it is very good, and he enjoys it. I hope you will like it."

He took the bottle to the dining room, filled their glasses while she dished up the *moussaká*, his in a generous portion. He sighed with satisfaction, sat down, and dug in eagerly.

She ate hungrily also; they said little, except to pass the salad, the hot French bread and the pats of butter, the *dolmáthes*. She had been in too much of a hurry to serve the meal in courses, and he did not seem to mind.

He ate, drank, sighed, murmured over the salad dressing. "A bottled dressing?—very good."

"No—I make it up myself. Do you like it?" A foolish question, he was on his third helping of salad, picking out the small black ripe olives and popping them in his mouth.

"You made it? You are a good cook. Is the *moussaká* frozen? Where did you get it?"

"I made it," she said patiently. "There is a good Greek grocery only three blocks from here. *Féta* cheese, always fresh—always have lamb—"

"Um—delicious—" He stared at the fast-disappearing

27

moussaká, and she dished up the rest for him. "I thank you. You are most kind. Where did you learn to cook?"

"In the convent. The nuns encouraged us to learn."

"Um. Delicious. You would care for more wine?"

"No more for me, do finish the bottle. The wine is delicate, and does not last long."

He was not reluctant, and the wine disappeared. She went to the kitchen for the coffee, brought it in with small cups for the black thick mixture of Greek coffee, brown West Indian sugar lumps.

"Cream?"

"No, I thank you."

He drank three cups. She apologized that she had no dessert. "Charmian goes crazy if I keep desserts around," she said. "But there is fruit—white grapes?"

"If you would be so kind—"

He ate all the rest of her grapes. She would have to go to the grocery as soon as possible, but it was satisfying to feed a man with such a big frame and such an appetite. She felt more kindly to him, as one does to someone one has fed.

She left the dishes and accompanied him to the hallway.

"I am sorry I must leave so quickly. Thank you for the excellent dinner. When I return to New York, I hope you will give me the pleasure of taking you out to dinner."

When he smiled, he was so attractive she could feel a little quiver of awareness. "You are most kind," she said politely, having no intention of seeing any more of this big black panther than necessary. Now he was fed and content, his long tail swishing in friendship, but she would not trust him as far as she could throw him, and he was twice her size.

He hesitated at the door. "I should say good-bye for now to your sister."

"She left half an hour ago," said Iris flatly, having heard the stealthy whisper of heels as Charmian had fled.

"Hum. Well. Tomorrow, you will be here?"

"I work."

"Where?"

"At the House of Nadia." He looked a question, and she explained, "It is the fashion house of Nadia Egorova."

"You are a model?" He was looking her up and down again, from her smooth black hair to her dark heeled shoes. She blushed.

"No. Models must be at least five feet seven inches, and I am five feet three. No, I make dresses, suits, coats. And sew and make patterns."

"Oh, I see." He nodded. "You have talent."

"Thank you."

"You will not be here when I come at five, then? Farewell, then, and again thank you for taking pity on a hungry man." The big hand was held out, she could not refuse him, and reluctantly allowed him to swallow up her hand for a moment. His hand was huge, strong, but gentle, lightly squeezing hers.

She took her hand quickly back to herself, he looked a question. She could not explain that she hated to be touched. She said quickly, "May I ask? Is—is your island very beautiful?" It was the first thing that came into her head.

He did not reply conventionally. He said, "The sands are of cream, warm to the body in the mornings. The seas are blue and white waved, cool and pleasant. The rocks loom high over one's head in red crags that have stood from the beginning of time. God's sculpture. And always there is the scent of flowers. The lime, the jasmine, the honeysuckle. And dotted on the fields of wheat are the scarlet poppies like drops of Greek blood shed for our precious freedom."

He spoke in poetry, this hard, tough man. Wide-eyed, she

gazed up at him, unable to speak. He smiled abruptly down into her eyes, touched her cheek lightly with his fingers, and said, in Greek, "Farewell, eyes of iris. Until we meet again." And he went out the door, and was gone.

Slowly she closed the door after him, and went to do the dishes. Later she curled up in the little sitting room next to her bedroom at the back of the house. The big drawing room was formal, for guests. There was the dining room, and the kitchen, her own domain.

Charmian had the big master bedroom, necessary for her closets of clothes. She had the huge bathroom also, for her many experiments in makeup, as well as her baths and soaks for relaxation.

But in the back of the large apartment were Iris's rooms, a lovely bedroom overlooking a small back garden. The bedroom was done in her favorite blues, whites, and yellows. Next to it was a small sitting room, for a maid, but they had none. Iris had taken it over, and furnished it with a comfortable couch and chairs, hassocks, a small worktable for her sketches, a sixteen-inch television, and her stereo player and growing collection of classical records. It was her sanctuary when Charmian entertained in the front room.

She sat with her sketch pad on her lap, curled up on the sofa, and stared blankly into space. Why could she not see visions of lovely unusual garments? All she could see on the blank wall where one day she would hang a new painting was the face of a dark tough man who had an unusually gentle smile, a smile that enticed where his frown repelled.

She got no work done that night. Sometime in the early morning, she heard Charmian come in, the soft murmur of voices, a door closing. She turned over and went back to sleep.

In the morning, she rose early, bathed, and dressed in her scarlet suit. She felt like a more daring outfit today. Nadia's words about her blue suit had stung. But was this one more chic? She eyed it dubiously: the bright color, the peplum pert at her slim waist, the fluffs of white lace at her throat. Oh, well, it must do, she had no time to brood. She ate, and then popped her head warily into Charmian's room.

She was relieved to see Charmian was up, clothes scattered about, two suitcases open. She was really going!

"Hello, Charmian, good time last night?"

"Marvelous! Met the great director and he is interested in me!" A cat-satisfied smile, a stretch of the graceful limbs. "Good eats, I made a pig of myself, loads of champagne. Met all the right people!"

"That's great."

"What a dictator Alex's cousin is! How did you get along? Did food soothe the savage beast? Alex calls him his demon cousin, you know!"

"He enjoyed the food," said Iris thoughtfully. "Look, I have to go. Do you want help packing? Shall I come home early to see you off?"

"Don't bother, love, I can manage." A quick sly smile, that wakened all of Iris's doubts. "Poor Alex, to be blind, I am sorry for him."

Iris set off for work in a thoughtful mood. Was she mean to be suspicious? At Nadia's, she told her boss something of the evening. Madame Egorova was interested, listening to all of her story keenly.

"He sounds like a Russian, yes! So dynamic. So tough. Did you like him, eh?"

"The way you like a panther in the zoo, with bars safely between you!"

The dark eyebrows rose, Madame looked alert. "Ah, one of that kind of man, eh? I do like a masculine man. One meets so many wishy-washy ones!"

Iris got down to work, and managed to do a good job of the

gold dress, which pleased her and Nadia. At three, she said diffidently, "You know, I think I had best go home and help Charmian pack. I want to be sure she gets off all right."

"Dear child, you are courageous," said Nadia dryly. "I have a feeling your sister is not so unselfish as to go and look after a blind man! But go, satisfy yourself, but do not let the panther chew you up!"

Iris laughed, and thanked her. She set off with a feeling of unusual excitement, and enjoyed the relatively uncrowded bus on the way home.

To her surprise, the silver Rolls-Royce stood in front of the apartment and Alex's cousin leaned on the door. His brow lightened when she appeared. He straightened, and smiled.

"Ah, you have come!" He took her packages efficiently, she fumbled for her keys. "It is very kind of you. Will she need help packing?"

"Perhaps," she said. "I can at least make coffee."

"It is good of you." He marched up the stairs behind her. There had been no hesitation either time, but today he seemed to own the building as he walked up the stairs. He did take over so easily. He had the keys, he opened the next door, and swung it open. He set down her sketch pad and parcels on the hall table. "When does she come home?"

"Anytime," said Iris, stilling her flutter of unease firmly. "Coffee?"

"Most kind."

His eyes were going over her again, seeming to approve of the scarlet suit, and the lace ruffle at her throat. He was the most noticing man she had ever met.

"I'll have a look in Charmian's room, and see how far she got with her packing," she said, as they finished the coffee.

"Thank you." He stood up and paced the room. "Is there somewhere to phone her?" He shot back his cuff and studied his large flat square gold watch.

"We could call her agency and see where her last appointment was, but only in emergency. They are very busy, and don't like it if relatives call to trace people," she explained.

"It is past four o'clock."

She did not try to answer. She walked down the hall, to Charmian's room, and by the prickle at her neck she knew he followed her. Sure enough, as she stepped into the other girl's bedroom, he was right at her heels. Iris stopped short, and he bumped into her, holding her by the arms firmly from behind. She was intensely aware of his male scent, his warmth at her back.

"Oh—no," she moaned. "I knew it was too good—"

"What?" he barked.

"She had two suitcases out this morning—" The room was neat, unnaturally so. Charmian's room was never so neat. It had been cleaned out in the suitcases: her handbag, the cosmetics from the top of her dressing table, and her jewel box.

Charmian had disappeared. She had funked out. Iris mentally blazed some fury at her sister.

Both saw the white folded note at the same time. Iris reached for it, he was faster and plucked the paper from the small table. He unfolded it, both read it, she looking over his arm as he stood beside her.

"Darling Iris," read Iris aloud. "I cannot possibly go to Greece. Have so many engagements, cannot cancel out. Worth my career! Do explain to Alex's demon cousin! Love, Charmian. P.S. Love to Alex."

Gregorios said something in Greek, violently. Iris flinched.

"Do you speak Greek?"

"Some. But not those words," said Iris firmly. "Oh, I am sorry, Mr. Venizelos."

"She had no intention of coming! She is selfish, coldhearted, a bitch of the first degree, she is a—"

"She is my sister! Please mind your tongue!"

He stared down at her, as she stared right back at him, her cheeks pink, her eyes blazing. "She agreed to come, then backed out—"

"If you will think clearly, Mr. Venizelos, she did not agree to come. You took it for granted that she would do exactly as she was told. She did *not* agree."

He was silent, thinking, she could feel the heat of his fury, though he said not another word for a time. Should she offer him food again? No, there were limits to what food could do.

"This is your sister's room?" he asked then, glancing about. He strode to the long wardrobe, opened the doors, looked over the beautiful gowns, the suits, the fur coats. He shut the doors again, wandered to the dressing table, opened drawers and closed them.

"Yes, and she will not thank you for going through her possessions. If you will go now—"

"No," he said. "Where is your bedroom?"

She stared, but he pushed past her and went out the door. He strode down the hall, found the door to her room, and went inside. What was he going to do? Unable to think clearly, she panted after him, "Now wait one minute—just wait one minute—"

He seemed to take in her room in a comprehensive glance, the blue and white cotton cover on the bed, the pretty white draperies with blue braiding, the desk with the sketch pads and white lamp, the closets—he opened the closet door, found a suitcase and took it down. He reached again into the closet, chose the blue suit, a couple of white blouses—Iris was reacting.

"What do you think you are doing?" she screamed, her voice an octave higher than normal.

"One sister will do as well as another," he said, his mouth tight. "Pack! We leave for the plane in one hour, as I had planned!"

"You are insane! Do you think Alex will be pleased to have *me* instead of Charmian? He will see in a minute—"

"Alex is blind, and your voices are alike!"

"If you think he will be fooled—" Iris's voice died, he was folding her suit neatly and was about to stuff it in her suitcase. She snatched it from him.

"Pack," he said. "One suitcase. Oh, you can take your sketch pads and stuff also. We have no time for more. I mean it, you are going with me. I will not go back empty-handed! I will not be made a fool!"

He was in a cold fury. His eyes blazed black fire, his nostrils were pinched. Iris's heart sank. She would be the lamb of sacrifice for Charmian. She bleated, "But this is wrong—I cannot go—my job—"

"My blind cousin is more important," he said flatly. "Pack, or you will go with no clothes at all. I might enjoy that," he added insolently, looking down her body slowly.

She packed, shaking with fury. He stood over her as she stuffed in a couple of nightgowns, a robe, her underclothes, which he looked at with detached interest, shoes, blouses, another suit with a matching slacks outfit. . . .

Then she got down another small case. "Must you?" he growled.

She paid no attention, her shoulders stiff. She put in her sketch pads, swatches of material she had been working with, her watercolors and oils, her palette box, pencils, pens, a couple of books on fashion design.

"I must call Madame Egorova."

"Make it quick. It is ten until five o'clock," he said, shooting back his cuff once more, to glance at the gold watch.

That reminded her. She put in her small alarm clock, a few cosmetics, a box of tissues, though he growled, "We are not going to the ends of the earth!"

Then he carried the cases to the door while she dialed Madame Egorova at the fashion house.

She explained quickly. Nadia wailed, "You must not go, child! It is madness. You are not your sister, that painted one! I am worried about you, who is this man?"

He was standing over Iris, so he probably heard every word Nadia had said. He took the phone, "Madame Egorova, I am Gregorios Venizelos of the hotel chain. My office in Athens can contact you and confirm who I am. I assure you I will take every care of little Iris."

Iris burned. Just because she was not five feet eight—

"Yes, fine, thank you for your good wishes. She will phone you, I shall see to it. Good-bye." He dropped the phone, picked up the suitcases. "Come along," he said brusquely.

Iris followed him out the door, made sure it was locked, then she wailed, "I have not left a note for Charmian!"

He said something wicked in Greek, the equivalent of letting her stew in her own juices. Then he raced down the stairs and put her suitcases in the front beside the chauffeur. He opened the door at the back, snapped something at the chauffeur, who had no time to get out of the elegant car.

He half shoved Iris in the backseat, and got in beside her before she had time to move over. She felt his heavy warm body pushing at hers.

She felt abused, indignant, half scared, swept away by this impossible Greek.

"You know," she attempted, turning to him as the car slid away from the curb. "I cannot possibly—you must see—"

"Sorry," he said, and picked up the telephone from an enclosure before him. He dialed, as she watched fascinated; she had never seen a telephone in a car before. He spoke on the phone in Greek, so rapidly she could not follow it. He hung up, took a portfolio from the floor of the car, and opened it. His dark brows were frowning. She sank back in the seat, in resignation. He would never hear her now!

They sped out of New York, and to the highways, and the sleek Rolls-Royce made its way through the traffic like a gray bird that did not need to touch the asphalt. Others parted before it, yellow taxis, all color cars, battered ones and smart ones, and curious ones, staring. There were on the highway to Kennedy, she recognized the route.

At the airport, they did not turn in to the usual airport gates. The car made its way across back lanes, and to the place where a beautiful white and blue airplane stood. It was smaller than the other huge jets, but had a distinguished air of its own. With a shock, she realized it was a private executive jet, probably like the one her father owned—Charmian had told her about that.

"Ah, we made good time," muttered her escort, and closed the portfolio. "May we have a good flight," he said cheerfully.

Chapter Three

Iris was escorted up the steps of the executive jet, and Gregorios followed her. Their luggage was next, in the hands of a blue and white uniformed crew.

The interior was more spacious than Iris could have dreamed. There were seats and a couch like a living room, only everything fastened down to the blue and white Greek-patterned carpet.

The steward smiled at Iris, seated her, placed magazines near her, and murmured, "What would you care to drink, madame?"

When she hesitated, he suggested whiskey, or orange juice. She took orange juice gratefully; it came in a chilled bowl of ice; the slim glass had little fingerprint designs, so it was easy to grip.

Mr. Venizelos was talking to the two pilots in the front and Iris caught a glimpse of a formidable panel of instruments. Presently he came back, sat down, and strapped himself in.

The steward strapped Iris in, and sat down in another chair. They taxied out to the runways, got in position and halted. Gregorios was deep in an oversize report that contained drawings of what looked like a hotel.

The steward said to Iris, as Gregorios ignored her, "There are three planes ahead of us, madame."

"Oh." She didn't know what that meant.

They waited. Presently the jets roared again, they moved forward, so smoothly it looked like the scenery moved outside and they were still. They passed incongruous land of weeds and grass, more cement runways, and then with a little jolt they were up in the air, roaring smoothly higher and higher, circling over some blue water with small white boats sailing over it.

They flew into the sunset, a rose and yellow sunset that held Iris enchanted for half an hour. The eastern sky was echoing the sunset in the west, then it faded to purple and deep blue.

Presently they were above a sea of white clouds, and all grew purple black. The steward was moving about. He came back with white wine and plates of hot and cold canapés. Gregorios set aside his report with a sigh, and looked across at Iris.

"Enjoying the flight?" he asked conventionally.

She nodded. She was not. She was sitting there worrying about what would happen when they got to Greece.

He seemed to be thinking the same thing. "You will pretend to be Charmian," he declared. "I will not have Alex disappointed."

"I am sure Alex is not an idiot," said Iris, biting off some of the hot chicken liver wrapped in bacon. It was delicious, especially when washed down with chilled white wine. "He will not be fooled. I am not so tall or shaped the same—"

His eyes moved as he looked her up and down, as she sat

neatly with feet together in the comfortable blue and white chair. "No, you have nice curves, you are not a broomstick," he said with a cheerful grin. "But your voices are alike, he will think you are Charmian." His chin was set; she shook her head with a sigh.

She was fairly sure Charmian had slept with Alex; the affair had been violently passionate while it lasted those three months. Charmian had been out all night with him, and almost lost a modeling job several times because of his attentions. Iris had no intention of keeping up some farce by going to bed with Alex. Besides, he would surely know then she was not Charmian!

She kept her plans to herself, and gave her attention to the plate of bits of lobster, shrimp, and clams, served with breadsticks. Gregorios was eating heartily.

When the steward returned to take their plates, Gregorios remembered his manners. "This is Myron—Miss Patakos, Myron. She will be accompanying me to Greece, to stay with my mother."

The smartly attired steward bowed low. "Happy to meet you," he muttered.

"The message was sent to Athens airport, about the plane to be ready?" asked his boss.

"Yes, sir. All should be ready by morning."

"Miss Patakos will have the white room, I'll have my usual."

Iris looked her question. The steward took her back into the next compartment, where she was amazed to find a tiny neat bedroom, all in white, a narrow but long bed, a compartment for her clothes, a table with a raised rim for her bag and cosmetics.

She was glad to freshen up; she unpacked a suit for morning, and breathed a grateful sigh for the thought of sleeping in a bed rather than sitting up all night, as Charmian told her usually happened. The trip to Europe and the Orient was made painful, Charmian had said, by the long airplane rides sitting up, where her ankles got swollen, and she never really rested. But this was marvelous, to have a little bed to sleep in while the airplane soared on through the skies.

She returned as the steward was bringing the main course. She sat down, to enjoy the tender medallions of veal in a rich brown wine sauce, small new potatoes, green peas and mushrooms. She refused any pastry, content with a fruit compote of fresh pineapple, grapes, strawberries, and pears.

She sipped her hot coffee as Gregorios leaned back with a sigh. He did not light up any cigar or pipe, she was grateful. Come to think of it, he did not reek of tobacco smoke.

"You do not smoke?" she ventured.

He smiled at her. "No; you do not either. Good. One must have disrespect for one's body to do that. I intend to live a long time. A healthy mind in a healthy body, eh?"

She nodded. The steward removed the remains of the trays, brought steaming fresh coffee, and hovered.

"Anything else, Iris?" said Gregorios in a friendly tone. "Wine? A liqueur? Bring a coffee liqueur," he said to Myron without waiting for Iris's reply.

She found it delicious, thick and sweet, with a blaze that sent heat through her, and made her a little sleepy and comfortable.

"Good, eh?" said Gregorios, watching her. "I wish you to call me Greg," he added unexpectedly. She blinked. "When we reach home, it will be necessary."

She had her own plans, she did not bother to reply.

"You will have to play your part well," he added, watching her face. "Are you a good actress?"

"No," she said serenely. "I am just Iris. You are thinking of Charmian. We are quite different."

"But you are sisters. You were raised together?"

"No," she said.

42

He frowned at her brief reply. Just then the pilot came back to report on their altitude, their progress, how soon they would land in Athens in the morning. As the men talked, Iris picked up a magazine, and buried herself in it. She did not want to answer Greg's questions! He had to know everything, but he had no right snooping around in her mind.

She had found a new *Vogue* in the pile, and studied the pictures carefully, reading some of the articles. There was also a new *Elégance*, which she saw sometimes at Madame Egorova's and she went through that, studying each picture that attracted her.

Presently, Greg said, "If you want to sleep, go to bed. The hours are different in New York and Greece—we will lose seven hours, approximately."

"Thank you, I think I shall retire."

"The steward will call you in the morning, in time to dress and eat some breakfast before we land."

She nodded, and retreated gratefully to the little white compartment. Surprisingly, she slept hard, to waken to the tap at her door. She rose, washed hastily, and put on her blue-and-white-checked suit with a white blouse, and her blue shoes.

The steward had chilled orange juice ready, ham and eggs, hot pastries, black coffee. They ate, and the airplane was already circling to come in at Athens airport as they finished.

Iris deserted her coffee to lean at the window and exclaim with delight. She could see below her the whitewashed buildings, the dark sienna brown, and the red roofs, and suddenly on a hilltop was a familiar shape.

Greg was pointing. "The Parthenon," he said, with a caress in his voice, as though he showed a beloved mistress. "So old, so beautiful still."

"Oh, I cannot believe I am seeing the Parthenon!" she cried, clasping her hands tightly together. Her eyes drank

43

greedily of the lovely remains, the graceful pillars in the golden sunlight, the arches against the vivid blue sky, the glimpse of gardens and modern buildings of Athens. "Athens. Athens. How long can we stay?"

Greg looked surprised. "Oh, we cannot remain," he said brusquely. "We are going right on to the island."

She could not help it, her mouth drooped, her eyes lost their sparkle. "Not stay—after coming all the way here?" she exclaimed. "I am not to see *Athens*?"

He put his big hand on her arm. "Oh, I am sorry, Iris," he siad quietly. "I did not realize—I am anxious to return to once at Alex. But I promise you—in these next weeks, I will bring you to Athens, and show you all around. I promise you!"

Her father had made her promises, and had not kept them: *We shall be together again one day—you are so like your mother—do you think I would desert you? I shall come on your birthday next year—next year—*

"It is all right," said Iris, drawing away from him carefully.

"We are landing—if you will fasten your seat belt—" He reached for her belt.

"I have it," she said quickly, pushing his hands away. "I know how." She fastened the belt with a decisive click.

After a moment, he leaned back and fastened his own belt. She felt him studying her face; he was frowning; she refused to look at him.

In minutes, they were landing, coming in with a big swoosh, and a clean settling down on the runway. The steward took out their luggage; Iris had only to carry her pocketbook on her shoulder strap, and manage the little stairs down to the ground.

The clean air swept across the runway, and carried some faint scent on the breeze. Safely on the ground, she glanced about with eager longing. She was in Greece, the land of her ancestors, the homeland of her dreams. The sky was so vivid a blue, the air so fresh and sparkling, it seemed different from New York, different from Chicago, a land all its own. Greece! She was here, in the blazing sunlight.

A car had rolled up nearly to the airplane. The luggage was being piled into it. She wondered, but everyone was too busy to ask. Some man had come up to Gregorios, and was handing him a huge portfolio, answering his questions. She stood quietly, forgotten.

Myron touched her arm. "The car is here, madame." He guided her to the huge limousine of shiny black. Why were they going in a car? She was sure Gregorios had said they would be in another plane.

She waited, the car was hot, she wilted. She wiped her face carefully, put a bit more powder on her nose. Then Greg came, and got in, and the chauffeur got in and started the car.

They drove across the runway. Just as she was beginning to enjoy the ride, and looked about to the airport with its white buildings and the gardens, they halted again.

They were next to a plane that looked like a toy. It also was blue and white, but there the resemblance to the first plane ended. It was terribly small! Her heart sank down to her shoes. "Are we going up—in that?" she quavered.

"It is quite safe," said Greg brusquely. "Come along!"

The luggage was put inside, then she had to be lifted up inside the little plane. Greg got into the pilot's seat, and she could have screamed. Was he going to fly them? Him? Did he know how?

She could not help it. Settled in among the suitcases, she cried out, "Is this little plane safe?"

He glanced over his shoulder at her, and his lip curled, she thought in contempt. "Of course it is! Don't panic, Iris!"

"I am not panicking," she said, with dignity. "I am just

too young to die. Isn't there some other way to go to your blasted island?''

"Only by boat," he said, and laughed. "And that would take thirty hours! Be quiet, this is safe." And he put on some earphones, and shut her out.

She clutched the edge of the small seat, resolving to die with dignity. Oh, if she had only not come. What would Charmian have done? Refused to come along? Refused to fly this little thing? Or like it and laugh with pleasure at the experience?

Greg was talking, but not to her, she heard voices in his set. A man gave him permission to take off, and the miniature plane ran across the runway, and took off smoothly into the vivid blue sky, over Athens. She peered out, entranced for a second time with the Parthenon—the pillars, the yellow gold stone from ancient times—then it was gone as the plane turned. She wondered if she would ever in her lifetime see Athens.

Maybe she could come here sometime with Nadia Egorova on a fashion trip. Maybe Nadia would show her Athens. Nadia understood her, Nadia would know how Iris craved to see these beautiful places.

For a time there was no sound in the plane but the loud humming of the engines. Greg seemed happy, relaxed at the controls as though he drove a high-powered car. Iris sat at the windows, peering out at the sparkle of the sunlight on the blue green ocean waves. One island passed below them, she strained to see the tall flamelike cypresses, a small plot of grass, a white block of a house—then it was gone, like a toy God played with.

They were so much closer to the ground, flying in this little plane. It was fun, she finally decided, to see the sea and the islands, the little skimming boats that they passed over, a few fishermen who waved. She waved back happily, knowing they could not see her, but wishing to wave anyway.

Abruptly the plane sounded different. Greg said something in Greek. He was gazing down at the panel.

"What is it? What is it?" Iris gasped, as he pressed buttons, and said more things in Greek.

"Damn it to hell—I'll kill those mechanics—careless bastards—"

"Oh, God, are we going to die?" Frantically she began to pray aloud, "O God, our help and assistance—look down upon me a miserable sinner—deliver me from this trouble—deal not with me after my sins—"

Gregg had pulled off one of his earphones and glanced about to her. "Stop praying, Iris! Look out the window and watch for some land—an island—anything—"

She knelt up on the seat and stared out. He was looking about, but his view was confined to the front and part of the sides.

Then she saw a strip of blue, then a broader one to the left. Far over—it was brown—

"To the left," she cried. "Turn left!"

He turned automatically, searched with her. She pointed. He nodded, and a broad grin broke over his face.

"Now pray, honey!" he said.

She prayed, and watched, and clutched the crucifix at her throat, on the silver chain. He flew the plane closer, and began to descend. The plane was coughing and choking.

"You belted up?" he snapped.

She sat down, and belted up tightly. She closed her eyes and prayed hard. "O God, deliver and protect us from all danger—"

The plane set down hard, bumped up into the air again, and

then down. Her heart was in her throat, she could not swallow.

"Unfasten, and get out, and run!" he yelled at her.

The door swung open beside her, pushed by his hard hand.

She saw the land about three feet below her, brown hard earth. She threw out her two cases, and her pocketbook, then herself, landing on her knees in the dirt.

"Get out of my way!" he yelled, above her. She scrambled to her feet, grabbed her cases, and half stumbled, half ran to the edge of the woods. They seemed to have landed in a field that had been plowed up.

Behind her, Greg ran, his cases in his big hands. He caught at her as she paused. "Come on—farther!" he panted.

They ran, she was sobbing for breath. Why did they need to run? He caught at her shoulder, she dropped a case, and he pushed her to the earth, and flung himself on top of her.

Then the explosion came, a loud blast of heat on their backs. "God, God Almighty, thank thee," Greg whispered in Greek. And he crossed himself as he struggled to his feet. He looked back at the small plane.

Iris sat up slowly, covered with dirt, but alive. She began to murmur the prayer of thanksgiving. Greg's voice joined with hers as they stared at the burning plane. "Almighty and merciful God, I most humbly and heartily thank thy divine majesty for thy loving kindness and tender mercies—graciously vouchsafed to deliver me—" They recited it together to the end, then panted into silence.

Greg flung his arm about Iris and hugged her tightly. "God, we are safe," he said. "That was too damn close!"

She gazed up at him reproachfully from their seat on the ground. "And you said the plane was safe! I'll never fly in one of those things again!"

"Don't say that," he said, and laughed. "Of course you will! It's the only way to get around the islands!"

"I'm going back to the States, and never leave!"

"Nonsense. But I'll fire that damn lazy mechanic. The dial registered full; it was out of order, the plane could not have been half full of fuel."

She shuddered, her mind refusing to deal with what would have happened if they had had to land in the sea. It was so deep, she could not swim so well, she had not been wearing a life jacket—she would have gone down with the plane, and Greg also—drowning. No, she could not think about that.

She looked about. "Where are we?"

He was standing, shaking himself like a big cheerful puppy. "Have to look about—" Then he paused, frowning, as some men came slowly out of the trees. He called in Greek, "Friends! We are friends!"

She wondered at his alarm, then saw one man carried a huge shotgun, others carried farm tools pointed at them, picks, rakes, shovels.

The men came closer. One, with the shotgun, bolder than the rest, or their natural leader, came up to them, the others remaining behind him.

"Come with us!" he ordered in a sort of Greek dialect. His gesture held more meaning.

Iris stood up with Greg's help. He gathered up his cases and hers, but she clutched her case of oils and sketch pads. They followed the men silently. Greg seemed very quiet. Why didn't he ask them where they were? The men seemed shy, giving them wary looks. Probably they didn't see many strangers, and surely not ones who descended in such a fashion.

"Let me do the talking," Greg muttered to her.

She gave him a glance. She was not anxious to talk to them. And she knew the traditional attitude of Greek men in America. The Greek men on Greek islands were probably even worse. Women were made for one purpose only, and that was not for talking back to men.

They walked into a small village, some whitewashed buildings of one-story design, with tile roofs, and a few thatched roofs. A dirt road down the center, winding between the houses. A chapel in the middle of the houses, with a tall black steeple. A roadside shrine, with a gold Madonna icon. Dogs trotting alongside them, several cats lazing on a low wall. Pigs in one wooden enclosure. A single town well.

An aged woman stooped from her house, dressed in a dusty black gown. Her white hair was drawn back from her wrinkled face. She stared at them, her fist clenched in the air. She cursed them picturesquely. Iris was puzzled. Did all Greeks treat strangers so? Worse than New Yorkers! *They* could be kind.

Another woman came out, in a black gown, her age indefinite. Other women joined them, shaking their fists, and calling something. Something about taking their land.

The small procession went on the dusty road, down a few steps, to the right. A small whitewashed building stood there, much like the others. There was a brief argument, the man with the shotgun won. Someone opened the wooden door, it creaked from its low sill to allow a little sunlight to enter the dark interior.

"Go in," said the man in Greek, jerking his black shaggy head, his small black eyes peering at them.

Iris hesitated, then went inside nervously, glancing about. One bed, a table, a few pots, a few pegs nailed to a wooden wall rail. Nothing much else but the dirt floor.

Iris set down her cases her arms aching; she felt bruised and dirty and frightened. She turned about. Greg stood in the doorway, trying to question the man, his tone calm and reasonable.

"What island is this? Where are we? You could see we landed because of trouble. Pray, call the priest, or the mayor, or someone of authority. We would leave—"

The man shouted, "Filthy pigs! Trying to take our land!"

"We do not want your land. Where are we? We wish to return to our home. What is your name?"

Unexpectedly, a man shoved at Greg, he stared down his nose at the man. Another man shoved also, and unwillingly Greg stepped back into the little dark house. The door was slammed shut, and locked with a key in the rusty lock.

Greg shouted at them, "Come back. Tell us what is wrong. We ask only to be allowed to leave the island—"

Footsteps in the dirt. They were going away! Iris gazed at Greg with wide eyes, scarcely able to see him in the light of one window high up on a wall. A small window, too small to crawl from—they were prisoners.

Chapter Four

"I don't care much for their hospitality," said Iris. She watched Greg curiously. He seemed more cheerful for some reason.

He prowled about the small room, like a black panther around his new cage. He tested the bed, examined the mattress, said, "Clean," with satisfaction.

"What island is it, I wonder?" Iris felt weary, her arms hurt from when she had yanked them, jumping from the small plane. She rubbed them briskly.

"Cold? We'll have to have blankets for the night," he said.

"'The night'? Will they—they keep—us—here?"

"Don't worry. We'll get out eventually. It might be a day or two until someone in authority gets here and straightens them out."

"Why do they keep us?"

He shrugged his broad shoulders. His hair was ruffled, black as night, forming into little curls from his exertions.

His bold nose was alert, as though he sniffed at the new environment. She studied his tanned face, his dark features, the wide black eyebrows, the sharp black eyes.

"They kept yelling about the land, the land. My guess is that some land developers have been coming about, trying to buy their island to build hotels or expensive villas. It is a pretty island, and they are probably right to be suspicious. In the past ten years, the islands have changed amazingly. Some have been made into expensive resorts."

"Is that the kind of hotel you build?" She sat down wearily on the side of the narrow bed.

"Yes. But I have just one island resort in Greece. The others are in the Caribbean. Also several hotels in New England. They are quite popular again, old-fashioned hotels that look like nineteenth-century America. Is that your father's work also?"

"I don't know," she said simply.

He frowned at her. "Are you so absorbed in your own career that you don't care what your father does?" he asked sharply.

"I mean just what I said. I know nothing about my father's work." She met his look steadily.

"I suppose some men don't talk about their work at home," he said, evidently trying to draw her. She opened her pocketbook, and looked at her face in the little compact mirror.

"That's right, primp," he said, not unkindly. "We have just been rescued from a fiery death, or death by drowning, we are prisoners, but you have to check how your face looks in the mirror."

"Your face has a streak of red dust across the forehead," she said, and held up the compact mirror toward him. He frowned, took the little blue compact, and made a futile swipe at the dust with his hand. She laughed. "Primp, did you say?" she teased.

The frown broke into a grin, he looked down at her with more friendliness. "You're a mischief!" he said naturally.

"We will have to have water to drink," she said practically, when he returned the compact to her. "We can live without food, I read about that once. But we have to have water to live."

"And blankets," he added. "This room will be damn cold tonight. It is only April; the island is mountainous. It could get down to fifty or forty tonight, by United States reckoning."

"I have a couple of sweaters with me."

"That's good. So do I. We have our cases. But we'll need blankets. If nobody comes by nightfall, I'll start yelling."

He sat down on the bed beside her, and they were silent for a time. She was thinking how lucky they were to be alive. She did not know what he was thinking, his face was absorbed in deep thought.

Presently, he said, "To them, you are my woman. That will be best."

She knew she was blushing. She nodded. "All right."

"No fuss?" He grinned at her.

"I understand how it is. I have read books about Greece. And for a time in the convent school there was a Greek nun who talked to me and helped me practice my Greek studies."

"So that is how you know the language."

"Yes. The nuns told me the more languages I knew, the better, in a career as fashion designer," she explained. "I studied French and Spanish, and a little German and Portuguese. That can get me around Europe and South America."

She could not help the excitement that crept into her voice. He looked at her speculatively. "You intend to travel around the world as a fashion designer—alone?"

"I doubt if I will be alone," she told him. "One usually

goes with models and fashion photographers. And Madame Egorova would probably be there. She enjoys travel, and knows everybody.''

''You will probably marry,'' he said, with flat emphasis.

She shook her head. ''No. I mean to have a career, and marriage would interfere.''

''Nonsense. I don't think you are like Charmian at all!''

''I don't either,'' she said reasonably. ''But I still want my career. I have studied for years to get where I am.''

They were both startled when a key rattled in the rusty lock, and the door was pushed open. A new man stood in the doorway, a huge man in rusty black, who glared at them.

He rumbled something at Greg, who stood to answer him in a calm tone. His dialect was thick, but Iris understood some of what he said.

''You come to steal our land! You think to fool us by landing with a burning plane! But we are not fooled. You are bad, wicked! We will never sell our birthright!''

''We are not here for that. We are on our way home, my woman and I,'' said Gregorios Venizelos. His hands were calm, he moved them slowly in small gestures. The other man was waving his big arms; behind him stood others peering in at them, their faces scowling.

''I do not believe you!''

''Send for a priest, send for the mayor. Send for the authorities. I will tell them my story, they will telephone to Athens, and find out who I am,'' said Greg.

''I do not care who you are! You will die here! Nobody will come!''

Iris felt chilled at the ominous words. She saw Greg stiffen, he seemed to choose his words the more carefully.

''I am not a stranger to the Greek islands. I am no foreigner come to rape the lands,'' he said. He watched the man's face shrewdly for the effect of his words. ''I and my family have lived for many years on an island of our people, we have some land where we have built houses for us since one hundred years ago. Why do we want more? We do not."

"Fine words of an educated man," the peasant grunted suspiciously. "Other men came and talked in fine words, and now they say they own half our island on the other side near to the mainland. We can do nothing to save the land, they say. Sold for a few drachmas! Do you think we will sell the land which sustains?"

"No, you are not fools," said Greg calmly.

That seemed to stop him for a minute.

Greg went on slowly, "We must have some water to drink. While you send for the authorities, we will stay here as your guests. You will soon know the truth of us."

The man hesitated, scowled, then nodded. Greg pressed it.

"And water to wash in. My woman wishes to wash her face, from the dust of the journey."

The man did not even look at Iris. He nodded curtly, and went out and slammed the door.

"So far, so good," Greg sighed, and went to sit down again. "The only problem is, when they check on me, they will find I am a hotel man."

"Oh—Greg!" she quavered.

"And you the daughter of another," he added, and grinned down at her, though his black eyes were grave. "However, I am not interested in buying their island, and I hope I can convince them of it. If we can only get a priest or mayor to talk to, we're probably home safe."

"If—not?"

"Don't borrow trouble," he advised.

The lock rattled, the door was flung open. A black-clad woman came in cautiously, the man stood behind her with a shotgun trained on Greg. Greg and Iris sat still as the woman put a pitcher of water on the table, a couple of mugs, and a basin.

She retreated, another old woman with most of her teeth missing came after her, shaking a little as she looked fearfully at the strangers. She set down a steaming hot pitcher of water, and fled.

Greg said loudly, clearly, "And blankets for tonight, if you will in the kindness of your good hearts! I thank you for your hospitality!"

Hospitality was a Greek virtue; they hesitated, glancing at one another and muttering beyond the opened door. Someone grunted, the big man waved his hands. The door slammed shut.

"Why don't you wash up," Greg suggested. "The water is hot, and I venture we don't get more until morning, at the least."

She flushed. The room was so small, and there was nowhere to hide from him. He got up and went to the window, and stared out, his back expressive.

She washed at the basin quickly, enjoying the hot water on her face and hands, on her bare arms. She decided that would have to do for tonight. She took a long drink of cool water also.

Then she exchanged places with him at the window. "Your turn," she said.

"I shall not be so modest," he said, and began to take off his shirt.

"How do you know how modest I was?" she demanded crossly.

"By the sound of your clothes!" he retorted, chuckling. "Did you think I peeped like a Peeping Ted?"

"Peeping Tom," she corrected automatically.

"Have you thought of becoming a school teacher?" he asked.

She chuckled, unable to keep from it. He could be charming and nice.

By the sound of his clothes, he stripped completely and washed from head to toe. He finally said, "All right, you can sit down again." But when she turned about, he was wearing only his trousers, and was drying himself with his shirt. His bronzed body was virile and very male, with broad shoulders, a strip of black curly hair in a V down below his waist. She blushed violently, and sat down hastily.

"Don't you see half-nude men?" he asked.

She frowned heavily. "Of course not!"

"I meant," he teased, with a grin, "do you not design clothes for men, and see them try them on?"

"No, only for women," she said, her head lowered, to scrabble through her pocketbook for a pen.

He watched her as he finished drying, then searched his case for a pullover. He yanked it over his head, and settled the gray fabric on his body.

"What are you doing?" he asked.

She had found a small sketch pad, and was drawing. "I am drawing."

"What?"

"The island," she said. "This little house. Anything!"

"Want to draw me?" he asked provocatively. "I'll strip again if you like!"

"No, no!" she said hastily.

"Didn't you do nudes in art school?"

"Only seminudes."

"That is cheating."

She did not try to answer that, hoping he would tire of baiting her. She sketched for a time. He finally sat down beside her, and looked at a report from his briefcase.

She could not forget the way he had looked, standing with strong bare feet, clad only in trousers, rubbing briskly at his magnificent body. She had seen some male nudes in art school, as he had said, but they had not been so beautiful as he. Yes, beautiful, his torso like brown silk, the muscles rippling on his arms, and his chest, the shoulders like those of a Greek statue. Only not white and marble. He was all warm flesh and bone, muscle and rippling skin.

Virile and alive, with mocking teasing black piercing eyes. His chest so broad, with the black crisp hairs on it, curling like the hair on his head. He had slightly long hair; it curled down his neck in back, and around his large ears. He was perfectly proportioned, not an ounce of fat on him, she thought. Six feet tall, broad shoulders, narrow of waist, and his thighs were round and thrust strongly in his narrow trousers.

And his feet were beautiful, tanned as though he swam often in the sunlight, arched—she could see him running on the beach, or gripping the wet wooden decks of a fisherman's boat—she longed to draw him, as he had prodded her to do. And she would—but not before him! She could see him in her mind, and when she was alone, she would draw him.

The key turned in the lock again; Greg turned alertly, with the grace and movement of a silent black panther. The door opened, and some blankets were thrown inside the room.

Greg shouted, "I would like some food, some bread and meat!"

"Not tonight!" came the answer. "Why should people like you be well fed and comfortable?"

"Because we are your guests! Ask Kyrios Sicilianos about me! He will tell you I am an honest man!"

Pause. A puzzled voice said, "I know no such."

"Ask Orestes, or Timotheos."

"I know no one by that name. Who do you think to deceive?" There was some heavy anger in the tone. "Tomorrow, we will talk!"

Then the steps moved away again.

Iris was watching Greg's face. He seemed relieved, stretching with a ripple of shoulder and arm muscles, and grinned at her. "So we have blankets," he said, and picked them up and smelled them. "Clean, I think."

They were thin and worn, though. Would they keep them warm tonight?

He tested the blankets with his hand, looked thoughtful, glanced at the bed. Surely he was not thinking he would sleep with her on this narrow bed!

"Tomorrow I will try for food. Then some laundry," he said.

"You are a trier!" She could not help it, she smiled, her eyes sparkling. He kept pushing, and pushing, getting what he wanted.

"That is the way. You ask for one thing, accept it with gratitude, ask for another, and another. Presently you have all you want," he smiled in reply.

He prowled around the room again, tested the small window. The wall was almost a foot thick, he found. She watched him, he shook his head. "You might get through, but I could not," he said. "And you would not know where to go for help."

"I have a feeling I am safer inside!"

"Probably. Though there would not be wild animals on the island, just some goats and donkeys."

"Men can be more wild than the wild animals."

He looked at her sharply. "True. Man is the only beast that deliberately sets out to kill his own kind. And invents more and more horrible weapons with which to kill. Did you ever stop to think how awful wars are? Or are you too young?"

She shook her head. "Mother's brother died in Korea, father's cousin in Vietnam. We are all touched by wars."

He sat down beside her on the bed, took the sketch pad

from her and gazed intently at the drawing of the small room. "Nice. Tell me about your mother."

"I would ask first—those names you said. Why did you ask them about Kyrios—what is the name?"

His dark face shadowed. The room was becoming darker, night was falling on the island. Presently they would not be able to see each other.

"Sicilianos. My feudal enemies," he said. "Shall I tell you a little something about the feud? I had thought it might be their doing that we are here, but I believe not. They did not know the names, they betrayed no knowledge, and they are simple people."

"A feud? That sounds—ancient. Like the old times."

"They continue. In Greece; in Italy—at least, on Sicily— in other Mediterranean lands, wherever family feeling is strong. Mine is worse because it was all within our family." He moved, sat on the bed with his long legs crossed before him, half facing her. "Mine dates to World War II, and the wars within Greece."

"No further back?" She was surprised, thinking they usually dated to the nineteenth century. Her father had known some people in Chicago who were involved.

In the graying darkness, she saw the white flash of his teeth and knew he smiled. "Not this particular feud. There were others, of course! All self-respecting families had their feuds. Showed they had warm blood in their veins!"

"Blood which spilled," she said gravely.

"Yes, like the scarlet poppies on the fields of Greece," he agreed, with a sharp sigh, and change of mood. "Well. My grandfather was Leander—I am named for him Gregorios Leander—"

"The lion man," she murmured. She had thought him a panther, a dark cat or lion!

"Um, yes. He was known as the lion man, the fighter, the

black panther of Venizelos, our island. He had a brother Ignatios, and also a cousin Ignatios Sicilianos, all very close. Now, Ignatios Sicilianos and my grandfather, and my father, Ioannes, who was very young at the time, all fought in the Greek wars of independence during World War II, the so-called second wars of independence, we called them on Venizelos. We hated the Germans, the Nazis, we always hated them. But the brother of Ignatios Sicilianos, named Esdras Sicilianos—he was bought by the Germans, and fought with them. He tried to betray us—my grandfather Leander turned on him, and brought evidence—the British raided their home and killed Esdras.''

Iris was silent as he spoke on, his voice rasping in remembered anger as he spoke of the old times, as though he had been there.

''Ignatios Sicilianos was very angry and upset. He did not think in his anger. Instead of keeping it in the family, he led the Germans to where my grandfather was, and there was a bloody battle. My grandfather was badly injured, but escaped, but many men of our island died in the battle. We were very ashamed that a cousin of ours had betrayed us and caused our men to die. The men who fought with us and trusted us.''

He was so close to her on the bed that she could feel the heat of his fury as he recited the events.

''Ignatios and Timotheos, his elder son, were both kept by the Germans for information, and they were forced to betray many Greeks. When the war was over, they had to retreat to their island, to a mountain fastness, for they would have been killed. Timotheos married, and his sons are Orestes and the handsome Nikolaos. Orestes—he was the one who attacked Alexander in Athens. He got away.''

Iris started. ''So—Alex was hurt by a feudal cousin!'' she

exclaimed, surprised. "I thought it was—I mean, maybe some street crime, or—"

"It was worse," he growled, his voice rasping more fiercely. "If I could get hold of Orestes—I would leave him in little pieces!"

"But all that was World War II—what years—in 1943, or 1944?"

"In those years, yes."

"Almost forty years ago," she reminded him gently.

"It makes no difference," he said, surprised. "The feelings are strong."

"But you were not even born! What about your father— how does he feel?"

He stirred beside her in the semidarkness. He cleared his throat. "My father, Ioannes, died in 1972, he was a good and gentle man. My mother misses him sorely. My grandfather, Leander, he died in 1978. And I had to try to take his place, in the family and in our company. His place is not easy to fill," he added simply.

"So you are the head of the House of Venizelos," she said.

"Yes, I am the head of the house, and it is difficult at times. But I enjoy it!" and he laughed with that quick change of mood he had shown before.

"And what about your father?" he asked, in the silence. "Is Patakos the head of his house?"

"The house is small," she said slowly. "He has no sons, it is his grief. He started the hotel business, and he built it up, and has no cousins with him. They are all distant, I know none of them."

"That is very sad!" he said, in genuine interest. "I do not know what I would do without my uncles and cousins, who are all part of the House of Venizelos, and are in charge of various offices and functions and departments. I miss Alex, I was just getting him trained to be dependable. And now he will not work much until he can see again, probably.''

She sighed, and shivered. The room had turned cold with the setting of the sun. He got up, and said, ''I think it is time to sleep. I can forget my hunger then. I think we will have no food until tomorrow.''

She got up also. ''There were four blankets. I could take two—''

''No,'' he said firmly. ''They are thin. Get in your nightgown and robe, and I will put one blanket on the bed, and we will both lie down and wrap ourselves in the other three. Our body heat will keep each warmer. It gets very cold nights.''

She had been afraid of this. ''I don't want to sleep with you,'' she said explicitly.

She had thought he would blast at her, but she was resolved to stand firm, even if she had to sleep on the floor.

She was not prepared for gentleness. ''Little Iris,'' he said, touching her elbow lightly. ''I am not a monster. You have gone through much the past two days, the long plane ride, another worrisome ride, with the crash and fire, and then those difficult Greeks. Come now, do as I say, I shall not vent my passions on such a little flower tonight! She might wither away by morning!''

She was silent, hesitant. He groped for her case in the darkness, she thought he had cat's eyes, that he could see. He opened it for her.

''Go ahead, Iris, get ready for bed. Tomorrow I'll try to get you some food, and tonight I will try not to dream of your *moussaká*!''

She had to laugh a little, a forlorn giggle. She was so upset and exhausted, she was not even hungry, but this big man needed to stoke his huge body regularly. He would probably he very hungry, and he could treat it lightly. Well, she would try to match his nonchalance.

She was embarrassed to find she had to use the small chamber pot in the corner. She washed her hands then, dried them on a small towel she had put in her case. She undressed in the darkness, hearing him discarding his clothes also. She put on the blue and white nightdress by feel, added the long robe, and was grateful for that much.

He had spread one blanket on the mattress. She lay down cautiously, to find it was as hard and uncomfortable as she had thought. She wriggled around, pushed herself clear to the side of the narrow bed.

"All set?" he asked, then put one blanket on her. He folded the others neatly nearby on the table, at hand for the night chill that would come. "Too bad I am not a beanpole," he said cheerfully, and laid himself cautiously beside her.

She stiffened, and lay rigid. She had hated to be touched since childhood, because of the memories. The times her father had held her and caressed her, and jealous Shelley had pretended to smile and said, "Give the sweet baby to me!"

Iris had soon learned what would follow. Shelley would hold her so tightly Iris felt trapped, then a little vicious pinch would hurt her arm or bottom or side. Whenever her father held her, the punishment would follow, until Iris learned to avoid her puzzled hurt father. She had learned to hide her emotions, hide her yearning for affection, and by the time she was sent away at five, her emotions were all bottled up and frozen inside her. They had never been set free.

"I am not going to rape you—not tonight!" growled a rasping voice beside her.

"I'm sorry, I'm not accustomed—" She ended in a gasp, as a big arm folded over her.

The voice at the back of her neck growled, "I am going to pretend you are a little cotton dolly, stuffed with fluff!" he said. "Now, go to sleep!"

It was an order. She lay rigid for a time, but felt him relax behind her as she lay facing the small high window. As the room grew black, the window showed gray, and she could hear the slight birdcalls of the sleepy island, as all folded up for the early night.

He was asleep, she knew by his regular slow breathing. The arm lay heavily over her, but it was a sort of protection also. His woman, his *yeneka*.

Weariness overcame her, and she slept also.

Chapter Five

Iris slept uneasily that night, waking frequently. She was all too aware of the hard masculine body next to hers, the movements of his long legs, the even breathing of his smooth chest. He was aware of her also, she knew. He tried to soothe her, patting her arm when she stirred, murmuring to her to be quiet, all was well.

She knew when it grew colder, and he leaned to the table, opened the blankets and put them over her. Without him, she would have been intensely cold, for the night air was freezing. But heat emanated from Greg, his body was like a furnace behind her.

She finally wakened in the early dawn light, the room grew brighter. He stirred, yawned, and slid from the bed. She opened her eyes, and he grinned down at her.

He looked like a pirate. His beard had started to grow, and the black hairs rasped as he drew his hand ruefully over his chin and cheeks.

"How do I look?" he asked.

She smiled a little. "Like you are about to lead a raiding party on someone's ship!"

He groaned. "At least you did not say a Turkish pirate!"

The Greeks and Turks had been blood enemies for five hundred years.

"Never. A Greek pirate, to be sure."

"Thanks so much."

She turned her back as he washed and dressed. Then he went to the small high window and peered out, with interest, as she got up, washed a bit, and donned the blue suit again, with a fresh white blouse.

Not a sound from outside. Her watch was way off, she had not changed time zones. She thought it was five or six in the morning, Greek time.

"We should exercise," he said briskly, and began to stride back and forth across the room. She imitated him, and in the rhythm of their walking across the small room they passed and repassed each other. She began to curtsy to him as she passed. Solemnly, but with a twinkle in his black eyes, he would bow deeply to her in return. Anyway, it did help to move about.

Finally, she sat down again on the bed. She had folded up the blankets, there was nothing else to be done. Greg did squatting exercises in the middle of the room, then sat down on the pile of blankets.

Presently the lock screeched, and the door opened. The big man peered in. "Come," he said, and motioned.

Iris hastily put garments in her suitcase and closed it. Greg gathered up his cases and her suitcase, she picked up her small case with sketch pads and her pocketbook, and they walked out behind the man. Several other men stood about, watching alertly and curiously.

They marched up a hill, and around a corner, and the man jerked his head toward another building. "Inside," he said.

"Have the authorities come?" asked Greg, hesitating.

"Not yet. You will wait!"

They were shown into another room, a little larger and finer than the first, the only room of a somewhat larger building. A room that had been an office, Iris thought, observing a desk and chair, posters on the wall behind the desk. A little larger bed had been moved in, a couple of chairs and tables.

Pitchers of hot and cold water were brought in, then several women brought food. Trays of hot ham, thick dark bread, goat cheese, cups of cream and sugar, empty cups, and two huge pots of black coffee.

Without a word except for thanks to their "hosts," Iris and Greg fell to. They ate and drank greedily, it tasted so good. One woman cackled with glee at their appetite, pleased that her cooking was welcomed by the foreigners.

Then the men and women withdrew, the door was locked after them. Iris poured out more coffee, and leaned back with a big sigh.

"Ah, better. When do you think we will be released?"

Greg shrugged. "I don't know. We'll have to take it from day to day."

"Day to day?" she echoed. "Won't they release us today? How far do they have to send for the authorities?"

"Most of their men have gone fishing, and will take their catch to Patmos on the mainland," he said grimly. "That probably means we will be here at least until the men return."

She had caught the words about fishing, but had not understood the rest. "But the men here—do they not have authority—"

He shook his head. "The big man is something of an

71

idiot," he said wrly. "And he is in charge because of his size! The women and children have no authority, of course."

"Oh, of course!" she said snappily. He grinned at her.

"Calm down, my woman!" he teased. "This is not America. Well, we might as well talk and get acquainted." He looked at her with his usual inquisitiveness.

She shrugged. "I would rather work," she said. Deliberately, she went over to the desk, and spread out her sketch pads, watercolors, paintbrushes. He looked annoyed.

The room was more pleasant. There were windows on two sides, one toward the mountains and a magnificent view of trees and rocks. The other was toward the blue sea, and even more thrilling sights. Iris studied the sea, and the beach, a cypress tree, a small boat tied up, and began to form a design in her mind.

She put a little water in one of the cleaned coffee cups, and began to work. Seeing her absorbed, Greg gave a mock-heavy sigh, and got out his portfolio, and began to study a report. Soon he was as absorbed as she was.

Iris worked much of the morning. She completed the sketch of the beach, then began an oil on a small bit of canvas she had with her. The sea was conducive to painting, it was as rippling as blue silk, as changeable as the clouds over it.

About noon, as the sun was overhead, more food was brought. The old women who brought it looked curiously at Iris's work, and muttered to each other. After they had left, Iris ate, then sketched a few quick sketches of the old women, emphasizing their beaklike noses, their flashing eyes, the black garments drawn up about their faces.

"So, you do not just draw fashions," remarked Greg presently, as she paused in her work.

"No. I have always liked to draw and paint."

"Does Charmian like to paint?"

Iris looked her surprise. "No, she has no talent along those lines. She is quite good as an actress, she has been in plays since grade school, she said."

He pounced on that. " 'She said,' " he commented, staring at her as though he would like to look through her. "Why do you say, *she said.* Did you not live together?"

"No," said Iris shortly.

He sighed. "Prying information from you is worse than prying a snail from its shell," he said whimsically.

"It is none of your concern, who and what I am," she told him rather rudely.

"But we are going to be living together for a long time," he said, twisting his mouth into a wry little grin. "Won't it be easier for us if—"

"What do you mean, 'for a long time'?" she asked quickly. "How long will they keep us here?" Her voice rose.

"Hey, calm down, hey, hey, calm, now! I do not know. It was not that I meant. I will be taking you to my island," he soothed her, watching her thoughtfully. "That is what I meant."

"After we get out of here, I want to go home," said Iris, controlling her quivering chin with an effort. "I do not want to go to your island! I want to go home!"

"You will like my island very much. Just wait until you see it," he said, his voice gentling. "The smell of lime and jasmine, of spruce and cypress, and the salt off the sea, you will enjoy it very much. And your artist's eye will be enchanted with the blues of the sea, the reds of the cliffs, the yellow of its stone, and the golden white of the marble. Mother likes her gardens, and she fills them with the scarlet poppies, the yellow daisies, roses, and others—and many iris. She will be delighted with the Iris I bring to her."

Iris felt immediately suspicious. He could charm birds off the branches, she thought crossly. She drew a black line on the sketch pad savagely. His voice was too practiced in its wooing. He wanted to take her to Alex as a present, all wrapped up and tied with blue ribbons. Well, she wasn't someone's dolly.

"I would rather go home," she said politely.

"Well, you are not going!" he snapped, patience suddenly gone. "You are going with me to my island, and you will stay there! So be quiet!" He glared at her, and she glared back.

"We are neither of us going anywhere," she mocked him. And she added another line and another to the pad, and looked in surprise to find she had made a sketch of his face, scowling and black-browed, the head thrust forward belligerently. She chuckled. "This is what you look like when you're mad," she said, and held it up for him to see.

He stared at the sketch in surprise for a moment, then flung back his head and laughed. "Oh, so you have a sting, like a nettle, do you?" he mocked. He pinched her cheek lightly, and returned the pad, and strolled restlessly about the room.

"I hope your mother has not heard about the plane crash," said Iris, drawing a few more idle lines. "She will worry, will she not?"

"Yes," he said. "She has known many sorrows, I would not add more. I was in communication for a few moments with Athens airport at the last, yet I think they will not find it easy to trace us. So they will think us dead, I fear." He frowned out the window to the sparkling sea. "Your father— he will worry?"

"I doubt if he hears about it for a time," she said indifferently. Worry about her? He never had. "Nadia will be upset, though. I think she likes me."

He turned and stared at her, and was ready to shoot questions at her.

Hastily she said, "May I see the sketches of your new hotel? Or are they secret?"

His face lit up, "No, not a secret from you," he said, and got out the sketches, laid them out on the desk, and explained them. They were for a holiday resort in the Caribbean, and she found them unexpectedly fascinating.

There was a huge main building, then cottages scattered over the wide grounds, around a large golf course. All were along the seacoast, and beaches, gardens, swimming pools were indicated. He had also several architectural drawings, one of the main building with reception desk, lounges, and so on, and those of several different-sized cottages.

Greg described the various aspects, and from his enthusiasm she knew he loved his work. That managed to fill much of the afternoon.

The bed was a little larger than the first one. Iris settled down cautiously, and hoped to get a better night's sleep this night. But Greg put both arms about her, and drew her to him, and kissed her cheek.

"Don't do that!" she choked, stiffening. She wriggled to try to get out of his arms, and almost fell out of bed.

"Hey, now, calm down," he soothed. "Don't you like to be kissed good night?"

"No!" she gasped. "Don't do that—I will sit in the chair all night if you do that!"

He was silent, she could feel his breathing on her neck.

"All right," he said quietly. "I'll be good. Damn it. Go to sleep."

She did not trust him, or any man. She lay stiffly until she heard his quiet even breathing as he slept, and even then it was hard to relax and go to sleep. She kept waking every time he turned over.

In the morning, he got out of bed; she was still tired. "Go

back to sleep, Iris," he said, and went to the door to receive the pitcher of hot water.

She shut her eyes while he washed, and went back to sleep, and slept two more hours she was so tired.

The day crawled past. She sketched and ate, an old crone came and Greg gave her their laundry to do. The two prisoners had little to say to each other. They seemed to have run out of small talk, and Iris had no wish to tell him her life's story.

Greg prowled back and forth across the room. He was getting very impatient. "I've got work to do," he muttered. "How long are we going to have to sit this out?"

Iris shrugged. She had put a chair beside the window, and gazed at the sea until her eyes hurt. His gaze lingered on her.

"You're very pretty," he said, his voice suddenly charming.

"By the end of a week, I'll look like Miss Universe to you," she said tartly. "Don't worry, you'll soon be back in civilization!"

"You think you look beautiful to me because there is no competition?" he asked, amusement in his voice.

"Absolutely! If we were in New York—or Athens—you would not give me a second look—or even a first!"

"I have given you first and second looks already," he said seductively. "Do you fear competition from your sister Charmian? Has she stolen boyfriends from you?"

Iris glanced at him in surprise, then flinched from the hot look in his black eyes. "No. In fact, she tried to take me on dates with her. She can be very kind," said Iris.

He mulled that over, but she refused any more baits.

That night, he put his arms about her in determination, after she had gotten into bed.

His chin was very scratchy, he had not shaved for several days now. He nuzzled at the nape of her neck. "Iris—you are very sweet," he said. His breath was warm on her flesh.

"Don't kiss me!" she told him fiercely.

He kissed her nape, her ear. She hated it that a little thrill went through her. She wriggled, but could not break the hard clasp of his arms. "Let me go! I'd rather sit up in a chair!" she told him angrily.

"Come on, honey!" His voice was husky and low. He was probably not accustomed to being fought.

His mouth roamed over her, his hands went to the soft fabric over her breasts. She tried to push his hands from her. She could not move them. One of his hands cupped a breast, as though he weighed it softly in his palm. His thumb stroked over the taut peak. She shuddered, feeling too much emotion.

She fought him more fiercely, more desperately. His arms were too hard, and now his legs came up around hers, holding her to him. His thighs were pressed against her body, she felt the rampant masculinity of him. Fear struck through her.

He had pushed the bed up against the wall. She could not even escape him by falling out of bed on that side. She fought, and scraped her arm against the rough whitewashed wall.

"Ouch!" she cried. "You let me go!"

"Don't fight me, then! Come on, what is an embrace? Have you not taken any pills?"

"What pills?"

"Don't be stupid!"

She kicked at him. He pushed her over on her back, and loomed over her like a black shadow in the night. His one hand worked quickly to unfasten her robe and then her nightdress. He put his fingers on her bare throat, and moved them down to the rounded breasts. When he cupped the breast again in his palm, he rubbed it with his palm.

"Ah, you are soft!"

Wild hot thrills were going through her, and that frightened her more. If she gave in, she would hate herself as well as

77

him. She struggled in his hard arm. He pressed himself down on her, slowly, until she felt his bare chest. He wore only his pajama bottoms tonight. Had he planned this? She had a terrible feeling that he had.

"Don't you find me attractive?" he murmured, his lips on her throat, while his hand cupped one breast. A skillful thumb pressed that taut nipple, and he growled a satisfied laugh. "You like me, I can tell! Come, Iris, come, darling—let us enjoy each other—life is so short—"

"Cheap words!" she flashed.

"Would you rather have jewelry? Diamonds, like your sister?" he asked, contempt in his tone that vied with the warmth of his hands. "Come, now, be nice to me, and I will find you something pretty when we get to my home."

"Will you ask your good mother for some gem with which to pay me for my services?" she cried. "Will you ask her to pay for my virginity?"

He went stiff. "Do not lie to me," he growled. "You are no better than Charmian! She sleeps with any who can offer her the price! She is notorious even in New York! She is crawling over men's bodies to her peak of the career she wishes! What can men offer to you, Iris? Payment for the apartment? Silks for your body, furs? Or sending customers of their mistresses and wives to your fashion house? Do not lie to me, you are like the rest!"

His words burned in her brain like hot coals. She felt besmirched by his actions and his words. He was treating her like a prostitute!

In her shock at what he was saying, Iris had stopped fighting. He held her down with his legs, and took advantage of her quiet to open the nightdress to the hem. He had her body opened to him, and his hard warm body was pressed to hers. He reached down, to open her legs, and for a moment she felt his hard fingers between her thighs.

She screamed, and flung herself about, so his fingers were dislodged. She fought so desperately that he had to hold on to keep them both from being flung to the floor.

When he kept holding her, and pressing her body to the mattress, she finally cried out, tears streaming down her flushed hot cheeks, "I am a virgin. God have mercy, Blessed Virgin, hear my words! As God is my witness—I am a virgin!"

Greg went stiff as a board. He lay sprawled on her for a long terrible moment, she felt every bit of him as he lay on her. She thought he would disregard her, and take her. Then he uttered some terrible words in Greek, and half flung himself off the bed, onto the floor.

He got up and stormed around the room in his bare feet, while she sat up and wept. Oh, God, it had been so close! He raged in Greek, using words she had never heard, and never wanted to hear again.

She fumbled for the buttons of her nightdress, and fastened herself in it again. Then she put the robe about herself, and cocooned herself in that also.

Iris did not feel safe on the bed now. She slipped off, and blinded by the dark and her tears, she groped her way to the chair behind the desk. She sank down in it, shivering.

"Here," said Greg, and slammed down a towel before her. She wiped her face carefully, sniffing. "By God, that was close. Iris, do you truly swear before the Virgin Mary that you are a virgin?"

"Yes, I do swear it, before the Virgin Mary."

He drew a deep sigh, and finally sat down in a chair nearby. She could not see him or his face, the room was almost black.

"I cannot sleep," he said, with a groan. "We might as well talk. And, Iris, it is time you told me about yourself.

There are too many mysteries. Why are you different from your sister?''

"We have different mothers."

"Go on. What about your mother? Is she dead?"

"Yes." The rough actions, the dangers, had loosened her tongue. Her control was about gone. "My mother died when I was born."

"Then your father married again."

"Not right away," she said carefully. "I was raised by a nurse. Then—when I was two—he thought I needed a mother. And I believe he wanted a son. He married Shelley. And they had a daughter, Charmian. I looked very much like my mother, father said so. Shelley was—jealous—of any attentions to me." Her voice was forlorn, he reached out in the darkness, but she drew her hand quickly from his touch.

"So—when I was five—he found a convent school that would take me. It was Roman Catholic, the nuns were kind."

She stopped. He prodded. "Why not Greek Orthodox—"

"There was none that father liked. At first—he came and took me to the church on feast days. I saw him then. He would bring me presents—then Shelley stopped that. She would cry—well, he stopped coming. When I was twelve, they moved to Houston."

Greg drew in his breath, she just caught the sound in the darkness. "He came—to visit you?"

"No," she said flatly. "I continued in my schooling. When I was twenty, I finished fashion school, and went to New York. Charmian—well, I should say, Shelley, left him and married Bill Roswell, and they lived with Charmian in Boston. Father married again, but he still has no son. Charmian left school at seventeen, she wanted to become a model, then an actress. Father came to New York, bought an apartment for us, and said I should look after Charmian."

"A sparrow looking after a hawk!" he exclaimed.

"Bill Roswell comes to New York sometimes. He is kind."

"But your father?"

"I have not see him since. He is very busy," she added vaguely.

"How many times did you see him between twelve and twenty?"

"None."

Greg swore violently. "He left you, a girl child, when he was responsible for you?" he asked incredulously.

"The nuns looked after me," she said quickly. "No one could have been kinder."

"But no men?"

"No."

"And you were ignored by the father who should have been your chief protector." There was anger in his voice.

"The nuns were my family. Sister Therese taught me to sew, Sister Angela taught me fashion design, Sister Mary Concepcione taught me Greek—"

"Well, you are no longer alone!" said Greg.

Iris came out of her absorption with the past. She had been talking in the darkness, as though to emptiness, as though to some vague shadow, like her talks to her doll in the night when as a child she had felt so alone and deserted. But she was not alone. A vibrant man was sitting across from her.

"Of course not," she said briskly. "I have my job, and my boss is very kind. I expect to make good, she has plans for me—"

"I have plans for you," said Greg.

"Oh, yes, to offer me to Alex!"

He was silent, she could almost feel his anger. She leaned back in the chair.

"I will sleep here tonight," she said. The chair was not at all comfortable, but it was better than rape.

"No, you will not. Go to bed!"

"No."

His voice gentled. "Go to bed, Iris. I will not molest you. I am a Greek, I give you my word your virginity will not be taken until your wedding night! I have respect for you, it has not been easy for you. You need not fear me now."

She hesitated. He got up and strode around, as though he could see in the dark. She saw his vague shadow at the window.

"It is incredible," he muttered, as though to himself. "A lovely child like this, and he discards her!"

"He did not discard me!" said Iris angrily. His words stung. "He paid for me, for my room and board and education. He sent me checks for my birthdays and for Christmas. I could not have achieved what I did, but for his financial aid."

Greg made a contemptuous sound.

"It is true!" she said earnestly. "It is just—he could not bear to see me—I look too much like my mother. He said it—when he brought Charmian to New York." The remembered pain clouded her voice, and choked her up. "She was Poppea, I am named for her, Iris Poppea. He said, 'You are so like Poppea, oh my God, I miss her still.' That was what he said."

"It was a love match, then?"

"The marriage was arranged, but they loved on first sight."

"I see."

He was silent, then repeated, "Go to bed, Iris. I shall not harm you, I vow it. From now on, you are under my protection. Your father has lost his rights to you, I claim them!"

She rejected that fiercely. "I belong to myself!" she cried. "I can take care of myself." She would not have this black panther claiming her like a lost cub.

"I shall take care of you," he said, and came to her. He

lifted her, and put her on the bed. "Lie down, we shall sleep now. Come now, be quiet, child."

He rearranged the blankets, laid her out on them, pulled down her robe and gown demurely about her ankles. Then he lay down with her, and pulled up a blanket about them.

"Sleep now, Iris," he said, and put his arm across her protectively.

Somehow she knew he would not harm her. She feared him still, but for another reason. She sighed, and turned over, and went to sleep. And in her dream she remembered the touch of his hands on her naked body, and they made her restless.

Chapter Six

The days moved slowly in their own deliberate rhythm. It was easier for Iris, the room was like her convent room—though she had not shared that with a black panther!

For Greg it was much more difficult. He was restless, furious over the interruption of his work, concerned about his family and his business, worried about the uncertain tempers of the Greek islanders.

They rose with first daylight, washed, dressed. They ate the hearty island food, then exercised.

Iris and Greg were doing bends and stretches one morning, when two old crones in black appeared with their breakfast. The women stared, gap-mouthed, their few teeth showing like old witches, unable to believe the antics they saw.

Iris caught the looks on their identical faces, and began to laugh. She plopped down on the floor and laughed and laughed. Greg tried to continue his exercises, and solemnly swung his arms and jumped up and down. But soon he also was laughing too hard to continue. The women shook their heads, and tapped their foreheads. The foreigners were mad.

Iris filled up all the pages of her sketch pads, used up all her watercolor pages, and her few oil canvases. She sighed and contemplated the whitewashed walls.

"You aren't going to start a mural, are you?" asked Greg, with a mock groan.

"If we are here another two days, yes! I could cover a wall with paint, the way I feel."

But fortunately or unfortunately for the future of the room, they were rescued. Several impressive-looking men of authority came; they were taken to a nearby village, and questioned.

There was a telephone, calls were made. When Greg's identity was known, there were apologies, and soon Greg and Iris were on their way, a plane was sent to take them back to Athens airport.

Iris had her plans, she made them silently on the way to Athens. Never again, never again! She would take the first plane to New York!

As they circled in the little plane above Athens airport, Greg turned to her. The pilot was humming, then talking on the monitors. Another man was with them, shooting them curious looks.

"I am told newsmen will be there to question us. We will have to go inside the airport, but I have asked for a special room. Leave the talking to me!"

"Gladly! They won't want to talk to me anyway," she said gaily. "All I want is a ticket to New York. I can slip away and get it while you're talking to the newsmen." She had her own credit cards, surely her father would help her out financially if necessary.

Greg gave her a heavy scowl. "You are going with me to my island!" he said emphatically. "Let me hear no more nonsense! Certainly you are not going to New York!"

"You are surely not imagining that I will act the part of Charmian for Alex—"

The other man was listening with intense curiosity. Greg looked as though he could choke her. "No," he said curtly. "Not that now! Be quiet! Just do what I tell you!"

She would have argued more, but he leaned to her, and jerked her seat belt to make sure it was tight. While he was close, he muttered, "Will you kindly just trust me to do the right thing? You will not be sorry!"

He looked tired and cross, his beard heavy, his eyes red-rimmed from weariness. Her soft heart betraying her, she finally nodded. He patted her hands, and leaned back in his seat, looking self-satisfied.

Well, she could stay a few days at the island, she might as well have a little holiday before she went home. It had been a bit nerve-racking as a prisoner. And she would paint some scenes at his island home, that was supposed to be so beautiful.

Thanks to the industrious black crones on the island, Iris wore a clean suit and a freshly ironed white blouse when she descended from the little plane. She looked neat and fresh. Greg looked more demonic, his beard heavy, his scowl heavier.

Newsmen rushed them as soon as they entered the airport lounge. Flashbulbs hurt Iris's eyes, she blinked, and put her hand over her eyes. Greg steered her through the crowd, pushing his way with his body. Several men had met them, and they were making a path through the crowd of cameramen and reporters.

"Mr. Venizelos, could you tell us—"

"Were they kidnappers—were they terrorists—"

"Is it true, there is a blood feud between you and—"

"Who is the pretty young lady? Is she your fiancée? Is she the daughter of—"

"Later, later," growled Greg, pushing, but they could not get him through the crowd. His bodyguard glared and cursed, but the crowd stood firm.

"The lady—who is the lady—the lady—miss, what is your name—"

A reporter pushed his face right at Iris, little eyes peering at her intently, while cameramen flashed and flashed their still cameras. A television camera loomed over her head, ducked down to get right at her. She flinched.

"Iris Patakos!" cried one man's voice firmly, and she looked about, and half smiled, thinking it might be a friend. Then she saw the satisfied glint of a newspaperman's grin, and realized she had given herself away. "Miss Patakos, why are you here with Gregorios Venizelos? Were you on the island together? Were you alone on the island? Why were you flying with him? What brings you to Greece?"

"Be silent," Greg whispered savagely, as she opened her mouth. She shut her mouth. "Miss Patakos is my fiancée," she heard Greg say with sudden suaveness. "I am taking her home to meet my family!"

"How long have you been engaged? How long have you known each other? What did you think when you crashed? Does her father know about you? Is her father the Hilarios Patakos"—they gave him the Greek pronunciation—"of the Patakos Hotels? Are you forming a merger?"

The crowd surged on and on. Iris finally realized that Greg and his line-blockers were moving inexorably toward a lounge area. A break, someone opened a door, and she and Greg were shoved inside into the empty room. She staggered inside, feeling like the football in a particularly vicious game. She sat down in a chair, breathing heavily, feeling tenderly for her case of sketch pads and watercolors.

Outside came an outraged scream as the frustrated newsmen

realized they had been outmaneuvered. "But we must talk to you—why are you here—what happened—who is—"

Greg said to Iris, "I'll go out and briefly talk to them, then make some phone calls. Don't leave this room! There is a ladies' room there, put on makeup or something, but don't walk out the door! I'll have a guard put here."

"All right," she said feebly, dragging off her white hat and fanning herself with it. He gave her a brief grin. "You take care of feeding the animals, just don't give them blood meat!"

He laughed, and went outside. A strange man slid inside and shut the door, and gave her a brief salute. She dragged herself up, and went to the ladies' room. Knowing Greg, she had better be ready to shoot off with him whenever he was ready.

She washed her face, put on makeup, took an aspirin for her increasing headache. Why did people scream so? She liked peace and quiet. What on earth was she doing here?

She returned to the chair. A hostess had brought in a tray of coffee and sandwiches, and some fruit. Iris thanked her, the girl hovered curiously, but did not dare question her.

Lights were flashing outside, she could see them through the frosted upper panes of glass in the walls. She could hear Greg's firm voice overriding the questions, but made out only a few words. She did hear over and over the Greek word for "fiancée," or "betrothed."

Finally there was a reluctant chorus of *"Efharistó"* as they thanked him.

Greg half fell into the room, saying, *"Parakaló,"* rather savagely. He looked about, spotted the phone, and the hostess.

"A call has come through for you—" she said eagerly, and handed him the phone.

"Efharistó." He took the phone and began barking into it. Then his voice and his face softened marvelously. "Mother!"

he said very gently. "Yes, I am alive, we are alive. I thank you for your prayers. Yes, yes. She is here, yes, I am bringing her. Have the Blue Suite made ready for her. Yes. Yes. The Blue. No. I will take care of that when I come. Alex? Ah. Well—perhaps—no."

As he went on, Iris poured out a big cup of hot coffee, added sugar and cream thickly, and put it at his hand. He grinned a thanks up at her. He sipped at it thirstily as he listened.

The call finished, another came right in. Two men came in while he was talking. He paused, barked something at one of the men. Iris stopped listening. They talked, listened, one man shot out of there as though his shoes had caught fire.

All this hurry and rush after a week of quiet! She supposed Greg had a lot of suppressed energy he just had to use, like an oil gusher.

Greg was on his fifth or sixth phone call when the air hostess went to the window. She was pretty, thought Iris, tall and black-haired, with huge lovely eyes, a nice figure in the blue and white uniform. Greg was looking at her also, absently. Well, Iris had told him he would not look at her, once he was back into civilization!

The girl came back. "The car is coming," she whispered.

Greg nodded, cut short the conversation, and began to gather up suitcases. The men rushed to take them from him. Iris stood up, ready to fly with them, bracing herself.

They went outside by the door on the other side of the lounge from where they had entered. Newsmen were hanging around in the corridor. A shout went up. But Greg hustled Iris into the car, the luggage was thrown into the trunk, and the chauffeur took off in a cloud of airport dust.

"Got away," said Greg, with satisfaction. He turned to Iris. She handed him a sandwich in a napkin. He began to laugh, the chauffeur looked at them in the mirror.

He ate four sandwiches, as she handed them to him.

"You are a wonder," he said. "Well, that is finished. We should have a peaceful trip."

The car had left the airport, to Iris's silent surprise. The smooth highway was under their wheels; they left the city, though they passed many houses, and clumps of gardens, trees, parks. Then they had left the suburbs, and were traveling along a road that skirted the sea. Iris leaned forward eagerly to look.

"We will get the boat at Piraeus," said Greg, half smiling at her surprise. "You said you didn't want any more of planes! We can't cut them out completely, of course, but I thought you would enjoy traveling by boat for a change."

"A fishing boat?" she asked dubiously.

He laughed and laughed, leaning back in the comfortable soft Rolls.

"I could hit you!" she said crossly. "I don't want to go anywhere but home, and you just laugh!" Her voice quivered.

He stopped at once, his arm went about her, he hauled her to him, and patted her head. "Now, Iris, be calm! It will be all right," he said soothingly. "We are going on a nice yacht, and you will have a little bedroom all your own, and can sleep, or look at the sea, and maybe we will see some dolphins!"

She perked up at that. "Dolphins!" she exclaimed. "I have always wanted to see them!"

"I thought you would like that," he said with satisfaction, and let her go regretfully as she pulled away.

He pointed out some sights to her as they rolled along the highway. There was the huge home of a wealthy man often in the news. That was the private airport of a multimillionaire. That yacht basin held the ships of a dozen nationalities. This was a little village still sleeping in the sunlight, though wealthy homes grew up about it.

Finally the Rolls pulled up and drew into a parking lot

beside a marina. Half a dozen fine yachts rolled at their moorings. Iris looked from one to the other with fascination.

"Mine is the one with the blue and white and red flag on it," said Greg, opening the door and hopping out neatly. The Rolls had come up nearby. They had only a few feet to go.

Another car was pulling up behind them. Several men got out, and came to talk to Greg. Iris stood aside, and looked at the boats, and admired the blue shiny silk of the sea. The land behind them rose in red dusty crags, only a few tall pines swayed in the cool wind. She sniffed. There was a keen salt taste to the air. She looked at the men. They were all tall, black-haired, capable-looking, but Greg was the one that stood out. Perhaps it was the air of command, some subtle lift to his chin.

As she watched, he jerked his head, and they nodded and chorused something. They scattered as he left them and came to Iris, smiling.

"Ready to go aboard?" He took her arm and drew her to the little gangway. When she hesitated at the steps, he lifted her easily and carried her on board, to the great beaming pleasure of a young uniformed steward waiting on the deck.

"Greg—I can walk!"

He put her down. "This is my fiancée, Miss Patakos," he told the steward. "Iris, this is Aleko. He will take care of you. Come along, I'll show you your cabin."

He caught at her hand, and drew her with him along the side of the cabins, then down some rubber-edged stairs into a narrow hallway of dark shiny wood. The fittings were brass, rubbed to gold. She admired them as they walked to one door, which Aleko flung open with a flourish and bowed her inside.

Her suitcase was there already. She set down her other case and handbag, and admired the neat bed with its blue and white coverlet, the little fitted dresser and mirror, the set-in cupboards, the tiny bathroom with washbasin.

"We may not take off for another hour, I'm waiting for some packages from Athens," said Greg. "Why don't you lie down and rest a bit? Or come up on deck—change to a sundress and get comfortable. Whatever you like!"

He was giving her a choice for once! "Thank you very much," said Iris, trying to keep the sarcasm out of her voice.

He ruffled her hair quickly, grinned and left. The steward said, "Allow me to unpack for Madame," and had her case opened and the clothes hanging up before she had wandered around the tiny room and peered from the round window.

Aleko hung up a bold blue and yellow-flowered sundress she had made with shirred bodice and narrow ties for her shoulders. "This for luncheon and afternoon," he beamed.

She nodded. When he had finally left, she took off her shoes and dress, and lay down on the bed. It was amazingly comfortable, and she soon dropped off to sleep.

She wakened to the soothing rock of a cradle. It took minutes for her to remember where she was, and that the bright light was the sun glinting off the sea. She got up, washed, and put on the blue and yellow print. It seemed very bare of neck, showing her honey skin of shoulders and arms. She finally flung on a thin cotton stole, and went up on deck.

She leaned on the railing for a long time, enchanted. Her sunglasses perched on her nose, she gazed and blinked at the brightest blue sea ever, with white foam on the waves. She thought she saw fish and dolphins, maybe enchanted mermaids. There was not a cloud in the vivid sky, nor an island in sight. The little white bobbing yacht was alone, quite alone.

Bronzed arms came to the railing beside hers. A deep voice said, "Better than a plane?"

She turned to beam up at Greg. "Oh, thousands of times better, millions of times better."

He smiled down at her. "You are a true Greek, then. You love the sea. It is our womb, we came from the sea. We live by the sea, it sustains us like a mother."

Contentedly she leaned on the railing as he spoke slowly, about his own love of the sea, how he enjoyed fishing with the night fishermen, how Greeks had always sailed the seas, how their love of adventure took them on many seas about the world. Not by land did they adventure, he said, but by the sea. He talked of Greek legends, of stories she knew and others she did not.

Presently he gave her a tour of the little yacht, and she could see how proud of it he was. No wonder. The walls were of shining teakwood, the brass beautifully polished. The wheelhouse with the sailor at the wheel was as neat and trim and clean as any proud cook's kitchen. There were half a dozen cabins below, two with their own bathrooms. On the main deck were two large rooms, one furnished as a study and one as a dining room. It was a luxurious ship, but a working one, she thought.

Only one thing marred her pleasure that day. Greg kept introducing her to the men as his fiancée, and they would beam and stare shyly, and touch their foreheads to the future Madame Venizelos.

She must get out of this engagement quickly, she thought. A few days in his home, on the island, then off to New York. The engagement allowed to break, cautiously. No way would she remain engaged for long to this dominating man!

Not that such a man, a millionaire, an Important Man, a Very Important Man, would want to remain engaged to Iris Patakos. Much less marry her. But Iris had a queer little twinge of worry. It would be fatally easy to fall in love with a man like Greg, dominating, caring, surrounding one with comfort and protection—

Oh, no! What was she thinking! She was going to be an independent woman. A Career Woman, needing nobody! That way led to safety. When one depended on a man, one invited trouble! A man would make promises and promises, only to let one down! No way would she trust a man again! Not her father, not her sister's stepfather, not anybody. They could be nice, but it did not do to trust them and depend on them.

And wait until Greg saw one of his beautiful women again! Iris just knew he had dozens tucked away ready to be pulled out to amuse him. He was much too experienced.

In the study, Iris sat with her legs up on a comfortable lounging area, looking out the large windows to the sea. Greg had excused himself, and was poring over some papers at the desk. One of the men at the airport had brought them to him.

A week wasted! Yes, that is what he must think. But she would never forget that week alone with him. They had laughed together, fought, talked, she had told him things she had never told another soul, and he had sensed her loneliness and been gentle and kind.

It was over, but she would never forget that. She propped her chin on her hand and gazed at the sea.

They had luncheon at a beautiful polished wood table in the dining room, served on white china with blue and gold rims. Aleko brought platters of fresh fish, grilled in a lemon butter sauce. He served tiny new potatoes, fried mushrooms, green salad with a multitude of black ripe olives. Iris ate greedily of the greens, her system craved them after a week of mostly meat and cheese and bread. Greg watched her sympathetically.

Greg told Aleko to bring her fruit juice instead of wine,

and the steward brought glasses of a mixture of a biting tangy flavor. Pomegranate, fig juice, lemon, orange, delicious.

Greg seemed aloof that day, thinking, as they proceeded to his island. She left him to work, wandering on the deck, daring to take off her stole in the hot sunlight and smear suntan lotion on her honey skin to absorb the sunshine for a time.

By evening, she was rather pinkly flushed of face and shoulders. She washed, and put on a plain blue silk gown, hoping that would be fancy enough for Greg. What in the world would she wear at his home? If he dressed up on a yacht, what was his home like, and his mother? Very formal?

Greg wore a white naval jacket, smartly piped, with dark blue trousers, and white ruffled shirt. He was very courteous, pouring her white wine, making conversation. But again he seemed very thoughtful and rather serious. She thought he was absorbed in his work. Just as well, she thought. She had best retreat into her shell again, and when she got home to New York she would start forgetting him.

She was sleepy again, and went to bed early. He just rose from his chair and wished her a courteous *"Kaliníkta,"* with a kindly smile.

"Kaliníkta, Greg," she said shyly, and went off.

She slept well, rocked like a babe in the bed of the yacht. She woke early, bathed, and dressed in her blue suit, which was looking rather old to her now. He would have let Charmian take two suitcases with her! But even that would not be enough. Iris sighed, and decided she was guilty of the sin of vanity.

She brushed her blue black hair long enough to dry it after shampooing it in the shower, then tied it up in a demure chignon. The sun brought out unusual lights in it, deep blue against the black. And her dark blue eyes looked brighter and more sparkling.

With the checked skirt, she wore a sleeveless white low-necked blouse, suitable for the heat. When they arrived at his island, she could don the suit jacket and look proper.

She walked the deck until the steward came to smile and tell her *"Kaliméra,"* good morning, and beckon her to breakfast.

Greg was there, smart again in navy blue and white. He seemed very cheerful today, she thought he was glad to be coming home. They ate fried fish and tiny tomatoes, hot sweet bread and fresh butter, fig jam, with cups of hot sweet coffee.

"What time will we arrive?" she asked finally.

"About six this evening, with luck and the seas."

As he came closer and closer to his home, he seemed the more Greek, speaking in poetry, with a deeper accent. His black eyes gleamed, his black hair was ruffled into wilder curls. "I hope you will enjoy my home, and be happy there," he said.

"Thank you," she said formally.

But she dreaded it. She did not want to feel at home in his home. She did not want to get better acquainted with him, and like his family. She remembered Alex, so nice and charming, so handsome and gay and bright.

It would be best if she went home very soon, before she came to like them all—and not want to leave.

Chapter Seven

A sky blue Lincoln Continental met them at the small dock as they landed. A curious crowd of islanders had gathered to greet them, and calls rang out to Greg, while they stared frankly at Iris.

A British Land Rover also had met them, and Greg ordered luggage and packages piled into that for the trip uphill to his home.

Greg issued orders, flashed a bright white-toothed smile, ruffled the heads of small boys who darted about his long legs, and acted very much the master come home.

The village was a good size, of whitewashed homes sprawling along the dock and straggling up the hillside along with silvery green olive trees, tall black cypresses, and reddish dusty roads. A goat baaed in a garden as it was shooed from the vegetable patch. Some fishing boats were tied up near the great white Venizelos yacht, and the smell of fish was strong on the dock.

"My fiancée, Miss Iris Patakos," Greg was introducing her cheerily to some of the men at the waterfront. He said their names, but in her confusion she caught none of them. Why did he keep saying he was engaged to her? It was no longer necessary, really. It had been a farce for the guards of their "prison.' Perhaps Greg thought it was necessary for her reputation, as he had announced it to the newsmen. But didn't it make more trouble than it prevented? She must have a firm talk with him!

In the car, she tried. "Greg, when we meet your mother, I do not wish to be introduced as your fiancée. It is not necessary—I am not—I don't want—"

He patted her hands absently. "It is necessary for a time, Iris," he said. "We were alone on the island."

"But Greg—nobody believes—in this day and age—we don't need—"

"Leave it to me!" he said firmly. "Now, Iris, do you wish to telephone your father tonight?"

She had to collect her thoughts. "No, it will soon be about three in the morning there—better to wait until tomorrow morning."

"Good." He leaned back, and began to speak to the chauffeur.

Iris leaned back also, with a great sigh, and glanced about her. Even with sunglasses on, she found the light overwhelming. The houses shone with the whitewashing, reflecting the bright light. The sky was a vivid blue with only a few white puffy clouds. The earth was a dusty red, sand flew up from the car wheels. It was a hot land, surrounded by the silken blue of the ocean. The color contrasts, the contrasts of sunlight and purple shadows, of heat and cool, were all fascinating to her.

She caught glimpses of little gardens, flowers and vegetables, and some gray green shrubs of herbs. In windowsills were small pots of basil, larger ones of scarlet geraniums, and in one the curled-up form of a black kitten, blinking bright green eyes.

She must come down here and sketch.

The road wound uphill and around a curve, and then slid to a dizzy dip, before winding up again and around a smooth stretch of road. Then she saw some enormous houses, not unlike the ones below but so much larger.

The limousine moved around two houses, and came to a halt before a huge unusual building. Greg helped Iris out, and stood proudly as she gasped at sight of the place.

It was built on the top of the hill, on a level of several acres Tall golden white columns of stone held up the terrace roo. of tile covered with purple bougainvillea. Some cane chairs were placed about, and some glass-topped tables, and a lady was rising from one of the chairs.

Behind her, lights from oil lamps illuminated the interior as the sky grew dusky gray blue. Iris could see that the inside was all open, one large space, the second floor and ceiling upheld by more stone pillars. Then the lady in black came toward her.

"Mother." Greg stepped to her, and took her in his arms. They hugged, kissed each other's cheeks affectionately. "You are well?"

"Now that you are safe, my son," said the slow musical voice in Greek, in a sort of husky murmur. Then both turned to Iris.

"Mother, permit me to introduce to you my fiancée, Miss Iris Patakos." His voice rang with his pride.

Iris blinked. That he should deceive the mother he evidently loved! "I am happy to meet you—" she began. "However—I should tell you—"

"That it is very sudden," said Greg, with a warning scowl to her. "All that later! Mother, I wish the Blue Suite for Iris. Is it ready?"

"As you asked, my son," said his mother, and smiled, and took both of Iris's hands in her firm brown ones. She was tanned by the sun, about Iris's height, with shrewd black eyes so like those of Greg. She had graying black curly hair, a rather plump figure in the handsome black gown, a single silver chain and ornament at her throat, silver earrings set with blue stones. "I welcome the betrothed of my son. I have longed for him to marry and give me grandchildren. Welcome, Iris Patakos." And she kissed Iris ceremonially and warmly on each cheek.

Now Iris did feel guilty and a cheat. She wanted so badly to explain that it was a mere expedient until they got away from the glare of publicity! Surely his mother should know the truth!

Iris had been vaguely aware of others coming behind the matron. Now Kyria Venizelos turned her gently to meet them. First was a girl about Iris's height, only much younger, with long brown hair and wistful big brown eyes, and a sweet gentle face.

"Iris Patakos, may I introduce to you our little cousin, Melania Venizelos, who lives with us."

The girls shook hands, Melania gave her a sweet smile. "Welcome to our home, Iris. We prayed for your safety!"

"It was most kind of you!" Iris gave her hand an extra squeeze impulsively, sure she was going to like this girl. "How do you do, Melania."

Several women in black, and a girl in gray and white had come up, evidently servants in the household. Kyria was just introducing them when a wheelchair rolled around the edge of the gardens to them.

"This is Sophronia—my maid, and with me always. This is Chris. This is Esmeralda—and Joseph, her husband, the gardener—"

"How do you do? How do you do?" Iris was shaking

plump hands, returning broad smiles as the servants looked her over with the frank curiosity of people who belonged.

The wheelchair rolled right up to her. "Charmian!" cried Alex's well-remembered bright voice. "It is you—you came! Greg—I never thought you would bring her—give me a hug and a kiss, Charmian!"

There was a dreadful pause. "I am not Charmian!" said Iris in a loud firm voice before Greg could make her pass as Charmian. "Charmian could not come, she had many modeling engagements. I am Iris, Alex. How do you do?"

"Not Charmian? She did not come?" The brightness died from the thin face, his arms dropped to those of the wheelchair. Iris gazed down at him gravely. He had changed. He was much thinner, and his legs seemed to be helpless in the chair. Worst of all, dark eyeglasses, enormous ones, covered his bright eyes completely, and from the way his head turned, she knew he could not see.

"I am sorry, Alex. She—she sent her love to you."

He gave a bitter laugh, and his handsome mouth twisted. "Oh, she sent her love, did she? So kind of her! I would rather she had brought herself without her love!"

"Now, Alex, do not take it out on Iris, who came in the kindness of her heart," said Greg firmly. "And events worked out well, we are now engaged to each other. You may congratulate me!"

"Surely. Give me a kiss, Iris!" said Alex devilishly.

"She is not so close," said Greg dryly, and his hand prevented Iris from moving to the wheelchair. "I will keep her kisses for me, I thank you! Now, let us go inside."

Joseph moved to push the wheelchair, Alex followed them sulkily as the little procession moved inside. Iris gazed with bright eyes, removing her sunglasses, as the interior presented itself to her.

The building was an irregular oval shape, with a central

staircase curving up to the second floor. She could now see that the stone pillars were set about to hold up the roof, and to set apart certain areas of the first floor. Also, Greek rugs in red and sand color spelled out certain places: the dining area, several living areas, and in the far side there was a huge desk, and some curious electric equipment, including a telephone, stereo, radio, and so on.

The huge couches and chairs were of comfortable warm sand colors, with puffy pillows of sand-colored silk. The effect was that of the outdoors brought inside and made comfortable, and the living areas spilled out onto the terrace and into the gardens. When Iris looked more closely, she could see inconspicuous glass doors ready to be pulled shut to protect the house against wind and rain storms, but for now they were all open to the air.

"Do you like it?" asked Greg's mother, with a smile, watching her face.

"I have never seen anything so unusual, and so lovely! It is like part of Greece, the cliffs, the earth."

Greg was smiling broadly, pleased. "I thank you! I designed it, with my grandfather. It was completed shortly before he died, so he did see it finished. It was almost as good as living in the open, or in one of the cliffs, he said. And he would tell us stories of the war, when he did live in the mountains."

His mother's face shadowed.

"It is truly beautiful," said Iris warmly. "You are very talented! Did you plan the couches, the tables—"

The tables were of Greek stone, set in place near the sofas and chairs. A few occasional tables could be moved, those of a pale yellow pine, smoothly polished to show the grain and patina of the wood. Only a few items were on the tables: a small Greek statue in reddish clay of a woman, a Pentelic marble bowl, several wrought-iron candlesticks. Against the beige walls of the staircase stood several Greek vases of antique orange and black, stunning in their simplicity of design. And near the front door stood a huge stone archaic Greek lion, snarling, his fur showing curls and tufts, looking almost real.

"I will take you to your room, Iris," said Kyria Venizelos. She motioned to the servants, they went their way. Melania followed them, evidently with duties to do. But Greg followed his up the winding stairs, to the second floor.

This was also in simple curving clean lines. Set into walls were doors, the floors were of stone, with red and blue Greek rugs on them. Kyria Venizelos led the way to a nearby door, and opened it, and motioned Iris inside.

She gasped as she went in. For the color schemes were of those colors and shades she would have chosen for herself, and had in the apartment.

Most were blue and white: sea and sky blue, clear white of the stone houses. The large bed was old-fashioned, of a dark shining wood, with four tall posts beautifully carved with little figures and flowers. Over it were draperies of white linen with borders of blue in the Greek key design. And drifts of white muslin protected, ready to be drawn against mosquitoes.

The dresser and tall chest of drawers were matching, in the same dark shining wood. A dresser scarf was of white, embroidered with red and blue designs in a primitive pattern. A comfortable chair sat plumply filled with cushions of white silk that matched its own cover. The rug was of white with blue Greek key design, matching the draperies, and the ones at the window matched again.

Greg had crowded into the room, following his mother. Now he watched Iris's face eagerly. "Do you like it? Do you like it?"

"It is perfect," she said spontaneously. "It is so comfortable, with such lovely colors! Thank you!"

"Greg designed this also," said his mother. "Here is your bath, it is for you alone." She opened one door in the near wall, to reveal a grand bathroom, of white porcelain fittings, whitewashed walls, stencils of blue and red figures like those of ancient times. The towels were huge and white.

Madame Venizelos opened another door, to reveal a huge closet. Iris's clothes were already hanging there. A maid had been very quick.

"I did not give Iris time to pack more," said Greg, looking dubiously at the clothes. "She sews well, perhaps Charis will assist her in making up some dresses."

"Of course, there are many lengths in the sewing room next door," said Madame Venizelos, showing no surprise. "I will be happy to help, and there are women in the village who would be glad of the work in embroidery."

"Oh, I shall not be here that long!" said Iris quickly, flushing. Madame looked her surprise. Greg scowled heavily and took Iris by the arm.

"I'll show you the sewing room. Come with me!" and he dragged her with him. As they went, he hissed, "You will stay! Do not say such things! Do you wish to upset my mother?"

"I must talk to you!" said Iris, under her breath. "I cannot remain for long—"

He shoved open the next door, and they entered. Inside was a complete sewing room, with a dressmaker's dummy, a fine new sewing machine, an embroidery kit that would be a dream to work with, and shelves of lengths of fabric.

More packages lay on the floor, unwrapped. Madame Venizelos followed them into the room. "Oh, more have come—Greg, did you order some?"

"Yes, from Athens, as we passed through. There are also some lengths for Iris especially—you will know them! And, Iris, I saw that you had finished your sketch pads. Here are more, open them when you wish! Also, I had the men buy an easel for oil painting, some oils, and brushes, and such. I wish you to be happy here!''

Iris gazed blankly at the formidable array of parcels. ''Well—that is very kind,'' she said.

Greg interrupted her when she would have protested further. ''Good, good. Now, excuse me, I must go down and make some phone calls.''

And he departed hastily. Iris returned to her room, his mother followed her.

''How does he make phone calls? Surely no telephone lines,'' Iris began.

''No, we have a radio-telephone set, like the ham radio operators have,'' said Kyria Venizelos comfortably. ''It is most useful, even the storms scarcely interrupt the transmission. And we can phone to Athens, to Europe, even to America, most easily. Now, if there is anything you wish— no? Dinner will be served about nine o'clock, but pray come down earlier if you will, we must become acquainted!''

After her hostess had departed, Iris took off her suit and lay down for a time. The cool comfort of the blue and white room helped her feel more composed.

Charis, one of the younger maids, tiptoed in presently, took Iris's blue silk dress and soon returned with it beautifully pressed. She helped her dress, and fluttered about her curiously.

Iris went down about eight, and Greg met her at the bottom of the stairs. He wore tonight a cream-colored silk suit with a deep blue ruffled shirt opened almost to his waist. She could see his golden body with the crisp black hairs, and a gold chain dangled from his throat and ended in a gold saint's pendant. He smiled at her and took her right arm.

He also took her right hand in his, and slipped on the ring finger a gold band with a beautiful oval sapphire. ''Your engagement ring," he whispered. "It was my grandmother's. Do you like it?"

"Goodness—it is lovely—but I don't want a ring! I don't want—"

"Hush, hush, you will distress my mother!" And he firmly drew her over to one of the little islands of rug and sofas and chairs. Some of the glass windows had been drawn shut, the flames of candles fluttered in the night breeze.

Kyria Lydia Venizelos greeted them with a smile, busily working at some crocheting with her skilled fingers. Melania was also making something in red and white.

"Does your grandmother's ring fit your fiancée?" asked Kyria Venizelos, with a significant look and smile at Iris's small right hand, where the Greeks wore engagement and wedding rings.

"It fits well. It is a good omen," said Greg, sitting down next to Iris possessively, on the soft deep couch.

Oh, there were so many threads now to untangle! She felt more and more desperate. Why did Greg persist so?

"Alex will not come to dinner," said Melania, as Iris looked about. "He is very sensitive. He does not like us to see him try to eat."

"He is selfish," said Greg with a scowl. "He deprives us of his company, rather than make the effort to learn to eat though blind."

They discussed that briefly. Melania looked distressed, her aunt changed the subject. Iris had soon formed the notion that Melania had a crush on her handsome cousin Alex. Greg seemed protective of her.

"What have you done while I was gone?" he asked her.

"Oh, I have been sewing, and visiting the sick—"

"You must show Iris about. Take her to the village, introduce her to the priest and to friends there. Iris is a fine dressmaker. Help her choose some lengths to make up for herself, and help her sew," ordered Greg.

"I will not need—" Iris began. Greg squeezed her ring hand, and the ring dug into her palm.

"Some evening gowns, some day gowns," he said. "A couple sundresses. Those are not difficult to make, eh?"

"We might invite Petros Diophantus to come," said Lydia, clipping a thread. "He is a fine dressmaker, he has a house in Athens," she explained to Iris. "He will come and make many garments especially for Iris. He would be happy to be asked to make her wedding dress."

"Not now," said Greg. "Later. We will go to Athens, you and I and Iris," he said to his mother. "I have promised Iris a view of the Parthenon, and other sights."

She sat there, unable to break into their conversation politely, as they planned her future. Melania worked in silence, and once caught Iris's eye, and smiled shyly at her, as though to say she understood.

Lydia Venizelos seemed to Iris like a mother superior she had known: kind, motherly, ruling by force of her character. Even her bold, dynamic son listened to her. She had a gentle voice, but one listened when she spoke. At the table, she never raised her voice, but the servants slipped in and out, brought dishes, removed them. She was aware all of the time what went on, even as she spoke of other matters.

They lingered long at the table. Alex joined them for coffee, and teased Iris and Melania, and asked his brother about business in the States. He seemed impatient to return to work. Could he work again?

Iris returned to her room about midnight, and Charis came to help her retire. She slept well, her dreams of waterfalls of fragrant flowers, and butterflies hovering over phlox in blue and pink and mauve.

In the morning, she rose early, still off schedule, the

meaning of time changed for her. She did not have to rush to the bus to get to work, she did not have to worry about traffic and crowds. The day was peaceful, she could hear bees buzzing among the bougainvillea as she came down the stairs. The glass panes had all been rolled back, and a fresh morning breeze filled the open first floor of the large Venizelos home.

Greg was already at his desk, listening to the telephone, and some panels were lit up before him. He smiled and waved his hand to her absently. She waved back, but deliberately went over to the dining table where places were set.

Melania smiled a greeting, halfway through her meal. "We eat when we wish in the morning," she said shyly, when they had exchanged "kaliméra" greetings.

One of the maids came, and Iris asked for a boiled egg, and fruit juice, and helped herself to hot breads and coffee.

Lydia was outside, kneeling on a mat in the flower beds. Iris admired the sight: scarlet poppies and blue and rose lupins, against the vivid blue sky, and the woman in a pink cotton gown kneeling with her hands lovingly in the flowers.

"I would like to paint her so," she murmured, her gaze on the sight.

"Aunt Lydia enjoys flowers so much," said Melania. "And she can grow anything. She has the green—fingers?"

"Green thumb."

"Yes. So. I like to help her, but sometimes I pull up the wrong thing!" She giggled a little, her brown eyes flashing with mirth. "She does not scold, but she looks sad!"

"I fear I would do the same thing. I had best keep out!"

There had been a few flower gardens at the convent, but they were practically owned by the nuns who gardened. Others were not allowed to help or pick flowers. Iris gazed outside as she ate, and drank her coffee. This was a different life here, different from the long convent years. What must it be, to have a mother like Lydia Venizelos, so good, so concerned, so sweet? Iris would never know. She did not intend to marry, no man should have power over her as her father had had—to order her life, for good or ill, with no chance of protest. No, she was free now, and she would remain free.

Alex had come in, and was talking to Greg over in the study area. Now he rolled his wheelchair excitedly partway to where the girls sat in the dining area.

"Iris—telephone—your father!"

"Good heavens," gasped Iris. She rose, and went to them warily. She looked at the confusing metallic panel with its dials and lights.

Greg seated her in a chair, handed her the telephone. "Just talk naturally," he advised, and patted her shoulder. Alex was listening, so was Greg.

Iris took the phone. "Hello—father?"

"Iris!" Hilarion Patakos bellowed, so loudly that she winced and took the phone partly from her ear. "What happened to you? I saw the papers today, and they are full of pictures of you and some strange fellow in Athens—who is he? Where are you? What are you doing?"

She wondered how to answer all his questions at once, and decided not to. "I am well, father!" she called into the phone.

"Well, are you? What happened to you? Who is Venizelos? I have not met him! How can you be engaged to him? I have not approved of this! I tell you, I will plan your wedding! There will be no such foolishness! I shall plan your marriage when I find the right man, and you will listen to me!"

Iris felt quite shocked. She had scarcely seen her father for years, and he talked blithely of planning her marriage!

"No, father, I do not mean to—father! Listen to me—can you hear me—"

Everybody in the room could hear her father, his voice

111

yelled into the quiet curious air of the large room. Alex was grinning, and making rude signs to his Cousin Greg. Greg was scowling, and finally took the telephone from Iris firmly.

"Mr. Patakos, this is Gregorios Venizelos," he said, sounding very Greek, his voice rasping. "I am the fiancé of your daughter, Iris Patakos. How do you do?"

"What? What?" Even without the telephone at her ear, Iris could hear him clearly. "Who are you? How dare you engage yourself to my daughter! You have no right—"

"We must become acquainted!" said Greg, loudly overriding the other man. "Come to Greece!"

"Eh? What—what did you say?"

"Come to greece! Come to Athens, and I will have you met by a plane and brought to my island. Our families should become acquainted! I wish to meet the father of my future wife!"

"No—no—no," said Iris urgently, trying to get the telephone back. Greg easily kept it from her. "No, tell him I'll come home at once—that I will break the engagement—"

Greg shook his head at her. Alex was chuckling openly.

"Gregorios here yet, yes, sir. . . . To be sure—your wife and you will be most welcome! Let me know the time of your arrival in Athens!"

He hung up, smiling broadly, rubbing his hands.

"Well, well, we shall all meet, and I will see the father of my fiancée," he said, and winked at Iris. "I have things to say to him! Yes, I do," and he looked fierce suddenly.

Iris groaned. She loved peace and quiet, and she thought all the peace of the island was about to be destroyed. "Please Greg, call him back, tell him I will come home—there is no need to come—"

The phone was ringing. Alex reached over and answered it.

"Yes . . . yes . . . yes . . . Iris, it is for you again!"

She reached for it urgently before Greg could grab it. "Hello? Father? . . . Oh, Bill!"

It was Bill Roswell, the stepfather of Charmian, the man who had married Shelley. "How are you, Iris! I saw the papers, and I must say I was very shocked! Had no idea you were in Greece—plane crashed? Oh, that is terrible!"

"Oh, Bill, I am fine, thank you. It is all right. We were stranded for a week on an island, but we are fine now. No, we had no injuries, thank God for that."

"I tried to find out from Charmian what had happened, but she had no notion you had gone to Greece! Even Nadia Egorova did not know you had crashed. This was a mighty big shock, let me tell you!"

"Oh, Bill, kindly call Nadia, and tell her I am all right! I had meant to call, but hoped it would not be in the newspapers. . . . Yes, kindly call her, tell her I am well and fine, not injured. . . . Yes. Yes, she is very kind. . . . Oh, dear, she was crying? I am so sorry—"

Greg managed to get the phone from her once more. Iris cried out in exasperation. "Let me have the phone, Iris. Tut, tut, don't be angry!" and he grinned down at her. "Hello? This is the fiancé of Iris Patakos! You are Bill Roswell?"

Iris could hear the other voice going on. "Yes, I am Bill Roswell, mighty happy to meet you! Wish we could meet in person! Iris is a mighty fine little girl—does her father know?"

"I have invited her father to come. Why don't you come also? Our families should meet. My mother will be happy to have you as our guests!"

"Oh, no!" breathed Iris in genuine horror. "Not all of them together! They will—please, Greg! Don't invite them all!"

It was too late, he completed the arrangements, and hung up, looking very pleased with himself.

"There. We shall all meet and become acquainted!" said Greg.

Iris stood up, shaking out her skirts as though to rid herself of the dust of conflict. "I must say, you are arrogant and bullying!" she said bitterly. "You don't know what you have done! They all hate each other! And I will spend my time trying to keep them separated! Oh, a fine family reunion that will be! I could scream at you!"

"Now, Iris," Greg tried to soothe her, catching at her arm. "It will be all right. Why should they not all come? All divorces are not bitter. Besides, they are both concerned about you."

"I could reassure them on the telephone! But, no, you had to interfere!"

Alex glanced in amazement from one to the other, as though at a particularly torrid tennis match. His dark glasses glinted in the sunlight, as he kept turning his head, trying to get every nuance of their voices.

"Iris, you must trust me and do as I wish—"

"I am tired of doing what others wish!" she flashed, and ran from him, up the stairs to her room. She paced for a time, fuming. But it did no good.

Presently, she heard the maids in the next rooms. She went over to the storage room, and found the material Greg had ordered for her, the sketch pads, watercolors, oil paints, and easel and camel's hair brushes. She should have been mollified by the vast array of material he had bought, but instead she was infuriated anew at the thought he had done this because he meant to keep her here for a time.

And what for? To amuse Alex? Or to amuse himself? He seemed to enjoy her temper!

Well, he would get more of a taste of it, if he kept interfering in her life!

She chose a sketch pad, and fresh brushes and watercolors,

and jammed a straw hat on her head. Then she went down to the gardens where Lydia worked, and sat down to work.

The gardener brought her a folding chair, and she worked the rest of the morning sketching the scarlet poppies, and the figure of Lydia moving about in the garden. Lydia said not a word, she seemed to understand Iris did not want to speak.

The low growl and grumble of Alex's and Greg's voices came out to the gardens, but did not disturb them. She would forget them for one morning, thought Iris, and soon she would figure out some way to get out of this vexing fix and away from this island, beautiful though it was.

Chapter Eight

Iris had noticed there were several buildings about, near the Big House, and seemingly part of a complex.

At luncheon, Greg and his mother spoke of where to put their guests. "In the Long House, I think," said Greg, and Lydia nodded.

"Yes, I will have the women to clean the rooms this afternoon," she said. "Do you know when Iris's father will be coming?"

"Not yet, probably in two days from now."

"What is the Long House?" Iris ventured.

Lydia smiled at her and patted her hand absently. "Greg shall show you about, my dear. You should see all the houses, I believe. Ask her to approve the arrangement, Greg. After all, this will be her duty one day," and her black eyes twinkled suggestively at Iris.

Iris fumed inwardly. She would never say anything in front of Lydia, but, oh, how she longed to blow up at Greg.

"After luncheon, I'll show you around," nodded Greg. "Alex can listen for telephone calls. Do him good to be useful."

"Yes, he broods too much," said Greg's mother. "He has brightened up since you and Iris came. He was dull with us."

Melania hung her head. "He misses his friends," she said softly. "He is accustomed to beautiful women and bright conversation, and many sports."

"He is in danger of losing all sense of values," said Lydia, shaking her graying head. "You have earned too much money for the family, Gregorios. Alex thinks only of how to spend it lavishly!"

Greg looked thoughtful, but did not dispute that. Lydia turned to Iris.

"In the old days, we all had to work hard, it was good for us. During the war and after, times were hard. Yet we laughed and were close. All helped. Now, one hears only that someone has more jewelry than another, or more lavish clothes. Or someone must go to the Caribbean for the winter, to Norway for the summer, or not be fashionable! Gregorios's grandfather used to explode!"

"He certainly did," said Greg, with a grin that showed his white teeth. "Leander would not put up with foolishness. All must work, and earn his bread. And the money went back into the firm. But what does one do, when one earns more money than can be used in the firm?"

"One gives to the poor. One builds hospitals and trains doctors and nurses for the sick!" said Iris fiercely. "It makes me ill, to see the wealthy of this world with their silly games, trying to outdo the others in outrageous play. All that waste! And others are dying of hunger and disease!"

There was a little silence.

"You are right," said Lydia mildly. "There is much waste

in the world. Still, there is room for play, though, as you say, it is very expensive play, such a waste.''

"And some men like women who play expensively," said Melania, blushing as they gazed at her. "They do not . . . care for women . . . who think only to work hard, to be faithful . . . and have babies—that is no longer in fashion!''

"Never think so!'' said Greg roughly, smiling at her kindly. "Some men are so foolish as to say that, but it is not true. The true women of this world are those who are good wives and mothers, who love their men and their babies and care for them devotedly. That will always be true! The essential things and values of this world will remain forever! Men will work for their families, and women will care for them, and all else is the frills on the sturdy garments of life.''

"Hear, hear!'' Alex had rolled his wheelchair to them silently, and pushed himself accurately up between Greg and Melania. "Pour me some coffee and tend to my needs, woman!'' he teased Melania.

In silence, she poured his hot black coffee, added sugar lavishly, and put the cup near his right hand. He groped for the cup, stirred the sugar slowly with the tiny spoon, and drank thirstily.

Iris was eating a pomegranate cake. She enjoyed all the new flavors and exotic fruits and foods she was encountering. The cake was yellow, round and fluted, and over it had been poured rich pink pomegranate juice, which gave it a refreshingly tart flavor. Greg was watching her with a curious smile.

"You like it?''

"Very much, I thank you.''

"Now you must remain for at least six months of the year!'' he joked.

She remembered the story of the daughter of Ceres, or

Demeter. Hades had fallen in love with the beautiful girl Persephone, and carried her off. Because she broke her fast, and ate some seeds of the pomegranate, she must remain part of the year with Hades, her husband, and part with her mother Demeter.

"You speak as though it was a punishment to remain with us, Greg. Does Iris feel so? Do you not like our beautiful Greece?" asked Lydia gently of Iris.

"I think your island is lovely; that is all I have seen of Greece, except a brief view of Athens from the air, and the island where we crashed," said Iris.

"You will see more of it, and come to love Greece, your homeland," said Gregorios decisively. He shoved back his heavy armchair, and it scraped on the stone floor. "Come, Iris, let me show you about your new home."

She came with him, partly because he demanded, partly because she wanted to talk to him. Alex was left in charge of the telephone, he could make the wheelchair whiz across the stone floor to the complex of the study.

Greg looked down at Iris as she walked with him. He seemed to admire her in the dusty pink blouse and skirt, the sandals with straps wound around her ankles. "You look very lovely," he said. "You have a little tan now."

"Yes. Greg, I wish you had not invited my father here. It will be so awkward to break the engagement—"

His face hardened into a bronze mask. "I do not wish to break the engagement," he said. "Leave all these matters to me!" They walked across the driveway to the Long House. "Now, this house was built by my father, Ioannes, on the occasion of his marriage to my mother, Lydia. It was build just before World War II. They lived in it here—whenever father was home from the wars. It was good that it is one floor, for father was injured after the war, in the Greek wars that followed, and he was much of the time in a wheelchair. As you see, the floors are even with the ground outside.''

They walked into the hallway, a simple arrangement that divided the rooms on one side of the Long House with those on the other. Greg pointed to one door.

''Alex and his valet are there, a self-contained unit with bedrooms and bath, and a small dining room. I thought to put your father and his wife across the hall, and then Bill Roswell and his wife in the other corner rooms.''

He opened the door on the right, and Iris went in. Some village women were there, busily scrubbing out the rooms in the small suite. The bedroom was large, the parlor small, the bath adequate.

''They were all remodeled when the Big House was built,'' said Greg more cheerfully, after exchanging greetings with the women. ''Baths were put in, so we can entertain guests. The kitchen was no longer needed, for there is a separate kitchen in a building behind the Big House. How do you like this one for your father?''

Iris nodded. ''He likes red and bright blue very much. And the beds and chairs are big, he is a big man. This is fine.''

''And your stepmother?''

''Maria Ardeth? I don't know—I have never met her. I heard she is blond, with gray eyes, that is all I know.''

Greg looked disgusted, whether at her or someone else, she was not sure. They moved to the next rooms.

The corner suite for Bill Roswell was decorated in a sand color, with accents of rusty red. Iris approved them, though she knew Shelley was very particular and critical. Well, she was a guest, the rooms were clean and large, and she should be satisfied.

She did wonder about one point. The rooms in both suites had large double beds. And she thought all of them slept in

121

single beds, and in their own rooms! The modern way. Well, if they were uncomfortable, perhaps they would soon leave!

Greg caught at Iris's hand, and clasped it in his. "This way, to grandfather's house," he said. "This is the earliest house, it replaced one built a hundred years ago. Grandfather tore it down, and built one for himself and his bride, about 1920. We call it the Cottage, though it was large for houses at the time."

They came to the Cottage, and entered. It was a house much like those in the village, whitewashed with red slate roof. One entered into a tiny living room, with simple slits for windows. The furniture was old-fashioned, dark straight chairs, some plump armchairs, hassocks with embroidered tops, a white stone fireplace in which coal was ready to be lit. Behind it was a kitchen with a sturdy yellow pine table. On the other side of a narrow hall were two bedrooms, with narrow beds and coverlets of native embroidery on white linen.

A modern bathroom had been added at the back of the house, connected to the hallway. They returned to the front. Greg pointed to the front bedroom, opposite the parlor.

"This is where my father was born," he said.

"I like this house very much," she told him softly. "It is the kind of house where I would like to live!"

Greg looked rather stunned. " 'To live'? This is a guest-house, but if you would wish it—"

"No, no, I don't mean to move about, I shall not be here that long!" she said firmly. "I just mean—if I could have a little house like this in America, I should be content!"

He put his arms about her. "You are very sweet, Iris," he said huskily. "You know, I wish I could give you everything in the world that you wish!"

And he put his lips very gently on hers, in such a sweet

undemanding kiss that she did not think to fight him. She stood unresisting as he kissed her again, very softly, moving his large mouth over her pink lips. Her hands rested on his broad bare arms, he had rolled up his sleeves in the warmth of the day. She felt the muscles under the golden bronze of his warm skin. It was pleasant to rest for a moment in his strength.

Then he kissed her again, harder, and gathered her closer in his arms, so her body was pressed against his, and she took alarm.

She tried to push her hands against his body and move back from him. She might as well have tried to move the stone lion in the doorway of the Big House. His mouth turned greedy, he drank thirstily from her mouth, pressed it open with his lips, and sipped at her lips.

She could feel his thighs against her body, and felt the hard masculine stirring there. She remembered all too well how he had tried to take her in the little cottage on the island, where they had been prisoners. His passions were too easily stirred!

"No, Greg—no!"

"Just a moment—one moment more—"

His mouth closed again over hers, and his arms crushed her up against him so that her toes left the floor of the cottage. She was swung off her feet, up into his arms, and held helplessly there against his chest while he kissed her mouth, her cheeks, her throat. She felt him nuzzle back the cloth of her blouse, and press his lips to the warmth of her shoulder, and then down, trying to find her rounded breast.

She struggled, though it might mean falling. She fought him, pounding her small fists against his chest and neck.

"Let me go—let me go—Greg—if you don't let me go—I'll scream—I won't let you do—Greg—I don't want this—I will leave—I swear I will leave—"

Her flailing arms and wriggling small body finally accomplished what her words would not. He had to set her down before she fell.

"Oh, Iris," he mourned, as he set her on her feet. "You are so little and sweet. Let me kiss you!"

She was hot and flushed and furious. "No! I don't want you to touch me at all!" she stormed. "Why won't you listen to me? I don't want to be engaged to you! I want to go home! Let me go!"

She pressed her hands strongly against his chest, and finally he allowed her to slip out of his arms.

"But, Iris, why go home, when there is no one there to love you?" he asked softly.

She gazed blindly up at him, wide-eyed but unseeing. No one there to love her! No, there had never been, there never would be. But here was passion—here was lust—it was not enough!

With a little cry, she turned and ran from the Cottage, and out into the hot still air of the golden afternoon. Greg easily caught up with her, and put one possessive hand on her shoulder.

"And here is the family chapel," he said, as easily as though he had not been kissing her wildly a few moments before. "The priest usually comes once a week to us, for liturgy."

He moved her firmly to the small building beyond the Cottage of his grandfather. When they entered, the narthex was filled with a soft golden glow from the yellow candles, illuminating the Madonna icon.

Iris bent and kissed the icon, and murmured a prayer. Greg followed her example, and then they entered the sanctuary.

It was tiny, but in the usual form of a Greek cross. There were a dozen seats, and around the walls in niches were several statues. Iris wandered about, examining the statues, the murals, the beautifully wrought black iron candlesticks and candelabra. The statues were of her favorite saints: Saint John of Pátmos, Saint Luke, Saint Sophia, the Virgin Mother of God, and Christ the Pantocrator. The images had an even more Oriental look than those at home in Chicago, she thought, but something about them gave her the same feeling of *déjà vu* she had felt on arriving in Athens.

She had seen them before, or known of them, or lived here at one time in some other life. She felt at home here, and as she gazed at the images she had the strange feeling that she would be gazing again and again, for many years. Perhaps her people had come from near here.

She breathed it to silent Greg at her side. "I feel—I have been here before, seen them before—known this place."

He nodded, unsurprised. "You are Greek. You belong here. The land and the sea are your home. You have come home."

She moved her head in a negative, suddenly aware of what she had said to him. However, Greg had moved forward, and taken an unlit candle from a supply of white candles. He gave one to her, and took another for himself.

They lit the candles from the flame in a red glass vase before the Madonna, knelt and placed the candles in the candle stand and prayed.

Iris was praying silently in gratitude for their safe journey. They had been in grave danger, and the Blessed Virgin and the Christ her Son had saved them. She gazed up at the grave face of the dark-skinned Virgin and her solemn Son, and thanked them again and again that she and Greg had not died in the fiery small plane. As she turned her head slightly, she saw Greg had his hand on the Medallion at his chest, as he prayed to the Virgin and to his own special saint, probably his name saint, Saint Gregory.

In the flickering light, she saw what she had seen many times before. The eyes of the Virgin in the flickering light seemed to move, and to answer her own, and gaze deeply into her own eyes. She was answered, and she was content.

They rose, and left the chapel in silence, and returned to the outdoors. A light breeze had sprung up, Greg gazed at the sky.

"A storm will come before night," he said. "Look at the clouds gathering over the land, to the north. We need rain."

"Are the storms violent here?" she asked.

"Sometimes. At this time of year, we have some mild ones. Toward late summer and autumn, we have more violent ones. But I enjoy them all," and he laughed aloud at some memory, his eyes sparkling. "I have been out on the open sea, and it is frightening! But exciting!"

He showed her around the remainder of the buildings. The kitchen she had seen briefly, a separate building with ovens of the usual kind, and some brick ones, many tables for work, a dry sink, and piped-in water.

Beyond were several other small houses, for some of the servants. Others lived in the village below, and came only when needed.

A large garage that had been a barn housed the luxurious limousines and a couple of Land Rovers, and a full toolshed so they might repair their own vehicles.

After the tour, Greg returned to his study, and Iris went upstairs to see about cutting out some dresses. Melania and Charis followed her to the sewing room, where she set the dressmaker dummy to her own proportions. Then she began to examine the full shelves of fabrics.

Melania explained, "Greg keeps us supplied, we all like to sew. Sometimes it is necessary to make black clothes for funerals, or supply veils quickly. It is not always easy to go to the mainland for material, and the village store is limited.''

Charis added, with a nod of her black head, ''Kyrios Gregorios brings many more materials this time, he says they are for you to make clothes, which is your work. Eh?''

''Yes, at home I am a dressmaker,'' said Iris thoughtfully. She puzzled over the fabrics. Why did Greg supply all these for her work? Did he think she would be here long?

Happily she delved into the bolts of fabric. A length of blue green silk caught her eye, and she held it against herself. Charis and Melania approved, and so she draped some of the fabric over the dummy, cut and basted, and soon had a full-length evening gown in a classic style ready to be sewn. Charis was amazed, so was Melania, at the quick movements of her hands.

''I have done this for years,'' she explained.

''But even Kyrios Petros Diophantus does not work so fast, when he comes to make clothes for us,'' explained Melania. ''He is a very good dressmaker, but he fusses, and worries over details.''

''He is probably a genius,'' said Iris, with a laugh.

''But I like your work,'' said Melania. Charis took the lengths of silk, and began running up the seams on the modern sewing machine. She was very deft and soon had the main seams done.

Meantime, Iris had chosen a raspberry-colored silk, and made that up into a short afternoon dress. The bodice was a simple one, the skirt attached with a length of elasticized tape, so that the full skirt hung in little pleats. Melania offered to sew that by hand, and sat down to thread her needle and get to work.

Iris seemed to be living in her flowered sundress; so she decided to run up a couple more. She quickly cut out one in a bright yellow cotton, and one in a periwinkle blue cotton crepe. She basted them easily on the dummy, tried them on to make sure they fit, then set them aside.

"Melania, would you like a new dress?" she asked, fondling the lengths of silk fabric. Her eye had been caught by a silk of sherry brown shot through with a gold thread.

Melania's brown eyes shone. "Well—you will be busy—"

"Not with such able assistants!" laughed Iris. She pulled out the fabric, and began to drape it over Melania. The girl stood still for her, and soon Iris had a lovely sleeveless gown cut out, of a classically simple slightly full skirt and a pleated bodice like a Greek statue.

They completed the work on the sewing machine as the dusk closed in. "Surely it is not late evening," said Melania, glancing out the deep-set window.

"No, the storm comes," said Charis. "I must go light lamps, I think."

She excused herself, and departed. Rather than light a lamp here, Melania and Iris gathered up the fabrics, a sewing box of thread, needles, and pins, and went downstairs to one of the couches before a stone table, and prepared to work there.

Gregorios and two menservants in rough blue work clothes were moving about among the pillars, closing the glass panes; and, on the north, closing and bolting the rough white-painted shutters that would protect the glass. Lamps had been lit in the sewing area, giving off a mellow golden glow.

Lydia came down from her room to observe the girls' work. She praised the dresses, and asked to embroider the yellow sundress. "I would put on white daisy petals, so that the yellow fabric will show through for yellow centers," she said, and soon was busily working the white daisy petals onto the fabric.

Charis brought trays of hot tea and small sandwiches. Greg came over to join them, and Joseph wheeled Alex in. The men teased the women for their work, though Greg seemed to take a personal pride in Iris's work.

"She makes a dozen garments with the ease of another woman making one," he said, watching Iris sew the hem on the blue green silk. "Iris, make me a dozen shirts! I should like some white ruffled ones, and a blue one like that—"

She wrinkled her nose at him. "I do not make clothes for men," she said primly. "They are too particular, at least some men such as one I know are particular!"

"Make one for me, then, fair Iris," teased Alex. "I would enjoy just having it from your fair hands!"

Greg scowled unexpectedly, and took exception to Alex's remarks, which made his cousin tease him the more. Lydia stopped them placidly, and changed the conversation.

"The rooms for Iris's family are ready now. When do they come, Gregorios?"

"In two days, mother. I have ordered more food from the village, and two lambs will be brought."

"Good. I have ordered more bread to be made and brought to us. Half a dozen women will come to work, including two with experience as maids."

Iris felt it was a lot of work, and said so. "I am sorry there will be so much more work to be done because they come."

"Nonsense. It will be a pleasure, and everybody in the village will be ready to help."

"She will make a good wife," said Greg, with satisfaction. "She worries about my expenses! And she is mature, she has gracious manners. And she will make a good housewife, see how she sews, and makes use of the hours of lightness!"

Lydia did not take it as teasing, as Iris did. She said placidly, "Yes, Iris will make you a good wife. She is genntle of nature, she has religious feelings. I am glad you did not choose one of those modern girls who think only of their careers!''

Iris shot upright on the thick plushy sofa. "But I do think of my career!" she retorted. "I am a dressmaker, and a designer! If I do well, Nadia Egorova will make me her assistant! I plan to make many designs, and make a fine name for myself!"

Lydia patted Iris's knee, and smiled at her. "You have a fine talent," she said mildly. "It will help you with your own family and your children when they come. It is pleasant to make little garments for your babies. And one day you may make some little dresses for yourself and your daughters, the mother and daughter dresses I have seen in magazines! That will be sweet!"

Iris blushed violently as Greg smiled over at her. "I am serious about a career," she insisted. "I mean to make very fashionable garments for the New York markets. Madame Egorova will make me very famous!"

Melania listened, wide-eyed, over sewing her sherry-brown dress. " 'Famous'?" she murmured. "You wish this?"

"When she marries, she will change her mind," smiled Lydia. "She is a homebody, I know it."

Nobody listened to her! Nobody believed she meant what she said. Iris fumed in silence, as the conversation changed to the coming storm, and the winds howled about the large sturdy building.

They did not know her, thought Iris. Well, they would see! She meant what she said. Her ambition was to be a magnificent famous dress designer, and she would do it!

They dined together, even Alex, to the sounds of the howling winds, and a rainstorm that drenched the gardens. Melania patiently cut up Alex's meat, soothed him when he spilled French fried potatoes on his suit, made sure his wineglass was half filled, not full. Her musical low voice seemed to calm him when he became furious at himself.

After dinner, they listened to the storm, and to the music of Beethoven on the stereo. The combination was magnificent. The ladies sewed, the men talked together in low tones or were silent. All listened to the satisfying music.

It was the last peaceful evening for a long time.

The next morning, Iris was sewing with Melania when the telephone rang. Alex answered, and motioned to Greg. He took the telephone, and talked in it, while Alex made frightful faces and motioned with his arms slashing in the air.

"What is it?" asked Melania from across the room.

He mounted, "Xanthe and family!"

"Oh—good heavens!" she gasped, letting her sewing fall into her lap. "They are not coming!"

He nodded violently, making horrible faces at Iris and Melania, only half joking. He seemed disturbed and upset.

Iris watched Greg's face. He seemed quite calm, half smiling as he talked on the telephone. He hung up, rang another number and another, then stood up.

"Melania—kindly tell mother that Xanthe and Vanessa and the girls are coming up from the dock. I'll see to the servants—they must be told to prepare the Cottage." And he strode out.

Melania ran out to the gardens, where Lydia was working with the gardener. They talked briefly, then Lydia came inside. She did not seem happy, but her placid face was not as angry as Alex's.

"What is it? Who is Xanthe?" Iris ventured to ask Alex as he wheeled himself over to her.

"Some cousins, about fourth cousins, I think. Very Greek and passionate!" he grimaced. "Xanthe was raised on a farm in very poor circumstances. This was the years before Gregorios made us all rich! We had money, though, and some comforts. Well, Xanthe vowed to escape the farm, somehow, and she married a German, a very nasty fellow as he turned out. Greg was worried about it, tried to stop it, but it went through.''

"And he was—not kind,'' said Iris thoughtfully.

"To put it mildly!'' Alex had picked up some American expressions, and sometimes used them forcefully. "It was a riot! Xanthe is a very bossy character, but her husband had her—er—buffaloed! He was a brutal fellow. Karl Grassmann.''

"And she has children?'' Iris finished an armhole, and began to gather up her sewing. She had best put it all away, if guests were descending on them.

"Yes, two girls, Greta and Nora. Evidently Karl started beating them up whenever he got drunk, and Xanthe struck him. They might have killed each other, but fate intervened. He went up to Germany to visit relatives, and while there someone struck him over the head—killed him. Big relief all around!''

"How terrible!''

"Yes. Well—Xanthe is free now, but still unhappy. I wonder if that woman is capable of being happy. She has a younger sister, Vanessa, a beautiful girl. The two of them live together in an apartment Greg bought for them in Crete—their homeland. But Xanthe works from time to time, then loses her job. Her tongue gets her into lots of trouble!''

Iris grimaced involuntarily. They did not sound like comfortable guests. Alex laughed. "Well, I'm going to hide out in my rooms for a time! A privilege of being an invalid!'' And he wheeled himself away.

Iris put her sewing away, made sure she looked demure and neat in her yellow sundress with the white daisies, and came down to sit with Melania in the living room. Melania seemed nervous, twining her fingers together. Finally the sound of cars was heard, and both girls rose, and went out onto the patio.

The blue Lincoln Continental rolled up first, then a Land Rover filled with suitcases. "They mean to stay!" whispered Melania, who was never catty.

From the first car came a smartly dressed woman in funeral black. She had black hair and black eyes, her hair was caught beneath a thick black veil that must have been stifling in the humid heat of the day after the storm.

She had a strong face, with a long Greek nose, haughty chin, and lean cheeks. Bitterness lay like a yellow mask across her face.

After her came another girl, younger, and much more beautiful, with classic grave features and lovely huge eyes. Vanessa was in silvery gray, a smart traveling suit, with slim high-heeled silver gray shoes, and a smart black hat. After her came two small girls, to stand solemnly on the driveway, staring at everybody in turn.

Much kissing of cheeks. Iris noted that Greg's face was kissed most often, by Xanthe and then by Vanessa. Vanessa lingered over him, her gray-clad arms about his shoulders, her body pressed to his until he stepped back again.

"Aunt Lydia!" More embraces. "Melania!" More embraces.

Then black eyes turned on her, like pinning a butterfly. Iris felt a country cousin in her bright yellow cotton dress.

"We heard—we saw in the newspapers—yes, we saw that Gregorios Venizelos—he is engaged—it cannot be!—not to an American girl!"

Greg beamed. "Yes, I am the fortunate man! Permit me to introduce these cousins, Iris! Iris Patakos, this is my cousin, Xanthe Michaelides Grassmann—"

Brief touch of cheeks. Xanthe's sallow cheek seemed cold

even on that warm day. "Iris Patakos? But you are not Greek!"

"A Greek-American girl, is she not lovely?" Greg smiled, taking Iris's arm possessively, in a way that her right hand was shoved forward and they could see the blue sapphire on her finger.

Burning black eyes stared at the ring, stared at Iris's face. "It cannot be—you would always marry a Greek girl!"

"Americans are said to be very fast," murmured Vanessa, with a smile. She had strong features, a more relaxed look than her dynamic older sister. "But one can see little Iris Patakos is not like that!"

Iris smiled at her. She smiled back, and held out her hand. They shook hands, touched cheeks briefly. Her cheek was as chilled as that of her sister—the car must have had the air conditioning turned on.

"The newspapers were so vicious," said Vanessa brightly. "Of course, we all know reporters lie! But the stories—that you had lived together on an island before coming home! I could not credit it!" Bright eyes stabbed at Iris.

"I lost my position," said Xanthe to Greg, clinging to his arm suddenly, her face breaking up. "I cannot believe it—they gave me no notice at all!"

He looked embarrassed, for her, and worried.

"We will discuss it later. It shall not upset you like this!"

"When we saw the newspapers, we said it was fate," Xanthe continued, totally ignoring the girls behind her. The two girls, about seven and four, stood hand in hand, staring at everybody solemnly, like two lost from a storybook. The older one was dark-haired with a narrow sallow face like her mother. The younger one was unexpectedly yellow-haired, like a blond doll, with a round face. Like her father, probably, thought Iris. "We had to come to see if that could be true,

134

that Gregorios Venizelos could be marrying a fast American girl!''

"And you see it is not true,'' smiled Lydia sweetly. "He is marrying a fine, modest Greek-American girl, our Iris, who is beloved of us already.''

And she turned, and motioned them into the house. "Your rooms are not ready yet. You will be in the Cottage presently,'' said Greg, dealing with Xanthe's arm by removing it and picking up little Nora. "And how is my little precious?''

She stared at him wide-eyed, and put her thumb in her mouth, earning her a furious rebuke from her mother.

"The Cottage?'' cried Xanthe, giving a covetous look at the Big House. "I thought we would be in the new house! Surely the rooms are ready for guests now!''

"We knew you would be more comfortable with the children, in a place by yourselves, so you will be in the Cottage,'' said Greg firmly, going inside with them.

"Or the Long House, surely the Long House!'' wailed Xanthe. "The Cottage is so primitive!''

"Alex is in the Long House, also some relatives of Iris are coming to celebrate our engagement!''

Xanthe's complaining voice died away. Melania had caught Iris's arm, to prevent her following them. "Come with me—for a walk,'' she whispered.

Gladly the two girls walked away. "Whew,'' said Iris. "And he welcomes them! My respect for Gregorios goes up!''

"He is a good generous man,'' said Melania. "When my parents died, he came for me, took care of all arrangements, and said I would live with him, and his mother would be my mother. I have been here since then, five years now. He opens his heart and houses to us all. Some reward him with gratitude, others with—'' And she jerked her thumb backward toward the Big House in a rather vulgar gesture for her.

They walked in silence for a few minutes. The recent rains had dampened the wild flowers in the fields, but they were trying to spring up again. Iris admired the scarlet poppies, the blue gentians, the yellow coreopsis, the white daisies with yellow centers like her dress.

"I wanted to warn you, Iris," said Melania. "Confide nothing in Xanthe or in Vanessa. Xanthe is openly bitter about her lot in life, she likes nothing better than to drag down others to her state of misery. Vanessa seems more kindly, but she has malice in her. Be careful. They came not because Xanthe lost her job, but because Greg is engaged."

"Do they think to break us up?"

"They hope," said Melania, with a grimace. "Xanthe is fond of her younger sister. She wants a fine marriage for her, and has tried for five years, while I have been here, to entice Greg into an engagement with Vanessa. They have come again and again, using all kinds of tricks and stories. She loses her jobs regularly, to come here and live off Greg while she tries to get him and Vanessa engaged to be married. I'll warrant she did not lose her job, but quit to come."

Iris was silent. She would not mind losing Greg to a nice Greek girl—so she told herself. But she did not think Vanessa was the right one for him! He was too fine a man to have a malicious spiteful wife. However, Vanessa was very beautiful, and Greg seemed attracted to her. Had there been something between them, perhaps an affair?

The two girls stood on the rusty red cliff overlooking the sandy beach and the ocean below them. A glint of brightness caught their attention at the same time.

"What was that?" asked Iris.

"I don't know. The sun shone on something . . ."

They searched, then Melania pointed. "There—two fishermen in blue—see them?"

The men were gazing up at them. But they were not simple

fishermen, thought Iris. One was a huge man in rough blue clothes, yet he was holding to his eyes a pair of binoculars! As they watched in surprise, he handed the glasses to the other man, a slimmer dark man.

"Oh—they are watching us through their glasses!" exclaimed Melania. "How—rude! Oh—I wonder—if they might be—" All at once, she grabbed Iris, and drew her back from the cliff, out of sight of the men.

"What is it?"

"They might be—the men of Sicilianos!" said Melania. "Oh, I must tell Greg—"

Chapter Nine

Later in the evening, in the brief silences, Iris wondered about the event of the afternoon. Melania had reported to Greg about the two men, and he had gone out at once in one of the Land Rovers, with a rifle and two menservants. He had not returned until almost dinner, and had a grim face for a time.

"Those Sicilianos—they are very dangerous," Melania whispered to Iris with a shudder. "One hurt Alex very much, as you see. They have no mercy!"

"But it is so long for a feud to go on," Iris protested. "It has been since World War II!"

Melania only stared blankly. "But men were killed, and blood was spilled in betrayal," she said. "Of course the feud goes on."

The memory haunted Iris's dreams that night also. Or perhaps it was the realization that her father and the others would arrive the next day. Xanthe's shrill complaining had gone through her head all evening, and given her a headache. Iris had retired early, while Lydia smiled at her with comprehension.

Iris's dreams were filled with images of red blood, a vicious Nora who kept pinching her and screaming at her. She wakened in early morning to the welcome sight of her blue and white peaceful room. The windows were open to the dawn light off the sea, flickering on the whitewashed walls, and the stuccoed ceiling. She finally rose, and turned on the water in the bathtub.

When she returned to the room, wearing her terrycloth white robe, Charis was there, going through her clothes.

"Kyrios—he said you shall wear a nice dress today," said Charis, beaming a greeting. "*Kaliméra,* Miss Iris! Shall you wear the blue silk, or your new raspberry silk?"

"The raspberry, I believe. Does he know when my father arrives?"

"The telephone has rung already from Athens," said Charis. "The plane came in, and they will take the little plane from Athens to the island this morning. What happiness!"

The cheerful maid evidently envisioned joyful reunions between father and daughter, between stepmother and stepdaughter. Iris shivered. More likely thinly veiled dislike, jealousy, watchful eyes alert from both Shelley and Maria Ardeth to make sure Hilarion Patakos did not show his daughter favors that might belong to them. So it had been when Iris was a small child, and the girl could not cope with it. Iris did not feel much more able to cope now, at twenty-two. Jealousy was such a sick, distasteful emotion to counter. It was so unreasonable.

Charis brushed out Iris's long black curly hair, and began to tie a bow about the thickness to keep it back.

"Up in a chignon, I think, Charis," said Iris.

Charis's smile did not falter, nor did her hands. "Today

you look young and engaged," she said gaily. "Kyrios says so!"

She had her orders, and Iris sighed and gave in. Looking like a girl just out of the schoolroom rather than a crisp businesswoman and dress designer, she went downstairs, her sandals with the ties about her ankles making little sound on the broad stone steps.

Greg came from his desk to take her hand, and draw her to himself. Before the approving gaze of several maids, and a beaming Joseph, he kissed her lips tenderly.

"How beautiful you are!"

"Thank you. *Kaliméra*," she said shyly. His kisses were not so distasteful as they had been. Could she be getting used to him? She almost liked the feel of his strong hand on her waist. It was warm and reassuring as he guided her to the breakfast table.

They were alone, it was early.

"Your father comes soon," Greg smiled at her. "He shall be welcome in my house!"

"Thank you, I am sure," she said conventionally.

"So why are you worried, and have a little line between your lovely black brows?" And he gently touched the little area above her nose.

"Shelley and Maria Ardeth," she sighed.

"Ah. Leave them to me!"

She would gladly have done so. For now, she could do nothing. A maid brought pomegranate juice, fresh and tart. She drank it, and felt refreshed. Then she dug into the crisp pieces of fresh-caught fish, laced with lemon, and the hot buttered croissants. How delicious they were with the Hymettus honey, tasting of the wild thyme in which the bees had delved. Cups of hot black coffee completed her pleasure and the meal.

Greg was eating as hungrily as she. "I like to see a woman

enjoy her meals," he said. "This eating cups of yogurt only is disturbing!"

"I'm afraid I enjoy food too much to do that," said Iris. "I like our apartment so much, because now I can cook what I wish."

"I must arrange that you shall do some cooking for us when we marry," said Greg thoughtfully. "I wonder if I might buy an apartment in New York, where we will stay when we visit."

Crash! went her mood of content. She looked at him reproachfully.

"I wish you would not say things like that, Greg. I do not intend to marry you! I am going home soon, as soon as this mess is cleared up. I am sure Alex does not need me."

"No, but I do," said Gregorios, and his large Greek mouth looked firm and haughty. "You are right for me, you suit me very well. And I am thirty-four, it is time I married and had sons! And also daughters," he added hastily. "Yes, I shall enjoy daughters as well."

A typical Greek male, thought Iris, when the baptism of the son was a much longer, more joyous occasion than that of a daughter. A son meant the continuation of the family name and line and business, one to carry out the pride and *philotimo* of his family.

A daughter meant dependence, the worry of finding an adequate dowry or *proika* sufficiently big to persuade a Greek man to marry her and be faithful to her and her children. There was no equality of the sexes in Greece. A woman could not even start a business without the permission of her husband, and that permission was not usually given. It might make her too independent and not submissive.

"You are quiet. Do you not look forward to having my sons, sweet Iris Poppea?" he asked softly, into her ear. He kissed the earlobe, and left a bit of honey on it, and laughed

142

as she scrubbed at the ear. A maid giggled, and left hastily as Greg glanced at her.

In midmorning, Iris and Melania were sitting sewing on the front loggia, facing the sea. It was peaceful there. There had been loud noises and fussing earlier as Greta and Nora raised their voices to Xanthe, and, having gotten slapped, wept and screamed. Melania had winced.

"She should have had sons," said Melania. "Perhaps her husband would not have been so mean to her."

"It is the husband who determines the sex of the children," said Iris, snipping off a thread viciously. "He could not blame her for that!"

Melania's brown eyes were surprised. "Is that so? It cannot be! I have never heard of such a thing. Nobody in Greece would believe it."

"And I know that!" muttered Iris. "It would offend their male ego!"

Presently a small blue fly buzzed high in the blue sky. The girls glanced up. "It is the plane from Athens!" cried Melania. "Look how it circles and comes down at the little airport below!"

They watched until the little plane disappeared, in the valley, where an airstrip had been cut from the red earth. Greg had gone an hour before to meet them and pick them up in the cars. Xanthe and Vanessa had been sulking all morning, hating the idea of the relatives of Iris coming there. Now they came from the Cottage, and headed for the chairs where Iris and Melania sat.

Within a minute, Lydia came from the house and seated herself next to Iris. Iris had the feeling she was there for her protection, like a shield left by Greg for his fiancée.

"Your father comes with word of your dowry?" asked Xanthe, with a sour smile.

"I don't believe in—"

"You know that is a private matter, Xanthe," Lydia cut in smoothly over Iris's words.

Black eyebrows rose in the sallow face. "But we are all family. Why should we not know? What money has she? It is a matter of grave importance!"

"Not to you," said Lydia bluntly, continuing to embroider on a little dress for Nora. "Gregorios will not thank you to interfere in his affairs, you know that, Xanthe. He is courteous, and fond of you and Vanessa and the children. However, there are liberties he will not permit, and I advise you to remember that."

"My sister is always pleasant to him, and would not insult or interfere!" exclaimed Vanessa passionately. "Do you hint we are not welcome here?"

Both sisters were drawn up, ready for attack. Lydia managed to look both haughty and faintly surprised, always the lady. "My son has welcomed you all! Do you doubt his hospitality?" She neatly turned it back on them.

Xanthe finally turned to Iris. "What work do you do? You seem to sew all the time. It is your lifework, eh?"

"Yes, it is. I enjoy sewing and dressmaking," said Iris.

"It will be useful for her family," said Lydia suavely.

"But you cannot cook and clean, eh?"

"She is an excellent cook, my son has told me," said Lydia.

Vanessa smiled, a wide false smile. "Iris has no tongue! She cannot answer for herself!"

"She is a modest girl, who does not praise herself," Lydia smiled back at her. Melania swallowed a chuckle, and almost choked on it.

"Your Greek has a poor accent, you had a poor teacher, eh? That is a shame. All Athens will mock you, I fear!" said Xanthe.

"She was taught by a nun in the convent where she had her

schooling. The accent is pure Greek, not Cretan,'' slashed Lydia with ease. ''No wonder you do not recognize it!''

Xanthe and Vanessa rocked violently in their chairs, brooding, while silence finally fell on the women. Gregorios's mother was protecting her future daughter-in-law, it was cause for thought.

Finally the blue Lincoln Continental and a couple of Land Rovers drove up the dusty red path to the houses, slid onto the asphalt driveway and pulled up near the Long House. Hilarion Patakos and Bill Roswell got out and helped their wives to alight. Greg came from a Land Rover, he had evidently elected to drive with the luggage rather than with his guests, thought Iris, with a little laugh to herself.

Iris braced herself, and went to greet them. Her father held out his arms, she eyed him warily and held out her hand to press his briefly. He looked disappointed, but she could not bring herself to do more.

He was graying, she thought, and he had gained weight, he looked as though he worked too hard and played too hard.

Bill Roswell came forward, smiling, held out his hand. He knew Iris disliked being embraced. He pressed her hand warmly. ''How are you, my dear?'' he said.

''Fine, Bill,'' she said, and caught the cold dislike in the blue eyes of Shelley Patakos Roswell. The same look as she remembered when a child.

She nodded to the two women. ''How are you?'' they chorused, then glanced at each other as though they hated each other.

''You know Shelley,'' said her father uncomfortably. ''I think you have not met my wife, Maria Ardeth.''

Iris nodded. Neither woman extended hands. ''Maria Ardeth,'' she murmured.

Greg had been watching with frank interest. ''Come and sit down, and meet everybody,'' he said hospitably. He shooed them all with him to the small group before the Big House. He made short work of the introductions, and Lydia sent for refreshments.

Perhaps fortunately, Xanthe and Vanessa spoke little English, Shelley and Maria Ardeth spoke little Greek. Greg and the men carried on the conversation. Bill Roswell was his usual genial uncomplicated self. Hilarion Patakos fidgeted.

Finally Hilarion turned to Greg. "I hear you were alone on an island with my daughter, Iris. What do you say?"

"We crashed on the island, yes," said Gregorios, looking down his big nose. "Fortunately, we did not die." He paused significantly.

"Yes, yes, God is good," muttered Hilarion. "But what happened then?"

"We were taken prisoner by Greeks who thought we had come to steal their land. Some—foreigners—are trying to do this, to build expensive resorts." Gregorios glanced from one man to the other.

Hilarion looked very impatient, ready to explode. Iris remembered that her father did not have much patience. "But I mean—were you alone for a week in a room with my daughter? What happened, Venizelos? I will not stand evasions!"

"Father, I do not think it is your concern—nothing happened between us," Iris began firmly, but her voice was drowned out, to the disappointment of the women listening avidly.

"You will have to marry my daughter, you understand that!" cried Hilarion. "She is a good girl! I will not have her disgraced!"

"Of course she will not be disgraced." Gregorios was looking all the more haughty and aristocratic. "I will be happy to marry Iris. We are engaged," and he picked up Iris's right hand and showed the ring.

Hilarion looked, and was somewhat appeased. "We must discuss this!"

"Before everybody, father?" cried Iris, embarrassed and upset. "Do you wish everybody to hear all the conversation and pass judgment on me? Well, I do not! I have done nothing to be ashamed of—"

"Shameless!" muttered Xanthe, with satisfaction.

"What are you talking about? Speak English!" cried Shelley.

"We are engaged, and will be married soon," said Greg calmly, in Greek and then in English. Xanthe gasped, and Vanessa looked furious. Shelley and Maria Ardeth looked cool and blond and above it all.

"We must discuss the dowry," said Hilarion Patakos, a little appeased.

"I don't want a dowry, I don't want—" Iris began.

Gregorios stood up. "Come, Mr. Patakos, we will discuss this in my study. Iris—take our guests to the Long House, and show them their rooms, if you will?"

And he took Hilarion by the arm and they escaped into the Big House. Iris stood, furious, ready to follow them, but Lydia shook her graying dark head slightly. Her mother-in-law-to-be stood, and came to Iris. "Yes, my dear, let us show our guests to their rooms."

Iris whispered urgently to Lydia as they walked ahead of the others, "I don't want a dowry! Oh, Kyria, get me out of this, I don't want to get married—I just want to have my career—let me tell my father nothing happened—"

"Leave it all to the men, they will decide all," said Lydia comfortably. "They wish to talk it out, I am sure all will be fair."

Iris fumed inside, but would not show her feelings to Shelley and Maria Ardeth. Bill Roswell caught up with her, and said, "You look well, Iris. The air is very agreeable here, you have a little suntan already."

"Yes, one cannot help it," she said vaguely.

He made small talk, and praised the rooms, while the

women were muttering under their breath and talking of single beds. Before they could complain aloud, Iris and Lydia made their escape. The luggage was there, they could unpack and rest, said Lydia.

Outside, Lydia whispered, "They sleep apart?"

Iris shrugged. "Probably."

"An American custom?"

"The women have their way," said Iris wryly.

"It is best you come to Greece and live with us!" Lydia shook her head. "A woman feels unloved in America, eh?"

Gregorios and Hilarion were indoors a long time. None dared disturb them. They made telephone calls, talked, had coffee and drinks.

Lydia and Iris tried to cope as the others returned, looking rather put out at the small rooms and the double beds. Iris attempted to soothe them.

"You will find it cool at nights. When the sun goes down, soon there is a lovely breeze, and it even turns cold by morning. I hope there are enough blankets."

"Yes," said Lydia. "You will be glad of your husband then!"

Iris dared not look at Lydia, for the remark was very pointed.

"What a long journey it was, I am very weary," said Shelley. "I don't see why we had to come, but Bill insisted."

Maria Ardeth was not to be outdone. "When Hilarion heard about Iris being in—trouble—he had to come at once! Naturally, I came along. A woman can be of more help sometimes."

"You were both very thoughtful, and most kind to me," said Iris, trying to make peace. "I did not expect everybody to rush over here. Yes, it is a long journey. I hope the plane was comfortable."

"Very luxurious," said Bill Roswell. "Now Shelley will

want a plane like that! I warn you, my very dear, I cannot afford one! And to keep it up, mechanics and all that—it would be very expensive! Your Greg must be rich, Iris!'' And he gave her a wink, his balding head shining in the afternoon sunlight.

The blond women looked thoughtful. Xanthe and Vanessa understood the word "rich," and looked ready to give battle. They saw Greg slipping away, thought Iris, and were desperate.

Finally Greg and Hilarion completed their talk, and came out. Iris had run out of small talk, but at least the relatives looked somewhat more calm.

Lydia at once served luncheon outdoors on the terrace, on little tables, and everyone seemed to feel better. The maids brought trays of appetizers, rice and meat in grape leaves, some sliced sausage with grated orange rind, shrimp stuffed with crabmeat, tiny bits of shish kebob especially hot and spicy. This was served with a local white wine that was crisp and distinctive.

Next, trays of fresh fried fish were brought, casseroles of *moussaká,* and some small tender fried steaks. With this course was served huge bowls of Greek salad: crisp lettuce and other greens, red tomato chunks, small black ripe olives, and chunks of *féta* cheese. Iris had made her own dressing for this.

One of the cooks had spent all morning on the pastries. Her specialty was fresh tarts with tiny new sweet strawberries in them. She had also made some with almond crème, and some with coffee custard.

By the time hot coffee and coffee liqueur were brought, the guests were rolling sleepily in their chairs. They talked for a time, then left to get some sleep. Iris hoped they would rest until dinner that evening.

"Be sure to arise in time to see the sunset," Lydia

reminded them smilingly. "The sunsets have been glorious lately, all rose and salmon pink and mauve."

They thanked her and departed for their rooms. Greg took Iris's hand when she would have gone inside, and said, in a low voice, "We must speak."

She nodded, and went with him. Alone on the cliffs out of view of the house, she tried to drop his hand, but he held hers the more tightly. "You have reassured my father that nothing happened?"

Her father had looked quite complacent during luncheon. He seemed satisfied, so had Greg.

"I can go home with them, then?" she insisted.

Greg looked faintly amazed. "Go home? You are home, Iris, my dear."

"You know what I mean! There is no need for a marriage, we did not—you know! Didn't you tell father?"

Greg shook his head. "He would not have believed me," he said. "Besides—we almost made love completely, Iris. You know this. I would be furious if I were a young man, to know that a girl I was about to marry had come so close to losing her virginity as you did with me!"

Iris blushed furiously, and did not know where to look. She remembered the warm feeling of his naked body next to hers, the heat of his passion, the way he had opened her legs . . .

"But nothing happened!" she cried. "I don't have to marry you—I am still a virgin—"

"I thank God for it," he said earnestly. "But, nevertheless, all is well. Your father is pleased with me to become his son. And the dowry is all set. He is giving you one of his hotels, the only one in New England. It is in Connecticut, and inconvenient for him to manage. So—he gives it to you. I will manage it for you. It is close to one I own in Massachusetts."

"What did you say?" she gasped in horror.

"He gave me—you—one of his hotels—in Connecticut—"

"But I don't want one of his hotels!"

"You prefer money? The hotel is a good one, I telephoned his accountant, and was reassured about this. We will visit it, also, next time we are in the States—"

She turned on Greg with tears in her eyes. "Greg, I don't want his hotel! I don't want anything from him! All I ever wanted from him was his love and affection, and he could not give it to me! I want nothing from him, nothing! Don't you understand?"

Greg put his arms about her, and held her closely to him. His voice rumbled and rasped against her hair as she buried her face on his chest.

"I understand, my darling, all too well. He could not give you love, and I am very angry about that. But never again will you feel deprived of the love and affection you need and deserve! You shall have from me, your husband, all of that and more to fill your body and soul to overflowing, I promise you!"

She sobbed a minute, then drew back, and dashed her hand over her eyes. "Greg, I cannot marry you! I am going to be a fashion designer! I don't want money or hotels, or marriage, or anything. I can manage by myself!"

"Of course you could, but why should you?" he soothed. "Here I am, a proud, sturdy, hard-working Greek, longing to take care of you and let you nag me and scold me, so long as you give me love and my children! Eh?"

She could not smile at him, as he teased her gently.

"I have worked all my life for this career! I have struggled and studied languages, as well as dress design. Greg, I have worked so hard to get where I am! I do not want to give it up! I want to design clothes! I have my goals, I am reaching them! This is a proud time for me, when a fine fashion designer praises my work, and tells me I will be her assistant if I can but come up with a good line! But a few more months—"

Gently he put his hand over her lips. "Iris, my darling, how can a career compare with love and a man of your own? You will have fine children, I know it, my mother says so! You shall marry me, and be happy! I vow it!"

But he made no protestations of love, to her. He would not listen to further arguments, he held her and kissed her, and made her dizzy with passion in the late afternoon sunshine.

He would never understand her, she thought mournfully, even as her father never had. He would only try to dominate her, and rule her, as a Greek husband did. She felt fearful of his domination, and unready for marriage.

Yet—his lips could be warm and sweet, and she could not help answering his.

Her body pressed against his for a time, until he drew back, and laughed, and said, "Let us not anticipate our marriage, sweet Iris Poppea! Rather, let us marry soon!"

Chapter Ten

Greg announced at dinner that his mother would give Iris an engagement party. It would be in a few days, he said, as soon as it could be arranged.

Lydia added, "I think we can manage it in about five days. You will remain, Kyrios Patakos, Kyrios Roswell?"

"Of course," said the men, beaming, and their wives looked cross.

Greg leaned back in his chair, looking very much the young dominating male, the patriarch, thought Iris crossly. She felt as out of sorts as the blond wives. She did not want to be married, she did not feel her honor had been smirched. She resented being sold for a dowry, and the whole affair was being handled badly.

But she had not a chance to tell Greg so that evening. She wakened early, when Charis came softly into her room with a suitcase. Iris saw her, and sat up in bed.

"What is it?" she demanded eagerly. Was Greg going to let her go?

Charis beamed. A little girl followed her into the room, with a breakfast tray, which was placed across Iris's lap. The little maid left, then Charis closed the door after her.

Charis put her finger to her lips in the universal gesture for a secret. Then she whispered, "Your betrothed is taking you to Athens! He will buy you a most beautiful dress for the engagement party! All of the women will be green with envy!"

Iris groaned a little. Yet she could not help being excited. "Why the silence?"

"Kyrios Gregorios does not wish for everybody to try to go! There is no room in the plane for everybody, he says! So you go very early this morning, with himself and his honored mother!"

Indeed, it was done secretly. Iris quickly ate her breakfast, drank the coffee as she washed and dressed. She was soon ready in the bright scarlet suit and crisp white blouse. Charis took out clothes and packed for her efficiently, then carried the case out to the waiting limousine.

Kyria Lydia was already there, tying a blue scarf about her neat black chignon. Only the servants saw them off. In the car Greg chuckled, "That was a near thing! I saw one of the little children of Xanthe stick her head from the door of the Cottage!"

"Melania knows nothing, they cannot blame her. And Alex can hide behind his valet!" Kyria Lydia said placidly, but her face had crinkled up into laugh lines as Iris glanced over toward her.

In the early morning cool air, Iris relaxed as the smooth-riding car sped down the mountain to the landing strip, where the blue and white plane waited. Athens. She would see Athens!

"There will be time for sightseeing?" she asked quickly.

"We'll see," said Lydia. "You must buy something gorgeous for the party. Greg, what about gold?"

Iris sighed audibly. She had seen so many dresses in her short lifetime, they held little excitement for her, not compared with seeing the Parthenon! Could she manage to slip away from them for a few hours?

Greg helped her up into the plane and saw her settled. Then he handed her an envelope. "From your father," he said briefly, then went up to sit beside the efficient uniformed pilot.

Iris opened the envelope curiously. It held a check of huge amount, and her eyes widened. She read the brief note. *For my dearest daughter Iris on the occasion of her engagement*, and her father's signature. She stared at it soberly, remembering birthdays and Christmases when the same had occurred. Expecting a visit from her father, or some personal present, something to show he understood and cared, she would receive a note and a check.

It had not changed. She put the envelope and note and check into her navy blue purse, and closed them away. Lydia was watching her curiously as the little plane lifted up into the blue air. But the older woman said nothing.

For a time Iris felt bitter and indifferent to the journey. The check was so large—she could go to an airline office and buy a ticket home. Why not? Why should she remain: a substitute for Charmian, an unwanted stepdaughter, a fake fiancée? Why bother to play all these parts for others? Why not be herself, forget them, be as callous and determined as Charmian? She should start to live for herself, think of herself!

Lydia touched her arm, and pointed to the window. Iris glanced out, and saw the Athens airport below them, and in the distance the golden pillars of the Parthenon in the noon sunlight! How they glowed, golden and shapely.

Oh, why run away now? Why not stay for a time and enjoy

her life here? She would have some sweet memories to take home with her. Greg was not serious about marrying her, she need not worry about that! He was a sophisticated man of the world, he would find a fitting mate, and that was not naive Iris!

Her heart lifted, she smiled joyously at the steward as he checked her seat belt. "Athens," she said.

"Yes, beautiful Athens, the center of the world," he said.

He was serious, and she nodded politely. Soon another luxurious car was speeding them into the city, and she put her sunglasses on her small nose and was absorbed in drinking in as many of the sights as she could. Palms and cypresses, tall and deepest green, like black flames against the blue sky. Spring flowers, gay and bright, in array against whitewashed houses.

They were caught up in slow-moving traffic, and the honk of many horns made such a din. But the pauses showed Iris the entrances into small dark shops, women in gay skirts and white embroidered blouses tending the shops, or men in gray or black with their pipes firmly in their mouths. A couple playing chess, intently, white heads almost together over the board. A boy and his puppy racing down the sidewalk. Trays of long tubes of bread, brown and delicious-looking. Outdoor cafés, with lounging Greeks and tourists.

Finally the limousine pulled up in front of a smart marble-front building. A uniformed guard came to open the door, and a smaller man to take the luggage. "Welcome to our Athens home, dearest Iris," said Kyria Lydia.

They went up in a silent luxurious gray-plush-lined elevator to the penthouse suite. The building was a dozen stories high, and Iris watched the row of lights curiously. What was an Athens apartment like? She would bet Greg had a beautiful one, he liked his luxuries now that he had made his pile, she thought. Yet even so she was unprepared for the sight when the elevator stopped, and they got out into a hallway.

Greg unlocked the large carved door, and went inside, then invited them in. There was no hallway as such, it was all open and lovely, with pale cream carpets in all directions.

In the far area a slim curving stairway curled up to the next floor. On the right was a large long dining table with beautiful rosewood chairs set about. On the left was a lounge area with low tables, couches, chairs, bookcases filled with an array of volumes: art, history, biography, fiction.

Beyond the lounge area was an informal bar with stools, and a kitchen area. "That is where we have breakfast frequently, with a view of the city," said Lydia, indicating it. "But over here is my favorite view," and she led Iris to the far right beyond the dining table, to an area of low couches of cream plush, cream cushions, and hassocks. She opened a French window of glass, and stepped out on to the balcony.

A rush of traffic noise, muted, came up to them, but also a view that held Iris spellbound. For just beyond her reach, it seemed, loomed the small hill that held the most splendid buildings of the Ancient Classical World. The Acropolis.

She gazed and gazed. Lydia smiled at her entranced face. "It is always here," she said gently, but Iris could not turn her back on it, and walk inside again. She clasped her hands to her breast, and sighed in ecstasy.

She started when two hands went to her waist, lifted her firmly, turned her and carried her inside the apartment again. Reproachfully she gazed up at Greg's laughing face.

"Later you may dream," he said, and put her down, then took her hand in his big one to lead her to the stairs. "You will wash quickly and be ready to come with us. We have many errands today."

"I thought you just wanted me to buy a dress for the party," she moaned.

"And some other dresses, and shoes, and a sun hat for the times you sit outdoors and sketch," he said with a grin. "Oh, mother has quite a list!"

"To waste time shopping—in Athens!" she reproached. He only laughed, and pinched her cheek.

He led her up the stairs, and in the hallway she admired the acres of more cream carpet, and the carved wood doors to the various rooms. "The master suite—which you will share with me—" said Greg. Then he laughed at her startled face. "After we are married, of course! For now, your room is here—"

He opened another door beyond the master suite, and she found a blue suite even larger than the one on his island home. Again it was in her favorite colors, blue and cool white, with a strong dash of sunny yellow. "Oh, it is lovely—thank you, Greg."

"Be comfortable," he said, and left her to the tender mercies of a maid older and more sophisticated than Charis, but just as kind.

When Iris discovered that her room had a balcony matching the one below, and a view of the Parthenon, she was beside herself with delight. But there was no time, the maid urged her smilingly to wash and change her shoes.

With a regretful backward look, she ran out of the room and away from the tempting view, and down the stairs, where Greg and his mother were ready.

The remainder of the day was filled. A chauffeur drove them around, they stopped at a bank, an office building where Greg left some papers and collected others, and more shops than Iris thought possible.

They looked quickly at dresses, Lydia shook her head. "Not glamorous enough," she said.

"But it doesn't have to be," urged Iris. "I am not a glamorous type!"

Lydia smiled at her, Greg shook his head and said, "I will not have you outshone by the other women. This will be your day."

Only to break the engagement and go home after a discreet interval, thought Iris. But she dared not say so. Looking at Greg's square jaw made defiance seem not only difficult, but ridiculous. She could only wait for him to regain his common sense. Iris was not a suitable wife for him, and other girls were right there, all lined up ready to fight for him! She saw Vanessa at the top of the list, handsome, a relative, and there was something conscious in the way Vanessa gazed at Greg. Had they had an affair, at one time, perhaps recently?

An early night was decreed, and Iris was glad to eat a light supper and fall into her comfortable bed. She had resolved to keep her eyes open for a time, and luxuriate in gazing at the Parthenon—right outside her window!—but fatigue deceived her, and she was asleep in minutes.

It was even better, however, to waken in the early pure dawn light, and see the buildings waiting for her. Something had wakened her. She stirred in the bed, and her head turned on the pillow.

The door was open, Greg's curly mussed head had poked in. "Iris—awake?"

"Oh—yes!" She yanked the sheet up to her chin, and he smiled at her.

"If you get up quickly, I'll take you to the Parthenon now!"

"Now?" she squeaked. "Right—now?"

"Yes, it opens early. We'll get there before the tourists!"

"I'm coming!"

She waited only until he shut the door before falling out of bed, racing to don navy blue slacks and a white pullover. She tied a red scarf about her throat, grabbed her navy bag, and tiptoed out of the room. Her sandals were comfortable, they would last for hours of sightseeing, if he would take her!

He was sitting at the breakfast bar, eating and drinking heartily. He insisted she should have juice and eggs, sweet rolls and coffee, then took pity on her and led her away.

The chauffeur was waiting for them, and he too smiled at her excitement. They drove through the slowly filling streets, and were among the first to line up for tickets to go up to the beautiful temples.

The chauffeur was sent away with orders to return in three hours. Iris was very grateful to Greg, and said so. He smiled and patted her cheek.

"For being a good girl," he said solemnly. She laughed, a bright sparkle of sound in the early morning air.

Athens was being good today. The early morning breeze had cleared the air of some of the smog and air pollution, and a violet light lay over the city. The temples glowed golden in the morning sunshine. They climbed the steep slopes slowly, enjoying each view as they turned each corner, to see the buildings ever closer.

Not many tourists were there yet, only a few poking over the ruins, admiring and marveling at the marks of the chariot wheels in the stone, gazing silently at the buildings that had stood so many centuries.

Iris wandered around the ruins, conscious of Greg's helping hand over the rough stones, his silent presence. When she asked a question, he would answer, showing he loved these monuments and knew about them. But he did not trouble her with idle chatter.

Finally they left the ruins, and went to the Acropolis Museum. She kept seeing sculpture and objects that she had seen only in art books before. It was so thrilling to see these same objects herself. The sculptured figures of young women, known as the *korai*, held her rapt attention for a long time. The faintly mocking smiles, the intricate garments, the mystery of their presence, enchanted her.

She was shocked when Greg indicated it was time to go. They walked silently down the hill, to find the car waiting. But he did not take her again to shops. With a smile, he directed the chauffeur to the National Archaeological Museum.

"Unless your feet are too tired?"

"Oh, no, no, please, do let us go!"

Greg slanted a smile down at Iris, and seemed pleased with her. He was protective of her, scowling away men's stares in the museum rooms, growling a warning when a young man tried to come near on the street. She knew she would have had trouble here on her own. Ladies did not go about alone in Greece.

Iris was glad of his shielding presence. It allowed her to become absorbed in the magnificent statues: the bronze Poseidon, ancient ones of Apollo, those of Demeter, and even a lovely one of Iris.

The messenger of the gods, Iris, was depicted with winged feet and a sweet eager expression. Greg studied her from his pose beside Iris Poppea, and finally said, "I am glad you do not have wings, Iris! You would fly away from me, I believe."

"How do you know I will not?" she asked demurely, feeling at peace with him today.

He chuckled, and put his arm about her. "Because I am stronger than you!"

"That is brute strength!"

"Whatever it takes," he assured her, a twinkle in his eyes. He was flirting with her, she did not take it seriously.

"Oh, I almost forgot your mother! Do we meet her for luncheon?"

"No, she is with friends today, and will go to the Plaka with us tonight for dinner and the dancing."

"Oh—the Plaka," she beamed up at him. "Greg, thank you!" He squeezed her waist, and looked self-satisfied.

They had luncheon in a restaurant that looked like a *tavérna*, but there were no prices on the exquisite menus, so she knew it was expensive. She studied the hand-lettered items, and let Greg choose for her. Much as she knew about Greek cooking, many items were strange, and she wanted to try new foods. He chose, and she enjoyed the many dishes brought, testing the dishes of squid, octopus, eggplant, spiced lamb, and many others.

As in most Mediterranean countries, the meals were very late. It was past four when they finished luncheon, and Greg insisted on taking Iris back to the apartment to rest. She had really seen much today, and was content.

She curled up on her bed to rest a moment, and wakened two hours later. The maid came in to pour her bath and add perfumed bath salts. Iris dressed in the white embroidered cotton dress the girl laid out, and put on gold-strapped sandals.

Greg was waiting for her in the lounge area, gazing out at the Parthenon and the late afternoon sky. He stood up, gazed down at her thoughtfully, then reached out and brought her close to him.

"You are very lovely, pretty Iris," he said softly. She watched him warily under her black lashes.

"But not glamorous," she said pertly. He grinned, and bent to brush his lips against hers. She disliked it that she felt her heartbeat quicken. She tried to pull away, but at the first sign of reluctance, his grip tightened.

He drew her closer, so she felt the heat of his very masculine hard body against hers. His thighs were like sturdy young tree trunks. And something stirred between them when he kissed her more roughly, his lips twisting against hers as he tried to make her respond. His hand thrust through her softly swinging thick masses of black hair.

"Kiss me, eyes of iris blue," he ordered her. She shook her head, and the black hair swung about her head like a glossy bell. "Why not, *hum*?" he coaxed, and brushed his lips along her smooth chin. "Why not, come, kiss your fiancé."

"We are not engaged," she said gruffly.

"We are, we are, and shall be married soon."

"Look around you at all the beautiful Greek women, and choose one of them."

"I have the Greek girl I want," he told her, and closed her protesting lips with quick kisses. "Warm, feminine, sweet, with soft breasts and silky legs—"

She blushed wildly at the frankness of his speech. She pulled away, he promptly pulled her back to him, off balanced her, and she was leaning against him before she knew. His lips nuzzled the hollow of her throat, near her shoulder, and sent wild thrills down her. He kept her off balance by the simple expedient of leaning back and pulling her up to him, so she was on the tips of her gold-sandaled toes. The cotton dress was modest of neckline, but he managed to touch the rounded mounds of her breasts before Lydia's voice came softly.

"Are you ready to leave now?"

Reluctantly Greg released Iris, to meet his mother's thoughtful look. "I am teaching her to kiss me," he said, as though in half apology.

"Time enough for that after marriage," she retorted. "Be glad she is a modest girl, not a bold one."

"I am glad of it! But she is my fiancée—"

"One does not take liberties," scolded his mother. She moved to the door, straight of back. Behind her Iris gave a triumphant look at Greg, he laughed at her silently, his black

163

eyes sparkling. He caught up with her, and took her hand in his.

The car soon took them to the Plaka region of Athens, and as they strolled up the steep hill to one of the nightclubs the sounds of *bouzoúki* music made Iris's feet long to dance. Like *tavérnes,* only more gaudy, the neon lights of the district beckoned like so many ladies of the night.

Greg took them to one of the more Greek places, and soon they were at a table for the three of them, listening to the music, and choosing their dinner from a bewildering array of dishes. Iris could scarcely eat her dinner, for gazing and listening.

She loved the strumming of the guitars, the typical Greek music, half mournful and half wildly gay. She enjoyed at least as much as that the dancing of the men, in white costumes and baggy pants, their arms about each other's shoulders, as they curved among the tables in the intricate steps of various Greek dances, to the music of the *bouzoúki.*

One girl sang, some song of lost love. Another, older woman sang a song of the soldiers lost in the war, and Greg listened intently, his face somber.

As they watched and enjoyed, Iris had a strong sense of *déjà vu.* She felt as when they had landed at Athens airport, and met the wild winds, and the blazing sunlight, and the vivid blue sky. She had been here sometime; she had listened to these songs, seen these dances, felt a part of the singing and speaking.

Greg took her hand, and pressed it. "What is it, Iris?"

"I feel—as though—I have known this before."

"You are Greek!"

"It is so strong a feeling—as though in some other life—I was here—felt—knew—"

He raised her hand to his lips, and kissed the palm. He was not laughing or teasing she realized as she met that intense black gaze. "I believe it. There is something in you that has known this place. You are Greek inside, your soul knows Greece. You have come home!"

Lydia was listening, curiously, gravely, but she said nothing. Iris sighed, and turned again to watch the dancers on the platform, but Greg did not release her hand. He held it until she needed it again for her dessert.

Presently there was music for dancing by the guests. Greg rose, and drew Iris up also, and took her in his arms. She was enfolded to him by his gesture, held closely against him as they danced. She could feel every line of his body moving against hers, and it was intensely sensuous.

Oh, how she longed to give in to him! He was so suave, he courted her with such skill! Even knowing what he did, she was tempted to give in, and not fight! She was coming to enjoy his kisses—all too much. She felt enchanted and attracted to him. Surely any girl would feel so—but even more a girl who was Greek, as she was. He was so handsome, with his black curly hair, his wide sensuous mouth, that unexpected booming laugh, his big build, his grace of movement, his intense masculinity.

Yet—she must be wary of him. She must get out of this farce soon. She did not really think he would go so far as to marry her—he was practical—he knew there were many girls much more attractive and sophisticated. Other girls who would be hostess, wife, mother, regent, for his small empire.

He could not want small, stubborn Iris!

How far would he go with this pretense? He had talked to her father about dowries! What a tease! He did not mean it! He could not mean to go through with this! When her father went home, the whole play would collapse, she knew it!

He put his scratchy hard cheek down against hers and rubbed the silk of hers. "What are you thinking, sweet Iris, the messenger of the gods?"

"That I should fly away!"

He rumbled a laugh against her, and she shook inside. It would be so easy to love him! She could give in and sink against him, and let him come to her room that night—but, no! He was the very kind the good nuns warned against most sternly! Charming, handsome, with honeyed words!

"You dance like an angel. Did the nuns teach you this?"

"Yes, at the convent," she answered demurely. "We also learned the polka and the waltz."

"The polka?"

"Yes, in Chicago one must dance the polka! It is very popular!"

He swung her around in the corner and pulled her back against him, frankly hugging her in the dimness. "I think you tease me."

She laughed against him. His lips brushed her hair. Around his broad shoulder she glimpsed his mother, sitting patiently at the table alone.

"We must go back to your mother," she said firmly. The music was ending then, and he nodded reluctantly, put his arm about her waist, and led her back to the table. Lydia eyed their bright eyes and flushed cheeks and sighed and smiled.

"Do you know, it is past one o'clock in the morning?" she asked indulgently. "Tomorrow we really must find a gown for Iris."

"I can make one," said Iris quickly.

"No, no, we must go to Petros Diophantus," said Lydia.

Greg was paying their bill, he frowned. "Not to him," he said brusquely.

As they walked down the steps, Iris asked, "Why not to Petros Dio—— what is his name?"

"Diophantus," said Lydia. "He is a very good dressmaker, he understands the figure of the Greek woman, and does not make garments only for tall skinny models dying of malnourishment!"

Iris chuckled, and looked down at herself ruefully in the dimness. She was small, rounded, and the model dresses were not for her.

"Then we had best go to him."

"I don't want to go there," said Greg, sounding like a cross, sulky boy.

"Why not?" Iris asked, puzzled.

"He will like you too much!"

"Oh, nonsense!" said Iris, startled. Lydia was chuckling.

"It is true, he will like you enormously. He will admire your figure, your Greek looks, and your talent. I knew Greg did not want to go! But Petros will have the right gowns for you!"

"There are other dressmakers!" said Greg quickly. He paused at their car, and unlocked it, then put Iris in the front. He put his mother in the backseat, and closed the door, and went around to the driver's seat. The chauffeur was not with them that night.

In the car, Lydia said as he started the engine, "Petros will be best. He will understand how to make Iris look glamorous."

"I don't want him."

Lydia said gently, "Do you not wish Iris to look her most beautiful? Especially when her stepmother will be staring at her, and all the others?"

Greg hunched his shoulders. Iris was about to protest when Greg said gloomily, but finally, "We will go to Petros tomorrow. Very well."

Chapter Eleven

When Iris came down the curving stairs the next morning, Greg was standing at the windows looking out toward the Acropolis. She went to stand beside him, as he drank his coffee and smiled down at her.

His gaze went quickly, possessively, down her slim rounded body; today she wore a cream dress with navy accents, and navy sandals.

"Good morning—*kaliméra*," she said shyly.

He bent and brushed his lips against hers. She tasted coffee on his, and the warm masculine breath. "*Kaliméra*, my darling," he said in Greek.

She blushed, felt the heat rising in her cheeks. She turned to gaze out at the Acropolis, sighing in rapture again at the breathtaking sight. "Must we go shopping today?"

"Yes, mother says so!" he laughed. "Did your father give you a check, sweet Iris?"

"Yes, I have plenty of money," she reassured, rather surprised.

He frowned. "And you carry it around in your pocketbook? I thought so. Today we stop at a bank, and open an account for you. You will not need the money now. Eh?"

She stiffened, and scowled. He smoothed the black eyebrows gently. "No, Greg. I will pay for any dress myself!"

"No, I will," he said flatly.

"But it is up to me—and father gave me the money for any gown—"

"If you pay, you will think of prices and such. We shall not do that today," he said gently. "Eh, you will please me?"

"It isn't right. I'll ask your mother!"

To Iris's surprise, Kyria Lydia sided with her son on this. They would pay for her engagement gown, and Iris must put her father's check into an account for the future. So on the way to the dress designer's, Greg stopped at a bank, and set up her account for her, over her whispered protests.

"I don't see why—" she began in the car.

Lydia patted her hand. "Gregorios wishes to do this. Whatever your father gives to you can be saved against the future. He has not treated you the same as Charmian, has he?"

Iris frowned again. "But that is nothing to do with you!"

"Of course it is," Greg shot back. "He has not treated you as a daughter. He has no right to buy your engagement gown!"

Well, that was a different idea to Iris. She finally shrugged, and left it for future pondering. Greg seemed to have an aversion to her father and stepmother. But what business was it of his?

As they got out at the dressmaker's, Iris tried to suggest to Greg, "Why don't you go and do some business? Don't you have to go to the office?"

"Trying to get rid of me?" he grinned.

"I cannot see that trying on dresses will be of any further interest to you!" Actually, she did not want his critical and possessive looks on her while she tried to choose a dress.

"I appreciate your consideration," he told her dryly. "If I become very bored, I will leave you, eh?" And his black eyes shone with humor.

He put his hand under her elbow, and led her inside, kept his hand on her while the dressmaker came forward to be introduced.

Petros Diophantus was in his late thirties, plump, of medium height, with an amiable baby face belied by the shrewd black eyes. He was charming, greeting them happily, bowing over Lydia's hand.

"So this is the dress designer from New York City!" he greeted Iris. She felt Greg stiffen.

"Where did you hear that?" Greg barked.

"From your gracious mother." Petros beamed at Iris. "I will be happy to see any sketches you might have—"

"Not today, not today!" said Greg. "We have come for a gown for my fiancée—for our engagement party!"

The rounded eyebrows of Petros raised high on the baby-smooth forehead. Greg outstared him, the man shrugged, raised his hands high, and turned to the business at hand.

It seemed that Lydia had talked to him after their arrival in Athens, and he had turned out a golden dress at her request. It was brought and laid across his arms reverently, like a baby's christening robe, thought Iris, with an inward giggle. It was part of the act, as she knew from behind the scenes at Nadia Egorova's.

However, the dress was gorgeous. She went to put it on in one of the dressing rooms, and eyed herself critically. The golden brocade fabric was softer than usual, and it lay in gentle folds about her legs. The bodice was simple, because of the elaborately patterned fabric, with rather full puffed

171

sleeves, a simple low-cut V neckline that was yet modest. Lydia's fine hand! The hem had been just pinned in, and was a bit too long. She swished out to the cream plush room where Greg and Lydia and Petros waited. It was a large but private room where his clients might be served in solitude.

She turned around slowly, so they might see the softly full skirt, the back of the bodice, the sleeves. Greg nodded in satisfaction. Petros bustled over, and leaned down to look at the hem.

"Up another inch, I think—" And clicked his fingers for a maid to bring him pins and ruler. She sat on the floor, and followed his direction while the hem was repinned quickly.

"Beautiful," murmured Greg finally.

"Elegant," said Lydia firmly. "Just what I wanted for dearest Iris."

Greg opened his portfolio, and took out a red velvet case. He snapped it open, and Iris gazed wide-eyed at the array of sapphires inside. He proceeded to set a necklace about her throat, of gold links and deeply blue sapphires. He handed her the long dangling earrings, and she put them on her small ears. There was a bracelet also, and a huge dinner ring of a mammoth sapphire in a square cut. He set them on her left hand.

She turned in front of the mirror. The golden brocade gown had been elegant, now it was rich and extravagant, set off by the jewels, and setting them also in turn. Her black hair in the prim chignon took on more importance; her face was beautiful with peaches-and-cream coloring, and the definite black eyebrows and blue eyes.

"With golden-strapped sandals," mused Lydia—"and a gold evening bag—nothing more."

Greg nodded in satisfaction. Petros fussed about, puffing out the sleeves a little more about her elbows, adjusting the shoulders. "A perfect fit," he said, pleased with himself. "A perfect size ten, I believe. Madame Venizelos was right."

Evidently Lydia had even given him her proportions on the telephone.

"You like it, Iris?" asked Greg.

She nodded eagerly, and opened her mouth to ask the price. She would pay for it—she had her account now.

He cut in quickly, "Then we take it. Have it finished and the hem put in, eh?"

"At once!" said Petros, with glowing satisfaction. "The simple design is best, eh, with this elaborate fabric. And now what else does Miss Patakos require?"

Iris was about to say hastily that she wanted nothing more, but again her imperious fiancé cut in.

"Another suit, I believe. What about cream? And a pretty sun hat, Petros. And a silly one for the gardens, eh?" And he grinned at Iris.

"A silly one!" she protested. "Well, I like that—"

But when Petros brought out his stock of straw hats, she had to laugh and give in. They *were* silly ones, and Iris had her choice of one with straw-lashed black embroidered eyes, one with a kitten face and straw whiskers, one with a gray donkey's head, or others more conventional with leaves and flowers. Greg chose the kitten face for Iris, and his mother took one of the flowered ones. Iris added one for Melania, of lovely blue flowers.

Then Petros Diophantus brought out bolts of fabric, and Iris went a little mad. She exclaimed in delight over the silks, the velvets, the bouclé cottons and wools, in all the delicious colors of the Mediterranean—poppy red, sand, cream, sky blue, the violet of the Athens sky at sunset, sage and olive greens, so many she raved until breathless.

She and Petros began to discuss the new suit. She took out a pad—always present in her pocketbook—and sketched quickly what she would like. Petros watched admiringly over her shoulder as she worked.

"The jacket—with exaggerated shoulders—and then a little peplum at the waist, for a jaunty effect. The skirt, straight and slim, with short slits at each side. Length a little long below the knees—"

"The skirts are longer in New York this season, eh?" asked Petros, intently.

"Yes, the lengths are in again. And after a couple of years of emphasis on pants for fancy dress, I think we are reverting to luxurious fabric skirts once more. The luxe fabrics are definitely in: brocades, velvets, cut velvet is very popular—"

Greg began to get restless. He peered at the pad, then walked away, and handled the fabrics on the table, then left them to stare out the window at the little patio garden outside.

Lydia was admiring some gold braid at a side table. "Iris, my dear, could you do something with this?" She held up a piece.

Iris went over to examine it. There were several designs of braid, links, chains, then some in Greek key design already cut and ready to apply. She exclaimed in delight over that.

"Oh, I can see them on the hem of a dress and on the sleeves!" she said. She sketched rapidly, a dress with slightly full sleeves, to show off the braided sleeves. On impulse, she followed the pattern from the back of the hand up to the shoulder. "There—that would be different—"

"What ideas you have," gasped Petros, in admiration. "I would not think of it!"

Iris laughed softly, in pleasure. "Oh, I think you would!" He did have much talent, she liked immensely the simple yet elegant gold dress he had made for her. He had not spoiled it with too intricate a design that would ruin the fabric design.

"Together, we could do wonders!" he said eagerly. "Would

you consider working with me? You would move to Greece anyway, eh? You are Greek, one knows it by your accent!''

Greg intervened hastily. "She is here in Greece as my intended wife! I will thank you not to make plans for my wife!''

"Of course, of course!" said Petros quickly. "Now, Miss Patakos, you would like the cream made up in—what fabric?''

She picked up a length of cream cotton bouclé. "I think this one, and a bit of gold design on it—on the collar and sleeves. What about a matching dress that could be worn with the jacket?''

She sketched that out, they discussed it, while Greg became even more restless. Lydia was fingering fabrics, watching her son out of the corners of her black eyes, visibly amused.

Iris finally turned to Greg, as Petros went out to get something. "Greg, if you are weary of all this—isn't there something else you wish to do?''

He glared at her. "Nothing else!" he snapped. "I am happy to be here!" He put his hands in his pockets, and hunched his shoulders.

"Well, then, perhaps I should stop—I really have enough clothes—''

"Not at all! Go ahead—order what you will. You will be here in Greece a long time, you know!" It sounded like a threat. Then he relented at her half-scared look. "Get some swimsuits also, Iris. Petros has a nice boutique, eh? You did not bring any. And those garments—what do you call them—to go over the suits.''

He caught her arm, and piloted her out to the little shop in the other rooms. They had curious looks from the other patrons in the shops. Iris heard whispers about them, they knew who Greg was, and one had heard of herself.

"Gregorios Venizelos—yes—in the newspapers—I saw him on television! Stranded on an island—alone—a week! Her

175

father is Patakos of the hotels—small, isn't she? I hear she works! Perhaps her father is not rich after all!''

Another woman whispered loudly, ''I thought she was a model and in the movies!''

''No, that is another Patakos—she would not be in movies— too small—insignificant—what does he see in her—''

Iris felt she could sink into the floor. Greg did not seem to hear them, but she could hear the words clearly. And she knew what they said in Greek, thinking she did not speak it. She said in Greek to one of the shop girls in the neat cream uniform of Diophantus, ''Show me that swimsuit there in blue, if you will.''

''Yes, madame!'' The girl took it out, the whispering stopped, but the women kept staring all the time.

Greg said to the girl, ''Please bring some of these one-piece models back to the other room. Also cover-up garments, some in blue and some in yellow. Also swim caps, and sandals.'' He nodded at her, took Iris's arm and marched her back to the private room.

In the private room, Greg said quietly, ''I am sorry, Iris.''

She shrugged, with pretended indifference. ''I wonder why gossipy women always look like vultures with red scraggly necks?'' And she laughed.

He laughed out loud, and Lydia joined them, though with a concerned look for Iris.

The shop girls came in with swimsuits, cover-ups, and some pretty sandals. Iris sat down to try on the sandals, particularly admiring some cork-soled ones. Greg sat down beside her, obviously admiring her small neatly shaped feet.

He murmured, ''Are you going to try on the swimsuits?''

''And model them for you?'' she snapped. ''No!''

''Well, then,'' he sighed with great show of hurt. ''Well, then, if you aren't going to show them—I think I will go for a couple hours. I'll go to the office and scare the hell out of a couple of young cousins, and see what they are up to. I'll come back for you and mother about two and take you to luncheon. All right?''

When he smiled like that, she melted. "All right, Greg. Thank you. And I'll try not to spend all your money today!"

He gestured largely, as Petros watched them curiously. "Spend it all! I have a clever fiancée who can support me if I become bankrupt!" And he strolled out, having had the last word.

Lydia admired the swimsuits, and Iris tried on and finally purchased four. Lydia assured her she would have ample use of them, for sunning and for swimming in some coves where Greg would take her.

Two were bright blue, one was yellow, and one striped of orange and yellow. She bought some sheer net cover-ups, a practical white and yellow terrycloth jacket that came to her shapely knees, and matching towels, for the beach.

An associate of Petros came in while they finished the swimwear, and murmured to him. She was a tall slim black-haired woman. "But of course," said Petros. "Bring them in at once." He turned to Iris, beaming. "Marta tells me more fabrics came in today, and there are some you must see."

Iris had a feeling it might be dangerous, but could not resist. Marta and a couple of girls brought in more fabrics, and they all exclaimed over the silks and smart cottons.

One silk was in a peacock blue brocade. "Just the color of your eyes," exclaimed Petros gallantly, holding the fabric up to Iris's face. "Yes, they match."

"Beautiful," said Lydia critically. "You must have it!" And she stroked the fabric lovingly.

"It looks Chinese," said Iris, draping it on her shoulder. Her eyes narrowed, she could just see the design. She picked up her pad, and began to sketch.

In minutes she held out the pad to Petros, who whistled,

and nodded in excitement. The dress was sketched with a neat mandarin-style collar, a small button at the throat. The bodice was simple, with sleeves straight and full. In princess style, the waist just dipped in, then widened to the modestly full skirt of an A-line shape.

"Lovely," he breathed. "You make it up just like that!"

"And a stole to carry about the shoulders on a cool night," she said, and added that on the side of the pad.

"I'll make it up for you at once!"

She could have sewn it up herself, but remained quiet. Petros would be glad for the trade, and it was his fabric.

They looked through the other fabrics. Iris found one for Lydia, and persuaded her to have a dress made with the silver-and-black-striped fabric. It glimmered like moonlight.

Petros sat down with the order pad, and made it all out. But he had things on his mind.

"I wish I could come back with you to your island, if you are not remaining longer," he said, with intent.

Lydia looked at him thoughtfully. "Can you spare the time?" she asked.

"Of course, of course! I leave Marta in charge, as I do when I go to New York, or Paris. But what a chance to work with such a fine designer. She can tell me what goes on in New York, what ideas will work now. Eh?"

"I have been thinking," said Iris, "about some ideas for a line of my own. I work with Nadia Egorova—"

"I know the lady! Very fine woman! Excellent designer!"

"Thank you. She is marvelous. She has said if I come up with an original line of my own in three months, she will place it with her own models this autumn! I am forming some ideas, I would like to talk to you—it may be we can have some sort of partnership about it—I know Nadia works with a Paris designer like this. Would you be interested—"

"I would, I would!" exclaimed Petros before she had

finished. "You are fresh, you are different, you will have marvelous ideas! And to have some such arrangement with Egorova—marvelous! I will have the designs here, she will have them in New York. Twice the sales, eh? Great—why don't I come back with you to the island—"

"We could continue to work out some ideas, enough for a fall line," said Iris, thinking it out, though Lydia was beginning to look dubious. "With your access to fabrics and dressmakers, and our combined ideas for the designs—"

"I should be most anxious to work with you!" Petros glowed, he rubbed his balding head with a white handkerchief. He looked more than ever like a benign baby. "You make a career of this, yes? You have such a talent! The sketches grow under your fingers, they leap from your brain to the page!"

They were deep in plans when Greg returned at two o'clock. He listened, with growing anger. "You mean—you think to come back with us to the island—and make my fiancée *work*?" He growled out the words. "Nonsense! I brought Iris here to plan her trousseau, not to plan future work! Come, Iris, enough of this nonsense! Petros, you make mischief!"

"No, no, truly I do not!" Petros spread out his hands beseechingly. "You know me, Venizelos! I am a serious man! This lady is such a talented designer! You cannot stifle her talent! She must not marry and forget her fingers!" He snatched up Iris's hand and kissed the fingertips gallantly.

Greg seemed to grow inches taller and much redder and more furious. The little cream-uniformed girls, and Marta in her smart black, all watched in wide eyes and fluttery little steps about the main antagonists.

"She is not going to work with you! She has no time for such long hours of work! She is going to marry me! Forget all this, Diophantus! Find your own girls to flatter and play with!

You have all Athens to search! All Greece! I give you leave to search out the Mediterranean and find your own girl!''

And he caught Iris's arm, and half dragged her to the door. Lydia followed them demurely, a half-smile on her mouth.

''Thank you very much,'' said Diophantus bitterly, following them to the door. ''You are most kind. However, Miss Patakos is the most talented, most brilliant, most beautiful—''

Greg opened the door of the Lincoln Continental, and shoved Iris in the backseat, and his mother after her. Petros was shouting after them, ''Thank you for your patronage! I send the dresses after you! They will be ready soon!''

Two little girls were putting boxes into the trunk of the car, all the swimsuits, and so on. Greg did wait until they had finished, waved to Petros.

''I will not forget this, Petros!'' he cried out to the man, who grinned and kissed his fingertips to the ladies.

''Nor I!'' said Petros. ''Come back soon, eh? All success, all happiness. Be happy!'' And he waved both hands at them as they slid away from the curb.

''What a man,'' sighed Lydia, watching Iris from the corner of her eyes. ''I knew you would like him, Iris!''

Iris exchanged a little grin with Lydia. Greg snorted. ''Out after all the women! Huh! I left you alone two hours, and he invites himself to my home, to chase my fiancée! Nonsense! One cannot trust him an inch!''

''But what a fine dress designer he is, and he recognizes talent in others,'' said his mother comfortably. ''And of course your Iris is very talented, one can see that at once.''

''Of course, of course, but she will have no time for designing when she is married! I will keep her busy,'' and Greg chuckled in self-satisfaction.

Iris stiffened, and gave a long thoughtful look to the back of his curly black head. How confident he sounded! And how much he reacted to opposition! If one was meek and gave in, he lost interest. If one opposed, he would be all the more obstinate and want his own way. Was that her path, to be meek? But she could not risk that!

She had enjoyed so much the hours of work at the designer's. For all his bluster, his charming acts, his flattery, she recognized in Petros Diophantus a truly dedicated designer. They could work together, they had similar tastes. He liked simple designs that showed the rich gloss of a fabric. He let the cloth speak for itself. He thought of the client and what would flatter her, rather than the display of his design on some dummy. Yes, they could work together. And from what he had said, she knew he longed for some contact with New York designers, some business association there.

Iris had no right to speak for Nadia Egorova, yet—yet it could work out. Nadia would not be angry if Iris made that first contact with Petros. She would consider it, she would think with her shrewd Russian mind, and if it suited, she would agree. If it did not, they would have a frank, honest no.

Greg halted the automobile at a restaurant, got out and opened the doors for them, not waiting for the chauffeur. "Come back in two hours," he told the man.

When they ascended in an elevator up to the top floor, Iris thought they would simply be going to some elaborately decorated restaurant. To her delight, they walked out into a sunny airy open-air restaurant, like a *tavérna*, decorated only with grapevines and whitewashed ledges, and pots of scarlet geraniums.

And the view was out over the Saronic Gulf, the water as vivid and deep a blue as the Mediterranean Sea could be, and little boats ducked and bobbed in the waters of the ports. Greg saw them seated near a ledge where they could gaze to their hearts' content at the lovely view. He ordered for them from a plump black-clad woman near the kitchen, then returned to the table.

"My favorite place, Gregorios, thank you," said his mother softly. He pressed her hand, smiling. She turned to Iris. "I used to come here with Ioannes. He loved it so. This view of the Saronic Gulf, the boats. And the food—" She kissed her fingertips and wafted them to the kitchen, smiling.

It was a happy afternoon. They dined on many dishes of Greek foods, some familiar and some unfamiliar to Iris. Rice in grape leaves, squid in tomato sauce, tender chunks of lamb on skewers with peppers and onions and tomatoes, bits of fried fish and scallops, and a lovely white crisp wine, were all she remembered later.

After an hour or two of rest at the apartment later, Greg took Iris and his mother back to the Acropolis in the moonlight. It was an enchanted time. They walked in silence among the moon-drenched stones of ancient times, gazed at the night-purple sky blazing with white stars and an enormous full moon. Other couples had come also, and kissed in corners.

"Ah, if I had but come alone with Iris," Greg mourned teasingly. "I could kiss her senseless!"

"Just as well I came to protect her," said his mother, dryly, clutching his arm as she stepped cautiously over some stones. "I do not think Iris wants to be senseless. A most sensible girl!" There was a warning in her words.

"Ah, but she thinks too much," said Greg. "A girl about to marry should not think too clearly. She should be satisfied to leave thinking to her fiancé!"

"Do I have anything to say in the matter?" asked Iris, in a high voice.

"No," said Greg, and laughed, a deep infectious chuckle. He reached out and pulled her closer to him into his arm, and hugged her frankly. "Tomorrow we go back home, and you will prepare for our wedding, eh?"

She was silent, surprised. She had not known they would leave so soon. Why were they going home tomorrow? Did Petros and his eagerness to work with her have anything to do with it?

"Are you sorry to leave so soon?" asked Lydia perceptively. "Your guests are there, and mine also."

"I know." Iris gave a big sigh, and they all laughed spontaneously. "But I have been so happy in Athens! Thank you for showing me so much, both of you."

"It was our pleasure," said Greg. "I promised I would show you Athens, did I not?"

"Yes, you did." And he kept his word, she thought the next morning as they flew back to the island. He seemed in high good humor this morning, eager to be back home. The little plane was stuffed full of packages, mostly clothes for Iris!

But even better, her mind was full of all the beautiful images of the places she had seen. And she thought often of the possibilities of working with a Greek designer, perhaps with Petros Diophantus. And she had a fresh idea for a line for Nadia Egorova. Yes, it had been a very good journey!

Chapter Twelve

When Iris and the others arrived back at Greg's island home, it was to find that relatives and other guests were already arriving for the engagement party. Lydia had set wheels in motion from Athens.

The guests came by airplane and by yacht, from other parts of Greece, from Italy, from France and England. They were settled in the small hotel down in the village, and in some private homes, or remained on their yachts. Limousines scooted about all day and half the nights, taking people where they wished to go.

The engagement party itself went on for three days. After all, the guests must be fed, as Lydia said. Also, the cousins and uncles and aunts, the associates and friends, all had much business and gossip to catch up on, and chattered in Greek, Italian, French, German, and English day and night. Some seemed to slide easily from one language to the other, and Iris was very thankful for her training in languages.

Iris had thought to help prepare food in the kitchens. Scandalized, the cooks and maids shooed her out. No, no, no, she must dress up, be pretty, meet everybody and be admired! And judged, she thought to herself, seeing the critical looks of some of the women.

Melania was quietly amused at the avid jealousy of Vanessa and Xanthe, of Maria Ardeth and Shelley. They might wear more elaborate clothes and jewels, they might talk brightly in high voices, but all the attention was focused on little Iris, as Shelley said one afternoon.

"It is all too amusing," said Shelley, tossing her blond head and not looking amused at all. "All this shower of attention on little Iris, who wants only to be a dressmaker!"

"And she would be a fine one," said Lydia quickly. "However, she will make an even better wife and mother," and she nodded complacently.

"Don't tell me she is pregnant already!" said Shelley, her voice deliberately raised.

Iris blushed violently, and bent her head in embarrassment. "No, of course not," she muttered. "There was nothing—I was not—"

"You were alone with him for a week, weren't you?" said Maria Ardeth, all too happy to join forces with her despised rival, Shelley. "It is only natural to think—and the haste of the engagement party—"

Lydia looked very stern. "I do not approve of this gossip," she said in her full maternal voice. "Iris is not pregnant, she has done nothing wrong. And it is good to have an engagement party when her father can be present!" She emphasized the word *father* firmly.

Shelley looked very sour. A movement out of the corner of her eye caught Iris's attention, she turned her head to see Greg staring thoughtfully at Shelley and the way her face looked so ugly with her jealousy.

Lydia changed the subject, and pointed out Iris's dress, today of white with gold trim. One of the cousins had brought it from Athens, with Petros Diophantus's regards.

"This is one of the gowns that Iris designed, and Petros made up for her. He is enchanted with her talent," said Lydia. "You can see for yourself what a gift she has for design. Petros Diophantus also made the gown for her engagement party, you shall see it tomorrow evening. He is a fine designer himself, and longs to work with Iris. Of course, she will marry instead, but if she wished she could have a magnificent career!"

Iris wished her mother-in-law-to-be would drop the subject, it only made the women jealous of her more furious. No woman like Shelley liked to hear other women praised before her. And Shelley had been jealous of Iris since the girl's childhood.

Some guests from France had come out to join them on the terrace, and to admire Iris's white dress and gold Greek trim. They talked of Paris and its fashions, and she enjoyed the conversation, especially when it became general.

Greg drifted away, and joined the men who were playing bowls on the front lawn overlooking the cliffs and the sea. Her father spoke to him, they nodded and looked at her. Iris wondered what they were saying.

Iris was wishing the whole situation would go away. She longed to return to quiet, peaceful New York City, with its harsh roar of traffic, street cries, and screaming sirens all muffled in her sanctuary, the workshop of Nadia Egorova. There was peace, there was calm, and she could think and dream her own dreams.

How had she gotten into this situation? She wished Gregorios Venizelos would use his magnificent brain to devise a way out of this mess, instead of pushing her further and further into marriage with him.

She wanted to be a dress designer, not a wife. She did not trust men, especially charming men. She did not believe their promises, their flattery, their plans. She wanted to live by herself, and make her own calm life work out the way she wanted to.

Perhaps when she returned to New York, she could get a little efficiency by herself once more. That had been small and cramped, but her own. She had not become involved there in Charmian's problems. If she had kept her own place, she would never have met Alex—nor Gregorios.

Not met him? She drew a deep unconscious sigh. What she would have missed—this nervous exalted quivering trembling uncertainty, this physical reaction to his touch and his kisses, this blurring of her brain whenever he was about. She could do without all this! She needed it like one needs a broken arm.

Iris's attention was jerked back to the present by the sound of Charmian's name.

"My daughter Charmian should be here," Shelley was saying, stretching out her lithe long body in the deck chair, admiring her painted red toes in the open sandals. The red matched her scarlet cotton dress. "She is so lovely, no one could look at any other girl! Only nineteen but already a top fashion model! She has silvery hair, vivid blue eyes like mine—a very stunning girl, isn't she, Iris?"

Her look demanded response. Iris nodded.

"Charmian is very beautiful, everybody turns to stare at her on the street," said Iris. "And she can wear clothes very well, designers love her. She has modeled for me—"

Shelley interrupted. "Her name is Charmian Angelina Patakos," she said. "Her professional name is Charmian Angel, and men have said to me she looks the angel that she is! She ought to be here, she would love Greece! She is Greek herself, though she looks very American."

"She must come to us sometime," said Lydia politely.

"And you are sisters?" Xanthe said to Iris, having managed to follow some of this conversation. Her eyes scorned Iris's small figure, her darkness. "She is blond and beautiful, and you are sisters?"

Iris knew that Xanthe was very well aware of their relationship. The woman made sure she knew everything there was to know. Now as Xanthe sat forward, her neck craned to see Iris, she reminded Iris of the vultures again, long scraggly neck, bulging eyes intent on carrion.

"They are half-sisters," said Shelley, frowning. "I am not the mother of Iris."

Her tone added "Thank God!"

Iris thought the same, and looked away to the distance. Her father had disappeared from among the men playing bowls, and Greg was coming toward the women again.

He came right to her, smiling, and held out his hand. "Come, I wish to show you something," he said.

Iris got up, taking his hand, glad to cling to its hard warmth. Sometimes women were too much for her. As they started away, Vanessa and Xanthe rose. "We will come also," said Xanthe brightly, her black eyes curious. "We need the walk!"

"Not with me and my fiancée," said Greg, and frowned them down. "We are engaged, we do not need chaperons!" And he walked away with Iris, half dragging her as he strode along.

"I would say that you do," said Shelley, and laughed disagreeably.

Out of hearing, Greg said, "What a nasty woman. If she were my wife, I would not divorce her, I would strangle her."

Greg walked with Iris toward the cliffs, then behind some stunted bushes, and out of sight of the big house. He marched her around, until she said curiously, "Where in the world are we going?"

"Shush! Shush!" He circled the chapel, and they came up behind it, at the back of the small building. He opened a small door at the back, that she had not noticed, and guided her into the darkened building.

She blinked, she could not see at first, until her eyes became accustomed to the dimness lit only by a few candles. The sunlight outside was blinding. She took off her sunglasses, and looked at the Christ icon near the altar, examining it with a happy contentment. The art was so peaceful, so reassuring, that calm expression, that goodness reaching out to one. She crossed herself, and knelt before it.

Greg had released her hand. She knelt by herself at the altar, almost forgetting he had said he wanted to show her something.

She sat up again on her heels, then stood and took a chair near the altar. Someone came and sat down beside her. She thought it was Greg, until she turned and looked.

"Oh—father—" she said, in surprise.

Greg had taken a seat at the back, and seemed absorbed in the Madonna icon there.

Hilarion Patakos cleared his throat. "I wanted to talk to you in private, but I am always interrupted by those harpies," he said.

She bit her lips to keep back a grin of understanding. She eyed him in the dimness. He seemed older, more gray, and in the dim light of the candle she thought he looked haggard. Well, he was in his fifties, but she remembered him the way he had been when she adored him, when she was so little that she had accepted all he said as truth. All black curly hair, and laughing eyes, and tossing her up in the air, and making promises, "We will be together one day soon. I will come to you at Christmas as before—soon you will come to live with us again—"

It had never happened, and she had had to still her restless heart, and accept meekly what she could not change. But it had hurt. It still hurt, to be unwanted.

When he was silent, she said gently, "What did you wish to say, father?" Perhaps he would admit he was wrong to press the marriage. She would be out of this tangle.

"It was wrong of me to send you away when you were only five," he blurted out, and wiped his face with his handkerchief. "If I had persisted, I might have made Shelley accept you."

Her hands clasped together, she did not want to discuss that bitter subject.

"Gregorios Venizelos has spoken to me at length. He is angry with me that I was so weak that I let the women influence me," he said unhappily. "The nuns assured me that you would be happy with them. And Shelley had her own daughter—"

"We cannot change the past," said Iris in a low tone. "Let us rather forget it."

"But I wish you to forgive me for the past. Let us love each other, and begin again."

She was silent, fighting herself. One could not change the past, and in the present she had gone far from him. It would be ungracious to say so, but she had no wish to involve herself with him and with Maria Ardeth.

"You cannot forgive me," he said mournfully.

"Of course I forgive you," said Iris quickly. "It no longer matters—I mean, I am grown up. It was probably meant to be. The nuns were always kind and gracious to me. They gave me a good education, and cared about me."

He sighed. "So you do not need me."

She hesitated. She had always been a peacemaker, she hated warring words among friends and relatives. "It was meant to be," she said again. "It is good to know you wish me good, and I wish everything fine for you. Let us be friends.''

" 'Friends'!" His voice rose in the little chapel, and Greg at the back of the room started and glared at them both. "Friends? Is that all? I am your father, and you are my daughter."

He remembered late, she thought with a sigh, and sought for words to comfort him without committing herself to more than she was willing to give.

"Yes, of course you are my father. I appreciate that. I am proud to be a Patakos," she said. "We have a proud heritage. I am most proud to be Greek and American. And I am proud that you have made much of yourself, your deeds are known."

She had slid easily into Greek, he responded also in Greek.

"Yes, yes, we are Greek and American. It is good. How I wish, however, that I could do more for you. I have given you a dowry, and I like your future husband. Is there nothing more I can do for you?"

Iris frowned. She wished he would take back the hotel-dowry, and let her alone, but she would have to fight herself out of this coil. "I would like," she said impulsively, "a picture of my mother. I have none. If you would kindly give that to me—"

He shifted uncomfortably on the small chair. "Shelley destroyed them all," he muttered.

Iris swallowed over the bile. *"Destroyed—"*

"Yes, she was jealous. However—" he brightened at a thought. "Your mother had an aunt who was fond of her. There might be something in her possessions—she died recently—I will find out if there is some picture of Poppea in her household goods. Yes, yes, I will telephone to her son, and ask him for this. I will be glad to do this."

She had little hope, but thanked him politely. "If there is a picture, I would be glad to have it. Thank you for your trouble.''

"Is there nothing else?" he begged.

All, all too late, she thought, and shook her head, and managed to smile and pat his hand. She withdrew her hand quickly, though, when he squeezed it.

"Nothing else, thank you, father."

"Well—well—" He got up, bent over and kissed her cheek. She smelled the tobacco and shaving scent, then he went out the side door to the sunlight. Greg came to sit beside her.

Tears were rolling down her cheeks. Her father had come to her in the darkness of the chapel, because he still could not brave the fury of his current wife. He said fine words, but did not mean them. She dashed the tears from her cheeks with her hands.

Greg took her hand gently. "He wished to be reconciled with you, Iris," he said softly. "I think he is a good man at heart."

"Yes, of course," she said dully.

"What is the matter, my dove, my dear?" His voice was coaxing and deep. "Why are you not happy?"

"He had to sneak in here!" she cried out passionately, unable to force down her despair. "He did not dare come out in the open, to let them see me with him! He is ashamed of his love for me! If he has any such love! It is the same as always! He is afraid of those women, his wives! He fears their biting tongues too much!"

Greg was silent for a time, stroking her hands, soothing her with his gestures. He put his arm about her, hugged her, but she was tight with the turmoil inside her.

"Come, it is cold in here. Let us walk in the sunshine."

He drew her with him, out into the air. They had scarcely walked a dozen steps, when Vanessa came to them, and joined them, clinging to Greg's other arm, as though she had every right.

Iris muttered an excuse, and left them. She went into the big house, and upstairs to her room, and shut the door. She flung herself down on the bed, and put her head in the pillow. She had no more tears, however. She lay quietly for a time, and composed herself. What did it matter? Nothing had changed. She must find more strength within herself, and go on alone, as she always had.

There was still the engagement party to get through. She changed her dress and shoes, washed her face and put on fresh makeup, a little heavier than usual, to disguise the dark lines under her eyes.

On the afternoon of the third day, Charis helped Iris don the golden brocade gown, the gold sandals, the sapphire and gold jewelry.

"Beautiful, like a goddess," cried Charis, with more like compliments. Iris accepted them for the usual flattery.

But Greg came for her, to escort her downstairs, and stared and stared at her. The golden dress flowed softly about her, the sapphires glittered in the soft lights of the big house. Her small feet in the golden-strapped sandals were like the feet of the Iris of the Rainbow, the messenger of the gods.

Charis had arranged her black hair in a new way, with long curly strands loose on her shoulders, some down to her breasts, some down her back, with a few golden pins to hold it in place. The gold shone against the blue black of her glossy hair. And the sapphires in the long dangling earrings glittered in the black locks, matching her deep blue eyes.

"You are—magnificent!" breathed Greg, and he seemed serious. He was strikingly handsome today, even more than usual. He wore a white tuxedo. A sapphire was on his right hand.

He took her on his arm, and escorted her proudly down the

194

curving staircase, to where the guests waited below in the huge open area of the big house. The chatter slowly died, all heads turned, they stared as the couple descended the stairs.

Hilarion Patakos gazed long at his eldest daughter. Tears came in his eyes. "She is the image of her mother," he muttered.

One of the older uncles dared to approach Iris first, and kissed her hand. "You are like a goddess today!"

She felt the flattery was very fulsome, until Kyria Lydia said to her quietly, "You are more beautiful than I have ever seen you, Iris. You do resemble one of the goddesses, or the little Iris herself."

Iris smiled, and thanked her shyly. She hated being the center of attention, having everybody staring at her. She felt self-conscious, scarcely able to eat the dinner and drink the wine, as she sat at Greg's right hand in the dining area. The oldest of the uncles and aunts sat with them, the younger ones were scattered about in the other areas, and out on the terrace. She was in the place of honor, deferred to, flattered, complimented, gazed at, envied—yes, she knew that look in people's eyes.

Shelley was madly impatient, furious. She could scarcely be decent to her own husband, and Bill Roswell had his patience sorely tried that day. "After all," muttered Shelley, loudly enough for Iris to hear, "it is only an engagement party, not a coronation!"

One of the young male cousins, silently admiring Iris, dared to say to Shelley, "But this is a family party, which will be long remembered! Today the head of the House of Venizelos is being engaged! In the old days, he would have a title, and a throne!"

Shelley could scarcely endure this. Iris was biting her cheeks to keep from laughing aloud at the earnest young cousin, he would be sadly insulted. But Shelley did not share her amusement.

"A throne, a throne!" moaned Shelley. "Oh, God, that is impossible, that is sickening! I cannot believe you! It is only an engagement party—"

Someone led her away. Iris smiled until her face was stiff. She had not seen her father in the background, watching her proudly, thoughtfully, and hearing all that went on. He was not accustomed to the background, she knew, when she did see him. It puzzled her that he stood there, hands behind his back, silently observing.

Sunset came, the party had been planned so that most of the dinner would be over in time to watch the sunset over their coffee and liqueurs. Iris was seated in one of the chairs on the terrace, holding a small court reluctantly. One of the elderly aunts wanted to tell her the history of the family, and was being gently dissuaded by another.

"Well, well," said one of the uncles. "It is sad to think that tomorrow this time we will all go our separate ways, and not see each other until the wedding of Gregorios and Iris!"

"Is it soon?" someone asked Greg.

"Soon," he confirmed. "However, it will be a small affair. This was large, so that all might meet my future wife. Enjoy it now!" and he laughed.

Iris thought he was fooling them, that he would break the engagement discreetly when the clamor and fussing had died down. Their time alone on the island would be forgotten, the gossip would go away.

The old uncle turned to Hilarion Patakos. "Hilarion, you go home soon? You live in Texas now?"

"We live in Houston, Texas, now, yes," said Patakos. "However, I have decided to stay over for a time. Gregorios Venizelos has kindly invited me to remain."

Shelley Roswell gasped audibly, and her vivid blue eyes

flashed with fury. But she could say nothing, he was not her husband now. Maria Ardeth stiffened and sat up straight. Hilarion was her husband, and he had said nothing!

"You did not say this to me!" she said haughtily.

The Greek relatives looked at her curiously, and shook their heads. Iris could hear the thinking that ticked in their heads. Bold, brazen American wife!

"I have only just made up my mind," said Patakos mildly, but there was a gleam in his gray eyes. "I have spoken to my office this afternoon, and there is nothing urgent to command my return."

"Well, I don't want to stay!" cried Maria Ardeth rashly. "I have many engagements. I dropped everything to come with you when we thought Iris in danger. Now that she is safely taken care of—" and she sneered over at Iris, "well, I see no reason to remain."

She had flung down the gauntlet in front of her husband. He let a small silence cool the air, then spoke gently, almost in a whisper. "Then I shall arrange your transportation back to Texas. All shall be taken care of. When do you wish to depart?"

She gasped. "I'm not going alone! All that distance! You are coming with me!"

"No," he said. "I am staying to get to know my daughter better. It has been many years—we have much to catch up on. Gregorios has kindly said to me I am free to remain. I shall stay."

The finality of his words surprised Iris as well as his wife, and Shelley. Before Maria Ardeth could catch the trend of the matter, Shelley had spoken up.

"Well, she is my daughter also, and we have not had a good visit for a long time!" said the amazing Shelley. "I think I shall remain, and get to know Iris better!"

"I am not your daughter," said Iris, blurting it out before she could stop herself.

There was an appalled silence, avid curiosity in the eyes of all the relatives and guests.

"But she is welcome anyway," said Gregorios quickly. He sat down beside Iris, and took her wrist warningly. "You must remain, Bill Roswell, if you can spare us the time."

Bill scratched his head, then nodded. "Reckon I could stay for a time," he drawled. "If I could use your phone for a few calls, reckon I could work it out. If Shelley wants to stay."

"Yes, of course," said Shelley tightly, with a bright false smile. "It will be a pleasure to remain here, in these beautiful surroundings."

Iris knew she would be hopelessly bored, and wondered why Shelley bothered. She did not want to become better acquainted with her stepmother, and did not think the reverse was true either. So why did Shelley want to stay? Did she think to get Hilarion Patakos back again? What was her motive? Something devious, Iris was sure. However, there was nothing Iris could do about it.

Maria Ardeth Patakos gave in sullenly, too smart to go home without her husband. "Oh, well, I suppose I should remain also, since we are invited so—kindly. I have not had a chance to know Iris either."

Iris would have been happier, much happier, without knowing this stepmother. She smiled politely, and wished she was not bound by courtesy to pretend pleasure in their remaining.

Iris had been looking forward to quiet and peace, after everybody left. And now they were all four remaining.

She caught Bill Roswell's quiet twinkle, and winked back at him. Well, she liked Bill, he was nice. And he understood.

Greg pressed her hand. "We shall all become better acquainted," he said. "I shall be interested in hearing all about Iris's childhood!"

Iris stiffened, and looked incredulously at her fiancé. He gazed blandly back at her. He knew darn well, she thought, that these four knew nothing of her childhood! Did he just rub it in, that they had ignored and neglected her? Yes, she thought, that was just what he was doing!

Oh, what a pleasant week to come, with them all here!

Chapter Thirteen

Most of the guests departed, by airplane or ship, and Iris was glad to wave them farewell.

However, several remained: her father, Bill Roswell, Shelley, and Maria Ardeth. And Vanessa and Xanthe and Xanthe's two small girls seemed permanent fixtures. Greg did not seem to mind at all. He was a genial host, whenever he was not working.

Hilarion and Bill Roswell made their business calls, fascinated by Greg's equipment. Alex did not reappear. He was still hiding out in his suite of rooms in the Long House, as they called the second building on the estate. He held a small court in his rooms for his young male cousins, and left the others strictly alone.

Melania and Iris envied him! "He has an excuse to avoid them," Melania whispered, then clapped her small hand over her mouth. "Oh, I am wicked!"

"If that is wicked, I am a devil," sighed Iris. "Where has the peace and quiet gone?"

The women rose late, then their shrill chatter filled the air like very noisy birdcalls all the remainder of the day until the late night. It spoiled the sunsets, Iris thought, to hear the gossip and malicious laughter.

She began to take refuge in drawing and painting. Every morning, after she had breakfasted, she gathered up her paints and brushes, an easel and some papers, and set out to find a place to work out of sight of the women. Greg frowned after her, but refrained from calling her back. Melania had her household duties, and fulfilled them conscientiously.

Iris would take off, and not return until the two or three o'clock luncheon. She would endure the talk, then disappear once more to some other place to work. She was achieving something also. She had created some little country scenes that pleased her. But even more important for her career, she had begun to design some dresses, some suits, and accessories, for a line of clothes for Nadia Egorova.

One afternoon after luncheon, she set off with her easel, firmly refusing all company. "No, I'm going to work!" she said shortly to Greg.

"You will tire yourself!"

Shelley was listening curiously to this exchange. "Let her go! Do sit with us, Gregorios, and talk of your office in Paris! I hear it is very beautiful, and you designed it!"

Greg turned his head, distracted, to answer her politely, and Iris managed to get away, walking swiftly into the fields to the south of the cliffs.

There was a view there she liked, and with luck the sun would be right, to gleam off the lemon trees, and sparkle on the field flowers. She wanted to try to capture the effect of the light on the yellowed fields.

She set up her easel with a sigh of satisfaction. What a

pleasure to be alone and silent! Only the bees buzzed around her, and two butterflies of yellow and white danced over some anemones and small scarlet poppies. From the nearby hills came the strong fragrance of the maquis, that scrub that feeds the goats and makes hiding places for outlaws.

She put down her camping stool, and sat before the easel, and soon was busily at work sketching in the fields. She was going to try oils today, but she must work fast to catch the slant of the light.

She became so absorbed that she noticed nothing, not the flying away of the bees, and the butterflies. Not the silencing of the soft field noises about her.

Only when the scent of the fields and flowers were drowned out by the strong smell of an unwashed man, and a dark shadow fell over her small canvas, did she glance up.

Then she screamed, and screamed! He lunged at her, knocked down her easel, and picked her up as easily as one would grab a child. He was a massive man, with black shaggy hair, like a bear, and his bull-like neck was reddened and dark with dirt. His big hands were black with the dirt of the fields he had been crawling through.

He grunted, in Greek, and shook her as she screamed. She was like a rag doll in his grip. He held her so she could see his dark face, the pockmarked skin, the small mean black eyes. He dripped filth from his twisted mouth, words she scarcely knew, only they were filth.

Frantic with fear, she kicked at him with her sandaled feet. He did not seem to feel the blows. Her arms were twisted, until she feared they would break off.

Then a shout! "Let her go!" a man yelled. "Let her go! I will kill you—"

The voice came closer, shouting fearful threats.

It was Greg, she caught a glimpse of him, his black eyes wide and fearful, his face reddish tanned, his fists uplifted.

"Greg—help—Gregorios—" she screamed. The bull lifted her high, and dashed her to the earth. She gasped, the breath knocked from her, and lay limply at his feet.

He pulled a long knife from his leather belt, and the sun glinted on the sharp blade. Terrified, she rolled over against his legs, trying to knock him off balance. It was like hitting a tree trunk.

He kicked her savagely with his booted foot. It caught her a glancing blow at the ribs, and she groaned, and rolled into a small painful ball. Then Greg was there, and he struck at the man, and knocked him backward, away from Iris.

She rolled over, trying to get out of the path of the two men as they fought. Greg caught the man's knife hand, and twisted it. The knife gleamed, then finally fell to the ground.

The bull let out a bellow of pain, and ran. Greg started after him, and yelled, "You will leave, get away—coward, bully—shameless one—" in Greek. "You would fight a helpless woman! You run from a man, bastard, jellyfish!"

He stopped abruptly, and returned to Iris, gently lifting her. His face was anxious.

"Iris, my dove, my dear—Iris Poppea—you are all right?"

Stupid question, she thought. She ached all over, especially in her ribs. Were they broken? "Hurt—" she muttered.

He gathered her up, and carried her uphill back toward the house. As he strode with her, some men raced down to them. "Who is it—what happened?"

"Go after him!" he yelled, gesturing to the man now in the distance. "It is Orestes Sicilianos—get him!"

Her father ran to meet them, as the other men ran past. His face was an odd color, tanned, but drawn and greenish.

"What happened—my daughter—is she—"

"Safe," said Greg between tight lips. "Get out of my way—call my mother—"

Greg carried her past the curious crowd on the terrace. Iris moaned in pain, then fainted.

"Take her up to her room—" said Kyria Lydia. She called to the servants, giving orders, and hurried after Greg and Iris.

Iris came to slowly as someone bathed her forehead with cool water, and gentle hands felt her ribs.

Voices murmured above her. Kyria Lydia, Charis—Melania—Greg—Iris stirred, and opened her eyes slowly. The pain was there, making her moan with it.

"Ribs broken?" It was Greg's concerned voice.

"I think not." Kyria Lydia's gentle hands moved over her bare waist, up to her arms. "But best to get the doctor from the village—"

"I'll send at once!" And Greg left the room, yelling his orders. Iris flinched at his loud voice. Her father bent over her, his face thrust near hers.

"Iris Poppea—how do you feel?"

It was difficult to talk, much less explain how she felt. She closed her eyes, and drifted away from them.

She faded in and out for the next night and day. The doctor came, and poked her painfully, but declared the ribs were not broken. She was bandaged, salved, questioned, made to drink liquids when she would rather sleep, and visited by an endless procession of the curious.

Finally she protested. "Get out—everybody! I want to be alone!" she cried. "Let me alone! I ache—I hurt—let me alone to heal!"

And she began to cry. She never cried, but she felt she had to. It got results. Kyria Lydia shooed out everybody, including Greg, and left her to the quiet care of Charis.

Then Iris could sleep, and rest, and begin to heal. From a distance, shrill voices rose to her, but she could ignore them. People asked about her at the bedroom door, but Charis kept them out firmly. Only the doctor came in, and Kyria Lydia for a time.

But the shock and the pain were breaking up something in Iris. She felt tears continually in her eyes. She sobbed over nothing. She had nightmares when she did sleep, and wakened with a jerk, sure that Orestes had returned.

"What is it, what is wrong with her? I must see her!" Greg's voice at the door disturbed her, she moved wearily.

Greg bullied his way inside, and gazed down at her with concern. She sniffed, and eyed him through tear-wet eyes. He groaned, and bent down to her, sitting on the side of the bed gently.

"Oh, Iris, I would do anything to take the pain from you!" His voice was unusually soft and kind. He stroked back the curly hair from her forehead, and gently kissed it.

"Oh, Greg—who was that—that horrible man—"

He scowled frightfully. "Our feudal enemy, my cousin, Orestes Sicilianos," he said. "But do not worry your pretty head about him, he shall not harm you!"

"Why—why did he—"

"He must be hiding here on the island," said Greg reluctantly. "He has heard probably of our engagement, and thinks to hurt me through you. But we shall find him!"

She trembled. "He was not—found? He is—loose—not captured?"

"I think not yet, but he will be! Do not worry—"

But she did worry and fear, and her tears flowed afresh. He bent closer, and gathered her up into his arms, and rocked and soothed her. He pressed her face into his shoulder, and she smelled the fresh linen shirt and the starch, and his masculine shave cream, and his own odor of clean outdoor man.

It was somehow comforting. He was so big, and held her

so gently, she felt like a small child in his arms. She stopped her weeping, and cuddled down against him.

He murmured to her in Greek. "There you are, my pet, my lamb. Nothing shall harm you, my darling, my dove. You are safe with me, adored one. You will be easy now, eh."

He stroked her hair and soothed her. It was night, and she could hear the cracking and humming of the cicadas, the sleepy calls of the birds. Faintly, music came to her also. Alex must be playing one of his records of classical music.

"I am all right now," said Iris, with reserve, and feeling she had clung to him long enough.

Greg only held her closer. "I do not mind," he said mischievously, and smiled down at her. "You are very sweet! I look forward to our marriage!"

That did make her feel uneasy. "That is nonsense, we shall break the engagement soon, when everybody goes home," she said tartly. "No need to continue the farce! Nothing happened!"

He frowned. "You need protection," he told her sharply. "I do not want you to go out alone again! Promise me this! You must never go anywhere alone."

Iris scowled, and evaded the demand. "I do not need protection in New York City!" she said. "I know where I am safe."

"New York is the most dangerous city in the world," said Greg firmly. "You shall not go back there and live alone! I tremble when I think how foolish your father was, to allow that! I have told him what I think of him!"

"It is not your concern!" cried Iris. "If I don't mind, why should you?"

"But, my woman, you did mind very much," said Greg. "You minded always! However, your father's chance is gone. You belong to me now, and I shall protect you! You are in my care from now on to eternity!"

Iris stared at him in growing alarm. He seemed to mean it. The trouble was, he was Greek and very possessive. And he had a high sense of duty. He had taken over Iris, and meant to protect her, whether she wished it or not.

She felt he was overdoing all this protection business. When he came to his senses, he would be sorry he had taken on a small brown bird like Iris, instead of a glamorous peacock! He didn't want someone like her for a wife, he could not! There were plenty of peacocks around squawking for attention, some gorgeous ones attracted to his wealth. Any one of them could look proud and jeweled as his wife.

She must dampen his feeling he had to protect Iris. Right now it was difficult, she ached all over, she felt weepy and frightened. It was sweet to cuddle into his arms, and be scolded and petted.

Charis came in sleepily, and Greg went away. Iris lay awake for a time, trying to think how to call off the engagement. However, her brain was not working too well, and she postponed thinking. It made her head ache the more.

The next day, she felt some better, though her bruises had turned to interesting patterns of blue, green, and purple. Greg swore frightfully when he saw the ones on her arms, and it was as well he was not allowed to see her ribs. They were reddish purple and swollen.

"Another day or two in bed," the doctor decreed. Iris gave in, and lay there, to be pampered some more.

Greg came in during the afternoon, and his frown was thoughtful. "There was a strange boat in the dock, it has now departed," he said. "I think it was my cousins. Someone who looked like Nikolaos Sicilianos was piloting the boat, a very handsome fellow. I do not like this."

Greg laid some flowers on the bed beside her, some white roses and fragrant lilacs. They must have cost the earth, thought Iris, lifting them to sniff luxuriously at the fragrant petals.

"Thank you, Greg, but you should not—"

He bent over the bed and kissed her lips, silencing her, then stood erect, grinning with pleasure. "I have discovered a way to silence you!" he declared.

Charis giggled and sat down demurely in a corner of the room, as chaperon. Greg seated himself beside the bed.

"Greg—tell me about the feud. You told me once, before I knew anybody," said Iris. "I do not understand—why it has lasted so long. Didn't you say it began in World War II?"

He nodded, his black curly hair mussed, an intriguing curl on his tanned forehead. "Some of the family were on either side of the war in Greece, both communist and fascist. Some were helping the Allies secretly. Very confusing," he said. "I believe there was betrayal on both sides, each doing what they thought best for Greece."

He paused, frowning in thought, idly caressing a white rose in his lean fingers. She had noticed how he loved flowers, and would carry one with him when he walked, or put one between his teeth when he was working on his boat.

"Ignatios Sicilianos and my grandfather Leander—the lion— were on the same side. However, the brother of Sicilianos, Esdras, was on the side of the Germans, and he died. Ignatios believed that my grandfather had betrayed Esdras. He turned against us. Soon after, Ignatios died in battle. His son Timotheos carried on the feud. Later, when he had sons, Orestes and Nikolaos, they also joined him in the feud."

"And it was—Orestes—" Iris shuddered at the memory of the dark reddish black face of the bull-like man who had attacked her. She could believe the stories of the Minotaur, half-man half-bull, that lived in darkness and killed men.

Greg put his hand on hers soothingly. "Yes, it was Orestes. I learned today that he had been on the island for a time, hiding in some caves. Nikolaos must have come with the boat to take him away. May they both remain away!''

"I hope so—'' she whispered.

"They shall not harm you!'' he vowed.

"I wish I could go back to New York," she said. He frowned and shook his head.

"The story,'' he said, obviously to distract her. "I will tell you the rest. My grandfather Leander kept up the feud. My father Ioannes was more gentle, but he also was involved. They had nothing to do with the Sicilianos family. We became wealthy, from the hotels, and hard work. We bought back some land we had once held, and the Sicilianos were very jealous of this. We have land all over Greece and many islands," he said proudly, with a toss of his black head.

"Jealousy makes for poor relations,'' said Iris.

Greg grimaced, and nodded. "All too true. But it was our hard work that achieved this. We are not ashamed of our methods. We worked hard, and were honorable! So—those who are wealthy become the targets of those unable or unwilling to work hard. Not only do the Sicilianos envy us, but also those scum called terrorists. Because of the hotel chain, many of my relations have become targets of such villains. Alex works for us, and his recent attack was probably the work of Orestes—Alex thinks he recognized the man. But it may have been unknown and strange terrorists. It is not a comfortable feeling," he ended simply.

Iris sighed. "No, it is very bad. I am sorry," and her hand sought Greg's big one, and touched it. At once, he caught her hand in his, and gave it a gentle squeeze, smiling down at her.

"My grandfather Leander, the lion man, was much admired, and I am said to look like him," said Greg. "He was stern and honorable and hard-working. He protected his whole family. I try also to do this. We have known much poverty, but we now have property, land, and many of my relatives I have settled on the land as tenant farmers. We do well. Many work in the hotels, all who show capability are given opportunity to learn and be promoted. It is a family concern. I shall put one of my young cousins in charge of your hotel, Iris!''

This reminder was not pleasant to her, it reminded her of her problems.

Later on, Iris tried to remember all Greg had said. With Lydia's help, she wrote down all the family names, and their relationships, and that helped her understand this feud.

''The feud should be healed,'' she said to Lydia, troubled. ''It has been a poison all these many years.''

When Greg came back, Iris repeated this to him. He scowled. ''It is they who carry it on,'' he said sharply.

''But someone should heal it, someone ought to stop it,'' she insisted. ''There is no sense in keeping it going—how long could it last, a hundred years? Wars are bad enough! But if men and families quarrel, how can nations be at peace? Hate is a poison.''

He brushed his lips against hers, and changed the subject. ''Your color is better today, my dove,'' he told her. ''You feel better, don't you? I shall carry you down to the terrace to enjoy the sunshine.''

He was as good as his word, carrying her down after Charis had carefully dressed her in a light sundress of yellow and blue. Greg laid her tenderly on a lounge chair, and the men made much of her. Lydia greeted her happily, so did Melania, but Iris did not flatter herself that the other women were glad to have her company.

''Well, perhaps we can now go home,'' muttered Maria Ardeth spitefully. ''Now the invalid has decided to come among us!''

Hilarion Patakos pretended not to hear her. He sat next to his daughter, and asked her tenderly how she felt.

"I am much better, thank you, father. I am sorry you felt you must remain."

"It was my duty and my pleasure to be here." He gave Greg a significant look. "Gregorios has explained the feud to me. It is sad that it has gone on for so many years."

"Yes, dreadful. There is no sense in continuing it." Iris turned anxiously to Greg, who leaned against a pillar near her, looking tanned and handsome and very much alive. "Greg, could it not be healed? Is not the father of Orestes much more sensible?"

"About many matters, but not this," said Greg. "He has his honor, of course."

"Honor!" said Iris. "How much honor is there in sneaking about attacking helpless women? Nonsense! It is foolish. Hate is such a poison, it turns men's minds!"

Even as she raged, she looked at Greg, and thought how tall and handsome he was, how strong and fine. Alex had joined them because Iris had come, and lay back, with dark glasses, and too slender limbs languidly on his lounge. How would she feel if Greg had been laid low as Alex had?

Xanthe was sneering, "You do not understand the Greek sense of honor! It is our obligation to carry on the feud! We shall one day wipe them all out—off the face of the earth! That is the only honorable way!"

Vanessa looked oddly troubled, and raised a slim hand in protest. "Let us not speak of such—" she murmured. "It is not lucky, it is unfortunate—"

Xanthe's burning look blazed at her sister. "You must never be weak and frail, Vanessa! The women of our family have always been as strong as their men required them to be! It is only those who have gone away to foreign lands and lived in decadence who became weak and unwilling to live in honor!'' And her stare took in Iris and Shelley and Maria Ardeth.

"Now, just a minute!'' said Shelley. "I don't find that amusing—American women are—''

In the argument that followed, Iris got a headache, and she let her mind drift away from the talk. Her gaze went to the small blue pitcher that stood near her on a glass-topped table in the sunshine. It was filled with scarlet poppies, the flower of Greece. Greg had picked one from the vase, and twirled it in his fingers.

Against his white shirt it shone like a drop of blood.

And it was like the blood shed by the feuding families, who could not keep peace among themselves. She longed to end this one feud anyway, and bring peace to Greg and his family.

If it was not ended, then one day that scarlet flower might lie on his shirt and blood would flow from his strong tanned body, in a life-ending flow. Greg might look like a strong god of Greece, but he was human. Those eyes so bright and mocking would close in death. That large carved generous mouth curled in a grin would straighten into everlasting silence. His body would lie stiffly to be put into the dark red earth of Greece, to belong forever to the land he loved.

She shuddered. She could not endure that thought. Greg— dead—and so foolishly, in a feud.

If only the feud might be ended.

For she loved him, she thought, and the shock of it was as blinding as the sunlight that poured over them on the terrace. In the brilliant light of the truth, she blinked and tried to shut her eyes and panic and say ''No, no, it cannot be!''

But her gaze went to the tall strong man, leaning against the white pillar, his black curly head as arrogantly handsome as any Greek statue. And she knew she loved him. Pride and arrogance, all that he was, she loved him.

It was as terrible a revelation, as blinding and shocking and earthshaking as one of the Greek earthquakes to Iris.

She had meant never to love, never to marry, never to put herself into the power and possession of a man. For that would mean more hurt and sorrow, she knew that. Best never to know that shattering love than to endure the pain a man could bring to a woman.

But unasked, unwanted, love had come to her in the shape of a Greek male, proud, possessive, and determined. Whatever he decided to do with her would be done, and she could not stop him.

She could not endure to think of him stricken down, killed. She could not endure to believe he would be killed by his feudal enemies. If only she could have gone away while she was free of his charm and allure!

He caught her gaze, and smiled slowly, deliberately, at her, and put the scarlet poppy to his mouth. It was as though he kissed her before them all.

Then he said to them casually, but not idly, "I will tell you what I have planned. While you are still here, I shall have our marriage performed in the village church. No point in you going home to America and having to come right back!"

Only Lydia Venizelos and Hilarion Patakos did not look surprised. Iris could not speak a word.

"What—what did you say? marriage—in the chapel—when—now?"

"Yes, in a few days, it is being arranged." Greg straightened, and came over to sit beside Iris on the lounge. "I want the right to protect Iris forever! She shall not be hurt again. I have spoken to the priest, he will obtain the documents. We shall be married before the week is out!"

And he took Iris's hand and raised it to his lips. His eyes searched her keenly, read her face and her willingness. She had just discovered that she loved him, how could she refuse him? And she was dumb and numb and unable to speak—she could not say him nay.

He knew it, and a slow smile spread over his face, and he looked so self-satisfied she longed to shout her refusal. But she could not. She wanted him, and the want was naked in her face and eyes, as it was in his. He did not love her, but he wanted her, and he would protect her, and that had to be enough for her.

Oh, God, thought Iris, the marriage would be bitter for her! But bitter or sweet, she must have it. She loved him too much.

Chapter Fourteen

By the next day, the marriage preparations were already in full swing. To Iris's surprise and anger, her wedding gown was already made!

It had arrived from Athens, and the hands of Petros Diophantus. Charis and Lydia spread it out in the sewing room, and the folds of creamy white silk brocade swished and billowed over the table and the floor covered with white cotton to protect the gown.

"He made it—sent it—but I did not agree to marry Gregorios!" cried Iris, in amazement, when she saw the dress.

Lydia looked faintly surprised, Charis gasped, "But you are betrothed, Kyria Iris!"

Iris swallowed hard. How to explain that she did not mind being engaged—but marriage was another matter! The thought that Greg had taken her so for granted that he had ordered her wedding gown while they were in Athens infuriated her!

She gazed in silence as the long veil was spread out, to foam in lacy folds over the silk gown, trailing out in wide waves after it. The veil would be fitted to her head, flow down her shoulders and back, and trail behind her a good eight feet as she walked up the church aisle to meet Greg—and the priest—

She tried on the gown, and the women murmured about her. Lydia and Charis, Melania and a couple of maids helped her put it on, adjust the veil, and then gazed at her admiringly.

The dress was a triumph for Petros. The bodice was simple, showing the beautiful silk brocade fabric. The neckline was high, demure in a mandarin collar with seed pearls sewn on the bodice. Tiny satin buttons fastened the gown from throat to waist, then the skirt billowed out to fall about her in puffy clouds to her heels.

The sleeves were puffed also, to her wrists, where they were fastened in a narrow band decorated with more pearls.

"You will be able to dance in this," beamed Charis. "Many will come from the village to see you! Everybody is coming!"

It would be a typical Greek wedding, thought Iris, with the solemn ceremony, the golden crowns over their heads, and afterward feasting and dancing, and many fastening money onto her sleeves. Everybody would be staring—and Shelley would sneer—and Maria Ardeth would make nasty remarks in Iris's ears—and afterward—after all that—Iris would be alone with Greg—and he would take complete possession of her—

She could not go through with it. He did not love her. He thought of her as one more relative to be taken care of. He had a strong sense of honor. Nobody took care of Iris, so he would! And he had wronged her by staying for a week alone with her. Yes, that was the root of it—

She changed from the white gown, which fit perfectly, even to the hem. She slipped on a sundress of blue and white, and went to hunt for Greg.

She still felt a little pale and languid, and her ribs hurt, but her brain was clear. She no longer wanted to cry and cling.

She found Greg working at his desk near the electronic equipment. Her father was talking on the telephone briskly, to somewhere in the States.

"Cannot you take care of such a simple matter?" Hilarion was saying in exasperation. "Have the plumbing repaired at once, pay them extra to work overtime—of course! It must be done. A hotel cannot operate if the pipes have burst! No, I am not returning until my daughter is safely married!"

He heard the patter of her sandals, and turned to beam at her, the scowl disappearing.

"Greg, I must speak with you," said Iris softly, not to disturb the telephone conversation.

"Oh, of course, delicious," he said absently. She bit her lips. Did he hand out flattery automatically? He stood, put down the papers, and slid his arm about her waist. "What do you wish to discuss?"

She motioned him away with her toward the stairs. They were alone in that area of the room. "I—I wanted to say—it is not necessary for us to go through with the marriage," she told him hurriedly. "It is all—too sudden—I mean—why not wait, let them go home—break the engagement—"

"I have neglected you," he said at once. "You are feeling unsure and it is difficult for you."

"No, no," she said, shaking her head vigorously. "No, it is just—well, I don't want to get married!"

He frowned, and caught her hand. "Come, let us go out for a time. We have not talked for a time." He led her out the back, and to the garages, where the sleek limousines rested.

He ignored them, to put her up into the seat of one of the sturdy Land Rovers. He came around to the other side, and started the engine, guiding the jeeplike vehicle out the back way and down the hill.

Iris was silent as he drove. She must collect her thoughts and persuade him with calm reason. And herself. Much as she loved him now, and knew it, she did not think their marriage would work. He needed a glamorous hostess, a marvelous Greek woman who would handle him and his life with icy efficiency, of whom he would be proud. All Athens and all Greece must stare at his woman, and she must be able to endure the critical looks. Iris did not think she could stand that!

And, besides, she had her career. She had put most of her lifetime into preparing for that. She would not give it up!

Greg drove in and out of the hills, then finally let the Land Rover slide to a halt on a patch of raw earth overlooking the valley. Behind them was a good-sized mountain, and the sunlight gleamed on the lemon and orange trees that dotted the slopes. She could smell the sharp clean fragrance of them, and of the maquis.

Greg helped Iris down, and they walked slowly through the scrub and the wild flowers to a patch of green grass. She sat down and he sat beside her, crossing his legs and getting comfortable.

He wore blue jeans today, and a blue checked shirt, and he looked so informal and American, she could have almost believed he was what he looked—a nice young man intent on marriage. But she must remember he was not that. He was head of the House of Venizelos, an immensely wealthy Greek with a hotel chain, a very busy man and a very important one.

"So," said Greg. "You have doubts, my Iris Poppea. Tell me about them."

He reached out and clasped her small hand in his big tanned one. He squeezed her fingers encouragingly. She drew a big sigh.

"You see, Greg, I am not the right wife for you. I am not interested in a social life. I dislike it. I am not a tall imposing woman. I am not a peacock," she said in a rush.

He was silent, his mouth folded into what could be grimness, or an attempt to conceal amusement. His black eyes questioned.

She looked away from his smooth brown cheeks and sparkling eyes, the carved mouth, and gazed beyond him at the valley that lay below them, and a small meandering blue stream that flowed among the little farms. The greenish gray olive trees swayed in the breeze, and their leaves turned to show the gray.

"You should have a woman as your wife who is a Greek woman of importance. A social woman. A woman who would be hostess for you."

He listened, and said not a word.

"You are an important man," she said. "You have many business interests all over the world, and an office in Athens, and one in Paris, and one in New York."

He said nothing, merely smoothing her hand gently.

"I," said Iris, "I want nothing but to have my career! I have studied and worked for years to be a dress designer. I am achieving that. I don't want to give it up!"

His gaze was on her steadily, she found when she glanced nervously back at him. She looked away, and concentrated on a gray goat who baaed nervously on a hill path some distance from them. He could not seem to decide whether to jump down the hill or go along the ledge. But a green shrub seemed to tempt him. He leaned his neck farther and farther, trying to remain on the path, and yet reach the shrub.

Iris stared at the goat, and talked rapidly. "You see, Gregorios, I have my ambitions also. You would not want to marry an ambitious woman. I want to be a designer, I have made up some designs for Nadia to present to her soon. As soon as—as everybody goes home, I can go back to New York, and give them to her—and we could break the engagement and—and settle it all."

Greg waved his free hand. "What is it to work? You do not need to work, Iris," he said impatiently. "You may make all the dresses you like for yourself, for my mother and for Melania, if you choose. Why ask for the approval of the world? You will not need that. I will take care of you!"

"That is not the point! It is my career. The work satisfies something in me. Would you like to live without working?"

"I might—for a time!" he grinned. "But, yes, I enjoy working, conquering the markets, deciding on new hotels—making my guests so comfortable they return again and again. You shall help me with that!" he exclaimed, suddenly inspired. "You may travel with me, and help me design some of the hotels!"

"No, Greg," she said firmly. "That is not my work! I am a dress designer!"

"So—you will stay home with the babies, then, eh? Whatever you choose!"

The thought of having his babies made her quiver. She must not think about that. She concentrated again on the silly goat shaking on the ledge, trying to reach the shrub without leaving the safety of the path. He stretched out his neck as far as it would go, but could not get a nibble. Before him was a steep drop, beyond that the shrub with the tasty branches.

"You shall live with us here—my mother will explain the work to you. In Athens, you will manage our townhouse, and train the servants. Mother will show you all. We often have guests—"

Oh, guests! Iris moaned a little as she thought of the long-staying Xanthe and others like her.

"You shall make them all welcome," he said imperiously. "They will enjoy your meals, the way you make them comfortable! And we shall travel together, I shall show you the delights of Greece that you wished to see! And we shall go to France also—you will like France—"

She could hear her father's voice over Greg's. "I will come for you—we shall see Chicago together—you shall come to us in Houston—we shall live together—"

Promises, promises, all forgotten.

She shivered a little, and Greg put his arm about her. "You are chilly! Come, lean on me, and be kissed! You shall forget your silly fears!"

His body was like a furnace, as he pulled her against him. Her chilled frame absorbed heat gratefully, before she thought. Tenderly he kissed her cheek, then turned her head to kiss her lips.

His mouth closed slowly over hers again, and he began to kiss her more deeply. Her lips opened, his tongue licked delicately at her tongue, then thrust into her mouth more deeply. She felt as though she were being absorbed into him, that her self and her personality, her will and her wishes, were all being taken over by him.

He was such a strong man, such a determined and possessive man. He would take her over and remold her into the way he wanted her, and she would have nothing to say about it! She felt alarmed, and tried to pull back from him. His arms tightened about her, he pulled her to him and seated her on his hard knees and firm thighs.

He had wrapped his arms about her, there was no escape. His mouth drank from hers, he rocked her in his arms, and pressed her closer to himself. She could feel the hard masculinity of his thighs, pressing to her soft rounded hips, only their clothing kept him from taking her. His face grew more flushed, his black eyes blazed when he drew back a little from her, and gazed down into her dazed face.

"I want you," he said.

He did not say he loved her. He wanted her. She knew that! He had wanted her before, and come very close to taking her.

"Well, you cannot have me!" she cried out.

"What?" He was incredulous. "What do you say?"

"You cannot have me!" she stormed at him. "I never wanted an arranged marriage! I am not for sale, not for a hotel, not for money! I don't want marriage like this—or any marriage!"

He was abruptly furious. "You are a crazy little girl! I won't listen to you! You don't know what you want! You are formed for love," and deliberately his hands went over her breasts and waist. "Your father did not deserve you. I will take you, keep you, care for you! You belong to me now!"

"No, no!" She tried to fight him off, bue he would not let her push him away. His folded arms enclosed her, his hands went over and over her hungrily, until she was about insane with passion. Heat had risen in her, passion had risen, and she began to answer his kisses with her own.

His big hand was around her breast, his thumb teased the tip through her thin cotton dress. She moaned, and he smiled in triumph, and pressed his mouth again to hers. "You want me, too," he whispered in her ear, and nipped the lobe with his sharp teeth. It was the most erotic sensation. She was remembering how he had tried to make love to her that night in the small house on the Greek island, when both were prisoners.

His lips moved over hers once more, teasing, tormenting, until she kissed him back. Their lips clung to each other, opened, with one breath uniting them. Her head was back over his arm, her hair had come loose and flowed over his hands. He pushed his fingers through the curls and tugged gently at her hair until her throat was back, and he could slide his lips down over her white throat to the pulse beating so madly.

The narrow straps of her blue and white sundress left her shoulders almost bare. He moved his head so he could nuzzle at the skin, and waken more erotic feelings in her. He pushed aside the blue fabric, and found the rounded breast, and kissed it.

"I can scarcely wait until our marriage night," he muttered. "Aye—aye—aye—three more days!"

She panicked, and tried to pull back, at the thought of what he would do to her then! And from then on—forever! She would belong to him, and he would boss her around mercilessly! And he did not love her! He just wanted her! What would happen when he became bored with her? Would he turn soon to his mistresses, to his pillow friends, as the Greeks called them?

Yes, of course! He was a passionate man, she would not be enough for him, not without love!

Tears formed in her eyes as he kissed her ruthlessly, wildly, from her forehead to her throat, to her breasts and over her arms. Tears spilled down her cheeks, and he finally drew back and stared at her.

"Tears? Iris Poppea, why do you weep?" He was not gentle, he was furious, ominously furious. "Is the thought of marriage to me so terrible? Eh?"

"I don't want to get married!" she wept.

225

Abruptly he turned her around, and gave her one hard slap on her bottom! Then he stood her on her feet, with a spine-jarring slam! He got up. "We will go home," he said grimly. "And no more such talk! I will be tempted to take you without marriage to teach you obedience!"

He strode over to the Land Rover, leaving her to follow meekly. She wiped her eyes with her skirt, then glanced over to check on that fool goat.

It must have taken the plunge. It was down on the slope below the ledge, munching contentedly on the shrub, sliding slowly on its sharp hooves away from it. For the sake of a sweet mouthful, it was losing its footing, its chance of safety.

"Oh, you fool goat," Iris muttered aloud. "All for a sweet bit of shrub!"

"Baaaa!" mourned the goat, as the ground slid away from it, and it went sliding down the hill away from the shrub. *"Baaaaa!"*

Iris watched to make sure it was not in real trouble. It slid until a slight change in the hill enabled it to get its footing, and with some dignity it came erect again, scrabbled around, and marched with slow dignity and disdain over to another ledge.

"And let that be a lesson," she murmured, walking over to where Greg waited in the Land Rover.

But, silly Iris, she thought. Just as silly as the goat. She looked at Greg's firm carved mouth, and thought she would marry him, for the sake of some sweet kisses. Though she would slip and slide and fall afterward!

The days went past very swiftly. The morning of her wedding day came. She was dressed in the white wedding gown, and taken to the church. She stood with Greg in the large entrance door, and accepted the lighted candle from the priest. She walked with Greg to the altar, and went though the ceremonies as they had rehearsed them. The solemn prayers, the hymns, the exchange of the rings went on.

The gold of the groom's ring was given to Iris and placed on her hand, to remain there. It symbolized the domination of the groom over his bride, and also his giving to her the seal of his household, to care for his goods for him. His hand received the silver ring of the bride, to wear from then on, a symbol of her sharing with him the toils and hardships of life. The rings shone on their right hands, as the priest laid his stole over their joined hands.

Then they approached the altar more closely, again holding the lighted candles. The priest swung the censer once more, to remind them that their good deeds must shine in the world, and rise to Heaven like incense. Psalm 128 was sung: "Thy wife shall be as a fruitful vine by the sides of thine house; thy children like olive plants round about thy board—"

The people answered again and again, in song, "Glory, glory to Thee, our God, glory to Thee."

Then Iris and Greg stood upon a rug, and they were asked the questions and gave the answers of the solemn wedding vows. The priest blessed them, wishing them chastity, well-favored children and joy in them, and a blameless life.

Iris listened solemnly to his admonitions, and thought that Greg did also. Greg's face was serious and glowing with light, his black eyes blazed at times as he answered the priest.

Then crowns of myrtle and olive branches were brought, and the priest held them over the heads of Iris and Greg. The crowns were tokens of their victory over their passions, and reminded them that they should guard the purity of their lives after marriage also.

Iris tried not to think with fear of all she was promising.

She seemed to be promising so much, it would be the remainder of her life!

And Greg's also—but perhaps men did not take all this so seriously. Yet—she stole a quick look up at his face—he did seem to be accepting the vows reverently.

The songs were sung, the lesson given, and the sermon preached. Then a cup of wine was brought. The priest blessed the cup, and presented it to Iris and Greg alternately, so each drank from it three times. The cup of wine symbolized the fact that they must live in a union that would not be broken, and would share with each other both joy and sorrow.

Then the priest led them three times around the lectern. Melania held the crown over Iris's head, and a dignified uncle of Greg's did the same for him, as they marched and danced about the lectern.

After this, the priest removed the crowns, and gave them greeting and good wishes. Then the record was signed, and Iris wrote her maiden name for the last time as a single woman. The marriage was completed, and then they were overwhelmed by kisses and hugs from the wedding guests.

From the church, the wedding procession wound through the village to the town hall. Everybody in town wished to attend, and only the town hall was large enough to hold them all.

The fiddlers played until late. The groaning boards of feast were visited often. An immense wedding cake was cut, and pieces given to each guest. The wine flowed and laughter rose to the rafters.

Iris danced with old and young, any who asked, and Greg beamed on his bride. He too danced with everyone, from the oldest crone to the youngest little girl dressed in a gay Greek costume.

Shelley and Maria Ardeth had tried to remain aloof, their noses in the air, but they were not proof against the merriment. When Iris saw them later, each was dancing gaily with a young Greek male, being swung in the air to shrieks of joy, bounced around to the music of the fiddles and guitars and *bouzoúki*, until their hair tumbled down and sweat beaded their elegant foreheads.

Sometimes the men caught each other's shoulders, and moved in the graceful Greek male dances, as the others clapped in rhythm. Greg led dance after dance, tirelessly. Alex tried to join in, blind though he was, and he was handled tenderly, until his leg gave way, and he had to rest. But he sat on his wheelchair and clapped in rhythm and beamed, as Melania sat near him and gave him bits of food from her plate.

Kyria Lydia was beautiful in a gown of deep purple with gold trim, her jewels amethysts set in gold. She glowed with joy in the marriage of her only son. Hilarion Patakos danced with her several times, to the sullen anger of his wife. He seemed not to notice, and laughed and joked and drank all he wished.

Melania had been bridesmaid, demure in a peach gown of silk embroidered in yellow roses. Her jewels were pink topazes, set in gold, and she looked older than her seventeen years. She was surrounded by the young men of the village, but they treated her with great respect. She was not for them, she was one of the House of Venizelos, they knew.

Xanthe and Vanessa and the small children enjoyed the wedding as much as their spoiled natures would permit. Greta fussed for more cake and was slapped. Nora was pretty in her costume, and kept smoothing her skirt self-consciously. They insisted on remaining with the adults, instead of joining the dances of the children, and Xanthe kept them with her, as though afraid they might be contaminated.

Iris laughed as men pinned money on her full sleeves and to her skirts. It was the custom, but it did seem odd for a man to dance with her, then put money on her. Greg joked when he saw her, "I shall not have to work this year, my wife will support me!"

An old village crone took his words seriously, and piped up, "Nay, nay, you must not spend it—it is for your children and their dowry!"

Greg laughed and agreed with her, grinning wickedly at Iris and her blushing cheeks.

Finally the hour grew late, and the people began to drift homeward.

Hilarion Patakos came to his daughter and kissed her solemnly on each cheek. "We go home tomorrow, Iris, I shall not see you again for a time. Be happy. I am glad for you."

She permitted herself a moment of weakness, and leaned against his hard shoulder. "Oh, father," she whispered. "I should not have married him!"

"Nonsense," he said. "It was a matter of honor. He did the right thing! And he will care for you, he promised me!"

He patted her back jovially, and wished her well. She stood back, managed a smile, and let Greg take her to the Land Rover. He whizzed her back to the big house on the hill, and the maids helped her change from the elaborate brocade gown to a simpler one of blue linen.

She had no idea where she was going. She only hoped it would not be somewhere they had to go by airplane!

Charis told her, as she helped her change, "It will be very quiet tomorrow! Everybody goes home!"

"Um," said Iris, wishing she could remain here peacefully in the pretty blue and white room she had lived in for weeks. It had been a refuge. Now after this, she must share a bedroom with Greg—

"Alex will be happy! He hates to stay inside his room," Charis giggled.

Iris grimaced. "He had an excuse!"

"I know it! Kyria Lydia will be pleased if all went home! But Xanthe and Vanessa will stay!" Charis looked very wise.

Iris wondered why. What did they hope to gain, with Greg married? Whatever it was, it would add up to mischief, probably. They adored making mischief.

Oh, well, She had enough troubles to worry about. Tonight was her wedding night!

Chapter Fifteen

Iris did not know how Greg could see to drive. It was true that the moon was big and round and glowing silver, and the brilliant stars glimmered in the night black sky.

However, the paths were in shadow, the mountains cast gloom about the valleys, and not a cottage could she see. They were not driving near the village, she was sure of that. And she could not see any boats with their swinging lights on the masts, so they were not near the docks.

Greg was humming some Greek dance tune as he drove. He sounded very happy and carefree. She clung to the side of the Land Rover as he went around a curve. He drove slowly, peering ahead.

"Almost there!" he said cheerfully.

"How can you tell where we are?"

He laughed. "I know every inch of this island! It has been my home always! As a boy I hid out and played guerrilla in the hills, I roamed the valleys and camped there. I went with my grandfather to the cottage I will take you to—we spent many a night there.''

"Then we are not going anywhere by airplane!" said Iris with relief evident in her voice.

"No, no! Did you think I would take you to a noisy city for our moon of honey?" he asked.

His words reminded her of the old Greek custom, that when a visitor came to the door, he was to be greeted with sweetness, a bit of candy, some sugared piece, or a spoonful of honey. Greg's mouth was like honey, she thought, when he kissed her.

Such thoughts made her shiver for the night to come. She loved him too much. She must hide that, she thought, for he would soon take her for granted, and the humiliation would be more than she could endure.

The Land Rover pulled up and stopped. She could see a dark shape nearby, but could make out nothing.

"Wait until I light the lamp," said Greg, and swung out of the vehicle, and disappeared completely. Then she saw a window take shape and behind it bloomed the soft yellow of a paraffin lamp. She got down and went in, gazing about with pleasure.

Greg brought in their two suitcases, and set them down in the one room of the small cottage. On one side was an immense bed, with fresh sheets smelling of lavender. On the opposite side was a dry sink, and a paraffin stove with a kettle of water, and a basin.

There was a small upright wood sofa with some thick cushions on it, a couple of tables with paraffin lamps, and a wool rug on the floor. Nothing else.

"There—how do you like it?" asked Greg, beaming, as though he conducted her into a mansion.

"I like it very much!" She wandered about, admiring the

cushions of wool, the rug, the filled lamps. "It looks very comfortable."

He peered down at her to make sure she was not being sarcastic, then he grinned at her, and patted her head. "Good girl. It is like the place where we stayed on the island, eh? After the plane crash? Simple and comfortable."

He indicated the open door. "In the morning we will swim in the sea. Do not go alone, Iris, there are sometimes sharks in the bay. Always wait for me."

She shuddered. " 'Sharks'?"

"Yes. But maybe not now," he said cheerily. "Maybe dolphins, would you like that?" As though he could produce them at a moment's notice. He examined the food boxes on the table. "Ah, plenty of bread, cheese, wine, fruit. I will catch some fish for our breakfast."

Breakfast—after the night had passed—

She drooped, eyeing the bed wistfully. If only she could lie down and sleep—alone!

Greg turned, and caught the look on her face. "Weary, eyes of iris?" he asked gently. "Put on your nightdress, and go to bed. Do you wish any wine, or bread, any cheese or fruit?"

She grimaced. "I feel I can never eat again!"

"It was a fine feast, eh? But in the morning we will be hungry again," he predicted with a laugh. He stretched out his long arms and rose to his toes, and down again. "Ah, I am tired also! What dancing, what fun!"

He glanced at her. She hovered near her suitcase, she had opened it and taken out a nightdress—she had packed the case herself, and put in a practical cotton gown that covered her from head to toe, not just the pretty frivolities bought in Athens.

"I'll go out and look at the sea," he said, and walked out the door. She sighed with relief.

Foolish to be modest when he had seen her completely, and tonight was to be—she shut off her thoughts in a panic. She would not be able to move if she started to think.

Iris found a covered jar, and used it, her mouth quirking at what Charmian—or Shelley—would think of this! she washed at the dry sink, from the cool water, and donned the long nightdress. Then she crawled thankfully into the bed.

Greg soon came in, and undressed, and came to bed. He turned out the paraffin lamp, and darkness filled the cottage. In a few minutes, the darkness was only gray, as the sky outside seemed to enter through the door and single window. It was never truly dark in Greece. The sky glowed.

Iris stiffened at the side of the bed against the rough whitewashed stucco wall. Now would come the pain—

Greg reached out and patted her shoulder. "Go to sleep, little Iris," he said. "Now is not the time for passion. We are both weary. Morning comes soon."

And he turned over and grunted, and sighed, and sank into the mattress. He seemed to be asleep in seconds. Amazed, Iris lay awake a little time. He could be so considerate!

She did not remember falling asleep. All she knew was when she opened her eyes the darkness was gone, the cottage was filled with a blue and golden dancing light. She lay idly staring at the whitewashed ceiling, and wondering at the beautiful silence.

A bird called, that was all. She sighed, turned over, stretched, saw the pillow dented beside her own. Where was Greg?

Iris got up and padded barefoot over the rug to the single window. She blinked at the glorious view, of a curve of creamy sand, the brilliant blue and green of the bay, waters rippling like shot silk, and Greg bounding up and down in it, his bronzed body like a god rising from the sea.

How handsome he was! He had broad shoulders, a sturdy chest covered with black curly hairs. His head was erect and proud, carved by a master hand, with large nose, imperious forehead, sculptured mouth, large ears, black curly hair all over his head to his neck.

And his waist was trim and slim, then his thighs were long and bronzed and hard, with dimpled hips, and as he bounded in the water she saw his long brown legs and the large arched feet.

As she idly watched him, it suddenly dawned on her. He was naked as a Greek statue! More naked than some that wore fig leaves of marble!

"Oh—my gosh!" muttered Iris, moving back from the window with a hot blush. She put her hands to her cheeks. "Of course—how silly—why should he wear trunks—but—how can I go out there?"

She debated staying inside, but that would be prudish. She got out her yellow maillot and the matching yellow terrycloth jacket. She donned them, hesitated, then went out into the sunlight. How good it felt on her body! The sunlight of Greece, glowing, alive, the pure light from the bowl of the vivid blue sky.

Greg waved and yelled at her as soon as she appeared. "Hey—good morning—*kaliméra*—come in the water!"

She waved back but did not try to yell. She left her yellow jacket on the sands beside a blanket and towel he had deposited there, and waded timidly into the surging white foam of the surf. She gasped again as the cool waters lapped her ankles.

Greg swam over to her, water streaming down his cheeks, his grin wide. "Come in, come in!" he invited her, holding out his hand. "Do you swim?"

"No, not really," she cried, shaking her head in the yellow rubber cap. "I cannot go in deep—"

He was patient with her, and held her waist while he drew her out farther with him. But he seemed to realize her need to feel the firm sand beneath her feet.

"I will teach you to swim," he said, and urged her to put her head down and try to open her eyes in the water. She could not yet, but felt excited that she could go out farther. She felt safe with him, he did not fool around or leave her stranded.

She kept looking about nervously.

"What are you looking for?" he teased. "There is nobody here but us, I have ordered everybody to stay away!"

"How—how do you know when there are sharks about?" she asked, with a quaver in her voice.

He did not laugh. He told her promptly, "When you see a triangle of fin above the water, head right for shore. It might be a dolphin, but more likely a shark. However, I have kept watch today, there are none about."

She gave a big sigh of relief, and he patted her hip reassuringly.

"I will take care of you, never fear about that!" he told her. He was possessive, but this morning in the water that felt fine.

When she tired, she went to the beach and stretched out on the blanket. He swam about more vigorously, then came ashore also, and lay down. He seemed to sleep again.

Presently he got up. "I must catch our lunch!" he said, and produced a small fishing line.

"No pole?" she asked, sitting up.

"No, not the way grandfather taught me. Come with me," and he caught her hand and drew her with him across the sands to a pool beyond the cottage some distance.

In the blue waters she could see the dart of brown bodies.

He let down the line, and sat patiently, with the end twined about one hand. They were silent, drowsing in the bright noon sun. She had pulled on a cotton wide-brimmed hat, he was bareheaded, not seeming to mind the sun.

The line jerked visibly in his hand. Greg came alert, and pulled slowly, bringing in a fine fish about eight inches long. He let the line down again, after putting the fish in a bucket of water.

He caught four fish, then said, "That is enough!" They went back to the cottage. He started a fire in a pit near the front door, and guarded it as gravely as a primitive man at the entrance to his cave. He slapped mud on the fish, and buried them in the ashes and coals.

Iris had gone inside, washed, and dressed in a sundress. Then she cut a long loaf of bread and some cheese, chopped tomatoes and let them soak in lemon juice and herbs along with slices of onions. She washed some peaches and set them on a plate. She set two places with the simple brown and white pottery plates, some silver, and cotton napkins of a local weave.

She was hungry by this time. The smell of the tomatoes and onions, and the fish, were drawing juices to her mouth. Greg took out a platter, cut open the clay-hard shell, and revealed the tender white flesh of the fish.

They ate hungrily in silence. The sunlight glimmered and shone on the whitewashed walls, a slight breeze wafted the scent of the maquis to them, and the salt of the sea.

Greg showed Iris the well where she could draw up fresh water. He helped her do the few dishes, then strode off into the hills by himself. He returned with some meat, from a shepherd, he said, some tender lamb for their supper.

There was little housekeeping to do. They lazed in the

shade during the hottest hours of the afternoon. Toward evening, they swam again, and admired the streaks of red and orange in the sunset sky. Before the sun went down, Iris cooked their simple supper, and they ate it, sitting on the sand and watching the last of the sunset. The sky turned deep blue, then purple, with a few last streaks of crimson, which shone on the sides of the maquis-covered hills.

Iris felt more relaxed with Greg now, but still the thought of the night ahead made her shiver. The unknown is always more to be feared than the known. Oh, if only the night were over!

Finally they went inside as a chill wind came up. Greg lit the lamp, and it gave a golden glow to the white walls, and made shadows flicker.

"Tell me about your life in the convent," he invited, holding out his hand to her as he seated himself on the wooden sofa. She came, and took his hand, and sat down against the plump woolen cushions.

"What do you want to know?" she asked warily.

"Anything you wish to tell me," he said comfortably, and that made it easier.

She told him about the nuns, the kind ones, the brisk ones, the devoted ones, the laughing ones. She told him about her girl friends there, and the mischief they could get into even in a convent school. It seemed very harmless mischief, compared to New York, and he laughed heartily at some of her adventures.

"You put salt in the sugar bowl, and sugar into the salt, eh? I shall have to watch you at home!"

"And there was the time we had a new little girl who cried at night. We took turns going to her, and sleeping in her bed, and sister found me one night—"

He listened, his face changing from laughing to tender, to

interested and deeper thought as she spoke about philosophy and the religion studies.

"It was not a bad way to grow up, Iris," he said, "compared to that of your sister Charmian. Oh, she was loved much, but she is spoiled, one can see that. The discipline was needed, and she did not have that."

Iris shrugged. "She did have discipline from Bill Roswell, but perhaps that was too late. Bill gets distressed about her—I mean—" She stopped abruptly, she was talking too much.

Greg drew her closer, into the curve of his hard arm, and she felt the heat of his body against her own. He put his cheek down on her thick black hair.

"You are a very lovable girl, Iris," he murmured.

She held her breath. Would he tell her he loved her? She knew he desired her, but love—love was different. Love was tenderness, compassion, wishing to live one's life with one person, being devoted, single-minded, not looking at other women—could Greg do that? Oh, she wanted so much!

Probably too much. She must be satisfied with what she received! Not be greedy, and spoil it all. She rubbed her cheek against his thick shirt, felt the uneven texture of it, the coarse fabric, the warmth of his body beneath the cloth. His hand came up and cupped her head, and held her gently against him. Then he turned her face up to his.

She saw the desire blaze in his black eyes. The golden glow of the paraffin lamp was the only light in the room. They were shut off from the world, alone in the plain simple cottage, listening to the *shush-shush* of the waves against the beach.

He bent his head slowly, and she felt his lips touch hers softly, with a tender care. He kissed her again, again, then his mouth grew warmer, and he pressed more deeply. He turned, and held her more closely against himself, and she felt the growing urgency of his body.

She was wearing a yellow cotton strapless dress with matching sweater against the cool evening air. His hand moved inside the cardigan and pushed the cloth back from her smooth bare shoulder, and his fingers closed over her shoulder and caressed it. Then he pushed again, and the jacket slid down her arms, and off.

He put his fingers under the shirred bodice of the sundress, and she was bare under the bodice of the gown. It was not necessary to wear much in this climate. He gently touched her bared breast, and cupped it in his hand, squeezing it softly, and thumbing the nipple. The peak rose against his fingers, hardening in his fingers. He bent lower and took a nipple in his lips, biting it softly with his strong white teeth, causing wild sensations to run down her spine to her thighs. She wriggled uneasily in his arms, and he lifted her onto his thighs.

Somehow she knew he was not just going to kiss her tonight.

As though in idle touch, one hand went to her knee, and pushed up her dress hem. His hand slid along her knee to her thigh, and down again, while he kissed her lips and nuzzled at her breast. She was uneasily aware again of his body, of the hard thighs under her soft hips.

The caressing hand on her hips brushed back the cloth of her dress, and touched the bikini panties beneath. Questing fingers searched, and she flinched and jumped.

"*Shush*, easy, Iris—eyes of iris—do not worry—" he soothed her. His lips gently teased at hers, coaxed for a kiss, and she answered his lips, almost forgetting his fingers—until they came too close to intimate parts of her. She jumped again, and gasped.

"Greg—what—oh, don't do that—oh, don't—"

She wriggled, and he said patiently, "Do not be worried, Iris, it is very natural. Come, let me feel you—it will help later—be easy—"

She allowed herself to hear his coaxing words and honeyed tongue. He drew her back against himself, and kissed her more deeply, holding her closely in his one arm, while the other hand searched her thighs. He drew off the bikini pants, and his fingers moved over her, slowly, finding the softest parts of her body.

Iris gasped again, and his mouth covered hers, and his tongue thrust into her mouth. His tongue roved her mouth, honey-sweet, and she could scarcely get her breath. He pushed down the bodice of her dress, and it fell from her to her waist. The hem was up almost to her waist, and she felt the nakedness of her body—then he drew off the dress, and she was bare from head to toes.

He lifted up and looked at her, sitting on his lap in the golden light, quite naked now, and shy under his staring. He smiled at her, triumphantly.

"Well, my little virgin, are you going to offer yourself to me?" His black eyes sparkled with mischief.

"Like a god?" she shot back, unable to resist. "No, I don't fancy the part of living sacrifice—"

"Tease! I have wanted you for ages now—since I first saw you! And on the island—my God, what a time I had resisting you! However, I am glad I had the strength of willpower to wait until our marriage!" he added arrogantly.

"Oh, you—I fought you—" she gasped. "I would not let you—if you remember—"

"Huh. If I had decided to take you, I would have," said Greg. "But your being a virgin held me back. Now I shall have my reward—wife of my being, mother of my children—"

And he picked her up and took her over to the bed. He laid

her down in the sheets, and she gazed up at him in the lamplight as he stripped off the coarse cotton shirt, and stepped out of his blue jeans. He left the lamp on, smiling at her, his eyes going over her from head to foot. He missed nothing, she thought, from her blue black curly hair spread out on the pillow to her rounded taut breasts to her slim waist, the wide thighs, the legs, and the arched feet—he seemed to like what he saw.

She remembered with her body the way he had touched her on the small island, and her breathing began to come more quickly. Shyly, she shut her eyes tight, and clenched her fists tightly.

She stiffened to prepare herself for the wild taking and pain that she subconsciously expected. He came to the bed, and gazed down at her, she felt his being was a burning presence beside her. Then he lay down beside her, and he touched her softly on the arms.

Greg's mouth moved slowly on her shoulders, and over her arms, following the caress of his hands. She felt his warm sweet breath on her throat, and smelled the sea salt in his thick curly hair.

Her eyes shut tight, she absorbed the sensations of his closeness. The heat of his limbs against hers, his bare and hers with the cotton sheet riding up her legs. Impatiently he pushed the sheet from her, and she too was warm and bare and shivering a little with the nightwind.

One hand cupped a breast, he held it like a chalice in his palm, and his thumb pressed the nipple until it hurt—not with his pressure but with a strange aching. She shifted on the bed, and opened her eyes.

The lamplight glowed on his golden body as he bent over her. She saw his strong shoulders, and the mat of black curly hair down to below his waist. Timidly she put her hand on his chest, and fingered the black curls. He smiled down at her, and his black eyes glowed like coals.

Greg was murmuring love words in Greek. Oh, how glad was Iris that she knew the words he said! He called her love, and honey-sweetness, darling, and flower for bees to suck, warmth of sunshine and brightness of stars—and much more she thought could not be printed.

Her whole body was on fire. She clutched his hair, and he came back to her, leaning his body on hers as he braced himself on his knees and elbows over her. He leaned down, brushed his hard body on her softness, and pressed briefly. She felt the hard, searching passion of his body, but now she did not care about hurt or pain. She had to have him, there was something in her crying out for possession. She wanted him to take her—now—

He kissed her mouth, twisting his lips against hers, so she must answer with her own passion. She wound her arms about his neck, smoothing the hard flesh of his back with her fingers, knowing him through his skin and bones. She could not get him close enough, she curled her legs about his thighs, and urged him tighter.

He pressed gently against her thighs, and she did not flinch. "Darling Iris—" he whispered. "It will hurt, my love, but not for long—"

"I want you—" she said wildly. "I want—" unheeding of the pain, knowing only wild passion. "I want—oh, Greg—you must—please—oh, I want you—I want—oooohhhh!"

The pain flashed through her, more than she had expected, a keen biting pain. She cried out, into his ears, clasping him tightly, her fingernails scraping his back.

"It's all right—darling—love—" he gasped. "Let me—once more—"

Another smooth pressure of his body, and he won entrance. The pain ripped through her once more, and then slowly died,

245

in the gentle movement of his masculine flesh. He soothed her, held her gently, swayed back and forth with her, then drew out carefully.

"It was harder than I had thought, my love," he whispered. He left her, to return with a cloth wrung out in cool water. He washed her thighs, and she saw the blood on the cloth.

He looked so anxious, she was impelled to calm him. "It is all right—Greg—I expected—"

"You were a virgin—I am very happy," he told her.

"Did you not believe me?" she cried, unexpectedly angry.

"Yes, but when one has proof, that is always good," he said so complacently she could have struck him!

She muttered, "Men!" And turned over on her side. He laughed, and washed her gently once more, then flung the cloth on the table. He lay down and took her in his arms.

Greg was restless. She could feel the tremors in his body. Finally he turned her, so she lay on her back on the bed.

"I need you," he said urgently. "Iris—my body burns for you. Do you ache too much—I must take you—please—"

Her own body still burned with passion. She did not answer in words, her arms reached up for him. With a groan of mingled desire and satisfaction, he came over on her. He brought them together, and began the movements on her.

She had never imagined such things. Her mind had refused to think about them. The nuns had not spoken of such, she had not talked with girls who knew. When Greg lay on her, and joined their bodies, and his movements were faster and faster, she was amazed. It seemed a dream, of closeness, passion, the way they fit together, as though she could never be alone again.

His hard thighs thrust again, and again, faster and faster, then longer thrusts, deep into the heart of her, Excitement built, passion burned in her, until she felt she was hanging on the edge of a cliff, and wanted to fall over with him—she was waiting, needing, yearning, begging—

"Oh, Greg—Greg," she moaned. Her hands dug into his back, her fingers stroked on his neck and shoulders. Her arms slipped over him, wet with perspiration. His body was so smooth and strong, he was like a god over her, taking her—

"More, give me—more—again—again—oh, please—"

He held back, with an effort. His breath was harsh in her ears, he could not speak. His black eyes glowed behind half-closed eyelids. His bronzed face was splendid as a god, blazing with light from the golden lamp. His body was wet with sweat, he slipped on her, and groaned, and found his place again, feverishly.

Then he was deep inside her again, moving more slowly and deliberately, holding high. She felt the little trembles coming once more. Absorbed in the sensations, she held him tightly to her, rolling over with him on the bed, and back once more on her back, to her side, and back. She was held so tightly, and he was so big and tight in her—

Something seemed to burst in her, and she felt the roll and rush of an ocean wave in her own body. Even as it happened, the tremors inside her became an earthquake, and she shook with the answering passion. She was crying out softly in his ears, begging him, loving him—little mewing cries came from her that she could not have dreamed of.

She was flung up on a high pink cloud, her eyes tight shut, explosions of joy in her. Then they floated together for a time, slowly, slowly down to the earth, still clinging tightly. She was shaking as though with a chill, and he dragged the sheet and blanket over them.

She could breathe only with difficulty, and it was a time before she was warm again and breathing normally. He too was gasping for breath, his wide chest heaving. He lay beside her, his arm flung across her, possessive even as he closed his eyes in sleep.

Sometime in the night she wakened. He had risen, and was turning out the golden glow of the lamp. He moved around, naked, godlike, his magnificent body a shadow in the small white cottage.

He went outside, and then returned, and came back to her, a little chilled by the outdoor air. He knew she was awake, and his arms closed about her hungrily.

"Iris—you were so precious—may I—again—you are not hurting?"

"It is all right—" she reassured him sleepily, and her hand moved shyly on his matted chest. Oh, to have the right to touch him like this, to know the hard skin and firmly muscled body with her fingers—

She caressed him slowly, and he lay over her, and touched her more and more urgently, until they had to come together again. This time it was more brief, he brought them together, and slowly thrust against her, his powerful legs churning against hers.

This time she did not know the ecstasy she had felt before, but there was a deep satisfaction in the gripping and thrusting of his body on hers. he moved deeply, and groaned, and came hard, and lay helplessly on her for a time, his heavy body sprawled on her soft one.

What satisfaction she felt in his pleasure! It was as good as knowing the ecstasy herself, to know how he felt in her, how he wanted her, desired her, and needed her.

For now, that was enough. When he had finished, and sighed, and kissed her breasts in gratitude, she drew the blanket over him, and let him sleep in her arms.

The deep blue of the night seemed to creep into the cottage, and she lay and watched for a time how the stars sparkled beyond the doorway. The soughing of the waves was a part of her honeymoon night, and the soft breathing of the man who lay against her, his arms about her.

All in the hours of the night she had changed. He had become a part of her, and she was part of him. She could not leave without a rending of her flesh and her heart.

Chapter Sixteen

Iris was sitting on the blanket, her legs stretched out so her toes curled in the warm sand. She had her sketch pad before her, and she was busily drawing Greg as he bounded up and down happily in the surf.

She felt content, relaxed. She enjoyed sex with him! She admitted it.

She held the pencil over the pad, and frowned slightly. The only problem was—could sex alone be the basis for a good marriage?

Greg had never said he loved her. She thought he did not love her, not the way she thought of love. He did desire her, he felt possessive about her, he spoke of their future together, he wanted her children.

Could that be enough? Well, it had to be. There was no use crying for the moon.

And during the days they had the bright golden sun, and the clear pure light of Greece, that made mountains seem close, and gave one the feeling that if one were careful he could see out of the corner of his eye the shape of a god walking on the hills.

Iris picked up the pad again and sketched, finishing the magnificent head of her husband, a gesture of his arms that showed his delight in the water of the bay. She studied it. Could she do an oil painting of that when she returned home? She hoped so. If only she could capture the brilliant sparkle of the blue green waters, the bubbling of the white foam, the spring of Greg in the air as he bounded delightedly in the next large wave.

"What are you doing?"

Greg had come out of the water, had run up on the creamy sand, and now he flung himself down beside her, sprawling out at full length. He reached for the pad, after drying one hand on the towel. She gave it to him diffidently. He studied the sketch intently, his black eyes shadowed by his long curly black lashes. (Would their son have such lashes? Would their daughter have such eyes?)

"It is good," he pronounced gravely. "You have a fine talent, Iris."

"Thank you." She accepted the pad again, and laid it down on the blanket. She gazed down at him as he stretched out beside her and yawned, and propped himself on his elbow.

"You are happy?"

She nodded, and brushed back her long strands of wet hair. She had not worn her bathing cap this morning, and it took ages for her hair to dry. But she did not mind. It felt good, wet and clinging to her neck and shoulders. "Very happy."

"I please you?" he asked softly, a little devilish smile curving his sensual mouth, and he caressed her arm with his fingers.

"You know that!" She was blushing, and deliberately she looked away.

"It would be nice if you would say so," he complained, his voice high like a little whining boy.

She laughed at him, and brushed his thick curly hair with her hand, so that water sprayed from it. "My tongue is not full of Greek compliments!"

"I must teach you some!" He sat up unexpectedly, and pushed her back on the blanket, and bent over her, his face shining bronze and golden. She closed her eyes slowly against the sun and the blaze on his face.

His mouth closed over hers, and his lips were warm and damp and salty. They kissed, and she felt her breath coming in short gasps between his kisses. Oh, he caught her breath, took her mind away from her, made her forget everything in the world but himself!

His wet body pressed against hers, his fingers toyed with the straps of her orange-and-white-striped bathing suit. He began to draw down the strap over her arm.

"Don't," she murmured.

"Always 'don't'!" he complained, kissing her arm. "Take off the suit, let me see you in the sunlight." He pulled the strap lower.

She had never gone naked outdoors, she was too inhibited for that, she thought ruefully. "No, I cannot."

"Why not?"

"Because the shepherds in the hills will see me naked," she invented quickly.

He shot up straight, and glared toward the hills. "What—what shepherds! Are they up there? You have seen them?"

"No, but they could see us," she said reasonably. He frowned at her, and noticed how her lips twitched with laughter.

"You are teasing me!" he accused. "There is nobody there!"

"There could be!" He pulled her down, and silenced her laughter with his kisses. But she noticed he no longer tried to get her to take off her suit. Yes, there could be men up there, staring curiously at the couple on the beach.

He kissed her for a time, and stroked his big hands over her soft flesh, then finally he lay back, his arm across her, and went to sleep against her waist. She settled her broad-brimmed hat against the sunlight, and sat patiently with him, loving the drowsy moments, the sound of the bees humming in the wild flowers, the soft *shush-shushing* of the surf.

When he wakened he was hungry, and they prepared fish and vegetables again, with bread baked in the ashes with the fish nearby.

"More delicious than the most gourmet restaurant of Athens," said Greg with satisfaction.

"Um, delicious, and hunger is the best appetite," said Iris. She remembered one of the sisters saying that when she was a child. "The nuns encouraged us to play hard, work hard, and eat all on our plates," she recalled with a smile. "It was a healthy life."

"Without love," he reminded gently, glancing across at her curiously.

Her blue eyes shadowed. "Oh—well—one cannot have everything."

"No, but there are certain essentials of life," he said seriously. "Food, clothing, shelter, and love."

"There are many kinds of love," Iris reminded him. "Love of God—that is the highest. And love of fellowman, love of each other, wishing the good of another."

"Yes, those are good, and essential," he agreed, licking his fingers of the fish. "Love of God—how necessary is that. How I am sorry for those who do not know that love. The communists have tried to smash that love, and it but grows the stronger."

"They say religion is the opiate of the people—but it is rather our salvation. A man may endure much, if he has the love and faith in God he needs to live. I read about a prisoner of war who survived, and he said it was because he always kept his faith in God."

Greg listened thoughtfully as Iris told him what she remembered of the story. Their talk wandered on to other matters, things she had learned in school, some people he had met on his travels. He told her something of the way he had earned his fortune, helping his father build up the chain of hotels after the war.

His grandfather had been his idol, he said. "He was so strong, so firm in his faith. Poor or rich, it made no difference. He was the same essential being he had always been. When we came here—" He gestured to the cottage, the beach. "When we came, we could live as happily—more happily— than in the finest hotel of our chain. He would say: A man brings himself along on his travels; he must make sure he travels with a light heart or his luggage will be too heavy for him."

"I like that." Iris smiled and savored that saying. "I wish I had known Leander. And Ioannes. Your mother told me something of them both. She said Leander was more a father to her than her own father."

"Yes, mother had a sad time of it. Her father was wealthy, and absorbed in his work. Her mother raised her, but several deaths in the family made her sad and withdrawn. After Lydia married, she found laughter again, she told me. Even in the war and later when times were bad, she and Ioannes could always find things to laugh over together. They were well matched."

"And he did not mind—being—in a wheelchair?" she ventured.

"Oh, he minded it—very much! Really more than Alex, who growls and grumbles, but takes advantage of his condition to hide out and be alone when he wishes! Ioannes never hid from anyone or anything. But he felt less than a man, and that bothered him. He was very—Greek, very male, though a gentle soul and good. Not being able to have any other son, or to have a daughter, troubled him. He took in Alex, he encouraged us to have Melania come when that would be possible. He had always liked Melania, and said when her mother died we must have her. We carried out his wishes, and that was good."

Iris had picked up the sketch pad as they were talking. She had finished eating, and wiped her fingers on a wet towel. How lovely to be so casual, eating on the sand, scrubbing the dishes in a bucket.

She sketched Melania's face quickly as they talked. Greg watched over her shoulder idly, admiring the movements of her fingers.

"How swiftly you work, and you need only a few lines to show the character," he said. "There—you have Melania's face to the life—her gentleness, the laughter around her eyes. Have you drawn the children of Xanthe?"

"Oh—I tried—but they run about so quickly." She evaded the question. She had drawn them, but the crossness of Greta's face and the troubled look of Nora made the experience unpleasant.

"They need a father," said Greg, shaking his head. "Xanthe scolds them, and thinks that is discipline. But it is not. They need love and concern and firmness. However, she is so bad-tempered it would not be easy for me to find a husband for her. She has no dowry, I could supply that. But the best dowry for a woman is a good disposition!"

He rose, and gathered up the few dishes. "I will do them," said Iris quickly.

"Be easy! I'll do them—go on sketching if you wish." He went off whistling, and returned with the dishes clean and dried. He put them away in the cottage, and returned to enjoy the small fire.

When she stopped work, and set down the pad, he said, "We are almost out of vegetables and fruit, and we need fresh bread. I think I will drive to the village. You will come with me?"

"Um, yes, I should like that," she said, and got up lazily and stretched. She was wearing a brief yellow T-shirt and short yellow shorts, and only sandals on her long tanned legs.

He frowned at her absently. "Do you have a long skirt?" he asked.

She was about to tease him, and say she preferred to wear shorts. Then she saw he was serious. What was all right for a girl was not all right for a wife!

"Yes, I'll put it on," she said, and went into the cottage. She had a long white skirt with blue and yellow butterflies embroidered on it, and she put that on over the shorts, and buttoned it to the hem. Greg was getting out the Land Rover when she returned with the food basket. He nodded in satisfaction, and began to hum as she got into the seat.

It was a pleasant drive through the afternoon sunlight uphill and down, around the twisty curves, where every turn revealed another breathtaking view of the sea, the beaches, the mountains with silvery green olive trees almost to their peaks. She enjoyed the little gamboling lambs, the placid black-faced white sheep, the nervous goats with their sharp hooves.

And most of all she enjoyed the sunlight, the white and gold light of Greece, that burned on the hillside, that shone against the whitewashed houses, that made every scarlet flower stand out in the green fields, that seemed to bring the blue bowl of the sky so close. The white light of Greece. No wonder the gods loved it here.

She told that to Greg. "No wonder the ancient gods chose Greece as the center of the world, and the mountains here their home. It is the most beautiful place ever, with the clear light shining."

He smiled, well pleased. "I knew you would love it. You are Greek. I knew that first day."

"What did you think of me?"

He said promptly, "That you were obstinate, you were lovely without vanity, that you were set against me, that you could not be the foolish mistress of Alex, that you cooked like an angel and defied me like a devil."

She laughed aloud. "All that?"

"All that and more. I went home, soothed, wanting to see you again, thinking of your red mouth as you drank wine, and fed me. I was so glad you were not Charmian."

She was still smiling at his words, as she gazed across the fields. They were nearing the village. A few scattered white houses appeared, with neat vegetable plots about, and some lemon and orange trees.

A man and a woman stood in a field, a Land Rover parked nearby. Something in the way the woman held her head, and turned her body away from the man, caught Iris's attention.

Iris stared. The man was very handsome, tall and black-haired, graceful in faded blue clothes like a sailor. He caught the woman's hand, and they walked away from the whitewashed house, into the shade of a tree.

"Why—there is Vanessa!" said Iris, too late, for the Land Rover had spun past the house, Greg driving the vehicle easily around the rutted curves.

"Vanessa? Where? Impossible!"

"No, she is there—with a man!"

Greg frowned, and turned about, slowing the vehicle. No

one was in sight now, the tree was distant. "You imagine it," he said positively. "Vanessa never goes anywhere without Xanthe. And she would not be alone with a man! She is very conscious of her reputation. She is Greek!"

"The man was very handsome, tall and black-haired," said Iris quietly, on her dignity now her word was doubted.

"All Greeks are handsome!" grinned Greg, and pulled up in front of an open market stall. "Do you wish to buy some paints and an easel?"

"Oh, yes, I would like that—" Iris was distracted by his offer. "You don't mind?"

"That you want to paint on our honeymoon?" He shook his head. "You like it, that is enough for me. There is a store here—I'll take you."

He caught her hand in his, and they wandered up the narrow street about two streets over from the harbor. That handsome man with Vanessa, thought Iris idly. Could that be the handsome Nikolaos? Oh, no, of course not. But he had been so very striking in appearance, arrogant head high, profile like a Greek statue, perfect figure in the faded blue. Lean hips, narrow waist, broad chest . . . no, it could't be—could it?

If it had been Nikolaos Sicilianos, he would not be with Vanessa. And she knew it had been Vanessa. Her artist's eye was keen. She was accustomed to noticing the features that made one person different from another. Her hand and eye were skillful because she recognized the little things and big ones that distinguished one person from another.

Vanessa had a way of holding her head, just slightly on one side, as though one ear was not as keen as another. Her hair was usually in a black chignon, but she wore it much lower than other women, so the weight of it lay on her neck. And her profile showed that slight dent in the beak nose.

Iris had studied her, trying to draw her, but Vanessa had

not liked that. She was suspicious of anyone who could draw an image, as so many were.

A painter who could capture one's image might be able to draw the soul in that painting, and take it from one! And even worse was a sculptor who could make little images of people in clay or stone. Ah, that was wicked mischief! A sculptor had told Iris ruefully about an experience in a *pensione* in Italy.

"I returned to my room after a long day of work, to find the tray knocked over and all the clay images destroyed. The maid said she had done it by mistake, but I saw the look on her face. She and another had done it on purpose, because they feared the image making!"

He had changed *pensioni*, and kept his room double-locked after that. But he encountered suspicion and fear wherever he went, in spite of the beautiful work he did.

Iris had found that two of the maids would not pose for her, and several of the men would not. She had not persisted. She did not want them fearful of her. It had been odd to find that Vannessa did not want her portrait painted. But Iris had not insisted there either.

Vanessa was a handsome woman, with a flashing attractive smile for Greg. There was something between them; Iris sensed it, and it made her uneasy. Had they once been very close? Or did she imagine things?

"What are you thinking?" asked Greg on the way back to the cottage.

"Oh—of the Mediterranean peoples. I would like to travel some more, to see Italy, and Sicily, and Spain—it is all so glorious," she sighed. "The colors are stunning, the flowers, the sky, the light—"

"We shall go," he declared. "I shall take you where you wish to go. Should you have liked a honeymoon in Spain?"

"Oh—no, I like the cottage!" she said at once, which

pleased him. He put his big hand on her knee, until he had to remove it to swing the wheel of the vehicle on another of the tricky turns.

"We will travel, however. The House of Venizelos has many properties. You will come with me the next time I go to Paris, and we shall buy many beautiful clothes for you!"

She smiled, but did not answer. The word "clothes" made her recall her own work. She had designed a number of dresses, some suits, some evening gowns. When could she make up samples, and get someone to model them? Would she be in time to turn in a line for Nadia Egorova? Would Greg let her go on with her designing? He did not seem to leave any time for her to do this. However, she had set her mind on achieving success in her chosen field.

It was near sunset when they returned to the cottage and unpacked the Land Rover. Greg carried in the boxes of food. Iris put her paints and easel and canvases in a safe corner of the cottage, and went out to look at the sunset.

Greg came up behind her, and put his arms about her as they gazed, she leaned back against him. She felt the heat of his sturdy body against her spine and hips. His hands linked at her waist.

The sun splashed down into a pool of crimson and gold, spilling light all over the mountains and the white clouds.

Rosy sprays fanned out all over the deepening blue of the sky, and faded to violet and purple. The sea turned to inky blue, and a breeze came up to spin white drifts of seawater over the beach.

"We will fix supper indoors tonight, it is turning cool. We may have rain tonight," said Greg.

"Rain, really? I thought it never rained in perfect Greece!"

He turned her to the cottage, and spanked her behind lightly with his big hand. "Irreverent heathen!" he scolded, with a booming laugh. "Rain is from the gods, to bring drink to the grasses and the land! However, it is arranged to pour at night, when people are indoors!''

''Oh—really! Oh, how convenient! That is why it poured so heavily the other day?''

Greg lit the paraffin lamp, and the stove, for Iris did not have the knack of that yet. She fried some onions and chunks of lamb in a skillet, added peppers and herbs. Greg cut the bread, set the table, and fixed a salad of greens and tomatoes. With a chilled bottle of white wine, they had a meal fit for the gods on Mount Olympus, declared Greg.

''I thought they ate nectar and ambrosia?'' asked Iris, her eyes sparkling in the lamplight.

''When they could not get lamb and onions,'' declared Greg very gravely. Their laughter mingled as they drank wine from pottery mugs, and cut the *baklavá* with the kitchen knife to eat with their fingers.

The dishes did not take long, they let them drain for morning, and went out to sit on the sand and watch the moon glimmering on the sea. They talked idly, or were silent, or Greg would sing a song of Greece. The waves lapped near their feet, rippling up to them, and retreating again. One could watch the sea endlessly, thought Iris.

Presently Greg drew her down beside him, and leaned over to touch her mouth with his lips. His hands moved over her body, opened the jacket, and touched her over the T-shirt. His hands cupped her breasts, and the fabric was in his way. He slid his hand under the shirt, and touched her bare breast.

She caught her breath. She loved his touch, it was so warm and his fingers were hard and slightly scratchy on her delicate skin. It was all the more erotic to feel his work-worn hands on her body. She thought she would not like the touch of a man who did no physical work, she enjoyed so much Greg's hands—they showed he did not scorn work. Or was it because those hands belonged to Greg and she loved him?

A drop of water splashed in her face, and another. She looked up dreamily, to see clouds had come over the sea, and the sky had turned dark grayish black, instead of purple.

"The rains are coming," said Greg. He picked her up and carried her inside the cottage. He put her on her feet there, and closed the door for the first time. "It is blowing from the west, we are in for a storm," he declared with pleasure, as though the idea of a storm excited him. He propped the window shutter partly closed, and they watched the skies for a short time. The sky turned the more black, and the clouds roiled in the heavens, blown by a fierce wind. Rain pattered on the beach, and beat on the roof of the cottage.

"It is well made," he reassured Iris, who gazed up at the roof with a slight frown. "Grandfather and I lived through many storms! And the roof was rethatched not long ago."

"How long does it last?"

"A well-made thatched roof can last from thirty to fifty years," and he smiled at her surprise. "Sometimes the old ways are best. I have known buildings made of sun-dried bricks in the old method to last through a bombing, when the modern buildings fell into dust."

"Not bombings in Greece—in your lifetime?"

A shadow came over his face. "Not here, no. It was in the Orient. I was there in relief work for a time. Horrible. So many died of hunger and disease. The work was endless, sometimes I felt it was hopeless. I took sick, and came home, and never returned. Sometimes I see them in nightmares. However—my grandfather told me of the wars in Greece. It was so here also. How I hate wars, man against man, in a senseless killing of everybody. Bombs from the sky that ought to be a peaceful beauty. Blood and guns and screaming."

The rain beat on the roof as he talked, and he sat with his hands tightly clasped as he relived the experiences. She felt very much closer to him, and presently she put her small hands on his big ones, and persuaded him silently to unclench them, and to hold her hands in his.

"Was it after that that you went into hotel work?"

"I had worked in hotels before, and when I was well I returned to it. Father died, and grandfather needed me. It is enjoyable work, Iris," and his face lightened from its tension. "I like the planning of a new hotel, working out details to make the places more beautiful and enjoyable. I like visiting the hotels that we have, and making sure all goes smoothly. To be a good host is an art. There are some men who do it well, and those we promote, and encourage. Others are sour and disagreeable, and those we fire!"

He grimaced, and she knew he meant it. "That is for the best, I am sure," she said. "I have gone to hotels, and been so pleased to be greeted with a smile, and feel I am really welcome there. And when someone takes the trouble to ask if the room is comfortable, if I wish something as hot tea, or more towels—I feel as coddled as a kitten in a blanket!"

He smiled at her, and put his arm about her. "And do you now feel like a kitten in a blanket?" he asked, as they relaxed in the cottage with the rain beating down outside. They had only the paraffin lamp and stove for light and heat, but it was enough.

"Um, quite coddled and comfortable," she murmured.

He lifted her up onto his knees, and held her closely to him. Iris relaxed against him, curling up into his arms. His mouth came down on hers, and she opened her lips and let him taste the sweetness of her mouth. Their tongues touched and twined lazily, probing, teasing.

His big hand moved over her hips and thighs, soothing and exciting in one. He began to unbutton the long skirt, until it fell back from her legs, and he could reach the bare flesh of her limbs. He stroked her leg from foot to hip, and back again, kissing her lips and throat as he did so. She felt caressed from head to toe.

Finally as he kissed her, his hand went to her thighs. Excitement was building up in her body. Heat burned from her heart to her hips. Tonight she wanted him badly. She had been close to him all day, swimming with him, lying on the sand with him, talking with him more intimately than they had ever spoken.

He finished unfastening the skirt, and put it over the back of the wooden sofa. Then he managed to unfasten her shorts, and pull them off, then the bikini pants. He gave a murmur of satisfaction when she sat with bare thighs on his lap. He ducked his head, and brushed a kiss on her legs.

"Greg—"

"Um—"

Her hands were in his hair, and she pulled him urgently to her. He half smiled, passion glowing in his black eyes.

"Greg!"

"Yes, my darling. Now?"

"Oh—yes—yes—"

She thought he would carry her to the bed. Instead, he lifted her, and carefully set her down again on his hard thighs. She gasped, her back bending against his arm, as he pressed her with great care down onto him. Then he rocked her back and forth, and entered her more fully. She clasped her arms about him spasmodically, her hands gripping the cotton of his shirt in back.

"Oh, you are ready," he whispered in her ear, and bit the lobe. "Oh—you are so sweet and ready—my dove, my dear—oh, you are honey sweet and dripping with juices of our love—and you are so hot and pretty and soft—"

He put his head down into the curve of her shoulder, and held her tightly. She was moving on him, trying to get closer, wildly ecstatic with the movements in her. She bounced, and he groaned, and held her down tight, and came hard in her. Ripples of erotic reaction blazed in her, shooting in her like stars, so she closed her eyes tightly and saw heavens behind the lids.

She lay limply against him, exhausted by the wild impact of their bodies. Greg gathered her closely to himself, murmuring his reassurances.

Her head pressed against his chest, she heard the wild thumping of his heart as his breathing eased. His hand stroked over her hair, through the thick curly tangles, soothing her.

Her mouth sighed against his chest. "Darling, Iris," he whispered.

"Oh, Greg, Greg."

His lips brushed her damp forehead. "Sweetness," he murmured, and more Greek love words.

This was even better than the hot close embrace that made her feel she was dying of ecstasy. She loved to be cuddled by him, held gently and caressed by his hands and lips. He rocked her slowly back and forth in his arms, soothing her until they were both more calm and quiet.

The rain poured down, but the winds had calmed. The sound of the drumming rain on the thatched roof and against the door and window shutters seemed to enclose them in a world all their own. Greg's voice was singing in her ears.

Like a lullaby, she thought drowsily. Like the crooning she had missed when she had gone to the convent. No more nanny holding her and soothing her tears over the lack of her father's love. Only the cool bed, the silence, the sound of a nun's footsteps in the corridor, a quiet reproach if the girl was found awake.

Greg nuzzled his face against her breasts, and she cupped his head in her hands to hold him closer.

"Oh, Iris, messenger of the gods," he whispered. "Oh, you took me with you up to heaven tonight!"

He carried her over to the bed and laid her gently down. He turned out the lamp, and opened the window to the sweet cool air. The storm had passed over them, and disappeared. Then he came back to bed with her, and took her into his arms.

"Oh, if I had known what passion was in you," he whispered in her ear, and bit the lobe. "If I had known, I would have taken you that first night in your apartment!"

She laughed weakly, remembering how she had feared that stormy black panther stalking her in the kitchen. "No, you would not! I would not have let you!"

She curled into his arms, and his arms were so strong and hard and protective.

"No, you waited for marriage, sweet Iris. That is good. You will be my woman, the woman of my life, the wife of my bed, the mother of my children. Ah, what a lucky man am I! Gods, do not take this from me, or I shall despair!"

Chapter Seventeen

The honeymoon week was over, and they must return home to work and problems. Iris washed the dishes and pans for a final time, and put them away in the minute cupboards.

Greg filled and trimmed the paraffin lamp, and made sure it was ready for any chance visitor, or refugee from a storm. He restocked the small cupboard with boxes of crackers and tins of cheese.

They closed up the place, climbed into the Land Rover, and set out, rather silently.

"You are sorry to leave, sweet Iris?"

"Yes, Greg. It was a beautiful week," she told him shyly.

"For me also. A very lovely time alone with you. Aye, aye, aye, the problems that await me!"

He sighed heavily, but she thought he enjoyed his work, and looked forward to dealing with problems. He liked a challenge. By early afternoon they were back at the cluster of buildings, the House of Venizelos, on the hillside overlooking the valley and the sea, and the village below.

When the Land Rover pulled up near the terrace, Kyria Lydia was there to greet them, and the servants and Melania ran out to give them welcome as though they had been gone much longer than a week.

Vanessa and Xanthe and the two girls came from the Cottage, faces in scowls as dark as their black dresses. How unpleasant they could be, thought Iris.

Greg went in at once to talk to Alex, and discuss the work with him. The maids carried in the couple of suitcases.

Vanessa said jealously, following Iris inside, "I suppose you went to a very expensive hotel?"

Iris thought of the cottage, the sea, the curve of beach. "Very dear indeed," she said gravely. "Priceless!"

Xanthe said, horrified, "With all the poverty in the world! It is a scandal!"

Iris caught the eye of her mother-in-law, and it brimmed with laughter. Kyria Lydia knew where they had gone, though probably no one else did.

"And you dressed for dinner every night? Where are your gowns? What did you eat?"

Greg had heard the questions, though his attention seemed to be completely on his conversation with Alex. He said promptly, "Food fit for the gods! Nectar and ambrosia!"

Vanessa and Xanthe looked all the more sour. Iris went on up the stairs, and they did not dare follow. That was private quarters, upstairs. Melania came with her, giggling when they reached the upper floors.

"They are so silly, Iris!" she whispered as they reached Iris's blue suite. Iris pushed open the door, to find her closets still filled with her garments, her brushes and mirror and powder boxes still on the dressers. "They have pried and questioned endlessly about where you went!"

Iris looked about the room slowly, her heart sinking. The maids had not moved her possessions to Greg's room, the master suite. What did that mean?

Melania noticed her concern. "Greg ordered that the panel between your suites should be unlocked," she said. She turned to the wall just beyond the hall door, and moved a panel Iris had never noticed. It slid open easily, and showed the handsome masculine room beyond, Greg's bedroom. She gave a shy little mischievous smile. "He did not want you to know about this before!"

"Oh, heavens! He could have come in anytime!" gasped Iris, staring at the innocent-looking white panel lined in blue, like the rest of the wall.

"*Poh-tay!* Never!" said Melania, vigorously shaking her head so her long brown curly hair spun about her shoulders. "Kyria Lydia kept the key, and Gregorios did not ask for it! Never. He would not so dishonor his fiancée!"

"No. Of course not," murmured Iris, relaxing. "Of course not. He is a strong person, and a man of honor."

Melania gave a little satisfied smile. "Yes, he is. Now, do you wish anything? Luncheon will be served when you are ready."

"Oh, I'll come when Kyria Lydia wishes—"

Melania waggled her finger. "But you are now the mistress of the house, dear Iris!"

"I—of course not!" she gasped, whirling around to stare at Melania. "You tease me!"

"No. It is true," Melania told her gently, seeing her distress. "It is the wish of Kyria Lydia. From the moment you returned from the honeymoon, you are mistress here. All will take your orders. All must obey your wishes."

Iris sat down on the side of the pretty blue-and-white-covered bed. "My orders—my wishes—" She shook her head. "But I am not ready—I am not trained—"

"Kyria Lydia will train you. That is natural," said Melania. "Shall I unpack for you?"

"I shall unpack for the Kyria Iris!" said a mock-severe voice in the doorway, as Charis came in. She bowed to Iris. "Welcome, a million times!"

Iris took a quick bath in the unaccustomed luxury of a tub with hot and cold running water. She dressed in a blue linen dress and went down to luncheon.

Kyria Lydia insisted Iris must take the foot of the table. However, at Iris's request, her mother-in-law continued to direct the servants.

"I will instruct you," said Lydia with her sweet smile, and nod of her gray-streaked black head. "It is not difficult, you will learn quickly."

"Thank you, mother," said Iris. It was easy to call her mother, and Greg looked down at her with a smile.

Vanessa and Xanthe looked sour again, but dared say nothing.

During dessert and coffee, the telephones rang imperiously. Greg took his coffee over to the electric panels, and began talking again, briskly, making notes on his pads. The problems were flowing in to him, and he was dealing with them. Iris wondered how long he would remain on the island, or if he would have to fly away to handle their hotel chain.

Alex had disappeared, and did not return until after four o'clock. After a brief rest, Iris and Melania returned to the main floor of the Big House, and talked with Kyria Lydia.

Vanessa and Xanthe and the two girls appeared promptly for tea, just as Lydia was explaining some of the household routine to Iris. Lydia stopped, and ordered more tea to be brought.

Xanthe eyed the simple blue linen dress Iris wore. "I suppose such dresses are good enough when you have tea with us!"

"I would suppose you had bought many more gowns in Athens on your honeymoon! Or did you buy them in Paris?" Vanessa had a beautiful smile, but there was malice in her black eyes.

"I have plenty of dresses for my needs," said Iris, as patiently as possible.

"I did not hear the airplane returning with you this morning!" said Xanthe. Greta came over to look at Iris's sketch pad. "What is she drawing, Greta?"

"Another dress!" said the little girl, leaning so close Iris could not see the pad.

"You see? She says she has plenty of dresses, but still she draws more!" said Xanthe sharply, her nose in the air. "Has Gregorios given you more jewels? Some resorts are famous for their beautiful women in designer gowns and jewels!"

"Gregorios keeps many jewels in the safe in the Athens house," said Vanessa. "I have seen them. Have you seen them, Iris? Or perhaps he keeps them—for another occasion! He used to give some to ladies—in fact, he gave some sapphires to me—" She stopped abruptly, looking self-conscious.

"That is enough, Vanessa," said Lydia furiously, glaring at her flushed face. "Of course he will give his beloved wife many jewels on the appropriate occasions!"

Except that his wife was not beloved, thought Iris, sketching silently when Greta had finally removed her small self and returned to fussing with Nora. Greg had never said he loved his fiancée, nor had he in all their passion declared his love for her.

He did not love her. He had married her for honor's sake, and the dowry of yet another hotel! As though he needed another! Perhaps he was with his hotels like some wealthy women with jewels—one always needed another set of diamonds!

She glanced at him as he sat absorbed at the telephones and

273

talked to his cousin in Athens. He barked out crisp orders, asked questions, frowned over an answer. He enjoyed this thoroughly, the power, the wealth, his business. Yes, it was the House of Venizelos, and many relatives were involved, but Greg was the head of that House of Venizelos, and what he said was law.

How different he seemed from the passionate lover, the laughing swimmer in the surf, the tender teacher of Iris in the ways of making love. Making love, it was making sex, she thought bitterly. Yet—she had enjoyed it also, but she had dreamed it was because of love. Her love, not his.

Yes, she loved him deeply. He was a complex man, and she loved the part of him that was lover, gentleman, the man of honor. What about the businessman? The hotel owner? The wealthy man who commanded airplanes with a snap of the fingers, and owned so many limousines he did not know how many he had?

That night she slept alone. Greg had come up to bed very late, it was past midnight. She had not been sleeping, but he did not come to her. She heard him murmur in his bedroom to himself, sighing, as he turned over in bed. He had worked hard that afternoon and evening.

Was this the way it would be, apart once more? Or even more bitter, like a medicinal herb that was supposed to be good for one—would he love her and want her only occasionally? Or just enough to create a child to inherit his wealth? Just enough to have a son of a woman he knew had been a virgin, so suitable to be the heir of the House of Venizelos?

She slept, and wakened to find the sunlight streaming in the blue and white room, behind white curtains. She yawned and stretched, and felt better for the brightness. She must plan her life, and her days, so they did not drag.

Yes, she would return to her designing of dresses. She must

start making up models, to send to Nadia Egorova. The line she had dreamed of—yes, she would go ahead on that!

She put on the bright yellow sundress today, it would help her keep up her spirits. She loved blues and yellows, the colors of the sky and sunlight.

She went down to breakfast, to find Greg already at the telephones. He waved and grinned at her, and left the phones to Alex.

"Good morning, my darling!" he greeted her with a kiss on her cheek. "You look bright this morning. Are you rested?"

"Quite rested," she answered with composure. "And you also?"

"Yes, I am rested," he said, then bent to whisper to her, and bite her earlobe gently. "But I missed you in my bed! You were asleep when I finally came up."

She had not been asleep, and he had not even looked in her room! She managed a smile, and took her place at the table.

The maids brought hot crisp slices of bacon this morning, small creamy pancakes with honey and dripping butter, juice the color of pomegranates and tart along with its sweetness, and steaming hot black coffee.

Greg and Iris ate alone, in silence. He seemed to have much on his mind. He excused himself when Alex called to him, and went back to the telephones.

Iris went upstairs, and searched out the paintings and the sketch pads she had filled the past week. She studied them and then went over to the sewing room, where she worked alone for a time.

The maids came up to clean and make beds, and peered in at her in surprise. But they did not interrupt.

She set out bolts of cloth on the tables. She had decided all the garments would be white. There was lovely white linen, charming white cottons, sheer white muslins, white lace, white satin and silk, a few pieces of white wool.

She mused over them, then pinned the sketches to each one. She would make up a line of Greek-inspired fashions, all in white, with trim of gold, or blue, or red.

There would be lovely white dresses, with skirts like those of the *korai,* brief and pretty, with soft pleats. The bodices would be cut low and rounded, modest. She pinned those sketches to some white cotton bouclé.

More white cotton would be used for some matching shorts and short-sleeved shirts. Then some blouses of white muslin, with full sleeves to be embroidered in red and blue with typical Greek designs of small ships, butterflies, or the *Glastra* pattern of a stylized flowerpot. This would be more intricate, she wondered who she could find to do this.

She decided to let the evening gowns go for now, they would be in silks, white velvet—

Lydia looked in once during the morning, smiled and left again.

Melania came up, said, "May I be of any help, Iris?"

"Not at this stage, thanks," Iris told her.

"Then I will not remain to trouble you. Alex needs me," she said, and smiled radiantly, her brown eyes shining.

Iris smiled over her work as the girl danced downstairs once more. Alex seemed to be turning more and more to Melania. He did not resent her help in walking as he did that of others. And he let her read his letters, help with his phone calls and notes. She had the patience to disregard his grumbling and moods, and could laugh like a child with his teasing.

After luncheon, Iris went with Kyria Lydia to talk to the cooks about the evening meal. They discussed menus, and Iris began to learn that phase of the immense job of taking care of such a large household.

That set the pattern of her days; during the long mornings, in the sunlight when she felt fresh, she worked on dress designing. In the late afternoons, she worked with her mother-in-law with household duties, gradually learning and experimenting with various phases of that.

Evenings were for all the family. Sometimes Greg had telephone calls. More often he sat with them after dinner on the terrace, enjoying the spectacular sunsets, talking lazily, drinking endless cups of coffee and eating sugary sweets.

They talked some of the old days, and even Xanthe could laugh at some memories of childhood. They talked of the wars, the feuds, though Greg often shut off that conversation. They seemed to make Vanessa uneasy also. Iris wondered if Vanessa was still seeing that man, and if he was the feudal enemy, Nikolaos Sicilianos. Surely he was not, she would not be out walking with their enemy, would she?

She did hope Vanessa was seeing some nice young man, though. Marriage would be good for Vanessa, perhaps sweeten her souring disposition. She did not seem interested in work, or a career of any sort. And she was fond of the children of Xanthe. She could control them when Xanthe became exasperated. And Greg did not seem to consider training Vanessa for some career in business.

Iris drew several simple embroidery patterns on a couple of muslin blouses she had made, and the evenings were often spent in experiments in embroidery. She liked some of the traditional patterns, and used various arrangements of them. She often embroidered little sample pieces also, to the curiosity of them all.

"What are you doing? That is not large enough for even a doll's dress," complained Xanthe one evening.

"These are merely samples," said Iris. "I am trying out designs in various colors and designs."

"They are not nearly so fine as those the women make in the village," sneered Vanessa.

"Oh, do the village women embroider?" asked Iris, glancing up.

"Of course! They are world known for their embroidery! It is a pity they have no markets." Xanthe frowned and shook her head gloomily. "Such beautiful work, and only for the few tourists who stop here."

Iris was silent, the conversation changed. Vanessa was teasing Greg to take them to Athens for shopping.

"I don't have time now. I can send the pilot with you, if you wish."

But that would not do. They wanted Greg, Iris thought, not the shopping especially. They wanted him dancing attendance on them, showing his wife of how little importance she was.

The days were growing hotter. It was early June now, and in July it would be very hot, said Melania. One morning, Iris wakened to find it was already sultry and still. She would find it hard to sew today. The palms of her hands would be damp, the room warm.

The panel of white and blue between her room and Greg's slowly, cautiously opened. She had one eye opened sleepily, and she gazed in fascination at the panel. Greg's tanned face appeared, and white teeth shone in a big grin when she showed herself awake. She lifted a sleepy hand to wave fingers at him.

"Good morning!" he whispered, as though he could be heard. "Would you like to swim this morning?"

"Oh—yes!" she said, sitting up. His eyes approved the light blue gown that scarcely covered her body and slim legs. "Can we go out—"

"Yes, I'll tell one of the maids to pack a basket. And listen—would it be all right if I invite Melania and Alex? He could swim if I take him out—and he isn't exercising his legs very much." A brief line of worry crinkled his brow.

"Oh, yes, good idea!" She slid out of bed and reached for her robe. "I'll go ask Melania—you get Alex. I take it we are not going to ask Xanthe and the children?"

She laughed softly as he made a terrible grimace. The children had gone once with them last week in the afternoon. They were fussy, worrying about the sand on their small bodies, crying and angry before the afternoon was half over. Greg had given up in disgust and taken them all home.

Iris wakened Melania, then went to dress. She put on her yellow bathing suit, and over it the yellow blouse and long white skirt with blue and yellow butterflies. She found her immense bath towels of yellow and orange, put them in a straw basket with her straw shoes, some suntan oil, tissues, cream for her face, her blue cotton hat. Then she was ready.

She crept downstairs, to find the house silent but for one maid dusting the furniture in the large room. The maid beamed at her, made a wide swimming motion with her arms, and nodded as Iris went out to the Land Rover parked at the side of the Big House.

Melania soon came down to join her. Then Greg appeared, with Alex in his wheelchair. One of the men came also, to help Alex into the jeeplike vehicle. Alex was grumbling quietly.

"I don't know why you bother—I cannot swim any longer— what is the use of exercise, I'll never walk again—"

"Shut up, and get in," said Greg good-naturedly. "You just don't like to wake up early, you never did."

They got Alex into the backseat, and he held on to Melania as Greg started up the Land Rover. He backed down the hill, rather than drive near the Cottage where Xanthe and her sister and children stayed. He was taking no chances!

When they were well away from the cluster of buildings,

Greg began to sing, a big bellow of sound, some sea chanteys at first. Alex fussed at him, then laughed, and began to join in the singing.

Melania added her sweet small voice, and Iris joined in the lusty choruses. They were all laughing and singing by the time Greg had found the cove he wanted.

It was one Iris had never seen before. A creamy sand beach was crammed into a small space below some rocks, with just room for the Land Rover to park on a narrow rock ledge. Green waters filled the small cove, hemmed in by rocky triangles of land covered with green shrubs, a few little trees, and some scented maquis.

Beyond where the points of land almost came together was a deep blue sea, endlessly to the horizon, where a few puffy white clouds floated lazily. It was perfectly quiet, not a human being was in sight for miles.

"There—this is quite safe, Iris," Greg told her. "Sharks never come in here, and the water is never deep. I'll take Alex out for a time, you and Melania can paddle about."

Greg helped Alex out of the vehicle and set him on the sand. Then he put up a couple of colorful beach umbrellas of blue and red and orange and yellow. He set out the straw baskets of food, then helped Alex down to the water, and stripped off his jeans and shirt, to reveal the bathing trunks beneath.

Iris could not help looking at Alex. His legs and thighs were covered with deep reddish scars, scarcely healed, and he limped heavily even with Greg's help. Greg had Alex's arm across his shoulders, and his arm about his waist. His tall healthy unscarred body was in vivid contrast to the drooping lightly-tanned body of his cousin.

"It was a very bad accident," whispered Melania. "Not really an accident—he was stabbed—the car went out of control—they crashed—the fires—" She shuddered.

"A terrible thing, the feud," said Iris soberly. "It should be stopped."

"It will not stop until *they* are dead, those Sicilianos," said Melania with unusual fierceness.

The girls stripped off their skirts and blouses, and went into the water, to paddle around happily. The water was cool in the early morning, but already turning warm in the sunshine.

Alex and Greg went farther out, but finally returned. Greg started a fire, and cooked fish for them all, while Iris and Melania set out the platters of fresh sweet rolls, cheese, and hard-boiled eggs. They ate hungrily, the fresh air and exercise encouraging their appetites. They finished with cups of hot coffee sweetened with honey and lightened with milk.

Alex lay back on the blanket he shared with Melania, and handed her his cup. "Good," he said, and closed his eyes. "I'm tired." He put his head on her lap, and was asleep at once.

Iris saw Greg's look on him, tender and concerned. Alex was not improving as he should, she knew Greg was worried about him. Perhaps more fresh air and exercise would help him. He stayed too much in his room, brooding over his once-active life.

Melania softly stroked Alex's hair, and soothed him when he mumbled. Her look down at the man who rested against her was revealing. She loved him. And not as a cousin.

Presently Melania lay back, and slept also, in the shade of the beach umbrella. Greg took the suntan lotion, and began to smooth it on Iris.

"You will burn," he murmured, and his big palms smoothed the cool lotion on her back and thighs and long legs. His touch was firm and strong, stroking the lotion into her warm skin. "Now me," he said, and handed her the lotion with a slow smile.

She sat up lazily, and stroked some lotion into his neck and his back. He had a broad back, wide shoulders, long arms. There was much more of him to cover than there had been of her! She worked the lotion into his tanned skin, down to his waist. With a wicked twinkle at her, he pushed down the belt of his shorts, and silently encouraged her to rub lotion into his tanned hips.

Iris smoothed the lotion firmly into his thighs, trying not to stare at his male beauty. He was so handsome, so beautifully put together. Oh, God, she prayed, let him never be scarred and hurt as Alex was!

She poured more lotion into her small palm, and stroked some lotion down his long hard legs. She could feel the muscular strength of his limbs, down to the arched feet. She finally finished, and set the lotion down, just as Greg rolled over.

"Now —here—" he whispered, and motioned to his chest.

She sighed, in mock protest, and began to put lotion on his chest. Her fingertips lingered in the mat of black curly hairs and the male nipples enticed her. She touched them curiously, and Greg stared at her, his tongue licking his lips unconsciously. It was a sensuous experience rubbing lotion onto his chest. She rubbed down to his waist, his hand urged her further. She shook her head silently, her cheeks warm. What if Melania wakened while she was doing that?

She moved to the legs again. She rubbed the cool lotion briskly into his flesh, down to his feet. Greg stretched, and put his arms behind his head, and his whole body rippled with the movement.

Greg was so beautiful! She stared down at him when she had finished, and he grinned at her, his eyelids half closed. "Want me?" his lips mouthed.

Iris nodded innocently. Greg's black eyes flared with passion.

"To draw!" she said softly, and giggled at his disgusted

look. He pulled her down to him on the blanket, and curled her against him.

Into her ear he muttered, "Tease! You know what happens to teases?"

"In public?" she mocked, and deliberately brushed herself against his long body, letting him feel her softness against him. Her thighs were against his, she felt his instant masculine response to her. But she felt quite safe, Melania and Alex could waken any minute!

He groaned a little, and wrapped his long arms about her, to hold her close against him. She lay quietly, content, her head on his shoulder, the wet hair drying on his arm. It was a day she would put in her mental treasure box, to remember forever.

Chapter Eighteen

Several days later, Iris noticed that Greg was looking very absorbed and thoughtful, frowning into space, and muttering to himself. The mid-June days were heavenly, though growing quite warm.

Iris wondered if Greg was getting restless with this relatively quiet life, and longed to return to Athens—or Paris—or New York City! She wondered if he would take off, leaving her behind to learn her new duties as mistress of the household.

She frowned at her embroidery, and jabbed a needle into the muslin. Well, she must expect it.

That evening, she went to her room and was amazed to find Charis packing two good-sized suitcases! "What are you doing, Charis?" she asked.

"Packing for you, Kyria!" the maid smiled, and put her finger to her lips. "The master told me what to pack. It is to be a surprise for you!"

For one mad moment, Iris thought he was sending her

away. Then more practical suggestions occurred to her. They might go to Athens on business.

Greg poked his head in the door, then came in. "Are you about finished, Charis?"

"Yes, Kyrios!" She folded a thick sweater and laid it on the slacks.

"Where am I going?" asked Iris.

"We—darling. We are going—but I don't want the family to know about it, yet. So I am not going to tell you, and if they ask, you will just say you don't know!"

A mischievous sparkle lit his black eyes. She eyed him dubiously. "From the looks of the clothes, I think we are going to the North Pole!"

Charis had just laid out a smart navy blue coat and hat to match, in wool. She could see her blue slacks and gray ones in the cases. But there were also some beautiful gowns, her white and gold one, the blue silk—

"We leave tomorrow morning—for the North Pole," Greg laughed. "Say nothing to anyone. Just get up about seven, and be ready to leave by eight. The less fuss the better."

She heartily agreed with that philosophy. No one mentioned the trip that evening, though Kyria Lydia gave Iris an extra hug, and whispered to her, "Have a wonderful time!" as Iris was going off to bed.

Charis had set out a suit of light blue wool for Iris to wear on the journey. Iris put it on obediently, teamed with a lightweight white jersey. Greg had them down to the airplane by eight-thirty, and the pilot who lived in the village was ready to go.

They arrived at Athens airport before ten o'clock, transferred to a Venizelos company jet, and were on their way before half an hour had gone by. Iris relaxed into the comfort of the company jet, she found fashion magazines next to her armchair, and vistas outside her window that held her attention while they took off.

Then they flew above the clouds for several hours. Greg was absorbed in the contents of his black leather portfolio, and made notes of some items. The steward, Myron, served her coffee and orange juice, and later brought them luncheon.

Greg did come to then. He set down his papers, and smiled at her.

"When am I to know where we are going?" asked Iris, tasting the little dishes of appetizers. She especially liked the cold shrimp with hot red sauce.

"We are going to Cornwall," said Greg.

"Cornwall—England?" She grabbed mentally for her geography knowledge.

"Right you are," said Greg, eating hungrily. He took a long drink of his glass of chilled white wine. "I bought a fine hotel there recently, in the heart of some wildly beautiful countryside, overlooking the sea. A couple run it for me, Arthur and Meg Penhallow. You will meet their niece also, Yseult Penhallow."

"They sound like Old England!"

"Very old," he agreed gravely. "The time of Arthur Pendragon, in fact, King Arthur of the Round Table. His castle and the table itself are supposed to be there." He smiled at her wide-eyed amazement. "You know the story, I presume."

She nodded. She loved the old medieval tales that Tennyson had retold so beautifully. "Yes. But I never thought I would see that country!"

"It is lovely, you will enjoy it. Yseult will obtain paints and sketch pads for you, she is also an artist. While I am working, you can roam about with her, she will show you some lovely sights you can paint. I'll be in for a more difficult time. I'll tell you about it."

Delighted at his confidence in her, she listened intently, while Myron brought the next course, of crisp fried fish with lemon butter, baked potatoes, and a green salad.

"A little over a year ago," Greg began, "I was in the area, for a vacation of my own. I always keep my eyes open for hotels, and we were expanding then, I had none in England. I came to this hotel near Land's End, and Penzance—"

"Of the *Pirates of Penzance*?" she asked, entranced by all the marvelous names.

"The same. An old seaport that has seen a-plenty of history! I was enjoying the fishing there, when I returned cold and hungry, to find the dining room closed. The man at the desk was rude, tea was over, they didn't serve dinners on Tuesdays, or some such nonsense. I was complaining bitterly— when a plump lady came from the back area, cheeks like roses, skin like peaches and cream, grandmotherly with her gray hair. She said she would cook me a dinner, using some of the fish I had caught, and some good Cornish pasty, and so on. The man turned on her, and fired her!"

"Oh, no!" Iris stared at Greg; he nodded.

"I bought the hotel," he said simply. "I told him I would, asked the lady to go ahead and cook my meal. While she was cooking, I phoned from the kitchen to my London office, and put my people on it. By the next morning, the hotel was mine. I fired the manager."

Iris was laughing helplessly. "I love it, I love it!" she gurgled, as she wiped her eyes. She could just see Greg, starvingly hungry, being denied his dinner! Yes, he would act!

"The manager had been there for only a season, he was much disliked. The trouble was also that an American firm owned the hotel, and had not checked up on it recently. The cook, Meg Penhallow, practically ran the hotel for him. People came for her excellent food, and her gentle warmth of welcome. Her husband had been in an accident and lost his job—she was supporting the family.''

"What happened then?'' asked Iris, as Myron served tiny medallions of veal in wine sauce and green beans.

"I put Meg in charge. Since then the business has boomed. She hired someone for the front desk, got her niece Yseult to take small groups of people around to the local sights, and all went well. Then Arthur recovered from his injuries, and insisted on managing the hotel.'' Greg frowned.

"And does he know anything about hotels?'' asked Iris.

"I don't know. I just found out about this recently. I had some complaints from old-timers, who said the hotel had changed, the manager was rude, and so on. My policy in such matters is to get an auditor from our firm in to go over the books, and make it look like a surprise audit. Then I come in, and seem to go over the books also, while I have a look at the hotel itself as a guest. One can spot quite a bit that way.''

"And they don't resent it being done that way? They will know who we are?'' asked Iris.

"Oh, yes, they will know. But they will know also that we are looking over the operation with a view to improve it. If you see things, Iris, I want you to tell me, from little things about not enough towels, to any rudeness to the guests.''

"I'll try—I'm not used to this,'' she said doubtfully.

"Some managers can be driven, they must be told forcefully to shape up or get out. Others must be led. I think this will be the latter case,'' said Greg, and returned to his papers.

They landed at Heathrow Airport west of London in midafternoon, and skimmed through customs. Greg was well known, she thought. A silver Rolls-Royce was waiting for them, and a neat chauffeur in uniform, cheerful brisk Peter Rigdon. He was about in his thirties, she thought, and very efficient.

He had them into the limousine, and on their way very

quickly. "Now, sir, you said the scenic view to Winchester," he said to Greg, as they started out.

"Right," said Greg. "This is my wife's first visit to England, and I want her to see the gardens, and thatched cottages, the works!"

The chauffeur grinned in the mirror at them, revealing a pixieish expression. "That'll be grand, sir! And Winchester for the night, you have the reservations right enough."

He took the motorway called A30 southwest to Basingstoke, and Iris admired the houses and scenes she could see from the shaded windows of the Rolls. She knew the man was driving more slowly than necessary, in order to let her see the sights. She relaxed and watched the villages as they flipped through, the glimpses of steepled churches, reddish hedges—which she suddenly realized were masses of roses—and flower gardens in just about every cottage yard.

He turned off on to A33, and the signs pointed the way to Winchester.

"There's a lovely cathedral there, ma'am," said the driver, explaining the sights as they went along. "You'll want to have a look this evening. 'Tisn't far from your hotel, you can stretch your legs, you and the guv'nor, in the evening."

He soon was driving into Winchester, and Iris gazed into the narrow streets and lovely old buildings in great fascination. Their hotel was one of the older ones, gracious and old-fashioned with black and white architecture, like Tudor times. The beams were almost black with paint and age, and between were slabs of stucco whitewashed or painted. She resolved to examine them more closely when they got out.

The luggage was removed from what the driver called the boot of the car, and to Iris's surprise, they rode off once more.

"To see the Round Table of Arthur," Greg told her, with a smile at her surprise. "I told Peter you would like to see it."

"Just time before they close," the driver tossed over his shoulder. He drove them up to an immense castle, and took them inside. "Begun by William the Conqueror," said Peter briskly, as though that were just a little before yesterday. He marched through aisles and clustered columns of marble, then pointed to a table hanging against the wall. "The Round Table of King Arthur," he announced.

Iris stared at it. It was both smaller and more impressive than she could have imagined. To think of it lasting all those centuries. "Is it—really?"

"It could be," said Peter, "It dates from the thirteenth century at least, and is considered a relic of before then."

Iris took a last look at the painted wooden table, and tried to imagine the handsome genteel knights and King Arthur at the table.

They returned to the hotel along narrow medieval streets, and were settled into a handsome good-sized room. Iris was tired enough to want to lie down, but she readily agreed to go for a walk and "stretch her legs," as Greg suggested.

Peter had left them, taking the car. Greg took Iris's hand, and they walked out into the dusk of the beautiful city, to the cathedral. In silence, they entered the medieval church, and strolled among the pillars, along the nave. Iris admired the Norman architecture and the Gothic changes that had been made; the soaring arch of the main section was so beautiful.

They were walking along the north aisle, when Greg paused, and pointed to a window and brass tablet. Iris read, and her eyes widened.

"Jane—Austen!" she gasped. He nodded, they read the tablet silently. The tablet was to her, and she was buried in the pavement at that spot.

Iris had thought the statutes and monuments impressive, but this one touched her heart and mind. She had read the novels of Jane Austen in high school and loved them for their wit and intelligence, the descriptions of Regency life, the glimpses into the mind of a fine woman.

They finally moved on, to see the paintings, the windows, and the tablet of Izaak Walton.

"A great fisherman too," whispered Greg. There was so much to see they could scarcely take it all in, but wandered about for more than an hour, then strolled back to the hotel.

Iris was more tired than hungry by that time. They had supper in a dark-paneled room, and the fire crackled in the fireplace nearby, warding off the chill of the English June night. They had a thick beef and vegetable soup, some crisp toasted bread, local cheese.

Iris slept well that night, only briefly conscious of Greg's arm over her in the down-soft bed. In the morning, they ate a hearty English breakfast of fried eggs, fried tomatoes, sausages, rashers that seemed more like thin ham than bacon, toast, tea with milk, marmalade.

Peter Rigdon brought the Rolls-Royce around before nine, and they were loaded up and on their way with the early morning traffic. Peter whizzed them along, pausing only to let Iris and Greg admire a distant steeple, a particularly beautiful path of primroses, a field of wild flowers, a typical English thatched cottage with a yard full of hollyhocks.

Peter seemed completely familiar with the roads, and would drive them for a time on the motorway, then leave the highway to drive along a country road where the trees almost met over their heads. They drove through the New Forest, and saw some of the shaggy wild ponies grazing beside the road. Beyond the turnoffs to Southampton and Bournemouth, they began to smell the sea, and opened the windows of the Rolls to enjoy the scents of the ocean, the salt, and the grasses and flowers.

The farther they were from London, the more the scenes changed. Now the farms appeared, with green fields, and golden fields, and hedgerows separating one field from another. Some of the old stone fences fascinated Iris, the stones appeared to be piled on at random, but they had held for centuries, Peter said, with just a fixing of the stones from time to time.

They went through Dorset, admiring the towns and villages, the old cottages and smart newer buildings. Then they left Dorset, and the many fascinating names of the towns and places, to enter Devon, with even more marvelous names, signs pointing to Dawlish, and Babbacombe Bay, to Maidencombe, and Torquay. Then went through Newton Abbott, and Totnes, to Kingsbridge, and Churchstow and Modbury and Brixton. Then they skirted Plymouth, and Iris gazed longingly in that direction, wishing to stop. There just wasn't time for every place she wanted to explore.

Greg squeezed her hand. "Another time, Iris!" he said.

She smiled at him. "I love it here. We will come back," she said confidently. He lifted her hand to his lips, and she caught a glimpse of Peter smiling into the rearview mirror.

Soon after Plymouth, they stopped for a late lunch, and Greg invited Peter to join them. He made a cheerful companion, and was full of local stories of Devon and Cornwall. "We crossed the Tamar at Plymouth," he told them. "And now some Cornish folks say we are out of England, and in Cornwall instead! Another country, different folks, different language, or it was once."

Peter told them about the smugglers who had haunted these coasts, and how they hid the rum in the church crypts, and cut the priest or pastor in on the proceeds. Napoleon's gold paid for English tobacco and weapons, even while English citizens waited on the coast with dread in their hearts against an invasion. Hard to stop smugglers, said Peter, and told about the times in the sixteenth and seventeenth and eighteenth centuries when the forbidden "trade" was more profitable than any farmland or town factory.

In the afternoon, they rode through towns such as Penpillick and St. Blazey, St. Austell and Tresillian, Truro. There were turnoff signs pointing to places like Tregony and Portloe, Trewithian and Penryn, Falmouth and Porthleven. Peter told them that *tre* and *pen* usually meant Cornish names.

Finally, in late afternoon, they arrived at the hotel, perched on a cliff high on the Atlantic Ocean, near Land's End. It was a large rambling building of reddish and gray stone, made as sturdy as could be against the fierce ocean winds and spray. The trees were bent from the winds of a hundred years, and it was amazing to see flower beds behind stone walls, still brilliant with color in spite of the salt spray.

Beside the porter in his apron, a plump lady came out to greet them. Greg left the car and the luggage to greet her warmly, hugging her and kissing each rosy cheek.

"Iris, this is Mrs. Meg Penhallow—Meg—my wife, Iris!"

The gray hair blew in the brisk winds, the smile was warm as a lighted fire. Did Iris imagine worry in the gray eyebrows over the sparkling blue eyes? Perhaps a little crinkle between the brows, perhaps a slight droop to the pink mouth.

"Come you in, come you in! The wind is chill today, and you don't want to stand about!" A plump arm urged Iris to the door of the hotel, and she stepped inside to a parquet-floored lobby with chintz-covered chairs set about in little groups. Fresh flowers stood in the vases of gray and blue porcelain. Meg was quick to notice her interest. "Local clays, Mrs. Venizelos! Yseult knows some potters hereabouts."

"The work is very fine, very lovely," Iris murmured. "Please call me Iris, and let me call you Meg, as my husband does."

A quick smile, and nod, and they were friends. She herself showed them to their rooms on the next floor, overlooking the sea. The huge bedroom was furnished in sparkling blue and white linens, with more flowers in vases, roses, and some red and yellow flowers Iris did not know. There was a smaller sitting room attached, with a view in another direction out over the small town. The bathroom was immense, with a huge tub suitable for swimming! Thick towels were warming over hot rods.

"Now, I'll be sending up some tea for ye?" It was a question.

"Some tea for my wife, if you will, Meg, and I'll go off and see the auditor. He's working in the office?"

Iris had noticed how Greg could take on the accent and feel of a local language. In New York he was crisp and quick, in Greece slower and drawly. Now in Cornwall, the lilt of the region was already in his tongue!

"Yes, he is. Now, Iris, is there aught else I can bring ye?"

"Just some hot tea—nothing much else, thank you."

The tea came up, a silver tray of it on a rolling stand. Not just hot tea in a pottery jug, with more hot water on the side, and a jug of hot milk, a pot of sugar. But there was also a covered dish of hot scones, some chilled butter, a dish of deep red strawberries, tiny and sweet, and a pot of thick yellow whipped cream.

"'Tis Cornish cream, miss," volunteered the girl who brought the tray.

"Oh, I've heard of that!"

The maid beamed. "All the world has heard of our cream, miss!" And off she went, pleased.

Iris was hungry enough and rash enough to eat half the scones and cream, and all the strawberries! She ate at the windows, examining the scene before her with fascination. The wind whipped the blue waves into white foam, dashing the sea again and again against the reddish cliffs. The trees bent almost double against the lashing wind. And this was

June! What must it be like in December and January? She remembered stories in the newspapers of this coast, where the lifeboats went out to rescue men off ships, the freighters that sank, the horrible times when not all the men in the lifeboats returned. The sea was a relentless mistress, beloved by the seamen, but tormented by winds, and luring them to their death.

She lay down for a time, then got up and unpacked for herself and Greg, hanging the suits and coats in the scented cupboards. Greg returned about eight o'clock, as fresh and brisk as a summer breeze.

"Well, it's Arthur," he said quietly to her. "A difficult chap. He wants to run the whole show, he is cock of the walk, with no training at all. Meg has her kind heart, but he says she is too soft. It is service people want in hotels, and an ear to listen to them."

"What will you do about it?" asked Iris, with keen interest. "Let Meg run it?"

"Would ruin her marriage, and she does love him," said Greg. "No, there's another way, I'll work it out."

They had a quiet dinner in the corner of the dining room. Greg was silent, Iris knew he was watching the service, the food, the reactions of the other guests. There was a good crowd, the waiters were too busy to put on a show of concern if they did not feel it. Iris was interested in one bustling waitress, with a Cornish accent as thick as their yellow whipped cream. She seemed immensely popular with her tables, and kept them laughing with her comments. Yet she served them speedily and well, not seeming to mind any teasing.

Greg noticed her watching. "A good waitress, born to it," he said, with a nod. "She loves people, and it shows."

Their waiter was a shy young man, eager to please, very aware he was waiting on the "big boss." He blushed when he served them, watched them anxiously when they took the first bites, his hands shook when he served the coffee, and the cups rattled in the saucers.

Meg seemed to be working in the kitchen; she came out toward the end of the meal and had a long look around, strolling among the tables, and speaking with the guests. She would nod, and smile, and say, "Now, I'll take care of that right off," and that pleased them.

She came to Greg, and he insisted on her sitting down and having coffee with them.

"Arthur's niece, Yseult, is coming tomorrow to show you about," she told Iris. "You'll tell her what you wish to see. Greg says as how you are an artist?"

"Yes, a dress designer. I also sketch and paint."

"Well, now! You have the talents, yes? Yseult, she is a painter also, not that she sells much. But she says she will one day! Hangs about with a rather scruffy crowd, if you ask me! But good-hearted some of them, and with some talent. Soap costs money, I says, true, but cleanliness is next to godliness, and it wouldn't hurt them to take the scissors to their hair!"

Iris enjoyed her comments, and so did Greg. She finally left them, with a kindly, "Good night to ye, and sleep well!"

Yseult came the next day, with a small brilliantly red Mini car, her very own, she said. She drove Iris about, and knew every little port, every colorful town in the area. They sketched in silence, or chattered away half the day, visiting the cliffs at Land's End, the bay at St. Ives, Portreath and Perranporth and Newquay. Iris was enchanted with the pretty little blue bays, with bits of town scattered about them, and halfway up the cliffs all about. Some of the beaches were nice for swimming, others were all shell and sharp stones.

Yseult was a tall black-haired girl, with her long hair tied back with a red or a yellow ribbon, her long legs in blue jeans. A photographer wouldhave adored her, thought Iris, but the girl had no vanity about her fine figure, her peaches-and-cream complexion, her long-lashed black eyes, her fine hands.

No, she was an artist, she lived for drawing and painting. Summers, she took tourists about for her Aunt Meg, and showed fishermen where to fish, and artists where to sketch, and gardening enthusiasts the prettiest flowers and hedges and fields of wild flowers. She loved Cornwall and quietly enjoyed showing tourists about.

"Some can be quite decent, you know," she said to Iris. "Only a few can be—well—toffy-nosed."

When she found Iris a serious artist, she melted from her quiet dignity, and became eager to show her the best places. One fine blue-skied day, they drove far to the north, to Clovelly and the steep sliding cobblestoned road down to the port, to Woolacombe and Ilfracombe, and down again through wildly beautiful Cornish moors. They would stop and sketch, or make watercolors of various places, until their portfolios were full of ideas.

Since Greg was deeply absorbed in his work during the day, Iris had no compunction about spending entire days with Yseult, sunny or rainy, and finding places to sketch. Yseult introduced her to a few of her artist friends, evidently choosing the nicest of them. Iris met a potter, a worker in Cornish jewelry using local stones, a painter, several girls who did embroidery and made lace. She enjoyed talking with them, showed them some sketches of her dresses, suggested blouses to show off their embroidery.

Often she and Yseult stopped for luncheon wherever they happened to be. They would have a simple soup and sandwich luncheon in a pub, at a corner table, while workmen sat at the bar and drank their dark beer, and talked local gossip. Other times, they would stop at a "teas" place, in some house, where the housewife, to earn a bit of money, would have a few tables in her parlor, and show off her cooking with luscious biscuits, scones, small pies covered with fresh raspberries or strawberries, and the thick Cornish yellow cream. And always there was hot tea, pots of it. "I'll get fat," groaned Iris. "I can feel my belts getting tighter!"

Yseult rarely spoke of her relatives. Only once did she say, "It was a blessing when Mr. Venizelos came to our town! Aunt Meg cannot say enough about him." She paused, then added, "It was a shame Uncle Arthur got into it. He's my uncle and I love him, but he doesn't know damn enough about hotels. He was a hardware man, fixed things, ran the store. Hotels are a different business."

"If he is willing to learn, it may turn out all right," said Iris cautiously.

Yseult shrugged broadly, and flung out her expressive hands. "One hopes! Well, where shall we go to—or have you had enough for the day?"

It was almost five o'clock, so Iris said she would rather go back to the hotel. Yseult took her there, and promised to pick her up the next day at nine. Then Greg came out to the car, and stopped her from driving on. He had a smile on his face, and seemed more relaxed.

"Hold up, Yseult! I'll have my wife's company tomorrow!"

She gave him a shy smile. "All right, then. Want my Mini?"

He paused, then nodded. "Yes, I'll take it, thanks! I want a chance to go about with Iris for the day. We'll be leaving the day after tomorrow. I wanted to thank you for keeping Iris company these days. She has really enjoyed herself, I think."

"Yes, I have, Greg."

Both girls kept looking at him, and he grinned. He poked his head closer to them, inside the car. Iris had not yet stepped out. "You'll want to know what happened, in confidence,'' he said quietly. ''Arthur agreed to go to our hotel school right away. He'll be off in a couple days. I've arranged it with our people to put in some good words about service to people, and not being arrogant! You'll keep it quiet, Yseult, and help your Aunt Meg while Arthur is gone?''

''Yes, and glad to oblige!'' said Yseult quickly. ''You're a corker, Mr. Venizelos! I'm that relieved!''

He patted her shoulder, then helped Iris out. Yseult waved, and drove around to the kitchen area, and hopped out of the car. She had evidently gone to have a good talk with her Aunt Meg.

''So that is fixed,'' said Greg, with relief. ''Now, we'll have a day tomorrow free of problems, before we go back home!''

Iris felt she had learned much about her husband on this journey. How considerate he had been to her, showing her places that would please her, thinking ahead to her pleasures. He had planned to have Yseult show her about, rather than have Iris hang about the hotel, or try to find her own way about.

How wonderful he could be, in little ways as well as big ones. She was getting a different picture of Greg. Behind the facade of businessman and hotel man, jet-setter, and suave escort to beautiful women, there was another Greg.

He was thoughtful of people in his employ. She felt he was as concerned about the happiness of Meg Penhallow as he was about the profit of the hotel she ran for him. It was another side of him, and she liked it immensely, and found it brought her closer to him.

He was good to his mother and other relatives, but the most dastardly of men could be that! To find him with strangers, as gentle and concerned as for his relatives, was a distinct delight to Iris. And it made her love him the more.

Iris thought about it very much that evening, as Meg came

from the kitchen, and beamed about thankfully at her guests and at Greg. How tactful Greg had been, for Arthur did not seem dowcast, but rather more eager to please at the desk. He was much more pleasant to an elderly lady, as Iris lingered near the desk the next morning, waiting for Greg to come out.

"Yes, ma'am, there's a book about the local flowers at a bookshop in town. I'll write down the name of it for ye— you'll be able to match the flowers with the names. It is a good one, my niece Yseult uses it all the time in her painting!"

His florid face was even redder when he finished the little speech, but he seemed pleasant about the matter. Iris went with Greg to the tiny red car, and grinned when he moved his legs cautiously about inside the small space.

"Now, where would you like to go? It is your day!"

She had thought about that, too, she wanted Greg to see some of the beautiful places she and Yseult had seen. So they set out, and stopped at several of the coves, and watched the fishermen mending nets, and the children running about, the tourists riding donkeys. They had a fine luncheon at the best place Yseult had showed Iris, and Greg visibly relaxed that day. He was a good man, thought Iris, as she had been thinking. He genuinely cared about his people. He wanted things to go smoothly for them, and for the guests in his hotels.

She told Greg about the incident at the desk, about the old lady and the flower book. He nodded, pleased. "Yes, I think Arthur just needs some prodding in that direction, of service and considering the needs and wishes of people. You cannot make it all cut and dried, supply four towels and two teas, and one vase of flowers, and present the account to them. A hotel is a home away from home to people who travel, whether for business or for pleasure. If they have a special want, they should have it. If the tea room is closed, and the guests late, tea should be sent to their room with no fuss about it. If they got caught in a rainstorm, as happened the other day, they should have a fire in their fireplace, warmed towels, hot water, and fresh tea or coffee, as they wish, with no shouting. I think I showed Arthur this week what I mean when I want good service given to people. I stuck with him for eight days, and followed him about, and when he refused service, I offered it. He got a bit upset a time or two—'' Greg grinned down at her as he stretched out in the lawn chair beside the small restaurant patio.

''Yes, probably. but example is a good way of teaching,'' agreed Iris contentedly. Greg had solved his problem, he was happy, and so was she. ''I have enjoyed this time in Cornwall so much, Greg! Thank you for letting me come with you!''

''It was my pleasure,'' he said, and he seemed to mean it.

Peter arrived that night, and the next day they said their farewells, and set out to return to Greece. They stopped the night in Salisbury, saw the cathedral there, and visited Stonehenge early the next morning, and were awed by its strangeness.

Then Peter took them on to Heathrow Airport, and put them on the executive jet at noon.

''I've put him on the payroll full-time,'' said Greg, on the plane, as they buckled themselves in.

''Peter? Oh, how nice!'' exclaimed Iris.

''You don't often meet such a knowledgeable chap, such a good driver and proud of his country, and all that. I asked him if he would like to work for us full-time, and he agreed. I was quite pleased. He'll report to our London office, and be available to drive our people about the country, and up to Scotland and over to Wales.''

''Do you ask for references?'' asked Iris curiously.

''Oh, we had those before he drove us the first time,'' said

Greg, his smile disappearing. "Wealthy people cannot be too careful. Too many terrorists about."

Iris swallowed, and the plane zoomed up into the air. Every time she was about to be happy and carefree, something happened. Just the word "terrorists" made her feel chilled all down her spine.

The jet landed in Athens in late afternoon. They transferred at once to the smaller plane, and flew on to the island where Greg's family lived. The sky darkened, and it was dusk in the late June evening before they circled to land at the small landing strip.

The Land Rover and the Lincoln Continental were there to meet them. Greg turned to Iris when they were well settled in the car.

"Iris—I did not tell you before. There is a surprise waiting for us at the house."

By his tone he did not think it was a pleasant one.

"A 'surprise'—" she said. "What is it?"

"We have guests," he said, and told her. So she was braced for it when they arrived, and got out of the limousine a little stiffly.

Charmian ran out onto the terrace, her white dress fluttering, looking like some blond goddess out of the Greek past. Iris knew her sister was aware how the lights flattered her.

"Darling sister! How good to see you!" cried Charmian, and hugged her, kissing the air next to her cheek. "I brought your clothes! Mother said you were lonely!"

With that she flung herself into Greg's unwary arms, and smacked his face with her lips. From the house came also Kyria Lydia, and Iris kissed her lightly.

Then someone else came out—Petros Diophantus! His broad face beamed, he held out both arms.

She held out one hand, and coolly shook his. "How are you, Mr. Diophantus!"

"Well, I am well and happy!" he boomed. "Now we can make progress about our line of clothes!"

Greg's eyebrows rose, he disengaged himself from Charmian's clinging arms. Vanessa and Xanthe came out, in black.

"The widows have greeted me," said Charmian, and gave Iris an outrageous wink. "You really should encourage them to wear colors! Widow's weeds are so passé!"

So, she was making trouble already, thought Iris, as she saw Vanessa's furious look. Vanessa was not a widow, she was not even a wife! She would resent Charmian's remarks, and even more her blond beauty. Trouble ahead. The holiday was over.

Chapter Nineteen

Iris was glad to go to bed that night. The long plane journey was always tiring to her, even though she did nothing but sit and read and eat! There was something about the jet noise and rumble, the hurling from one vehicle to another, the confusion and sensations, that was somehow exhausting.

The next morning, she rose late, and had breakfast in her bedroom. She had heard Greg taking a shower earlier, so knew he was up and probably working.

She was reluctant to face Charmian. From long experience, she knew Charmian's capacity to make trouble. Last evening at dinner, Charmian had managed to monopolize the attention of both Alex and Greg. Alex had come to dinner, unusual for him, and ate little, but talked eagerly to Charmian, asking questions about New York and mutual friends.

What did Charmian want? She would not willingly leave her modeling assignments to come for an indefinite stay in Greece, except for some important reason.

And her mother, Shelley, had sent her, had insisted on her coming. Iris had gathered that much. Shelley was not kindly to Iris, so the motive would be malicious, something that would take away from Iris.

Well, time would reveal what Charmian wanted. It always did. Usually too late to prevent her grabbing with both hands what belonged to someone else.

Charis was unpacking for her, and gave her a sympathetic smile when Iris finally got up. "Long journey, very tiring?" she asked, hopeful for gossip.

"Yes, long and tiring, but very beautiful, Charis. We were in a most beautiful place in England, with wild flowers and the sea."

"More beautiful than Greece?" asked Charis incredulously.

Iris laughed. "No, not so beautiful!" she appeased her.

Her spirits lightened. She was not alone, Greg would protect her! She might resent his orders at times, but he had an eye out for all his own, and Iris now "belonged" to him!

She put on her yellow sundress, sorted out her sketches from the journey and put them away in a drawer. No time now to work them out into paintings, but later she would.

Kyria Lydia was in the living room area with Melania when Iris came downstairs about ten-thirty. Greg was working alone at the panel with the telephones. He gave Iris a wave and a smile, she blew a kiss to him along with a giggle. He mocked a lunge at her, then the telephone rang and he sank back into the seat with a sigh.

Kyria Lydia and Melania broke into smiles at the sight. Lydia looked pleased and happy.

"You had a good journey! You are happy!" she said, with satisfaction.

"It was lovely! Greg worked and I sketched!" She sat down with them and told them some of the sights, her blue eyes sparkling. "But when did Charmian arrive?"

"Two days ago, in the company jet of your father," said Kyria Lydia, a slight frown on her forehead. "I did not know she was coming. And to bring Petros with her! Well—I telephoned Greg in England, and he instructed me what to do. I put them in the Low House with Alex. Charmian was displeased. In fact, she wanted your Blue Suite!"

"That is like her," said Iris dryly. "Pay no attention. Greg is the boss, and he knows her, I think."

Melania said softly, "She went upstairs before we knew it, Iris. I did not know what she was doing. The first thing we knew, she came downstairs, and asked why you did not sleep with your husband! And she demanded the Blue Suite be made ready for her!"

Iris sighed. They were letting her know what she was in for. She picked up some embroidery, and began working on it mechanically.

Presently Charmian came. Seeing Iris there, she sent two maids over to her room and they returned with elaborate boxes tied with golden ribbons.

"Mother said she had no chance to get wedding presents for you, Iris. The wedding took place so quickly! So she bought some things in New York, and asked me to bring them with me."

"You are both very kind," said Iris formally. She began unfastening the boxes. Greg left the telephones, and came to see what was in them.

One box after another revealed a rainbow of silks, all undergarments and nightclothes. Pink and blue and yellow silks in camisoles and teddies, with lace inserts, negligees and nightdresses so brief they made Iris blush to see them. She did like one blue nightdress, a simpler one of blue cotton and white lace, with matching gown. "I chose that," said Charmian. "I told mother that Greece must be hot, and you do like cotton."

307

"You are very thoughtful, Charmian," said Iris. Charmian came over and hugged and kissed her, though she knew Iris did not like to be touched. So she was putting on an act of sisterly affection. What for?

"I'll help you take them upstairs to your room," said Charmian. Greg returned to the telephones, and Iris began to gather up the pretties. Charis came to help, and Melania folded garments neatly into the boxes.

All four girls went upstairs to the Blue Suite. "I was amazed to find that you were not in your husband's bedroom," said Charmian, giving Iris a sly look.

"Were you?" asked Iris coolly. She set the boxes on the small table. "Charis, would you put these in the drawers sometime today? The gowns can be hung up in the wardrobe."

"Yes, Kyria Iris," said Charis softly. She began to smooth the garments into the bottom drawer of the chest.

Charmian stopped Iris as she turned to leave the room. Melania hesitated, then sped away on her sandals, with the effect of flight. "Iris, I want to speak to you!" Now the old imperious tone was back.

"What is it, Charmian?"

"You know what Greg's mother did to me? She put me way over in that other house, that ancient one! Across the hall from Alex! I think it was insulting! As your sister, I should be in the main house, right here!"

"Your mother and father were over there, Charmian. It is quite comfortable."

Charmian frowned. "You don't understand! I ought to be here! I am your sister. And it isn't—well—decent! I mean, I am alone in that house with two men!" She managed to sound fearful!

"I am sure you can manage that," said Iris. She turned and left the room. Charmian hastened after her.

"Iris, listen to me! You should be in the bedroom with

your husband! Don't you want your marriage to last as long as possible? If you are doing your old touch-me-not act, he won't like it! I warn you."

"My marriage is not your concern, Charmian," Iris found the courage to say.

Charmian tried to put her arm about Iris, but Iris slipped from under it, and started down the stairs.

"But I want your Blue Suite, it is perfect for me!" said Charmian plaintively. "If the other bedrooms are not furnished here, let me have your bedroom! I won't be any trouble. But I want to be in the Main House. It is only courteous to me!"

"It was Greg's decision," Iris said wearily. "If you want it changed, ask Greg!"

"All right! I'll tell him it is all right with you!" and Charmian smiled radiantly. She sped past Iris on the stairs, and down to the telephone panels. She came up to Greg, and stood behind him, and put her hands on his shoulders possessively.

"Greg, darling, Iris says I may have the Blue Suite!" She hugged him, and tried to kiss his cheek. He stood up, and the chair was between them.

"What do you say? You want my wife's bedroom?" he roared. "Absolutely not! Are you out of your mind!"

His mother's mouth twitched, she studied her embroidery intently. Alex was wheeling himself in the door, and could hear it all.

"No, no, Greg, I know she would rather be with you," smiled Charmian. "But I want to be in this house, it is— more convenient! And I don't want to be alone in that other house with just two men about!"

"You don't feel safe?" asked Greg gently. Iris knew that tone, Charmian did not. Iris sat down on the couch, and picked up a scrap of white material.

"No, not really," said Charmian, managing to look helpless. "I mean—the lock is not secure—"

"Oh, that can be fixed!" said Greg. "I'll get a man on that right away. We'll put a double lock on that, so that my cousin in a wheelchair will not break down your door and rape you!"

The expression on her face was not pleasant. Alex cried out, "Charmian, what are you saying to him?" in a reproachful tone.

Charmian flounced away, right past Alex, though he tried to catch her hand. She hated being laughed at, it made her furious.

Iris took a scarlet poppy from the vase before her. She dried the stem, and laid it on the white cloth. It stood out beautifully. She sketched it, looking into the scarlet heart of it, then sideways, with the petals lying gently against each other, and the green stem curving down.

Finally she had a small sketch she liked. She transferred it to the cloth, and began to outline the pencil lines in scarlet thread. Melania and Lydia watched her.

She finished it quickly, and handed it to Lydia. "There. I thought I might make this the symbol of my dresses. What do you think? Does it look all right?"

"It is beautiful, Iris!" her mother-in-law praised, smoothing the thread. "A scarlet poppy! The symbol of Greece."

"Yes, my love for Greece, the scarlet courage of her people, the scarlet blood they have shed for their country."

Greg heard them, he seemed to hear everything, even when he was absorbed in his work. He looked at the little embroidered scarlet poppy and green stem thoughtfully, and picked up the cloth. "This is beautiful, Iris. It would be your symbol? Yes, the symbol of Iris Poppea."

Petros Diophantus came in later, and heard the idea, and

was pleased with it. "Let us work on dresses today, Iris. Surely you must have many ideas."

"Yes, I do, Petros," she said. Greg's standing up against her sister had pleased her, and calmed her nerves. He had bested Charmian so easily! Perhaps her marriage would work out after all. "I brought down some of my sketches."

They looked over the sketches, and Melania and Charis brought from the sewing room some of the blouses and dresses Iris had begun. Petros looked them over critically, liked some, made suggestions for others that would make them more practical for mass designing.

"These are single items," he drew out two of the gowns. "Designer items, to be handled singly. But the others could be mass-produced, maybe making a dozen or so and having them embroidered. They would be sold then in Athens and in New York, should sell very well. Yes, yes, I like this immensely!"

"Thank you, Petros. Did you have other ideas?"

They talked through luncheon, though Charmian tried to monopolize the conversation. Greg had a suggestion. "There is one more bedroom in the Low House, Iris. Why not turn that into a sewing and designing room? Petros could work there, if he must!"

"I must," grinned Petros. "I will work beautifully with Kyria Iris! Together we will go places!"

Greg frowned heavily. "My wife is going nowhere with you! I am allowing you to work with her only for a short time! She wishes to design some dresses, very well! But I do not wish her to continue a career!"

There was a heavy silence. Iris at the end of the table lowered her head, and felt tears sting her eyes. He still did not understand her need to design and prove herself! She had dreamed of this for so many years! And now he waved it away like a butterfly!

"Well, well," said Petros uneasily. "We will work out one line, the white line with embroidery that Kyria Iris has planned. We shall see how it works, eh?" And he brightened up. He thought Greg would come around, thought Iris.

But Greg was stubborn, he knew what he wanted, and was determined to have his own way, she knew that. Charmian looked from one to the other alertly, as though picking up clues. She must see that this issue divided Iris from her husband!

She worked with Petros the rest of the day, and then the next morning, Kyria Lydia had a suggestion for Iris. "Let us go down to the village, Iris. I want you to see some of the beautiful embroidery done by the women there. It is quite unique."

Iris hesitated. "I should like to go, but Petros—I promised to work with him today."

"We will be back by luncheon. He never arises early," said Kyria Lydia with a mischievous smile. "Come along, Melania, we shall need your good advice. You know the village women."

Melania brightened a little. She had been unusually sober and quiet since Iris had returned, since Charmian had come, Iris knew.

"Thank you, I shall be happy to come, Aunt Lydia."

As they were setting out, with a couple of boxes of Iris-designed blouses and two dresses, they saw someone at the doorway of the Low House. Charmian stood there, yawning, stretching, very lovely in a green negligee and nothing else, her silvery hair streaming about her shoulders. And Alex was in the wheelchair behind her, they had obviously come from his room.

Melania turned away, tears in her eyes. Lydia curtly told the chauffeur to start the car. "She is shameless," Lydia muttered to Iris, her eyes blazing.

"It might mean nothing," said Iris. "She likes to make a scene, she is a model and actress, you remember." She had seen the look on Melania's face, the hurt distress in her eyes.

"Did they have an affair in New York?" asked Lydia bluntly.

Iris shrugged. "She does not confide in me."

Iris deliberately changed the subject, and questioned Lydia about the embroidery. "I did not know whether to make up patterns for them, or ask what they could supply."

"I think you should see the designs they usually make," said Lydia. "They are typical of this island. There are three women who are—what you would say—leaders of the women on the island. If they accept the work, you will win over all the women who can embroider well. They could start with their own patterns, then gradually you might introduce others for the American trade."

They discussed this animatedly. Melania was even more quiet than usual, but finally joined in. "I know one girl who is especially skillful, and she likes to experiment with designs. She studied it in a special school in Athens, then returned home when her mother became ill. Nike is very talented."

In the village, Lydia directed them to one large cottage, with tile roof and beautiful pottery jars in the cottage yard. The small flower beds were brilliant with scarlet poppies, blue iris, and some yellow flowers like daisies or coreopsis. Two women in black sat in the doorway, embroidery hoops in their wrinkled hands, busily at work on some white cloth. They rose to greet the women courteously, and bowed to Kyria Lydia.

Lydia asked them to show Iris their work. Iris examined it eagerly. It was beautifully executed, with designs of the double-headed eagle, typical of the freedom symbols of the Greeks. It was in blue silk on coarse white linen, in chain stitch, satin stitch, and backstitch. Lydia told Iris the patterns were being done for tourist shops near the docks.

Iris did not care for the double-headed eagle design, it reminded her too much of the German and Austrian war symbols. But their work was so good.

"Do they make other designs?" she asked. She could not understand the strong dialect of the women, their thick speech was studded with local words unknown to her. Lydia translated.

"Yes, they can do the ships, the stylized birds, and so on," was the answer.

One of the women went inside the cottage, and returned with several bits of cloth, showing what they could do. Iris showed them the blouses, and asked if they might do some flowers on the sleeves of the blouses, and around the yoke. They talked about this for a time, and finally agreed. Yes, they would do it for her, the Kyria Iris, who had married Gregorios Venizelos.

They could complete the work in less than one week, they said, and finally smiled, showing yellowed teeth. They would be glad of the work, one added. Not many tourists came to the island this year.

Iris left one blouse with each of them, and they went on to see Nike. Melania led them to a small cottage about two hundred yards away. A lovely girl came to the door when they approached.

Melania greeted Nike with a kiss on each cheek, then introduced her. Nike was about Melania's height, but very slim and drawn. Iris thought she had been working hard, her young hands were wrinkled.

She invited them into the cottage, and gave them small honey cakes and hot black coffee. She was treated by Melania and Lydia like an equal, Iris noted. It was probably her education that caused this, or perhaps they were distantly related.

In the bedroom, Iris glimpsed a narrow bed, and an elderly woman lying with closed eyes. This must be her ill mother. No signs of a man about. Nike probably had to earn a living for them both.

Nike's black eyes lit up at the idea of doing embroidery for them. "You mean it? There is so little market here," she said. "Let me show you what I have done. I meant to send these to Athens, but have not had a chance." She opened a box, to show them squares of cloth with beautifully embroidered designs. "These are for pillow covers, they need not be done on special cloth, so long as they are washable," she said.

Iris grew more and more enchanted as she turned over the cotton and linen squares. Nike had designed these with talent and charm. One matching set was of a small stylized shepherd and shepherdess, with little stick arms and legs. Another was of several little animals, one of a pig, one a cow, one a goat, one a lamb. She showed imagination and humor and they would be adorable for a child's room.

There were others that Iris could use, of roses, carnations, poppies, iris, willow leaves, olives and their leaves, and so on.

"Could you do this one on the sleeves of the blouse, here?" Iris showed her a blouse with very full sleeves. Nike took the blouse and examined it.

"Yes. I think a narrow band from the shoulder to the wrist, a rose alternated with its leaves, then another rose, and so on. The material is very thin. I believe it would be best to space them wide apart."

Nike showed a keen understanding of the fabrics, and a willingness to try new patterns. They discussed it for a time, and Iris left the two dresses and blouses with her, to do patterns they had decided upon. One dress would have the gold key design on wrist and hem, the other dress would have deep blue butterflies and pale green ones. The blouses would be done in floral motifs.

Iris gave her the embroidery thread she had brought with her, and Nike promised to have all the work done in a week. This would be much faster than the older women.

On the ride home, Iris expressed her doubt to Lydia. "I hate to think of her staying up all night working. She looks exhausted!"

"Do not trouble yourself. Now that she has this work to do, she will hire someone to do the heavy work in the cottage and in the vegetable plot. One of the fishermen who is too injured to go out, he will be glad of this work. So you are helping several people."

"Oh, I'm glad." Iris was relieved. Nike looked too frail to do heavy work. "She is so lovely—has she no special man friend?"

Both of them looked at Melania, who shook her head. "There was a fisherman she loved, the marriage was set. But he died in a storm at sea, and she went to Athens to train for a career. Gregorios sent her. However, when her mother became ill, and there was no relative to nurse her, Nike returned home. She is a good girl, with a gentle heart. She is very happy to have the work to do that she loves. You will see that she does good work for you."

Petros was very pleased to hear that some village women would do the embroidery for them. He and Iris worked all that afternoon on some more dress designs, and a couple of suits. Her idea of an all-white line, accented by the embroidery, pleased him.

That evening after dinner, Iris was glad to sit back on the couch and listen to music. Petros was sketching idly on a pad, the telephones were quiet.

Alex had been trying to stand that day, and now he was out of his wheelchair, limping about, holding to Charmian. She teased him, smiling up at him intimately. His face glowed. Melania could not look at them.

Melania had tried so hard to help Alex, thought Iris savagely. Now Charmian would take over, and he would forget Melania. Men!

"Dance with me," urged Charmian, and persuaded Alex on his unsteady legs to dance with her to the music of the stereo set. Greg watched them critically, frowning slightly. Finally as Alex stumbled for the third time, his face turning white with pain, Greg went over to them.

"This is enough, Alex," he said curtly. "Come and sit down, it is foolish to press yourself. You are doing very well, but you do not want to reinjure that leg."

Alex sank into the wheelchair, gasping for the pain, but still protesting. Charmian glided right into Greg's arms, and had her arms about his neck before he realized what she was doing.

"Then you dance with me, Greg!" She smiled into his eyes. She moved sensuously against him to the music. "I just know you are a marvelous dancer!"

Iris glanced involuntarily at Greg's face. He was smiling, he had the taut expression of a man who held a lovely woman in his arms and enjoyed it. Charmian pressed herself against his thighs, and Iris saw there was not a bit of daylight between them.

Her lips compressed, she felt a fool for minding so much. Charmian always enjoyed men's attentions, she thrived on them, it meant nothing.

Only they were so closely pressed together!

Stop it, Iris, she said to herself. Don't mind—he doesn't really care, he doesn't really like her. She drew a deep breath, and concentrated on the embroidery in her hands.

"Again, darling?" asked Charmian, her hands clinging to

Greg's neck. He tried to detach her, smiling, and then oddly he glanced over to Vanessa!

The handsome Greek woman sat there, her black eyes glowing like coals as she stared at them. She and Greg exchanged a long look. Iris had the uneasy feeling he had forgotten Charmian in his arms. Charmian must have felt the same, for she slapped his shoulder lightly.

"Darling—dance with me! Don't waste the music!" Her startling blue eyes flickered from Greg to Vanessa and back.

Had Greg once had an affair with his distant cousin? Iris tried to crush down the thought, but it kept surfacing. There was something between them, she sensed it.

This time Iris could not look at the dancers. She closed her eyes, pretending to listen to the music, as Greg and Charmian danced in the space between two rugs. The tune ended, there was a slight pause between the numbers.

"Greg—I want to dance again!" said Charmian. Iris opened her eyes, to see Greg standing before her, his hand out to her.

"Dance with me, adored?" he asked, his eyes alight with mischief and passion combined.

She allowed herself to be pulled upright, and into his arms, he moved smoothly with her across the rug, to the bare marble floor. They danced slowly to the dreamy music, swaying in each other's arms. For the first time, Iris enjoyed being held by a man in the dancing. This was Greg whom she loved. She did not mind his touch, she enjoyed it.

Charmian sank down sulkily into a chair, watching them alertly. She looked ready to pounce when the music stopped. Petros was pretending not to pay attention, but he seemed interested in what would happen.

Greg turned Iris in his arms, and smoothly danced her to the terrace, into the dimness lit only by the moon. The music reached them softly, and Greg gathered her closer into his arms, both arms about her slim body.

"You do not mind my touch so much?" he whispered in her ear. She looked up at him.

"You knew about that?" she asked. "It was because—I mean—from my childhood—"

He nodded. "I understand, love. I am sorry you had a bad time of it, yet I am not sorry you do not wish the touch of any other man on you! I am a little possessive, you know."

She giggled, she could not help it. " 'A little'!"

"You laugh at me?" He lifted her face with his hand under her chin, and pressed his mouth on hers, teasingly, brushing his lips back and forth on her mouth.

Both heard the click of high heels on the marble. Charmian was brazenly coming out to them! Greg caught her hand, and turned her, his arm about her waist. "Come," he said. They walked past Charmian, her mouth opened to speak, they were past her.

In the hallway, near the stairs, Greg said cheerfully, "*Kalinikta! Kalinikta,* all!" And walked Iris up the steps with him.

It was very obvious where they were going, and Iris's face burned hot with embarrassment. But she had to giggle when they reached Greg's room, and he opened the door and ushered her inside. The thought of Charmian's amazement was rather sweet.

Greg shut the door after them, a grin on his face. "There are times when one must be firm," he said, and Iris burst out laughing.

His face grew more serious as he took her once more into his arms. "Why did you tell your sister she could have the Blue Suite?" he asked. "I was hurt by this."

"Oh, Greg!" Amazed by his confession, Iris hastened to reassure him, her hands on his bronzed cheeks. "I did not agree, that was another of her little truth-twisting statements. She kept after me and after me, until I finally said, ask Greg. I thought you would say no, and make her accept that. She listens to nobody when she wants something. She keeps after me, and goes on and on, until I find it hard to convince her I mean no.''

"Ah, So that is the way of it. She is very spoiled, she needs a man with a firm hand,'' said Greg disapprovingly. "Perhaps I shall help her father arrange her marriage.''

"If she didn't get what she wanted, she would get a divorce,'' said Iris soberly. "Shelley did.''

"So? So that is not the answer, eh.'' He shook his black curly head. "Too bad. Well, forget her for now. I did not bring you to my bed to discuss others!''

He turned her about, to unzip the fastening of the blue silk, and soon had the dress off her. He tossed the dress over a chair, then found the way to remove the bra and teddie, from the sets Charmian had brought to her, "Very pretty, eh?'' he breathed, as he pressed a kiss on her neck. "I am grateful for that, anyway!''

He laid her down on his bed, the covers had been drawn back by the maid, and his pajamas laid out. He ignored them, tossing them onto her dress. He stripped out of his white shirt and navy blue slacks, and soon was down to his bronzed skin. He was so handsome, he gleamed in the pale golden lamplight, and Iris admired him shyly.

He came and lay down beside her, putting his arm under her, and turning her to him. "Pretty Iris,'' he murmured, and moved his lips over her cheeks and to her ear. He nibbled at the ear seductively, and made a shiver go down her spine. "Pretty girl, lovely girl. I like marriage to you very much!''

He sounded very self-satisfied, and she giggled against his bronzed throat. "You do? Oh, you have all your own way! No wonder you like it! I do whatever you want. You said pack up and come, and I did. You tell me to go to bed, and I do. No matter what you ask, I do it, no wonder you like marriage!'' She managed to sound very plaintive.

"But of course, that is the way marriage should be," he teased. "The man is the boss, and the woman is glad to do what he wishes! As they say in the United States, I am the chief, and you are the Indian!"

Iris burst out laughing at his bland statement. He laughed also, then began to kiss her, starting at her throat, and moving down and down. Little delicious thrills went zinging up and down her spine as he continued.

His lips were honey sweet. He nibbled at her soft flesh, lingered over her firm breasts, and took a nipple in his mouth. He sucked it, absorbed, shaking it in his lips until the nipple stood up pert and proud. He moved down in the bed, to reach the soft waist, and down further to her thighs. His hands were stroking over her, down to her knees, and then back up again on the tender sensitive insides of her thighs.

His fingers caressed her intimately, and he smiled at her in the lamplight, watching her expressions. "You like this, eh? You like my touch now?"

"Yes—" she whispered it. "Yes, I like—your touch, Gregorios. You know me, I think, know what I—enjoy—"

He smiled, pleased. Her hands went to his head, as he bent over her thighs and kissed her there. Her fingers clenched in his thick curly hair, and tightened when he kissed her more deeply. She felt as though her insides were burning with heat, desire raging through her, melting her to a molten fire. She moved impatiently on the bed as he continued to kiss her, and tongued her with his clever tongue.

"Do you like this—and this—"

"Oh, yes, yes—" she moaned helplessly. "Oh, Greg—please—please go on—finish—"

But it pleased him to tease her more than usual tonight. He held back, kissing her, moving his fingers over her, tormenting her with his slowness.

She caught at his shoulders, finally, and dragged him to

her. He let her do it, otherwise she would not have succeeded, for he was much stronger than she. Her legs were parted, he came down between her slim legs, and settled himself into place.

He thrust gently, finding the soft places of her. He let his hard masculinity find her feminine sweetness, and mingle with it, slowly, teasingly, stroking up and down for a time, until she lifted her hips impatiently to him. She was blazing with fire, burning hot, almost unconscious of any modesty. She was all desire, all seductive womanhood, needing him to complete herself, to make the marvelous whole of which she was half.

He came into her, deliberately, sliding, sliding, until they were one person, one whole, complete, oneness that was so beautiful that tears slid down her cheeks. He kissed them and licked them with his tongue, and whispered love words to her.

"My dearest, my adored, my darling wife, my woman, you are all the honey in the world, you are the sweet honey I have longed for always—move with me—ah, yes, yes, move—like that—oh, ye gods! gods and angels—ah, it is good, it is good—ahhhh!" And he cried out, and they came together, and blazed up to the pinnacle of ecstasy as one person.

She wakened in the night, slowly, to find the blueness of the dark outside had entered their room and encompassed them. The stars blazed beyond the windows.

She stirred in his arms, and turned over lazily, to rest her cheek against the mat of thick curly hair. Greg half wakened, and his lips pressed on her forehead.

"Iris, adored," his sleepy voice murmured.

She stroked her hand slowly from his shoulder to his elbow. He murmured again, and seemed to sleep.

Then he spoke again, in a husky voice. "Vanessa," he said.

Iris stiffened. "What about her?" she muttered.

"Um, umm," said Greg, and rolled over, and she knew he had spoken in his sleep.

Iris had come sharply awake now, and it was unpleasant. Why had he spoken the name of his distant cousin? She thought of the blazing look in Vanessa's beautiful dark eyes as Greg had danced with Charmian.

Oh, surely, surely, if Greg had had an affair with Vanessa, it must be over, in the past. Except that the way they looked at each other—Iris covered her mouth with her hand, to stifle a hurt cry.

Chapter Twenty

The designs were going well. Iris and Petros worked several hours a day on them. The pile of garments grew rapidly, all based on white, with embroidered or braided designs on them.

"I have an idea, Kyria Iris," said Petros one afternoon. "I have been sketching and thinking, and working in the room in the Low House which Gregorios kindly set aside for me. You have an all-white line. I have thought of an all-black line to complement yours. It would be black blouses and suits, black gowns, very sophisticated."

"Black?" Iris echoed, trying not to show her shock. She did not care much for black, it meant mourning and death to her, though to some society women it was the basis for their very chic wardrobe. She glanced through his proffered sketches thoughtfully. She especially liked two of the suits.

"Yes, black. It would be a good contrast to yours. Your

line would be all-white basis, mine would be all-black. I thought to copy your idea—if you kindly permit—to use embroidery also on these, use Greek designs. What do you think?"

The more she looked at his sketches and thought about the ideas, the more she liked them. She had been a little troubled about her all-white line. Petros was helping her on the line, would Nadia Egorova think the work was too much that of Petros Diophantus? It must be Iris's work, or Iris was proving nothing, about her talent, about her ability to be an assistant to Nadia Egorova.

Lydia thought it was an excellent idea also. She loaned them not only Charis, who had been helping them already, but also two other women of the household especially skilled in dressmaking, and Petros began to turn out some black suits and gowns.

The first work from the village women came back beautiful. Gregorios also relaxed from his displeasure in their working his wife so hard. The thought of having real wage-paying work for his villagers was irresistible. He now approved of their going ahead to make one line of clothing. But he kept a sharp eye on Iris, to see that she gave him plenty of time.

The big problem was Charmian. She was making trouble, visiting Alex in his room, making sure she was seen by the disapproving greek servants and Melania. She kept trying to attract Greg, getting his "advice" on various matters, urging him to let up on his work and take her places, and so on.

"You really do work too hard and long, Gregorios," she would murmur, sitting on the arm of his chair in the late evening. "Why don't you show me the island? We could drive about tomorrow afternoon—or tonight! Show me the island by moonlight!"

"Not tonight," he said firmly, almost upsetting her bodily as he rose abruptly and went over to Iris. "Iris, darling, come for a walk with me!"

And he carried off Iris into the moonlight! They strolled about, drinking in the beauty of the scene, the huge white moon in the deeply blue purple night sky, the brilliant sparkling stars. She enjoyed the fragrant scents from the garden, as the coolness released their perfume.

"She is being a troublemaker," said Greg. "Does she not wish to return to her work in New York City?"

"She admitted the work had turned light this summer," said Iris, with a sigh. "She has done one good thing, Alex is standing and walking and exercising more."

"Um. She is a fascinating woman. Like Aphrodite rising from the sea," muttered Greg, and Iris felt a jealous pang. They walked in silence for a time, Greg's arm about her, but Iris felt distant from him, as he thought.

"I suppose Charmian photographs well?" asked Greg abruptly, and Iris had the unpleasant knowledge that Greg's deep thoughts had been of Charmian.

"Very beautifully," she told him. "The bones of her face, her slim body, the way she walks—photographers have told her she is a dream to photograph. She longs to act, she practices by the hour. I used to listen to her reading lines, and she does have a way of expressing them well. And she can get an innocent expression. I think she could do ingenue parts well. And that silvery hair—she is very beautiful."

"Um, yes, she is most beautiful." He sank deeply into thought again, and said little more as they walked.

Iris thought also. She could not permit Charmian to wreck her life. Nor that of Alex and Melania. Charmian would never tie herself to a helpless blind man. She was too much like her mother. Why should Charmian tease Alex into thinking she adored him, only hurting Melania, and leading Alex into later despair?

Charmian loved to act, loved troublemaking, and adored modeling. Well—Iris could offer her modeling! When they went back inside, Charmian was trying to get Alex to dance with her. His face was lined with weariness, he shook his head.

"No, I am too tired, I am sorry. I should not have tried to dance earlier." He was ashamed, his head drooped. He began to wheel himself to the doorway. His ego was being smashed to bits to amuse her!

"Charmian, I wonder if you would help Petros and me tomorrow," said Iris clearly, sitting down on the edge of a straight chair. "We are at the stage when the dresses should be tried on live models to see how they move. Would you be willing—"

Her sulky face lit up. "Oh, yes, I'd love to! Have you made some in my size?"

"Of course I have, naturally!" Iris managed a smile. "So has Petros. What about eleven tomorrow? Can you be ready?"

"Oh, earlier than that. What about ten? I'm so hot here, I really cannot sleep late!" Charmian was standing alertly, her startlingly vivid blue eyes shining. She tossed back her loose waves of ash silver hair. "What are you working on? When can I see them?"

"At ten tomorrow," promised Iris. "We'll bring down some of the gowns. We could set up a screen—a little changing room for you, Charmian. Do you have some suitable pumps to wear? And some silver sandals? For Petros's gowns, you will need some black-strapped sandals!"

"I'll get them out tonight! How shall I do my hair?"

Petros chimed in gallantly, he had been witnessing the antagonisms of the past week.

"You look stunning with your hair up or down, Kyria Charmian! However, in order not to detract too much from my gowns, will you kindly humor me and wear your hair in a chignon?"

"I'll do it. Well, I'd better get to bed early if I'm to model tomorrow!" And off she danced to bed.

Kyria Lydia raised her eyebrows in some amazement. Iris winked slightly at her, and turned to Melania. "And you, Melania, I wish you would model some of the gowns also. I have designed some for people more our size and height. Would you help us out?"

"If you wish it," said Melania, in a low tone. "I am not experienced, you know. I do not know how—"

"We shall teach you," promised Petros gaily. He managed to catch Iris's hand and kiss it before saying, "Now I must go off to bed also, and be rested for the morning. I shall bring over my gowns by nine. They will not have the embroidery on them, but we can get some idea of how they flow. Eh? So, *kaliníkta*!"

And off he went also. Lydia folded her work and indicated she was ready to go to bed. Greg caught Iris's hand, and drew her with him up the stairs, murmuring, "Little peacemaker! Your sister will be happier tomorrow, and not so fussy, eh? She makes trouble when she has too much time in her empty hands!"

"So did Aphrodite," Iris told him sweetly, and he chuckled.

"My preference is for the messenger of the gods!" he teased her. He drew her into his room with him, and shut the door firmly.

As she lay in his bed later, while he slept on her breast, she reflected about Greg. He seemed to admire Charmian's beauty, while detesting her lack of character.

It was the old story. A man wanted his wife to be good and

virtuous, but that did not keep his eyes from straying to the glamorous sophisticated women like Charmian and Vanessa. I wonder, thought Iris, staring into the darkness, how long I will hold and attract Greg. Until I am plump with pregnancy? Or have one or two sons for him? Then what? Left here on the island, to embroider and sketch, while he travels about the world and has women like Charmian in little apartments wherever he goes?

It was a bitter thought, and she flinched from it. But it haunted her that night and many nights. All the more reason, she told herself, to have a career ready and swinging well, so she could lose herself in her work, and not be as hurt as she might be. Work was a great salve for the hurt soul.

Greg was handsome, attractive, and very wealthy. There had probably been many women in his life, the ones she had seen in the gossip columns—and Vanessa—

Iris was glad to lose herself in the dresses and suits the next day, and the following days. She kept herself so busy she could almost forget the somberness of her possible future. They had been married in church—but so had her father. Greg spoke of a future together—but she was sure her father had meant all he said to her mother also. But her mother had died, and Hilarion Patakos had turned from one woman to another.

Greeks could be faithful—but they were also very passionate. If Greg tired of Iris, or found her not emotional enough for him, he would soon turn to another woman. Charmian had gossiped about Greg and Alex when she had been dating Alex. Two men-about-town, only the town was the world— and they had often had women in every port, like sailors.

And Iris had seen how Alex had swiftly turned from gentle Melania to the more exciting glamorous Charmian as soon as

Charmian had appeared. And Melania was hurt by his neglect, she was retreating more and more into herself.

She deserved better than Alex! But like all women, she found it difficult to deny her heart once it was given away.

Charmian was all professionalism when she started work, and through all those days. She had good advice also. She swept back and forth along the hallway in a full-length gown, turned, moved up the stairs, and back again.

"No, the hem won't do, Iris," she advised. "At least three inches shorter, I'd say. With all its width, it is too awkward to be so long. I could not dance in it," and she swirled about in a beautiful waltzing movement to show. The skirts seemed to drag about her legs.

Iris sat back on her heels, studying the hem, and nodded. "You are right, Charmian. It is much too heavy. Oh, dear, I'll have to take it apart at the waist, and start again. How do you like the bodice?"

"That depends on what you do with the skirt," said Charmian. "If you make the skirt narrow and daring, you ought to lower the bodice."

"Um. Right."

Petros was listening, watching, making notes. They had a good session that day, and the next ones. Another short dress of silk with whirling pleats came under Charmian's critical gaze. She stood before the full-length mirror, and whirled again and again.

"No, darling Iris! It won't do at all! The bodice is Shirley Temple and the skirt is Marilyn Monroe!"

Iris caught that at once. Petros had to think about it. But Charmian was quite right, her quick mind had caught the contrast. Iris took the dress apart at the waist, and started again on that one.

The suits went well, both the white ones of Iris and the black ones of Petros. Charmian graciously showed Melania how to model the suits, saying, "Watch me, Mellie! Do as I do. You walk along the runway gracefully with long steps, then you pause, slowly remove the jacket—then you sling the jacket over your shoulder and hold it with a finger."

Melania watched intently, and tried to copy her. She caught on some things well, but the chin-up sophisticated expressions were beyond her. She could only giggle when Charmian advised her,

"Mellie, listen, love! What you do is think: Those snobs, those peasants, what do they know about clothes? You lift your chin, you think nasty thoughts, and lo and behold, your face gets a *Vogue* expression!"

"Oh, Charmian!" said Iris, as Melania broke out into laughter. "*Vogue* girls are lovely!"

"Sure they are, but you have to keep your chin up and your nose haughty, and make sure the best profile shows. Mellie, back straight, love! Watch me—don't try to take such big steps, though, your legs aren't as long as mine! Try for the little girl look." She mixed insults with advice and charm so swiftly she had them all wide-eyed. "There, that's it—wide-eyed little girl—now that is sweet—Mellie, lift your chin!"

Charmian even made a suggestion for a new gown. "Iris, darling, I've been wanting a white brocade with a very straight skirt, and slits up the side to my—you know what," she grinned as Lydia visibly waited for a naughty word. "Could you make me something glamorous, with a copy for your show?"

"Of course, Charmian. White brocade?"

"Yes, and a wrap—summerish, but warm—maybe white velvet?"

Iris got busy with sketch pad, and later went up to look over her fabrics. She did not want an obviously sexy look for her line. How to do the slits so they were not vulgar? She worked on that for several hours, and finally came up with a solution. She cut, and sewed, with the help of Charis, and by the next morning at ten, she had it done.

Charmian put it on, and was delighted. The bodice was of Greek simplicity, with one shoulder bare. The waist was princess style, with no obvious waistline. The skirt widened just a little over the hips, then fell straight in front and back, and on each side were three narrow pleats. Concealed in the pleats were the slits, so that when Charmian moved swiftly the slits showed. When she stood still or moved very slowly, the pleats moved with her.

"Darling, marvelous! So subtle," Charmian praised.

"Just beautiful," sighed Petros. "I would love to do that in my black also, Kyria Iris!" His dark eyes pleaded.

"Why not?" said Iris generously. "Do let us call it *Charmian*! Do you mind, Charmian?"

Charmian was very pleased, and strode back and forth again and again, showing the gown to everyone. The gown in black turned out even more sophisticated in appearance, dignified until one saw the slits. It was subtle, teasing, not vulgar at all.

"Embroidery?" asked Kyria Lydia. "I think not—it has a look all its own."

"No, not embroidery," Iris agreed. "We will use brocade fabrics in the finished gowns, so it is self-decorated. But the lines must not be spoiled by anything."

She whipped out a white velvet jacket, with a tiny raised collar to set off Charmian's white throat and sleek chignon. Greg admired that, and the *Charmian* gown, but looked thoughtfully at Iris. She was tired, did she look haggard next to Charmian's radiant beauty? She had a feeling that she did.

"Can you get away for a few days from your work?" Greg

asked her very politely on their evening walk. "I want to take you with me tomorrow morning."

"Oh, I would love to go!" She was not flattering, though she sounded very eager. The effort to keep Charmian from teasing Melania, tormenting Alex, luring Petros, and mocking Vanessa and Xanthe—it was all getting her down. "Where are we going?"

He smiled down at her. "A secret, my Iris! But put in your suitcase a couple glamorous dresses, some high-heeled shoes for dancing—and a couple swimsuits and cover-ups. We shall be in Greek islands—I will tell you that much!"

She was content. They said nothing that night, and were off the next morning with only Lydia and Melania to see them off. Iris had a feeling of escaping as they climbed into the small company plane waiting for them at the landing field.

They flew only about forty-five minutes, not high in the clouds, but so low that Iris could admire the wine-dark seas, the sandy coves, the windblown olive trees, some shepherds with their flocks and dogs. They skimmed over some mountain peaks, and Greg pointed out a volcano. It was dormant, but he said it had erupted some years ago, and could again. "No volcano is ever really dead," he told her. "Any one can erupt again. There is activity in the earth's crust, one must be aware of that at all time, and not take nature for granted. We Greeks know that, in a way you Americans don't."

The pilot landed the small plane at a landing field, much like the one of Venizelos. A blue Cadillac came to meet them, and a polite chauffeur. He greeted Gregorios by name, and bowed on being introduced to Iris. He wore a smart olive green uniform, with gold braid.

The drive was brief, less than half an hour, and they drove up in the curved driveway of a large sprawling resort, whitewashed and drowsy in the sunlight. It was all blue and white and olive, with olive trees planted about the area, and a golf course laid out among the trees. Small blue pools dotted the lush lands.

"One of yours?" whispered Iris.

Greg nodded: "One of the most luxurious, where we might have spent our honeymoon!" He grinned down at her.

She was glad they had gone off by themselves on that occasion. This place would have overwhelmed her. They entered by an open-air lobby, with slight breezes blowing the pots of geraniums, carnations, and coreopsis. Men in olive green came to take their suitcases from the driver, and a man behind the counter almost ran to greet Greg. He was a young man with an anxious handsome face.

"You came, oh, thank you, Cousin Gregorios!" And he kissed him on both cheeks. "What trouble, what agony—"

"May I introduce my cousin to you, Iris," said Greg dryly, and with a brawny arm prevented the young man from hugging and kissing Iris. "You may shake her hand only!"

Reproachful look from melting black eyes as the young man lingered over Iris's hand. Hector was evidently longing to greet Iris as she should be greeted.

"You have to watch those Greek men," said Gregorios, and laughed at his cousin.

Hector himself took them to their cottage, a small white building with its own bedroom, bath, and living room. Outside was a little blue pool and tile floor for lounging, and some yellow lounge chairs. They were partially screened off from the next cottages by a low whitewashed wall about four feet high. There was a feeling of privacy, yet it was all in the open, and caught the wind off the mountain, and the salt of the sea.

While Iris unpacked and took a little rest, Greg went with Hector, returning to take Iris to luncheon. They ate in a beautiful dining room overlooking the sea, with vines and potted plants to give the illusion of being outdoors. A wind blew constantly from the sea, and small boats rocked in the little frivolous port. The food was delicious, the service excellent, the guests seemed happy. Iris wondered what was wrong with the hotel.

After luncheon, Greg told her he had to return to work, and he looked grim. "That's all right, I'll sketch for a time," said Iris.

Iris was stretched out on a lounge chair, in her blue sundress, the pad forgotten beside her, for enjoyment of the sunlight and cool breeze, when Greg strode back. She opened her eyes, surprised, as a shadow fell across her.

She had not seen him so angry for a long time. His mouth was drawn down into angry lines, his chin very square, and the black eyebrows met over his nose.

"Let's go," he said brusquely. "I have borrowed the car."

"You mean—pack up?" she gasped, sitting upright.

"No, no. For a drive! I shall not stay around to be party to their foolish angers!" He stormed into the cottage, got a jacket and sunglasses, and a blanket, and came back. Iris put on her small blue jacket, grabbed her purse and sunglasses, and trotted after him. He finally remembered her presence, and caught her hand, and slowed down.

At the entrance, a driver brought around the blue Cadillac, and handed Greg the car keys. He was looking apprehensively at Greg, and Iris wondered again.

In the car, Greg was silent for a time, scowling at the scene before them. He seemed to know where they were going, not driving aimlessly. Finally the scowl melted, and he turned to Iris. "What idiots!" he said.

"Your cousin?" she asked timidly. She could scarcely enjoy the ride, until Greg slowed down, and allowed her to see the cypresses whirling past the window.

"Yes, Hector and my Uncle Nestor. They quarrel all the time now. I asked them to run this resort together, they love each other. Or did! Hector's mother died early, the men are very close. Hector's wife loves her father-in-law, all was harmony. Now she is expecting a baby, and the men fight all the time. Would you believe, they cannot agree on a name for the baby who has not yet arrived? And they fight over how to run the resort, what food to order, and so on. I cannot have this disorder! The guests will be affected!"

"Oh—that is too bad." Iris gazed out the window, and they rode in silence. The drive wound up and up into the hills, until they came to a small clearing overlooking the sea, away from the village and the resort area.

Greg slowed the car, and parked it. He got out, and so did Iris, and he took her hand. They walked off into the woods, and then came out into another clearing, so quiet and peaceful that only the songs of the birds broke the stillness. And there in the center of the clearing, overlooking the sea and the valley below, was a small perfect temple, with a goddess inside.

"Oh—how perfect," whispered Iris. Any louder voice would have been sacrilege. They walked slowly together, holding hands, to the temple.

It was about ten feet across, in a circle. Inside was a small raised marble floor on which the goddess stood. The building was surrounded by narrow white columns, fluted, and with simple Doric capitals holding up a wooden roof to protect the small marble figure inside.

Iris thought it was small until she stepped inside with Greg. Then she realized the goddess was taller than she was, about six feet in height, in white marble, with an exquisite face of exceptionally pure beauty. Her arms were held out, as though in greeting, or in supplication to the god of the sea. Her gaze went beyond them, to the sea beyond.

The goddess wore a white short robe, in marble of course, with gentle carved curved lines that indicated a slight breeze that blew her garments against her lovely limbs. her arms were bare, one shoulder was bare, the bodice seemed to flutter about her slight breasts.

"Who is she?" breathed Iris, touching lightly the hem of the marble garment.

"She is said to be Selene, the goddess of the moon," Greg replied. "Local legend says she is strongly attracted to the sea-god Poseidon, a very violent god. She remains up here, and looks longingly to him, and attracts him, but is afraid of him also."

"The moon does draw the seas, that is what makes the tides," said Iris thoughtfully.

"Of course. Many myths and legends are drawn from facts of nature," he said, in his deep seductive voice. All the gravelly quality of his anger was gone from his voice. He put his arm lightly about her, and turned her to where the sea could be seen from the little temple. "Look, she faces her master, and beckons to him, and holds out her arms to him. And he tries to come from the sea to her, but growls when he cannot reach her. She is too high in her little niche."

"So they stand and watch each other, and cannot touch," said Iris sadly.

Greg smiled mischievously. "Oh, we think so, eh? But who knows? Perhaps on some moonlit night, Selene slips off her little marble stand, and out of her temple, and runs off down the hill here—and Poseidon roars a mighty roar and lashes the cliff, and manages to reach her! Eh? They could mate, and no one know it but the moon which hides its face in the clouds."

Just then a cloud slid over the face of the bright sun, and darkness came to the temple. Did the goddess move? Iris looked up at her, eyes wide with wonder. It was so mystical here, anything could happen in the silent grove where even the birds had stopped their singing for a moment.

"Would you like to remain and see how the goddess looks in the moonlight tonight?" whispered Greg into her ear, and bit the ear lobe gently.

Iris nodded. "Yes, I would like to stay." She did not know what made her say that, it was some impulse from outside herself. Perhaps the goddess had spoken instead of herself!

Greg looked immensely pleased. "Good. I brought a basket of food. Let us eat and drink here, with Selene, she will not mind, so long as we leave a bit of food for her."

They went back to the car, and got the blanket and basket of food from the trunk of the car. They sat down in the grass before the temple of the goddess and ate, and drank the crisp white wine someone had packed for them.

There were little sandwiches of rich paté, pieces of fried chicken, a box of fresh tomatoes and lettuce and other greens. There was fresh bread, still hot in a napkin. And the pastries were the favorites of Iris, *baklavá* and honey cake and persimmon cake. They ate and drank and talked a little, and gazed at the sea, as the sun slowly slid into the sea and sent up a splash of crimson and orange.

Greg leaned back on the blanket and sipped at the wine in the crystal glass. "Ah, heaven," he sighed. "If only men were not quarrelsome!"

"I have been thinking about Hector and his father," Iris told him. "I think I know what Sister Angelica would say to them."

"Oh?" Greg twisted around to look up at her. "One of the good sisters in the convent in Chicago?"

"Yes. She was very wise and old. When there was a problem, even the mother superior would go to Sister Angelica and ask advice. I remember one time two nuns who had been very close began to quarrel, and fuss, and it distressed everyone. They worked together on making robes, and I was involved also. I felt very sad that they quarreled. And it was so silly, they quarreled over the material of the robes, and the kind of decoration to put on them."

"And what did the wise sister say to them?"

"She said they must be parted. One must go to the motherhouse in San Francisco, another to a house in Toronto, Canada."

Greg sat up. "What—parted?" He stared at her. "The sister advised that?"

"Yes," said Iris smiled. "She said that was her advice. The mother superior was sad, so were we all. In fact, we were horrified! To lose both of them! But the plans were set in order. Then each sister came to the mother superior and said she would go, but the other must stay, both loved that house."

"After all that—what happened?"

"Both sisters stayed. They agreed not to fight any longer. They admitted they had been silly. The thought of parting had shocked them to admission of their faults. The mother superior fined them many many Hail Marys and good deeds, which they did together, and everybody was happy."

"Hum. Worth trying, eh?" Greg grinned at her. "Yes, it might work! I shall try it tomorrow!"

"But you have to be willing to go through with it," Iris warned him. "If you say you will send them both away—and do not—"

"Oh, I'll do it, all right!" he said, more grimly. "I cannot have their bickering. Let me see—I'll send one to Canada, and the other to Hong Kong!"

Iris laughed so her bell-like peal rang through the little grove. Greg grabbed her and pulled her down on the blanket and kissed her. He nuzzled into her neck, and kissed her soft shoulders, and pushed down the edge of the sundress bodice, so he could kiss her breasts. "Oh—Greg—not here!" she said breathlessly.

"Why not? No one will see!" And he put his hand under her dress, and stroked her thigh.

"The little goddess will! Selene—might be—jealous—Greg—don't!"

He pushed aside the basket of food, and corked the wine bottle. Then he settled her on the blanket. "Little Selene will not be angry, she knows what it is to feel desire," he whispered.

Iris glanced up at the pretty face of the goddess. Was there a smile on that face in the growing dusk? She lay back, and put her arms about Greg's neck, and her hands clutched the cloth of his shirt.

In the dim grove, they made love, slowly, luxuriously, under the darkening sky, the cypresses and olive trees, and the scent of the wild flowers and wild grasses was in their nostrils as they kissed. His mouth lingered on her lips, then moved to her throat, and to the breasts he had uncovered. Lower and lower he thrust the dress, until he could take it off her feet, and leave her there with only a bra and bikini panties to remove. He took them off, and she was naked under the breeze and his breath.

He kissed her from her head to her feet, and back up again, and shivers ran through her, not from the cool air. She felt hot and full of desire, and a sort of mysterious frenzy from their surroundings. Was there a Pan in the bushes, urging them on? Did gods laugh silently in the grove? Did Poseidon in the sea growl impatiently at their slowness? Did Selene smile down at them secretly, remembering nights like this with her lover?

Iris felt her mind blurring with Greg's passion and her own. He covered her with his naked body in the darkness, and when she looked up past his dark head, she could see the moon rising out of the sea, a white and silvery moon, glowing and fresh washed.

Greg brought their bodies together, and they slipped on the

blanket, and rolled over into the grass, hands clutching each other's wet body, moaning with the passion that gripped them. He lay back, and let her ride him, up and down, her face above his, until he could not endure the wait, and pulled her with both his hands on her hips. He brought them tight together, and she cried aloud and began to feel the sweet grippings of ecstasy.

She fell down on him, bound tightly to him at the hips, and he moved himself smoothly half in and out of her, until the ecstasy shot through her again, in an even wilder response to him. He was breathing hard, his shoulders under her hands gleamed in the moonlight from the sweat that covered him. He groaned once, and said her name, "Iris—Iris!" and pulled her down sharply, and came hard in her.

It took a while to come out of this. They lay together in the sweet-smelling grass, and clung to each other, breathing finally slowing. He said eventually, "You will be chilled—let me dress you—" And tenderly he put on each garment, and wiped her with a towel.

They drank the rest of the wine, sitting together on the blanket in silence, eating a sweet *baklavá* with the wine, and saying nothing. They did not want to break the stillness, where even the birds had gone silent with sleepiness.

It was late then, and they must go. They packed the basket, put the empty wine bottles inside, and the little food that remained. Then Iris looked up at the goddess and curtsied to her, a slight figure in the moonlight, with the pillars casting shadows on the white marble. Did she move, she seemed to wave slightly in the small temple; one arm lifted, didn't it?

"Thank you, Selene, for being our hostess and sharing your sacred grove with us," whispered Iris.

She thought Greg might laugh. Instead he bowed low, and caught Iris's hand warmly in his. The basket was at his feet.

"Thank you, Selene. Thank you for a most memorable night!"

They walked away together, and did not look back over their shoulders for fear of the goddess's wrath if they caught her running down the slope to meet her lover.

Chapter Twenty-one

Greg and Iris remained at the Greek resort two more days. In the cool mornings, Greg drove them about the island, they enjoyed the lovely wild scenery, the hills and olive trees, glimpses of primitive cottages whitewashed against the blue skies.

In the afternoon, Greg worked with his relatives; Iris stretched out in her little private patio to sunbathe. In the evenings, Greg took her to dinner and dancing. There was a fine pianist who played for the guests, anything they wished.

Iris enjoyed the dancing. Sometimes she and Greg danced the waltzes, and tango, and so on. Sometimes Greg joined the other Greek men in the line dances, often in the lead. She liked to watch the emotional outbursts of joy and pleasure of the dancing, as the men showed the guests how the Greeks danced in the old days.

Then Greg issued his ultimatum to his cousin and uncle: Hector and his pregnant wife would go to a hotel in Canada,

Nestor would go to Hong Kong. Greg would find someone else to manage the Greek resort. They were shocked silent, staring at him with great black eyes in horror.

"But we must remain—my wife's family is here—they look forward to the birth of our child!" exclaimed Hector.

"Why should I not remain? Hong Kong! It is the end of the world! To live among the heathen!" exclaimed his father.

Greg shrugged. "I cannot have such dissension in my hotels. If you wish to find other posts, I shall not stop you. But you will both leave here. I can easily find someone who will manage this well, and appreciate the beauty of the place without ruining it with his quarreling!"

He studied their faces. He was not sure this would work, but could not think of anything else to do. He added, "I shall look for someone, you will have a month to pack before you go to your next posts. If you wish to resign, let me know. You know where to reach me."

It was brutal, but he would not take back his words. He put Iris into the car the next morning, and they took off to the small landing strip. Hector waved them off, his wife was weeping and scolding.

"It may work, it may not," Greg sighed.

"I hope all will go well," said Iris, feeling responsible for her suggestion. He patted her hand.

"It was a good idea, thank you, my wife," he smiled at her.

All too soon they were back home, and nothing had changed. Melania was reserved, Alex was chasing Charmian, Charmian was mocking Vanessa and Xanthe, Petros had retreated to his dressmaking room.

Lydia worked in the early morning in her gardens, avoiding all except Melania. She was visibly relieved to have them back.

Iris set to work with Petros again. The July days were very

hot, and in the afternoon often airless. They worked until the late luncheon, then retreated to their various rooms to rest until the sun went down in a blaze of crimson heat haze.

The work was going well. Iris discussed it with Petros, and they decided to have a trial dress rehearsal, with Charmian and Melania showing off the dresses to the family, and to the village women doing the embroidery.

They set it for a morning in late July. Vanessa and Xanthe were jealous of all the fuss. Iris had tried to persuade Vanessa to take part in the modeling. She refused, haughtily.

"What? You insult me! I would not flaunt myself before people in such a shameless manner!"

Charmian had to mock her. "What do you have to flaunt, Vanessa?" And the two sisters raged at her, and went off to the Cottage with Xanthe's daughters.

Iris rose at sunrise to prepare herself. She bathed, and was dressing in a blue linen, when she happened to glance out her window.

A man at the window of the Cottage! She stared. Those two prim, proper sisters with a man in their cottage? He was the same man, she was sure, that Vanessa had walked with in the field so long ago. Could it be Nikolaos Sicilianos?

Or was it just one of the estate workers, fixing the window? The man drew the shutter partly toward him, closing out the sunlight. Iris stared thoughtfully at the Cottage. Then she forgot it again. It could have been someone fixing the shutter, it might have been banging in the morning breeze.

She went down to an early breakfast, and was halfway through when Greg came down. "You are early—good morning, my darling," and he kissed her cheek, and patted the top of her head.

"I like the early morning hours," she smiled. Lydia soon came down, and Melania, and they had a pleasant breakfast together.

Charis and two maids were stationed upstairs to help Melania and Charmian change their clothes. Chairs were set in the ground-floor hall, and soon the village women came up in limousines. Nike was there, shyly eager to see the results of her handiwork. The black-clad older women whispered, and shuffled their feet uneasily at being inside the House of Venizelos. Lydia made them welcome, and served sugared tea and little cakes.

Alex and Greg were working at the telephones that morning. Iris was not sure they would stop and let Greg observe the clothes. He did turn about and gaze from time to time, absently. She felt a little "down" that he took so little interest in her work.

Not so the women. They nudged each other excitedly as Petros began to announce the garments. He had a big booming voice, and waved his hands as he showed the first suits.

Alex half turned his head, but of course he could see nothing. He went back to his work, murmuring into a telephone.

Charmian came down the stairs first, modeling a white suit of Iris's. Iris watched it critically, absorbed in how the suit "worked." It moved well, it was wide enough in the hem, and the embroidery on the sleeves and hem looked smart. Charmian removed the jacket to show the matching embroidery on the sleeves of the blouse. Nike smiled in pleasure at seeing her work all together on the attractive model.

Melania came down in a black suit of Petros's, looking more mature and even distinguished in his work. The woman who had embroidered that looked immensely happy.

Charmian returned in the sleek black suit of Petros's, with small slits in the hem, a more sophisticated look than Iris's white suits. The women were beginning to get the idea now, and murmured together over the Greek effect of their embroidery, and the smart look of the whites and blacks.

There were long pauses between the appearance of each garment. Iris knew that abovestairs there was frantic activity as Melania and Charmian changed. The women murmured, or worked briskly on other pieces of embroidery they had brought with them. Their worn hands were rarely still. Iris talked a little to Nike and to Lydia, but mostly she was absorbed in the overall effect of the show. Would Nadia Egorova approve?

About a third of the way through, Iris glanced up absently as a commotion grew at the doors under the stairs. Two men burst through—and she recognized them in terror.

One was the handsome man she had seen at the Cottage window. The other was the bull-like Orestes, who had attacked Iris in the fields!

She stood up and screamed. The women froze in their chairs as Orestes raced over and pulled Alex from his wheel-chair, slashing at the sightless man with a long gleaming knife. Greg turned and started to run to Alex's aid when the other man—he must be Nikolaos, Iris realized—caught him with a tackle that brought both men heavily to the marble floor. The gun Nikolaos carried spun out of his hand and went off. The report brought servants running. Alex, bleeding, had somehow managed to get his hands on the handle of the knife and was wrenching at it desperately when two men of the household grabbed at Orestes. Orestes smashed the knife handle into Alex's temple, he stood up, threw off his attachers and lumbered with surprising speed through the door. Greg and Nikolaos were grappling with appalling ferocity. Then Nikolaos pulled a knife. The blade flashed and Iris saw blood blossom like red poppies on the white of Greg's shirt, just as Greg swore and with a wrestler's move flung Nikolaos to the marble floor. His head struck heavily, stunning him.

"Tie him up!" Greg shouted at the servingmen, as he raced after Orestes. Iris had started to move toward him automatically when her gaze was arrested by the expressions on Vanessa's and Xanthe's faces. The two women had entered the Big House—during the melee? earlier?—and both looked excited and pleased. . . . Surely not, Iris told herself, and ran after Greg.

Outside there was a squealing of tires as Orestes sped away in a Land Rover that must have been waiting outside. Greg ran after it, heedless of his wound. "Come back!" Iris screamed. He ignored her and ran on.

Drawing a deep breath, she turned back into the hall. Alex lay limp on the marble floor. Melania knelt beside him, trying to stanch the flow of blood with an inadequate scrap of embroidery cloth. Lydia was sending servants flying in all directions. One woman came with a basin of cold water, another with bandages, a third with a little medicine chest Lydia kept ready at all times.

Petros, who had stood frozen at the bottom of the stairs, roused himself and hurried over to Iris. "What is it? What happened? How horrible!" Yet he looked excited and thrilled also; what a morsel of gossip back in Athens!

"A family feud," she said quietly, amazed at how steady her voice was. "I wish you would not mention it to anyone. The less said the better."

She moved to bend over Alex. His valet came, and two men helped carry him back to his rooms; Lydia followed hurriedly.

Greg came back grimly. He got a Land Rover, regardless of Iris's pleas, and followed Orestes with several of his men, but the late start foiled them. When he returned a couple of hours later, they had not found Orestes.

"However, I think he is still on the island. No boat of his has been found. So they have accomplices—their father, of course, but others too."

Greg went to question Nikolaos, but could get no information from him. Iris could hear the yelling, and the curses flung by the handsome young man locked in one of the little cottages used by the servants.

Nikolaos was cursing them all, the House of Venizelos, and Gregorios especially. "I will have vengeance!" he roared. "Your house against mine! We shall endure! You will all be wiped out! We will kill, kill!"

Iris shuddered, and went to Lydia. Alex was resting in the hands of his valet, he seemed only half-conscious. Lydia sat limply in her chair, a sorrowful look on her face.

As Iris came to her, she looked up, and indicated a seat beside her. "Oh, dearest Iris, it is so terrible! I had hoped it would not continue! Why must men persist in such dreadful feuds?"

Iris sat down, noted that nobody was close enough to hear them. "Mother Lydia," she whispered. "This morning, I wakened early, and looked out the window. There was a young man in the cottage where Vanessa and Xanthe live, he was closing the shutters. It was Nikolaos."

Lydia stared at her, paling. "You are sure?" Iris nodded firmly. "Oh, ye gods! Greg will go crazy and kill them! He is in a terrible mood! And to think a Venizelos would betray us!"

"I thought I saw them together once before, Vanessa and Nikolaos," whispered Iris rapidly. "They walked in a field together. I was amazed. Greg did not believe it could be them. But now I am sure. Should I try to tell him, convince him?"

Lydia slowly shook her graying black head, her eyes deeply troubled. "Not now. Let us wait. I cannot think why—but those women are very jealous and angry. Yet—to consort with the enemy! What price are they given? The Sicilianos are poor, I think."

"Nik is very handsome. He looks—charming," said Iris significantly. Their eyes met, Lydia nodded.

"Yes, we say nothing for now. But I will watch, and so will my personal maid; I am sure Greg will post guards over Nikolaos. Well—well—this is a development, to be sure," and she looked very thoughtful.

Greg came back from arguing with his prisoner. He looked dark, implacable. And his white shirt showed the dried blood of his wounds. He came over to them, and stood over them, darkly brooding, his black eyebrows meeting over his nose, like some vengeful god, thought Iris.

"You are both uninjured?" he asked. They nodded. "I feared they might try to kill us all," he added. "God, there is no end to this! I am tempted to execute Nikolaos!"

From the corner of her eye, Iris saw Vanessa and Xanthe entering from the terrace. From the way they started and looked wildly at Greg, she felt sure they had heard his words.

"Oh, no, no, do not speak so," she said to Greg hastily. "It is wrong. God says that vengeance is His, He will repay, it is not for us to take vengeance! It has done enough harm in your family."

She had feared they would all be killed by the two wild young enemies. But this would make sure of it—if Greg carried out plans to execute one of them! God would surely make them feel His wrath! Vengeance was interfering with their careers, look at Alex! And their lives were blackened by this. It seemed so futile and so useless. Whey did men let feuds carry on so?

And women sometimes also. She knew the stories of feuds that women shrilly encouraged, fierce in their fury when their men were murdered.

"It must be stopped," Iris continued, as Greg looked bleak. "Could you not speak to their father, ask him to meet with you?"

"Never. He is a tricky old devil," and Greg stomped away, up the stairs, to wash and tend his wounds. Iris followed him, to help, but did not persist in her arguments. Greg was in no mood to listen.

She helped Greg strip off his bloody white shirt, and then took ointment and smoothed it over the scratches and jagged wounds. Two went rather deep. She put on a strong disinfectant, and he winced, and made rude noises.

"They came armed, all right! What I would like to know is how they stole in so quietly."

"Everyone was watching the fashion show," she murmured. She evaded his eyes, still wondering if she should try to tell him Vanessa and Xanthe were betraying him. "There—is that better?"

His eyebrows smoothed, and he put a quick kiss on her nose. "Your hands have healing," he said poetically. "I shall be well from your touch."

She smiled slightly, still shaky from the horrible scene of the fight. "I put more trust in the disinfectant," she said dryly. "And if any infection develops, we must take you right to the doctor!"

"Yes, mama!" he laughed. She was so glad to hear him laugh, she said no more about the fight. "Now I must go see how Alex does."

"I just came from there with your mother. He is resting."

"Very well, I will wait until after luncheon."

It was very late in the afternoon by the time luncheon was served. Lydia had apologized to the village women, and sent them home. "I told them the fashion show would resume another time," she sighed, at luncheon. "I fear the fight gave them much to gossip about."

"What we saw was good," Petros mused. "I think I shall change the hem of the black gown, though."

Lydia and Iris looked at each other. What a one-track

mind! But Charmian was as bad, ignoring the fight now that it was over. She had little curiosity about it, merely commenting that she supposed some ruffians had got in, and wondered if they might move away from such a godforsaken spot where bandits lived!

Iris did not try to explain to her half-sister that the "bandits" were close relatives with blood feuds on their minds!

Chapter Twenty-two

The next morning, Lydia said that Alex was very restless. Iris and Greg went over to his rooms in the Low House to talk to him. He was dressed, but lying on a lounge, and he tossed and muttered. His valet hovered anxiously.

"He had a poor night," the valet whispered.

Alex opened his eyes, brushed his hand across them. He said, "Who is there?"

"It is Greg," said his cousin gently. He took Alex's hand in his big one. "Where do you hurt?"

"All over," said Alex with a grimace. "Who hit me, a man in the form of a ten-ton truck?"

"Orestes Sicilianos," said Greg very grimly, his sensitive mouth set in hard lines. "I have captured Nikolaos, but Orestes got away."

"Get him," said Alex feebly. "He is a madman. He will not rest until he has killed us all." His head turned wearily, his eyes blinked and blinked, as though they hurt. His head turned in the direction of Iris. The valet had closed the shutters, but some sunlight had crept in and lit her pink dress. "Iris?" he questioned.

"Yes, I am here, Alex." She stepped one more step toward his lounge.

He blinked, frowned, seemed to peer in her direction. "Are you—wearing—a pink dress, Iris?"

The question stunned them all. Greg recovered first. "Can you see it, Alex?"

"Yes—it is blurred—fuzzy—like a television picture out of focus. But I can see a blur of pink, and yes—I see her face—" His voice became more excited. "Yes, I see her face!"

Iris laughed with tears in her eyes. She wished it had been Melania whom he had seen first. But to see again—it was a miracle!

"We will take you to Athens, to the doctors," said Greg. "Can you travel, do you think, Alex? Shall we go today?"

"My God, yes, I can't wait long," he said simply. He brushed his hand in front of his eyes, then held his head still and tried to stare at it. "I can see something—" He closed his fingers into a fist, then opened them again. "Yes, I can see my hand!"

Greg wasted no time. He had the valet pack for Alex, and Charis for himself and Iris, and they were off by noon. Charmian was up and begged to go with them. Greg curtly refused.

"This is not a fun trip, Charmian," he said. "If you wish to return to the States, I'll try to pack you into the plane. Otherwise, your trip will have to wait."

"I want to see Athens!" she pouted. "I haven't seen a thing! I know they have marvelous shops, mother said so!"

"This is not a shopping expedition," said Greg, and scowled at her. "Come along, Iris!"

"Why does Iris have to go? I could go instead of her!" Charmian persisted.

"Because she is my wife, and I wish it!" Greg shouted at her. He kissed his mother good-bye, and set off so fast Iris had to run to keep up with him.

Greg had set several guards over Nikolaos, and Iris could see him at the cottage window as they went past. He was unshaven, darkly scowling, his head bandaged. He made some rude gesture as they drove by, watching them curiously. Greg scowled back.

Greg sat in the back of the Land Rover, holding his cousin tenderly, during the long ride to the landing strip. At the plane, they all worked to make Alex comfortable, setting up a stretcher and blankets across several seats, and strapping him in.

They arrived in Athens in midafternoon, in a blinding heat haze, and brilliant sunlight. Two silver Rolls-Royce limousines met them, and Greg and Iris took one, and Alex and the valet the other one.

They went direct to the private clinic, and Alex was examined by the doctors. One was teasing him as they came in.

"You look like you have been in some big fight, Mr. Venizelos!"

Alex said in Greek, "You should see the other guy!" and they all laughed. He was pale with excitement.

The doctors first dressed his injuries, and found them mostly superficial. Two stab wounds were deep, and they shook their heads over them. But Lydia had good medicine, they thought any infection could be halted.

Then they took him away to examine his eyes. Greg paced the floor, Iris sat in a window seat and looked at the gardens outside, scarcely seeing the flowers set out so beautifully around a clear blue pool. Could Alex really see again? It would be a miracle.

She thought of the sister who used to say over and over, "God causes good to come even from evil."

If Orestes and his fist could make Alex's sight return— what a miracle God had created, yet again!

The doctor in charge came back to them, as dusky shadows were creeping into his waiting room.

"There is some chance his vision may return," the doctor told them. "His sight comes and goes. We are sure the nerves are affected, but how much is still a question. We wish to keep him here several days for observation. We should know more in a few days. Do you wish to return home, and come back for him?"

"We will stay in Athens a few days, doctor, on this trip," Greg decided. "I'll come again tomorrow, and visit with Alex. He is allowed visitors?"

"Indeed, yes, we should encourage that," the doctor said. "He will want his loved ones about him. Loving families can do much to help one recover."

Greg and Iris went then to the penthouse suite of the Venizelos family high over Athens, and she was glad to wash and change, after the long exciting day. She did not want to go out for dinner, and was glad when Greg sent out for some food.

They ate in their lounging clothes, Greg in his light gray silk robe, and Iris in her blue pajamas and thin robe.

They ate at the table overlooking the side where they could see the Parthenon lit up by golden lights. There was *taramosaláta*, smooth and rich, with crusty bread, thin slices of spicy sausage, olives and *féta* and vine-ripened tomatoes, and a chilled bottle of *retsína*.

"A picnic dinner tonight," said Greg, with a smile. "If we had had food in, I would have asked you to cook some *moussaká*! Perhaps tomorrow we can get in some groceries. The cook will prepare it, however. I want to take you to some museums, and other sites I think you will enjoy.''

"Oh, we are going to tour?'' she asked eagerly.

"If you wish. I have the time. All seems to go well with the hotels.''

"Have you—heard yet from Hector?'' she asked timidly.

He shook his head. "No, not yet. I have asked around for someone to take over their resort. I have had everyone accept! There are many who would like that job!''

She was quiet, thinking it was too bad if Hector and his father could not settle their differences. But Greg would be implacable. Petty quarreling could upset the hotel staff, and then the guests, and he would not allow it.

The next days were set into a routine. Greg and Iris rose early, they always had, and enjoyed the early morning hours, when the heat was not yet burning. They started out in one of the Rolls, and drove to a lovely spot, sometimes along the sea, sometimes in the mountains, or to a place where they could see crumbling white temples of long ago.

They would return to Athens about noon, go to the clinic, and visit with restless Alex.

By the third day, he was eager to get out of the hospital. He felt much better, his wounds were healing, and he could see better.

He peered teasingly at Iris. "Yes, yes, as pretty as I remember! I think I shall court her!''

Greg scowled at him mockingly. "Too late! She has my rings on her fingers! Find yourself another girl!''

Iris was blushing at Greg's possessive arm about her waist, and his look at her.

Greg and Iris talked to the doctors. They were very encouraging about Alex's eventual complete recovery of his eyesight. "It might have happened anyway," one doctor said.

"The head injury was healing. But something about the blow—well, it is a miracle. Perhaps the retina—"

Alex had told them he had seen gray for a time, they nodded and looked wise. "He may return home in a few more days, when we are sure what is happening," said the chief doctor.

Alex was reluctant to let them go. "Stay for luncheon," he urged. "Talk to me! I am so bored here!"

So they stayed for luncheon with him. It was served in a pleasant garden patio, near a pretty pool. The table was set with gay blue and white and crimson linens. It was a happy occasion, for Alex was able to see his food, through his very dark sunglasses, and the smile on his face added much to the meal.

"I thought I would never see again," he flung out casually as they drank their after-dinner coffee. "I could not reconcile myself to that. I think I would have died."

"Nonsense," said Greg firmly. "You are too strong for that! You would have learned to cope with it. We are alike, eh? I like to think if I should become blind, I would manage somehow. As you have, Alex! You have helped me much, even without your eyesight. It is a matter of mental powers!"

Alex looked very happy, for Greg did not hand out compliments idly. Iris smiled at them both. It was good that the two men were friends again, and that Alex had conquered his problems enough to work again. He was stronger, he could walk sometimes unaided by crutches. And now his eyesight was returning.

Greg and Iris returned in late afternoon to the penthouse apartment. The telephone was ringing as they entered. Greg murmured an excuse, and went to the phone. Iris watched as a heavy scowl came over his face, and his voice went to deep gravel.

"What—Timotheos Sicilianos," he said in Greek. . . . "Yes,

I know your voice! . . . What—do you think I will hand back your son who attacked me and tried to kill me? And Orestes—just let me get my hands on that bull! He tried to kill Alex! No thanks to your family that he is recovering. . . . Yes, he is recovering. . . . No, I have no wish to meet with you. Do you think I would fall for your tricks?''

Iris stood still, hands pressed to her breast. She whispered. ''Oh, Greg, talk to him, do! You must meet with him—oh, please!''

Greg heard her, he gave her a very heavy scowl. He looked lika a dark angry god, he pressed his fingers through his thick curly hair and it stood up on end as though in a windstorm.

''No, I have no wish to discuss it! Your family is insane! Attacking us like that! Was it with your knowledge and permission? . . . You do not say, eh! Two wild reckless sons, you are truly unfortunate!'' His sarcasm was thick.

He listened, frowning.

''Meet you in a restaurant at night? Do you think me mad? No, I shall not come! If you want your son back, you will give me Orestes! . . . Yes, I want him charged with attempted murder! Both of your sons, murderers! They would kill in a wink! I am fortunate to be alive, the gods were with me. Think of that, Timotheos, the gods are on my side!''

They evidently exchanged several strong insults, then hung up in anger. Iris sighed and shook her head.

''Oh, Gregorios, how do you hope to end the feud, when you quarrel like that? Why not meet with him in some neutral place, and talk of your difficulties! Do you expect to feud with him forever?''

''Silence!'' he roared furiously, and stormed out of the apartment. He was gone several hours. She rested, and then sat and looked out the windows of the apartment for a time, sadly.

How foolish to continue the feud. Sicilianos and his sons

were poor, they were wrecking themselves trying to harm Greg and his family. Only pride and hate drove them. What could possibly be accomplished? Nothing good could come of this.

Greg returned finally, and gloomed about the apartment until time to retire. Iris was glad to retreat to her bedroom, and sleep. She wakened to the glorious sight of the morning sun shining on the marble of the Parthenon, and lay gazing at it contentedly. At least there was such beauty in the world!

At breakfast, Greg was silent and scowling. Iris finally said, "I should like to go to see Marta—at the Diophantus fashion house this morning. Will that meet with your approval?"

"Who am I to say? You are a modern woman, you do and say what you please!" he snapped.

The maid was so startled she almost dropped the coffee pot.

"Thank you," said Iris, and they were scarcely speaking when he let her off at the Diophantus place.

"I will come for you about eleven, and we will go to Alex," he said briefly. He left a man with her, who stationed himself near the door, and Iris was reminded again that a wealthy family had to be always on guard against terrorists.

It was unpleasant, and she had to shake herself to ward off a chill down her spine. Marta welcomed her happily, and they spent two hours talking of the new fashions Iris and Petros had created, talking of some new fabrics that had come in, and briefly the good news of Alex's returning eyesight.

They were looking over some fabrics, and Iris was wearing a new aqua linen suit when Greg returned. He approved the suit, and they bought it. Marta brought out the silky blue gown Iris had also tried, and Greg liked it at once.

"Buy it, and I will take you dancing tonight," he said, and Iris smiled.

"That I cannot resist," she agreed, and they took that also.

Greg seemed in a better mood. In the car, he told her, "Nestor telephoned, and begged me to reconsider sending his son to Canada. His daughter-in-law has been weeping, and she may harm herself, with the child coming soon. He asked me to let Hector remain at the resort, he will himself go to Hong Kong, or where I wish. Evidently they have stopped quarreling. I told him to come with Hector to Athens, we will discuss it. If they are sincere, that is settled! They shall remain."

He seemed very happy, and she hugged his arm. He grinned down at her.

"*Some* of your advice is not bad," he said. Iris laughed softly.

"Well, I am happy about Hector and his father and the baby to come," she said. "I do hope that works out well. As for me, I shall always prefer peace to war."

"The next time you resist me," he said wickedly in her ear, "I shall remind you of that! Give in, do not fight me!"

She laughed again, she knew she was blushing madly. If only all their encounters could be so sweet. He was very handsome and lovable. If only other women did not think so! How long would he be attracted to Iris? How long before he tired of her, and looked around for a mistress? A shadow crossed her mind. Her father had been charming also.

They had a good visit with Alex, whose vision had improved quite a bit. He had to wear a thick eyeshade during the sunny days, but one day he could discard that probably. He was enjoying sitting in the garden, looking at the flowers, the pool, the butterflies.

"It is odd," Alex reflected, as they lunched together. "In the old days, I scarcely noticed flowers and butterflies. But since my eyesight was restored, I rejoice in so many beautiful sights like this. The colors are brighter and more lovely, the shapes are more perfectly made, the sky is more blue, the mountains more magnificent. Before this, I looked at mountains as something to climb and to conquer. Snow was made to ski in, a meadow something to rest in on the way up the mountain.''

Iris wondered how he would look at Charmian now, and at Melania. Would women still be playmates to entertain him, and to be conquered? He did seem more serious since his injuries, and he worked harder. But how long would that last?

Greg said something like that as they left him. ''I wonder if Alex has changed and matured. I hope so. In the old days, I could not always depend on him. A job might be done, or he might be distracted by a pretty girl, or a fast boat to race, or a new plane to try. I sent him once to Hong Kong, and he cabled for more money from the middle of China, where he had gone to see some strange sight. One can only hope he will settle down somehow.''

''I do not know. He is twenty-six,'' said Iris. ''One would think he would settle down soon, or not at all.''

''No, no, for a man that is young. He has not sown all his wild oats,'' said Greg, with a teasing look at Iris. ''I am thirty-four, and I have just settled down this year! But I did not find you until this year! So I have an excuse.''

He took her hands and held them lovingly. She wondered how true it was, that he had settled down on finding her. He seemed sincere, yet—yet—he had had many women, many affairs. Charmian sometimes laughed and teased him about some women in New York. Could she hold him if she tried? She loved him, yet he had never said those vital words to her—nor had she said them to him.

He put one of her hands to his rough cheek, and stroked it softly against his skin. The chauffeur was stealing glances at them in the rearview mirror, with great interest. She wondered if that chauffeur had taken Greg to his various rendezvous with women, and was curious about his marriage to the young unglamorous American girl.

"What are you thinking about?" asked Greg softly, biting her fingers gently.

"That you promised to take me dancing tonight!" she answered promptly, with a sideways look at him. He laughed.

"So I did, but I have other, more fascinating things to suggest," he said mischievously.

"Food?" she asked wickedly. "A marvelous meal of *moussaká*, and seafood, some *oúzo*, and *dolmáthes*—"

He groaned. "My wicked woman," he muttered. He got that look on his face, of incredible hunger, and she laughed again. "You win. We will rest, get dressed, then go out and find somewhere to eat and drink and dance!"

It was a gay happy evening. Greg telephoned some friends, and they all met at a restaurant at the waterfront at Piraeus. Iris wore the new silky blue gown that hung to her slim ankles, and a pair of golden sandals, and her hair in a sleek chignon on top of her head. She liked the half a dozen women, wives of her husband's associates, and the men who clustered around them.

They drank *oúzo* and *retsína*, nibbling at bits of shrimp and squid. Waiters brought platters of food, *dolmáthes*, cheeses, dark bread, platters of hot lamb on skewers with tomatoes and peppers and onions.

Between eating and drinking, the men would spring up to dance in lively fashion to the music of the *bouzoúki* and clarinets. Or there would be a slow melancholy dance, which Greg often led, dignified and with immense leaps in the air and showing off of style and leg movements. Sometimes the women joined in when they were invited, otherwise they watched and applauded.

Iris was glad she knew Greek, for most of them knew only a little English. They were mostly distant cousins, all involved in the hotel business, and the shop talk was lively at times.

When the women learned that Iris was a dress designer, they were curious. "But all that will end," said one older woman, "when the babies come, eh? One does not have time for both! No, no, Gregorios will not permit you to work, when the babies come!"

Iris was too wise to argue with her in public, but she set her chin, and kept her anger down with an effort. Perhaps that was in Greg's mind, but it was not in hers! She had worked too long and too hard to give it all up without a murmur! And she thought it was good for a woman to have other interests in her life than a husband and babies.

If Greg tired of her, Iris was not going to be left weeping!

Presently the music changed to waltzes, tangos, even a cha-cha and a samba. She danced with Greg, and with a couple of other men briefly. Greg watched her closely, even when he danced with other women, and he soon returned to take her in his arms for the next dance.

They finally said good night at about two in the morning, and drove back to Athens.

The chauffeur drove, and the moonlight shone softly down on them as they sped past silent villages, empty fields, small ports with little boats bobbing in the lazy waters. In Athens, it was amazingly busy, with cars still bustling about in the narrow streets.

"Athens is a night city," said Greg. "Athenians like to stroll about, and ride around and see their friends, and sit in bars, when the night is cool after a long hot day. It can be the best time of the twenty-four hours."

But Iris was ready to quit when they got home about four in the morning. She yawned her way up in the elevator, and stumbled into her bedroom.

She took off the silky blue dress, hung it lovingly in the

closet. This was a dress for memories, good memories, it had started well. She would enjoy this town, she knew it.

She put on a sheer nightdress, brushed her teeth, washed off her makeup, and fell into bed. Then the door opened and closed after Greg.

"Darling?" he said possessively, and came to the bed.

"Aren't you sleepy?" asked Iris, as he lay down beside her.

He grumbled, "Do you not welcome your husband? Where is your wifely concern?"

"I think I left it at the seaport about four hours ago," she giggled. "Did I drink too much tonight?"

He pretended to groan. "Do not go to sleep! I danced with you until I burn with desire!"

He drew her to him, and Iris pressed her face against his bare chest. She too had burned with desire when he held her in the dancing. Greg had a way of holding Iris with one hand on her rounded hips, pressing her against him, until she had felt his swelling masculinity against her thighs.

His fingers teased against the cotton ties of her nightdress. She loved the rough feel of his hardworking hands on her skin. The slightly scratchy touch made the sliding of his fingers on her all the more erotic to her. Slowly he unfastened the ties, and gently pushed the fabric down over her rounded breasts, disclosing them for his hands.

One big hand cupped a soft mound, and he squeezed it very gently. His mouth went hungrily to the nipple, and he tongued it, rubbing his head against her chest. Her hands went to his head, and she twisted her fingers in his curly hair, her eyes closed dreamily. She was so tired, so sleepy, and more than a little dizzy with all she had had to drink!

Greg slid the nightdress to her knees, and then off her feet, and tossed it out of the bed. It landed in a white pool on a chair near the window. The moonlight shone on it, and on the bed, and the silvery moon glowed in the night-purple sky over the golden Acropolis.

Greg moved up slightly on her, and his face loomed over hers. She opened her eyes, and gazed up at him.

"Your eyes are deep as the night," he whispered. "Yet in the daytime, they are clear as the sky at morning. Blue eyes of iris." Gently he touched each eyelid with his lips, closing her eyes with the little nibble of his mouth.

Her hand stroked over his hard shoulder, caressed down over the strong muscular back. His lips slid over her cheeks, down to her chin, and over to her earlobe. He bit gently at the lobe, and it made an erotic thrill go down her spine.

Then his lips returned to her mouth, and he pressed on her lips with his. She opened her mouth to the touch of his tongue. He put his tongue inside her lips, and slowly circled her tongue with his.

She loved being caressed and played with by Greg. His love play was so sweet and prolonged. He seemed to enjoy it as much as she did, moving his hands over her body from head to toes, his lips searching out secret places to caress and make her thrill. He knew how she reacted. When she shivered, and clung to him, his deep chuckle of satisfaction was both endearing and maddening!

"So sweet," he murmured lazily against his waist. "So silky soft. I like this little dark mole here, a beauty mark."

His mouth caressed it, and she trembled under his lips. Her hips moved on the bed uneasily. His hand slowly moved over her thighs, as though he soothed her, but that was not the effect of his touch.

"You do not now mind when I touch you," he said, not asked. "That fear of being touched, it is going away, I think."

Yes, it was. Iris thought about it. Greg had a way of taking her fears out of the dark recesses of her mind, showing them to the daylight, and revealing them for what they were, nightmares of a child.

"Yes, I am beginning to enjoy being touched—by you," she agreed softly, and her hand slid over his arm from his shoulder to his hand. When she reached his wrist, his hand turned over and caught hers in his big one, and they clasped hands, and twined fingers together.

"Yes, by me only!" he growled mockingly against her throat. "Not by any other man! I am more jealous of you than I dreamed I would ever be!"

She went still. Dared she say it? "Not of any other woman you have had?" she asked, forcing her tone to be light.

He went stiff for a moment. "The women I have had were not virgin, not my woman," he said finally. "I always knew I would look until I found a girl right for my wife, the mother of my children. All those—those playgirls—they were only for the lighter moments. You understand? The Charmian girls are not for marriage and families. One plays with them, pays them in jewels, and that is done."

"And what about women like Vanessa?" asked Iris, made bold by drink. "Where would she fit in?"

Greg had gone very stiff and quiet. He rolled over, and lay with his head on the pillow, no longer touching her. "Why do you speak of Vanessa now?" he asked, and his voice was deep with anger.

"I—I wondered about her. Why she has never married. She is very—beautiful, dresses well is sophisticated—is fond of children—"

He was silent for a time, breathing deeply. Then he finally said gruffly, "Once she was young and lovely, and very vulnerable. She—made a mistake. One is sorry for her. I will arrange a suitable marriage for her one day, but it is difficult. I also made a mistake over her, and it has caused trouble. She—thought I might marry her. But she is not for me."

Iris tried to sort out his words. "Did you—Greg, did you mean, you had an affair with her?"

He bit off the words. "One does not speak of such! You will not ask again! It is enough that I married you! Do you question and question, Iris!"

He rolled over away from her, and hunched his shoulders. Iris felt as though she had been hit in the stomach. So he had had an affair with Vanessa—she had been his woman for a time! But perhaps because she was not a virgin, he had not thought her fit for marriage to him!

Oh, that double standard again! And there was still a strong attraction between them!

Greg rolled back, and touched her arm. "I am sorry, Iris. I wish you had not spoken of that tonight. Or ever. What happened before our marriage is not important!"

She could not answer that. But when he took her in his arms, and kissed her to softness, and caressed her, and whispered love words, she had to give in. She loved him—no matter what had happened in the past.

Chapter Twenty-three

Iris wakened slowly, to the feel of warm lips nuzzling over her smooth shoulder. A hard brown arm lay across her body, she was cuddled into a masculine body at her back.

"Um, um," said Greg "You are sweet in the morning also. And your body is beautiful with the sunlight shining on you. My goddess Iris! I am glad you are not of marble!"

His big hand stroked caressingly over her belly and thighs.

"Did you not get enough last night? Oh, what a miserable wife I am," teased Iris. "Such a demanding husband! He never lets me alone!"

A chuckle rumbled through his body, shaking her also. He turned her over on her back, and gazed down into her sparkling blue eyes. His black eyes shone, his large mouth had a wide smile. He bent to kiss her, and she closed her eyes, and put her hands on his head.

Greg put his hand on her hips, and drew her to him, and they came together so easily that she was surprised. It was like a kiss of their bodies, a meeting of their hips, so sweetly and with no effort. He held her to him, kissing her with his mouth, rubbing her hips with his hand to get her closer. The sunlight streamed on them from the uncurtained window, and the sun was high in the sky.

He did not try to complete the embrace, he lay with her, moving lazily from time to time. She gazed over his shoulder at the brilliant blue sky, the golden buildings on the Acropolis, the orange brown roofs of Athens.

Finally he was satisfied, and lay back, and stretched widely. "What time is it?"

She wriggled around in the bed until she could see the small golden clock beside the bed. "Twelve-thirty," she murmured, and then, "oh, twelve-thirty! Greg! We're so late to meet Alex!"

"He will have to wait for us. It will be good for him to learn patience!" murmured Greg.

However, he stretched widely, sat up, yawned, moved his hand almost idly over her body, then got up, and went to his suite to shower. She heard the water coming on, and his voice raised in unmusical song. He made up in volume for the lack of melody, and she grinned to herself.

She made herself get up, and showered. She sprinkled some violet powder on her body, and put on the aqua linen suit, and some white sandals. Greg was ready before her, going through the mail quickly. He laid it down, and they went down to the car and chauffeur.

It was one-thirty when they reached the clinic, and Alex was waiting impatiently. "Where have you been? You are late!" he complained.

"We slept late," said Iris unwisely.

Alex frowned. "Greg slept late? He never sleeps late! He always gets up at some ungodly hour—oh, I forgot! Greg is now a married man, he stays in bed and occupies himself! So, he slept late, eh, you both slept late?'' And he laughed.

Greg's face was red; Iris was surprised, she thought he was incapable of being embarrassed.

''We were out late—we didn't get in until four,'' she explained quickly.

Alex still laughed, and teased them. ''Four, it is nothing. Greg can stay out until dawn, shower, and go to work!''

''We owe him no explanation!'' said Greg stiffly. ''It is not his concern! Never explain!''

And Greg stalked away to talk to the doctors. Iris was left to face the mischief on Alex's face, but it was a kindly look.

''He is very happy with you, Iris, I am glad of it. I worried, so did Aunt Lydia, that he would marry some terrible woman, who would make him miserable! He has a gentle heart, and takes everyone's troubles to his bosom. He could have married some harpy who would tear out his heart from his chest,'' said Alex, poetically.

''I suppose he—dated—many women,'' said Iris, fishing.

Alex gave her a sidelong look around his thick dark glasses. ''Oh, the usual international women, nobody takes them seriously.'' But Vanessa was not an international woman.

Greg returned with the chief doctor, and asked when Alex might go home. ''Would tomorrow be too soon?'' asked the doctor, with a smile at Alex's excitement. ''I presume there will be people there to take care of him, and keep him from doing too much too soon?''

''We will take every care of him,'' Greg promised, looking highly pleased. ''You will give us instructions, and they shall be followed.''

''Excellent. I will have my secretary write them out, if you will excuse me. The main thing is to keep his eyes protected from bright sunlight and much strain. Heavy glasses with side pieces at first. Gradually change to lighter ones, but always wear sunglasses in sunshine, from now on.''

He went away to dictate his instructions, and the others stayed to talk and discuss plans.

The next day they flew back to the island, and Alex was so happy there was no repressing him. He bubbled over with his delight. ''To see again, to see again!'' he half chanted. ''It's a miracle! God did it!''

Iris did not remind him of the intervention of Orestes. Alex kept pointing out sights on the way, a favorite mountain he had climbed, a place he liked to ski, and island made for swimming. ''Of course, I must go slowly for a time, but I shall do all these again one day!''

Alex was very weary by the time they reached the Big House. He would need nursing for a time, and Melania would be devoted, thought Iris. And then what? When he no longer needed help, and Melania's devotion was not required—would he then desert her? Probably. After Melania's heart was thoroughly broken!

Charmian ran to meet them, and Melania hung back, watching with big dark eyes as Greg helped Alex out of the Land Rover.

''Can you see? Can you see?'' cried Charmian.

What if he could not? But he could, and Iris watched in silence as Charmian flung her arms about Alex's neck and kissed him enthusiastically.

Alex finally let her go reluctantly, his face was flushed, and his glasses half knocked off. He settled them, gazing at Charmian's exquisite face and the figure that had been photographed for many fashion magazines.

''You are so beautiful,'' he whispered.

Melania's hands clenched behind her small back. She had a closed pinched look. Then Alex looked round to her.

"There is Melania! Why don't you come to greet me?" he reproached, and held out his arms.

She came to him, but stood at a distance, and held out one small brown hand. She shook hands gravely. "I congratulate you on the recovery of your sight," she said formally. He gazed down at her with an odd look on his face, half teasing, half wondering.

Then Charmian took one of his arms in both her hands, and tried to drag him inside. "Come and talk to me, I have been so bored!" she cried. "You should have taken me to Athens with you! I would have entertained you!"

"He went for medical treatment, not entertainment," Greg said brusquely. "Alex, you had best lie down for a time."

But he did not wait to see if Alex did, he strode into the building, with a suitcase under each arm, not waiting for the servants to take them.

"Did you shop, darling?" Charmian asked Iris avidly. "Do show me what you got!"

"Not now," Iris evaded. "I just went to the shop of Diophantus and talked to Marta. I bought this suit and a new dress, that's about it."

"Oh, I don't believe you," laughed Charmian, with a pouting look to her. "I'll bet you bought out Athens! With a rich husband who won't deny you—come on, show me!"

"My wife does not spend all her time thinking of ways to impoverish me," said Greg dryly from the stairs. "Come along, Iris, there is something I would discuss with you. Alone, if you will!" As Charmian brazenly started up with Iris.

Iris smiled faintly, and went up, as Charmian finally stopped. At Greg's room, she stepped inside. "What is it, Greg?"

He peered past her, and closed the door cautiously. Then he took her into his arms, and kissed her mouth soundly.

When he drew back, his black eyes twinkled with mischief. "There. I had to rescue you from Charmian's scarlet claws! What a harpy she is!"

Iris was startled that he used the same word Alex had used to describe women who tried to attach themselves to Greg. Harpy! The winged women from mythology who devoured and grasped greedily—well, maybe it did fit.

He let her go to her own room, to unpack and rest. She stretched out, and slept for a time, glad to be home in her own blue and white room.

At the late luncheon, she found Melania had been nursing Alex, and was concerned about him. "Two of his wounds opened on the journey home," she told Iris, worry lines crinkled about her eyes. "Aunt Lydia has smoothed salve on them, but he is very exhausted. What did the doctors say of him?"

Iris told her all she could remember, and later Melania went over the list of instructions from the doctor with Lydia. Together the two women nursed him devotedly. The valet was with him at nights, the women took care of him days. He was in his wheelchair much of the time, and worked a little, but the injuries of recent date took much of his strength. Still he was cheerful, because of his restored sight.

Melania asked Charmian if she wished to share the duties of nursing Alex. She asked in all seriousness, for she herself considered it a privilege. Charmian stared at her, and grimaced.

"Nursing? I am not a nurse, darling! I'll help him recover, but only in my own way," and she winked at Melania, so that others could see them.

Melania did not blush at the innuendo, she seemed to go more pale, and nodded and went away.

"You know," said Charmian to Iris, not attempting to lower her voice. "Some people like nurses and martyrs, but they won't appeal to men like Alex! They want playmates! Rich men can afford to pay for their amusements!''

''Would you want him if he was still blind?'' sneered Vanessa.

Charmian mimed a shudder, she loved to shock Vanessa. ''Of course not, darling,'' she purred. ''It would give me the shudders, and besides he could not appreciate me if he couldn't see!''

But Alex could see, and he stared at Charmian by the hour, propped up on a lounge chair, and sitting in the shade of the terrace. When he had improved to that extent, Melania again took a backseat. Iris wanted to shake her, but she knew how the girl felt. Melania was not one to push in where she wasn't wanted.

''If he loved me, he would want me around him,'' said Melania, when Iris protested one day.

''You would make a good wife for Alex,'' said Iris. ''However, I would not want you to have your heart broken. I think it is in these Venizelos men to break hearts. They take devotion for granted!''

She spoke savagely, and Melania looked vaguely troubled. ''Alex, perhaps. But surely Gregorios loves you truly? He looks only at you with eyes of devotion. He thinks mostly of your comfort. Charmian does not attract him.''

Iris did not want to disillusion Melania. She shrugged. ''I spoke in general,'' she said, and picked up her sketch pad. ''I think I shall go out and sketch for a time this morning, while it is relatively cool.''

She went on, wishing to be alone for a time. Later in the day, the sun would bake the red earth, and cause the grasses and wild flowers to lie gasping. But now it was a little cool, with breezes that felt cool in the shade.

She strolled down the hill out of sight of the houses. She loved the feel of the wind in her loose hair, she felt almost like a girl again, running in sandaled feet through the thick dew-wet grass. She could remember, before her father had sent her away, the large lawn of the house where they had lived in a Chicago suburb. There had been a vast expanse of grass, and a pool with water lilies in it of white and gold and pink.

There had been no pools and water lilies at the convent, only concrete. No grass to walk in, no cool wet mornings and laughter and a small wriggling brown puppy. Odd, she had not thought of that puppy for a long time. It had disappeared, and she had finally blotted it from her mind.

She sank down in a meadow, and began to sketch idly, drawing lines that meant nothing. She was half hidden in the thick grass, she felt as though she could draw up the wild flowers about her and hide herself in the scarlet poppies and wild small blue iris, the yellow coreopsis, the white daisies with yellow hearts. She leaned to observe an iris closely, and draw it, in the exquisite lines of the soft purple.

Some voices aroused her attention. She lifted her head and gazed in the direction from where they came. Had that been the laughter of children? Yes, it was, but Xanthe's children rarely laughed, and never aloud.

But it was them. Greta and Nora were clinging to the hands of a tall handsome man, pulling on them, and laughing. It was handsome Nikolaos Sicilianos! Had he gotten loose from his prison! Iris stared in horror and fascination.

Then she saw that with them was a woman in black. Vanessa, with her bonnet swinging in her hand, and she was smiling. And nearby were two men with long rifles, watching gravely from a little distance.

Iris observed them curiously for a little time. They were walking slowly about, evidently he was being allowed to exercise. Vanessa would walk with him, the children ran circles about them both, in a manner most unusual for those quiet sulky girls.

The guards kept a wary distance, but he seemed to pay little attention to them. He was laughing with the girls. He would lift Greta, toss her in the air, to her shrieks of excitement, let her drop into his arms, then hug her. He would set her down, and do the same for little blond Nora, and she would cling to his shoulders, and once she flung her small arms about his brawny neck.

They strolled on, and the girls raced around him, then clung to his knees, evidently begging for more of his attentions. He sang for them, and they listened and tried to sing with him.

He was charming with the children. Iris thought it was not put on. Children knew when someone liked them. And it could not be faked for long. He played with them for almost an hour.

Then the guards motioned. He nodded, and they began to stroll back to the buildings. Within sight of the houses, he walked more quickly, turned and waved to them. Then he walked on, alone, with only his guards. Vanessa stood and waved to him, and so did the little girls. They did not want to be seen with him. That was evident.

Iris waited until Vanessa had taken Greta and Nora back with her. Then she picked up her sketch book and pencils, and started back, soberly.

She longed to discuss it with someone. She saw Kyria Lydia working in the shade of the garden on the north side of the Big House, and went over to her. Iris sank into a chair set on the terrace, and waited.

Lydia saw her, nodded, but continued her work, until she had some seeds planted. Then she sat back on her heels, surveyed her work, and stood up.

She came to sit beside Iris. No one was within listening range.

"Good morning, my dear."

"Good morning, Mother Lydia."

"Something troubles you. Your sister?"

"No, I think she is still asleep!"

They exchanged smiles. "A safe place to be," said Kyria Lydia dryly. "Thank God for the hours of sleep. So?"

"I was out sketching. I saw Nikolaos Sicilianos, walking with his two guards. And Vanessa with Greta and Nora. They talked, laughed, he sang, they played together for almost an hour."

"Ah." Lydia was silent for a short time. "I myself saw them together, walking, when you were with Greg in Athens. The guards asked if I permitted it. I said yes. However—I wonder—"

"I think it could do no harm, and perhaps good."

"My thought. The feud would be ended by this. If they loved, and married—"

They were both silent, thinking. Could it come about?

"Vanessa has had a sweeter temper recently. She was quite lovely when she was younger. In her teens, she was a beauty, radiant. She got into trouble," said Lydia slowly. "A fortune hunter—he compromised her—she got reckless. Greg was very upset, he had always been fond of her."

Iris gazed into a distance. It hurt, that Greg had had an affair with Vanessa. Would he have married her, if she had not acted in such a wild manner? If he had, then by now he and Vanessa would have been married for many years, have had sons and daughters—he would not have come looking for Iris.

"Her mouth smiles more," continued Lydia, after a pause. "The children like him. Xanthe does not trust him, but Vanessa—well, she hungers for a man of her own. And he is very handsome and charming. He does not seem very smart, though. Greg thinks he is below average intelligence, quite below.''

''What does she see in him? He is handsome, but that is not enough—''

''Who knows?'' Lydia shrugged. ''And what about him? He may be flattered that a well-educated woman like Vanessa is attracted to him. She has gone to college, Greg saw to that. Xanthe could have gone, but she rushed into marriage, and then her husband would not permit it, and she had Greta at once. What will become of them, I do not know. Vanessa is discontented, yet does not want to work at a job. She wants to marry and have children. It will give her status.''

''It might settle the feud. Yet—what will happen to Xanthe? She adores her sister, she wants the best for her. I wonder why she was not out walking with them.''

Lydia sighed, shrugged again. ''Well, Gregorios must settle this. He is the head of the house. But we will wait and watch. You have not spoken to him about this?''

Iris said, ''No, just the one time, when he was sure it could not be Vanessa in the fields.''

The two looked at each other, and laughed softly.

''Well, well, we shall see. It is growing warm. I shall stop my gardening. When do you wish the next dress rehearsal?''

''Petros and I thought soon. I think he is eager to send the finished dresses and suits to New York, to Nadia Egorova.''

''Perhaps on Thursday, then. I will see if that will suit everyone.''

Thursday suited everyone. The women came from the village, bringing the last blouses and dresses they had embroidered. This time the rehearsal went well, with no disturbances.

Vanessa and Xanthe and their daughters attended, with muttered criticism from the women. Lydia had seated them at the back, with the village women at the front, so they could see "their" work.

And Lydia had picked multitudes of scarlet poppies and blue iris, and set them in low creamy white vases all about the white halls. They glowed in the sunny room, and made a lovely setting for the black and white gowns.

Iris watched the gowns very critically. They had altered hems, and she and Petros had discussed them all very carefully. The slits were demure and not vulgar. The gowns were not cut too deeply at the bosom. Charmian was magnificent, the complete professional. Melania did a lovely job of showing her dresses, and they would be practical for the Midwestern trade. Nadia did a lively trade with some stores in Ohio, Indiana, and Illinois, where white was worn much more than in New York. And she often sent gowns to Florida.

Greg took more interest today. He would turn around from the telephones, where he sat with Alex at his side. He would study the dresses critically, and nod or frown. Iris watched him from time to time, and was amused how she could predict whether he would like something or not.

He did not like black any more than she did. He liked colors, especially reds and blues. The white dresses with red embroidery gained his nod of approval, and one a smile and decided nod: a lovely gown with wide gay sleeves all covered with red flowers.

Petros sat beside Iris, with him a sketch pad and pencil to make notes. But he made few notes, he seemed very self-satisfied with his gowns. He did make note of one suit, frowned over it.

When the show was over, Greg led the applause. After a moment, the black-clad women joined in eagerly, and Petros and Iris stood and bowed happily.

Refreshments were served. Charmian changed and came

down in a pretty, comfortable rose-colored dress. "Did you like it, Petros?" she asked eagerly. "How did it go?"

"Good, good. I am worried about that black suit, though. The one with the hem in silver. It is wrong, eh? How did it feel?" he asked Charmian He had come to like her opinions on clothes.

"The hem dragged at the back of my knees," she said, and explained it to him as he frowned and nodded, drinking some champagne that Greg had found for the occasion.

The village women ate and drank timidly, listening to the conversation in Greek and in English. They seemed to enjoy it all. Nike and Melania had their heads together, talking animatedly about something. Vanessa and Xanthe ate and drank, then disappeared with the little girls.

Greg came to get a glass of wine. "How did you like my gowns, Greg?" asked Iris timidly.

"You do fine work, fine work," he said heartily. "You are now satisfied, eh? It is finished?"

She looked at him warily. "Finished? Yes, that line. Now I must wait for Nadia's reaction to them. If they go well, and we take orders for them, some can be made up in quantity, and the village women will have enough work to do for a year!"

"That is good, that is very good!" His face lit up. "Well, well, I did not realize that would happen! They need the work. Are there other women who can do some work?"

"Yes, Lydia is talking to some others whenever we go to the village. Some can copy the designs of others, some are creative and can design their own."

"But you will not need to work so hard, now?"

Iris was disconcerted. Did he not realize this was her lifework, that she wanted to continue as a dress designer? She met his gaze. Yes, he did realize, but he was trying to wean her from it, she thought. He would not come right out, and refuse her, but he wanted her to stop. Oh, he did not understand her!

"I want to continue designing," she said softly, so others would not hear them quarrel. "You know it—I enjoy the work so much. I have worked on this most of my life—"

His face sobered, he nodded, and drained the glass of champagne. "I must go back to my work," he said abruptly, and patted her cheek. "Your day is a success, eh? I am glad." And he left her to return to the telephones.

She ate the paté sandwiches without tasting them, and could drink no more champagne. The day had gone flat.

Chapter Twenty-four

It was mid-August. Heat haze hung over the yellowing fields, it was very dry and hot by midmorning. Petros Diophantus gathered up all the dresses and suits, and took off for Athens.

He assured Iris, "I will pack them very carefully, and send them on to your mentor in New York. Madame Egorova shall be pleased with them!"

"I hope so," she told him, with a sigh. "My prayers go with you! It will mean much to me, and to many others."

"And to me," he reminded her. "I need the trade in America. The more money, and also the reputation—it is very chic to be presented in America. Well, well, we shall see. You continue to sketch more, eh?"

"Yes, however I shall not have much sense of direction until I find out if Nadia Egorova likes these. She may wish more like this, or she may say that I am not doing the right things. So I must wait on her word."

"Yes, yes, of course." He kissed her hand ceremoniously in farewell, and Greg scowled automatically at him. Greg took him to the plane, in the limousine, with the boxes of clothes piled in the trunk and in a Land Rover.

Iris watched them go, with trails of dust along the road to mark their way. She was hopeful she had fulfilled her promise to come up with a good line in three months. She wanted to be a good dress designer, she had wanted it for years.

This was her big chance. If she failed, she would be very disappointed in herself, and she was not at all sure Nadia Egorova would give her a second chance. They were both gambling that Iris had sufficient talent to make a career of this.

One must be not only a good dress designer but also one must catch the fancy of the fickle public. One thing that would help—Iris was appealing to a more sedate middle-class public, not the high-fashion field. Her gowns were not extreme, not gaudy butterflies that would make headlines but not last a season.

Her gowns were designed to appeal to those who wanted beautiful garments that would last for several years, and enhance the wearer. They would attract attention for themselves, but also the wearer would not be outshone. Iris thought her appeal would not be so much for New York City and Europe as for the Midwest, especially Chicago and the people she had known most of her life. She had observed what women there wore, and wanted to buy. Now her observations must pay off, or she was finished.

It was a great effort to hold on to her self-confidence. She thought the line was good. Petros had praised it, and wished to imitate it with his black line. And he was experienced.

Yet—Greg would just as soon she did not continue with her career. Iris did not know what her future would be with Greg. He seemed devoted. Yet he had never said those all-important "three little words." "I love you," had never come from his lips. Nor had she said them to him, she had to admit.

Her father had been deeply in love with Poppea, her mother. On her death, he had remarried, and seemed madly in love with Shelley. She had had her way in everything, until they divorced. At least, Iris had supposed Shelley had had her way. Iris knew Shelley had managed to get rid of Iris! And Charmian had had everything she wanted and demanded.

And then had come Maria Ardeth. Hilarion Patakos gave her all she asked for. He seemed devoted to her. She was hung with jewels, she wore the most elaborate gowns any woman could wish. The only time he had crossed her lately that Iris knew about, was when he had insisted on coming to Greece to see what was happening to Iris.

Iris had best make a career for herself, she told herself ominously. If Greg wearied of her, as her father had of Shelley, Iris might be out on a limb. Divorce was easy for the wealthy, even in the Greek Orthodox Church, and had been for Roman Catholics also.

So she began to sketch again, absently, trying to think of fresh new ideas. But she kept watching the mail, waiting for a letter from Nadia Egorova. She counted the days, how soon would the garments reach her? Surely Petros had sent them off at once.

Vanessa saw her working and teased her coldly. "So—you try again with something else? You are not sure your dresses are any good, eh?"

"That line is completed, Vanessa," said Iris patiently. "Now I must think of the next one."

"What does your husband think of that, eh? He allows you to work so hard, why does he? Perhaps the marriage is over, eh?"

Lydia gave her a look of pure dislike, and Vanessa stopped for a time, but continued her pinpricks whenever Lydia was not around. And Greg did not hear her for a time: Vanessa and Xanthe were always careful to mock Iris and Melania out of hearing of Greg.

Charmian gave as good as she got, she loved trouble, and was quick to mock them. They were easy targets for her.

Charmian came down yawning at about twelve-thirty one noon. Vanessa was quick to pounce on her, as they all sat with their stitching in the living area of the great hall.

Greg had gone out with a workman. Alex was at the telephones. Alex swung around to admire the tall blond girl as she stepped lightly down the stairs, swinging around like a model for their attention.

"How beautiful you are, the sun has risen!" called Alex.

Melania stared down at her embroidery.

"Good morning, Charmian," Iris managed evenly.

Charmian stood and stretched languidly before them, showing herself especially to Alex, as she moved in the very short black and white cotton dress. Her long legs were lightly tanned, she wore high-heeled black sandals, and her toenails were scarlet, to match her fingernails. When she stretched, the dress rode up to her hips. Alex was staring at her legs, and a smile curled Charmian's red mouth.

"How late you are!" cried Vanessa, looking at the clock very obviously. "It is past noon. How can you sleep so long? You spend half your life sleeping! It is a waste of God's time!"

"God must have meant for me to be beautiful, I haven't a line on my face," smiled Charmian, drawing a slow finger down her soft sleek cheek, faintly pink and white. She had made up carefully, her hair was in a coronet of ashen silver. "So I need my beauty sleep! For some, it does no good at all!"

Alex was foolish enough to laugh. Vanessa and Xanthe had colored to unbecoming red, and gave him a glare of dislike. They visibly drew themselves up, "girding for battle," as Iris thought of it.

"You are as beautiful as a butterfly," said Xanthe, poison dripping from her thin mouth. "It also has no useful purpose. It emerges from a cocoon, displays itself with great vanity, and dies quickly! The bee, on the other hand, works from morning to night, gathering honey and spreading pollen. It has a very useful place in the universe. We would be at no loss if all the butterflies disappeared!"

Charmian draped herself languidly over a chair near Alex. Her startlingly large blue eyes glinted with the challenge.

"You think the bees must work all day spreading pollen? Just think how many flowers they cause to have little children! You would have the world overrun with flowers—and weeds! Perhaps it would be better if the bees were not so busy, eh?" And she glanced at the two little girls, and laughed.

Xanthe gasped, open-mouthed at this overt insult to her daughters. Lydia was not there for once, and Iris tried quickly to avert the threatened battle.

"Charmian—are you not ready for some breakfast? Come with me, I'll get you some fresh coffee!"

"Just bring me some yogurt—fresh, please, darling! Someone brought me some sour stuff the other day, it was inedible!" Charmian made no move to get up.

Iris sighed, and laid aside her work to get up and bring yogurt to Charmian. Alex was frankly listening to them, his eyes curiously dark.

"Oh, while you are there," drawled Xanthe insolently, "I should like some coffee. And some cakes! And get something for my girls! They are thirsty."

They all watched Iris to see how she would react to being

treated like a servant. She shrugged, and got up to go to the kitchens. No maids were about at that time. She would be glad to go away.

Charmian watched with a slight smile on her lips, Xanthe with a harsh triumph, Melania with vague trouble in her face. Iris left, and went to the kitchens. The cook there prepared two trays, and when they were ready, Iris carried one and Charis the other, returning to the living area.

Greg was there, frowning down on them all. He whirled around when Iris came, and glared as though she were at fault.

"Why are you waiting on these lazy ones?" he demanded, his voice like deep gravel.

"Because I am their hostess," Iris replied sweetly, raising an eyebrow slightly to signify surprise at his anger. She handed Charmian her dish of yogurt. "Fresh as possible, Charmian! Just made."

"I don't care for those cakes, bring some of the poppy-seed cakes to me," said Xanthe, looking over the trays greedily.

Iris indicated to Charis that she should set the tray before Melania for her to pour. "I'll go see if there are some poppy-seed cakes, Xanthe," she said, and turned to leave.

Greg caught her arm. "No!" he said. "Go yourself, Xanthe. And never again dare to order my wife about!"

There was a sudden silence in the room. Alex smothered a satisfied smile.

"Well, I am sure I did not order her about," said Xanthe, sullenly. "Of course, I will go, only my leg is not well today, and it is an effort to move—"

"She is older," said Vanessa quickly. "It is for the young to wait on the older! And that one lounges about all day like a lizard in the sun," she indicated Charmian with a pointed finger. "Why should she not do something for her keep?"

"Lord God!" roared Greg furiously. "Be still, all of you! I should throw out all of you! Iris, you shall not wait on them. You shall sit and be waited upon. What is the world coming to? You are my wife, the first of the House of Venizelos after my honored mother!" And he glared at them all.

Charmian licked her spoon like a dainty cat, her pink tongue licking and licking at the yogurt on it. "But Iris likes to be a martyr," she said mildly. "Why deny her the pleasure of it? In the apartment, she just loved to pick up after me, and make sure I got my food. Didn't you, darling?"

Iris had to repress herself with an effort. "Well, someone had to pick up after you, Charmian," she said, as calmly as possible. "We would both have drowned in a sea of undies!"

Alex burst out laughing, and quickly turned back to the telephones as Greg turned his glare on him. "Let me make this very clear," he said, in Greek, to Vanessa and Xanthe, and Charmian frowned that he did not speak English. "Iris is my respected wife. She is to receive deference and honor. I have caught words you spoke to her in malice and anger. There will be no more of that. You will not make trouble for her. You will help when you can, for you are all of the House of Venizelos. You are welcome here, you know that, all my house is welcome here. But you will honor my wife!"

And he gave them a final glare and stalked over to the telephones. He picked up a small pile of messages, and began to look them over.

"What did he say then?" asked Charmian. "I don't understand much Greek."

"Let it be, Charmian," said Iris wearily.

Melania poured out a cup of coffee, added brown sugar and

thick cream, and handed a cup to Iris, with a slight bow of her head. The others watched, in silence, suddenly understanding what Melania was doing.

"Thank you, Melania," said Iris, and sat back to drink her coffee.

Melania poured then for Xanthe, as the eldest, then for Vanessa, then for Charmian. Then she poured out cups for Greg and Alex and took them over to the tables, along with a plate of pastries. Only then did she pour her own coffee.

Greg was watching her over the pad of messages. He caught Iris's look, and nodded.

Charmian said to Xanthe, "Greta's nose is running. Do you mind removing her?"

She said it so softly that Greg and Alex did not hear. Xanthe left her coffee, snatched up Greta, and left the house so fast her sandals flapped. Vanessa followed her with Nora, her back expressing her outrage. Charmian smiled at Iris.

"There, I did it. You should exert your authority, darling, then you wouldn't be inflicted with them!"

"Oh, Charmian, why must you cause trouble so?" groaned Iris. "I'll have to go after them—"

Xanthe slammed the Cottage door in her face, saying something dreadful in Greek. The two women refused to come to luncheon, making extra work for the maids to take food to them.

Greg was exasperated with them, and chided them for making trouble, the situation was worse than ever. Charmian sat and laughed.

"Oh, I could slam their heads together," said Lydia, furious.

Xanthe and Vanessa came to dinner, but did not speak to Charmian or to Iris. Greg's mouth set hard. Iris thought he would send them away, if he were not so generous. They all took advantage of him. But he could be pushed too far, she remembered Hector and his father. That had been settled; however, Greg would have gone through with his threat to send them to opposite ends of the earth.

She strolled that evening with Greg, in silence. The huge silvery moon was full. Perhaps that was the trouble! She had read about full moon and how that could affect people's minds. It sent some crazy; police said they had more trouble with crime during full moon. And she had read it caused some people to become more ill with ulcers and heart conditions. Perhaps Xanthe was affected by the full moon—in addition to her own bad temper.

"I have been thinking about Alex," said Greg after a time. His voice was a little gravelly, she was becoming very sensitive to his moods expressed by the quality of his voice.

"He is recovering well, isn't he?"

"Yes, and getting restless. Charmian drives him crazy, she sometimes visits his room, and sends the valet away."

Iris grimaced in the darkness. "Should we send Charmian away? By September the modeling assignments should be started again."

She waited for her husband to say yes, he would send Charmian away. He did not.

"I was thinking about Melania also. She should have a good solid husband, someone to make her secure. I think Alex and Melania should marry."

He said it so calmly. Iris frowned. She fought to keep her voice even. "I think Melania likes Alex," she said cautiously. "However, I do not believe Alex is ready to settle down. He could make her very unhappy."

She waited. Greg strode along, so fast she had to hurry to keep up, her sandals cooled by the damp grass. Finally he slowed down. "Sorry, darling, I was thinking," he said, and slid his arm about her waist, and paused to gaze at the moon.

"I think Melania loves Alex. And she will always be a steady sweet lady. She will be a good influence on him. He will become a fine husband. And when they have children, he will settle down well. There is nothing like a son to make a man feel responsible."

"What about afterward?" Iris blurted out.

"What do you mean—'afterward'?"

"When Alex becomes bored, and sees another Charmian, and chases her? Why break Melania's heart? She could find another man," said Iris boldly. "Someone who is good and kind and gentle, and not so likely to stray!"

She held her breath, waiting for his response. For she feared for herself what she had expressed for Melania. Would Greg remain loyal to her? Or would he stray, once the newness of marriage had worn off?

She had heard about Greek pillow friends, the mistresses they took on, not so casually as an American took a girl friend. The pillow friend could last for years, so long as she was a beautiful and clever woman. The Greek might set her up in her own house, go to visit her often, give her rich gifts, and all society would know about her. He would keep his family from her, otherwise she was as close to him as his wife. And if she had a child, he would raise that child also, and make sure it was well educated. If Greg took a pillow friend, Iris would leave him, she vowed it!

"I think Melania wishes to marry Alex," said Greg finally. "And Alex likes her, he always has. She will make him a good wife."

Iris started to object agin, Greg squeezed her waist.

"Do not argue with me over this, Iris," he said, quietly, but with strong warning in his tone. "I have thought about it a long time. Alex must settle down, or he will waste years. And Melania will not wait. She is ripe for marriage. I do not wish to lose her to another family."

"Don't you have some other unmarried cousin, who might be more faithful to her than Alex?" asked Iris fiercely.

Greg said grimly, "Alex will be faithful to her, or answer to me!"

Iris was silent. Greg marched her along with him, and it was not a peaceful walk.

He said then, "Iris, I do not wish you to influence Melania against this marriage! She does not wish to become a career woman. She will make a fine wife and mother, that is her destiny. She is young enough to be molded, that is what I wish for her. So do not interfere in this, I warn you!"

When she did not answer, he squeezed her waist.

"Iris?"

"I have heard you," she said in a soft voice.

"And agree?"

"I do not agree with you. But I will obey you," she flung at him. He laughed out loud.

"Always so stubborn!"

"I have had to be!"

"I know," and the gravel left his voice, and it became velvety soft and subtle. "You have had a bad time of it, and you do not trust men! Nor many women, I believe. You must take your fellowman on trust, little messenger of the gods. You flit here and there, and try to carry peace with you, dear Iris. But mankind is not always peaceful, and you must fail sometimes. Do not be distressed by this. There is peace in the heart of you, and there are ones who will be drawn to the peaceful places."

When he stopped, she frowned up at him. "I don't understand what you say."

"No matter. You will sometime. Just do not be so upset about everybody. Take things more calmly, as my mother does. I do not know how she managed during the bad times, but she did, by withdrawing to her gardens, I believe," he added. "There she found peace, and kept her central calmness inside her. There is that quality inside you also."

"Gardens? I do not work in the gardens."

"No, you draw and sketch, and find peace there. I think it was that I noticed first, about you," he said. "There was peace inside you."

She mulled on his words as they strolled back to the terrace. But she was also very worried about Melania.

Melania had not confided completely in her, but Iris loved her little cousin-by-marriage, and read her eyes. Melania loved Alex, and he had the power to hurt her, and he had hurt her often. Just as Greg could hurt Iris, so Alex could hurt Melania.

If they married, and Melania knew he had other loves hidden away wherever he traveled, she would hurt deeply, in her gentle heart. Why should she be hurt so? Why not allow her time to recover from her infatuation with Alex, and learn to love someone who was good and deserved her, and would be loyal to her.

Perhaps Iris could help her, not directly, but by delaying the marriage. Surely Alex would be reluctant also, to tie himself down. He had shown no wish to be married that Iris could see. Oh, he enjoyed being petted and pampered by Melania, but as soon as he felt better, off he chased after Charmian.

Or should Iris stay out of this matter? She considered her own situation. If she had not been pushed by her father, she would not have married Greg—and known the heights of love, and ecstasy. Would she have been better off, if she had rushed back to New York City, never married, never known what it was to lie in Greg's embrace? She knew the answer to that.

No matter what happened to her, she could not regret having known Greg's embraces, his kisses, his lovemaking. Even if he took a pillow friend, even if Iris left him in a fury of jealousy, even if they parted forever—she could not be sorry she had married him.

For her, it was better to have loved and lost, than never to have loved at all.

Chapter Twenty-five

Iris was awakened by shouts and yells, and the sound of a motor revving violently. Greg in the bed with her muttered a curse, and struggled up. She sat up as he went to the window and flung it wide.

"What is that noise? What is happening?" he yelled.

"It is Sicilianos—he has escaped!" came the answering cry.

"Oh, the devil and all his minions of hell!" yelled Greg in reply, and he ran downstairs in just his robe and slippers, and Iris heard the yelling in the courtyard for a time.

She was thoroughly awake, but did not feel like getting up. So Nikolaos had escaped. She had wondered what would happen. Greg had refused to let him go, and the man had been increasingly restless. And what could be done with him? Greg would not turn him over to the law to deal with. No, it was a personal matter.

Greg returned, furious and grumbling. He took off his

robe, and climbed into his blue jeans. "I have sent men after him, to find where he went. The devil with him. He probably had some help on the island. Maybe Orestes is still here."

Iris shivered at the thought of the huge bull man hiding out, perhaps watching them as they moved about. There was such hate in him.

Nikolaos was different, a man with humor and laughter in him, and singing. He could glare and hate, but it was not his usual nature, she thought. He enjoyed the children, and often walked and played with them.

Greg muttered to himself, then finally was dressed and went out into the darkness. He did not return until noon the next day. He had decided to go to the village and question everyone there, and see if anyone had seen them.

He came back, and reported somberly, "No one has seen them, no boat has been around the port. I think, then, they must hide somewhere on the island, and come and go at some lonely beach. We are all in danger. They must be found."

Alex was looking quiet and depressed. His sight was returning, he walked better. But he must dread being attacked again, thought Iris. Melania put her hand on Alex's shoulder in sympathy, and he put his hand on hers, and smiled up at her.

"You are worried?" he asked softly.

Melania nodded, her eyes dark and wistful brown. "There has been so much trouble already," she murmured.

Joseph, the husband of one of the cooks, Esmeralda, came into the hallway, and snatched off his cap as he waited for Greg's attention.

"Yes, Joseph, what is it?" asked Kyria Lydia. He helped her with the gardening, she must have thought it was about this.

"I would speak with the master," he muttered.

Greg turned from the telephones, and came to him. "Yes, Joseph, I listen," he said in Greek.

Charmian still slept, Vanessa and Xanthe had not come to the Big House except for meals since the quarrel. Greg and Iris, Alex and Melania, Lydia and a maid listened as Joseph told Greg,

"I was awake in the night from a soreness in my back. I got up, I saw the guards were sleeping at the door. They snored. I was concerned. I watched. I saw someone drive up in the Land Rover. It was a woman."

It took him a long time to get the story out, he spoke little usually. Greg asked him, "You saw this woman?"

"Ay, ay, ay, I did. It is the troublemaker, my lord, that woman Vanessa Michaelides. She unlocked the door, your enemy, Nikolaos Sicilianos, comes out, he kisses her. Yes, I saw him, and my good wife also."

Greg's face had darkened with scowling, his black eyebrows had drawn together. Alex listened in amazement, but left the questioning to Greg.

"It was Vanessa, you are sure of her face?"

"The moon was bright, my lord Venizelos."

"Aye, yes. What happened then?"

"She gives keys to him, he gets into the Land Rover, he drives away. She walks back to the Cottage and goes inside. I run out and call your worship. The guards sleep heavily. It was something in their food or coffee, my lord."

He sighed with the effort of telling all this, his wrinkled brown face, like a walnut, worried and haunted. His black eyes remained faithfully fixed on his master.

"I will get Vanessa," said Greg. "Will you ask your good wife to come and speak with us?"

"Aye, my lord," and he departed, in his shuffling walk.

Greg returned with Vanessa, her face smiling, but her black eyes darting here and there worriedly. "What is it? What trouble is there?" she asked brightly. She glared at Iris, Iris looked steadily back at her. Would that woman betray them all, when Greg had been so good to her and her sister? Yes, thought Iris, she had enough spite in her that she would. Greg had had an affair with her, then discarded her. That must burn. Or—perhaps it was for love of Nikolaos. Iris would prefer to believe the latter. She hoped that what had been between her husband and Vanessa was finished.

Xanthe hurried in, sandals flapping in her haste. The girls were left behind—fortunately, Iris thought. The little girls had trouble enough, with their mother and aunt.

"What is it? What is going on?" she cried dramatically. her black eyes stabbed them all accusingly.

Greg ignored Xanthe. Joseph returned with his wife, Esmeralda. Iris recalled that the couple had worked for the Venizelos since their marriage some forty years ago. Nobody could ask for more faithful servants, through bad times and good.

The plump cook wore her white apron, her brown hands were as wrinkled as her brown face. Her brown eyes were steady and excited, sparkling with interest. They all loved a sharp bit of gossip, and none liked Vanessa and Xanthe. All the servants had felt the sting of their malice.

"Now, Joseph, you will repeat your story before us all," said Gregorios Venizelos, his arms folded before him. He wore blue jeans and a white shirt with two buttons unfastened, his sleeves were rolled up in the heat, but he looked as stern and dignified as a medieval knight, thought Iris, as she sat beside her mother-in-law on the couch. Lydia had laid down her embroidery, and sat with folded hands, listening carefully.

Alex took care of the phones, but murmured only, so nothing would interrupt the conversation. Melania was beside him, at the long table, with pad in hand, ready to help.

Joseph fixed his black stare on his master's face and

repeated his story. "I was up in the night with the pain hurting me in my back. I heard a sound, I looked out the window of the cotage his highness kindly gives to us. It is facing the cottage where the enemy of his highness is placed. The guards are lying on the ground asleep. I call my good wife to witness this, we are troubled by it."

Vanessa snorted. "Sleep? or drunk? They are no good!"

Greg listened in silence, not trying to contradict her. Iris knew he was letting her damn herself, it was inevitable, but shivers ran down her spine.

Joseph went on stolidly. "A Land Rover is driven up, with a woman at the wheel, driving that large vehicle easily. She goes to the door of the cottage of Nikolaos Sicilianos, she unlocks it, and lets out the enemy of his highness. They embrace shamelessly in the moonlight, he kisses her mouth!" He glared at Vanessa, she was pale.

Joseph must be getting involved in the drama of it, he was embroidering his story with his own feelings, Iris realized.

"Go on, Joseph."

"Yes, your highness. My lord, she gives the keys to the Land Rover to that evil man, he gets in and drives away. She returns to the Cottage where she lives with her sister and the sister's children, and closes the door. I come out and try to shake the guards, my good wife dresses."

Greg said, "Esmeralda, you saw this woman from your cottage window?"

"Yes, your highness."

"Point out to us that woman you saw, if she is here in this room."

A long brown finger lifted, and she pointed steadily at Vanessa. Vanessa shrank from it, as though from a witch's occult finger, able to stab her to the heart. "She is the woman we saw, my lord!"

"And you, Joseph, you saw this woman, Vanessa Michaelides, and she did release the enemy?"

"Yes, my lord, I have said it, and I say it again. It was that woman. The same who walked often with him in the flowers, and did walk and talk with him many times, and laugh with him, the enemy."

"He is lying!" cried Vanessa. "He saw nothing! He never liked me, and his wife also! They gossip among themselves, those lazy servants, and hate me because I am of the House of Venizelos, and they envy me!"

Bewilderment showed on the faces of the servants. They did not even understand what she said of them. Greg brushed this aside. He turned to Vanessa.

"Why do you deny you helped him? You were seen by honest folk. Why did you do it? Do you wish to stab me in the back?"

Vanessa shrank from his fury. "I deny that I did it," she muttered. "They lie about me!"

Greg sighed with exasperation in the face of her refusal to admit what they had seen. He turned to Esmeralda. "Do you have any sleeping tablets?"

Her face showed confusion. Lydia said gently, "Do you have any pills or potions that cause sleep to come?"

"No, my lord! I need it not. I sleep well!" she protested.

Iris bet she did, after a long day of working hard. However, all knew of the problems of Xanthe in sleeping, she complained often that she had to have strong pills to sleep.

"And you, Vanessa, do you have sleeping tablets or potions?"

"No, I don't!" she said boldly, but her black eyes shifted from his face to the ground.

"And you, Xanthe, do you?"

There was a moment's silence, then Xanthe burst out, "What evil do you wish on me, Gregorios Venizelos? Do I not have enough troubles in my miserable life? How can you accuse me of such a wicked deed? God have mercy on you, God curse me if I would do such a thing. You are a hard man, Gregorios Venizelos!''

Greg's face had turned hard. Iris intervened hastily. ''She is upset, she does not mean this. That is wicked, to say this, Xanthe. Come, tell him the truth, and he will forgive you! You are his family after all!''

Xanthe gave Iris a furious miserable look. ''What have I to confess?'' she muttered.

''Why did you do it, Vanessa?'' Iris turned to the woman's sister. ''For hate of us here? Or rather for love of a handsome and charming man, who happens to be our enemy just now?''

A dark red blush went over the strong features of the Greek woman. She twisted her face, she turned away from them in embarrassment. Greg looked at her in sudden understanding.

''Is that it, Vanessa Michaelides? You love that man, bad as he has been? Do not be ashamed, more women than one have been misled by charming men!''

''I think she is not misled,'' said Iris boldly. ''I think he cares for her! I have seen them together, and there is some strong feeling there, I think. And with the little girls, he is very good and kind. Greg, why do you not try to settle this feud? You could contact their father, Timotheos Sicilianos, and talk reasonably with him.''

''I have admitted nothing!'' cried Vanessa, distracted. ''Do you think I am shameless? I would not walk alone with a man!''

Lydia looked at her coldly. ''I myself have seen you walking with Nikolaos. Vanessa, why continue your lies? We would think more of you if you were truthful! Joseph has told us what happened. Now, speak!''

Vanessa began to cry. Xanthe jeered at her, furious that it had all failed. ''You can do nothing right, foolish woman! I told you no good would come of this! That man only used your fondness for him to encourage you to help him escape! Now what will become of us?''

"I think Nikolaos is fond of Vanessa," said Iris quickly. "This can be settled peacefully, if you will all—''

Xanthe turned on her, glad to have another victim to attack. "You!" she spat. "What do you know of us? You are not Greek! You are a stranger, a barbarian! You come from nowhere and marry a Venizelos, and think you know all about us! You know nothing! You are nobody!"

"That will do!" Greg was raging. He stood with fist uplifted, and for the first time Vanessa and Xanthe looked frightened. "Go, both of you! Out of my sight! Shut yourselves in the Cottage and do not come out again!"

"He will throw us out! Us, his relatives! And my two innocent little girls, who have done no harm in their young lives!" And Xanthe began to weep, big dramatic sobs, her black eyes not managing to acquire any tears. "Oh, my sister, what evil you have done this night!"

"Get out of my sight!" yelled Gregorios, his voice harsh and rough, he spoke in some dialect Iris could scarcely understand. "You have disgraced yourselves! Go! Do not let me see you! I must consider what to do with you!"

That did scare them, both women scurried away, covering their black heads with black scarves, and hiding their faces. They ran into the Cottage and slammed the door after themselves.

"Women!" cried Greg. "Damn women! Troublemakers! I should have shut that foolish man away in some remote area—women always make trouble," and he gave a hard stare at Iris, his mother, and Melania.

His mother dared to answer, in mild words, "Gregorios, I think Vanessa would have found her way to Nikolaos, and released him. She hung about him many times, and he is also attracted to her. I think you might let Joseph return to his work now," she gently reminded him.

Both the servants had remained, ears and eyes alert. Greg, reminded, turned to them. "You may go, and I thank you for your faithfulness to me and to my house."

Both servants bowed as deeply as their years would allow them, and their creaking bones. Iris thought of the feudal days, and how Greece was still in a primitive time span, in spite of the modern years. They were happy to have served their master, they would die for him and his house. If only Vanessa and Xanthe had their loyalty!

Greg strode up and down the room, fuming. Iris watched him with troubled eyes, and finally went to him, and took his arm.

"Greg, I beg of you to contact Timotheos Sicilianos, and talk with him. That is the only way to end this feud. He wished at one time to talk with you. Take him up on that."

Greg frowned down on that. She could feel the heat of his body, he was still very angry. "I do not trust them, not any of the Sicilianos! They have hated us for years, and take every opportunity to harm us! I shall not speak with them. Instead I must think of some way to silence them forever!"

At his ominous tones, she shivered. "But that is wrong, vengeance is wrong, God will be angry with us," she said, in a low tone. "Greg, I beg you—speak with Timotheos, or send some man you trust to speak with him—"

"I wish you would not ask me! This is not women's business!" he said harshly. He held her hand tightly, and scowled. "Women should stay out of men's business! You can see what harm came of it!"

His words stung, his hand hurt, though he seemed unaware of that. "Greg. I think Vanessa is attracted to Nikolaos. We might encourage that—"

"What—a Sicilianos, to be married to one of the House of

Venizelos? He would harm her, he might kill her! I do not trust a one by that name!''

Iris sighed, Greg was striding out to the terrace, and she walked out after him, like a meek little wife, she thought ironically.

Greg glared in the direction of the closed Cottage. "I must consider what to do with them. If it were not for the two little girls, I would throw out the women!" he muttered. "What trouble they make! What gossip and slander, what tormenting and teasing and mischief they make! I am sick of them both! Perhaps I shall take the little girls from them, and send Vanessa and Xanthe away to some remote island to live on nuts!''

Iris giggled, she could not help it. He glared at her, turned on his sandaled foot, and strode away from her. She let him go, did not try to follow.

Lydia came out, gardening tools in hand. "I will work with my flowers, they do not scowl and answer me harshly," she said, her mouth twisted. "What did he say, why do you laugh?''

"Gregorios will send his female relatives to some island, to live on nuts," said Iris, and began to laugh again.

Lydia's brow cleared, she laughed softly. "So, so! Well, a good solution. Monkeys live on nuts, do they not? I feel sorry for the little girls, though," she said, and grimaced as right on cue a small wail came from the Cottage.

"Yes, they will take it out on the girls.''

Someone innocent usually suffered, thought Iris. She got her sketch pad, and seated herself near where her mother-in-law had settled on a gardening pad on her knees.

Lydia dug contentedly in the dirt, Iris sketched the scene of Lydia and her gardening trowel. Thank God for work, they both thought.

Chapter Twenty-six

Alex had turned to Melania somewhat. Iris noticed it with satisfaction. Melania had a sweet temper, and Charmian could be very moody. Also, Melania was helping Alex with the hotel work, taking notes, talking with him about matters.

Greg observed it with satisfaction also. Not so Charmian. She stared at them with sharp blue eyes, and delighted in breaking up their conversations. In the evenings, she insisted on having Alex dance with her to music, until his hip pained him, and he had to stop.

Iris found refuge again in her dressmaking. She had sketched some ideas, but they did not please her. So she went to the sewing room on the second floor of the Big House, and worked with the fabrics directly on the dressmaker dummy.

She was working early one afternoon, humming as she worked, when she heard steps on the stairs. They sounded like Greg's footsteps, they were heavy and sure. She waited, but he did not come to the open door. She got up from kneeling at the hem of the dress, and stretched.

It was early September, the heat was not so bad. Perhaps Greg would take her for a ride, they had not gone anywhere for quite a while. She would like to go down to the port, and look around.

Her sandals clicked lightly on the marble floor, as she crossed the hallway to Greg's room. His door stood open, and she started for it.

Then she stopped abruptly, just before reaching the door. She could see inside the room, and the sight shocked her to the heart.

Greg stood there, his arms clasped around Charmian! Her sister leaned against his chest, her arms wrapped around his waist, her face on his shoulder. Charmian was so tall as she stood in her high-heeled sandals that she could look up and be only inches from his eyes.

"Do not send me away!" Charmian begged. "You know how I feel. I cannot go now—"

"It is for the best," said Greg curtly.

Iris waited for no more. Eyes huge and disbelieving, she backed away soundlessly from the door, and fled to the sewing room. She shut the door softly, and sank down into the floor.

Greg—and Charmian! And she had been married to Greg only four months! She put her hands to her face. In spite of the September heat, her hands were chilled.

Charmian's musical voice had been broken and agonized. Iris had never heard her like this, not even when Charmian had been reading a part. She was not acting, she could not be. She loved Greg!

And Greg—he had been encouraging her! All the time pretending to desire her! Or perhaps he did despise Charmian, but was reluctantly attracted to her. Charmian was so beautiful, so bewitching—

Iris rubbed her face distractedly. What should she do? What could she do? Greg was evidently trying to encourage Charmian to leave, he wanted to end their affair. Should Iris ignore it, petend not to know? But how could she endure the pretense?

Perhaps she should try to maintain her dignity, confront him, and leave? She could go to New York, she could work again. Thank God for work, she had her career.

She remembered the tender nights in his arms. His kisses, his fervent caresses. She had even begun to hope he loved her, though he never said so. And she knew her own love had deepened and grown, almost too big for her. How could she leave him?

At least she did not yet expect a child! She had begun to want a child of his—oh, God.

She did not know how long she sat on the floor, staring at the hem of the dress. Finally she moved, she felt stiff. She got up, and went to her bedroom, washed and changed. It was almost three, they would have their late luncheon soon, though she had no appetite for food.

She buttoned the large white buttons of the blue-and-white-striped dress. How childish and unsophisticated it looked. Yet that was what Iris was, she thought bitterly. She had never wanted to be cynical and knowledgeable about men, to run from one affair to another. She had never pandered to men, she had never flirted and dressed to attract them.

Charmian had—and look what she got. One man after another! That was the way of the world, and Iris must resign herself to it. Men like Gregorios Venizelos could have any woman they wanted. And of course they liked the sleek attentions of beautiful women. They enjoyed the flattery, the caresses, the gowns with their slits to show long beautiful legs, and round bosoms. Who wanted a modest woman, who wanted virtue and goodness?

She had worked herself to a fury by the time she went down the steps to the lounge area. Lydia looked up with a smile that faded as she surveyed Iris's stormy face. Melania looked concerned, Charmian looked like the cat licking canary feathers from her smooth chin.

"You are late, Iris," said Gregorios in lordly fashion. "You work too long on your dressmaking! We have been waiting for you!"

"You should have gone ahead!" she said curtly, and marched to the foot of the table, as he stared at her in surprise. Her white sandals hit the marble floor with a slap-slap that sounded like Xanthe's, she realized, and it made her all the more curious. To be like that nasty woman! She tried to curb her tongue, and found she had to be silent to do so. She fumed inside, and could eat little.

Alex was at the table, beside Melania, eating with them now. His dark glasses with side pieces had been replaced by lighter ones, and his eyes glowed behind them. He had his sight back, and he was happy. He talked business with Greg, the women were mostly silent.

Charmian ate a good meal, Iris noted. Did that mean she had convinced Greg to let her stay?

The maids padded around silently as they served dessert. They seemed to feel Iris's dark mood, and cast curious sympathetic looks at her. Did everybody know about Greg's affair with Charmian?

Greg drained his coffee cup, and looked at Iris. "You received a letter in the mail today," he announced. "It is from your former employer, Nadia Egorova. It is on the desk there. I wish you to tell me—"

Iris cried out, interrupting him. "I have a letter from Madame Egorova! Why didn't you tell me! Where is it? It is important!'' And she glared at him reproachfully. "I have been waiting for weeks for this!''

His black thick eyebrows raised. "Why, the gowns were sent only two weeks ago—''

She jumped up from the table, and ran to the desk where the wide white letter lay, with the fine black handwriting. She sat down on the edge of the chair, and tore open the letter, to devour it eagerly. This was fate, this was probably her solution! To think the letter from Nadia Egorova had come on the very day she had discovered her husband's infidelity!

The letter read:

Dearest Iris Patakos Venizelos:

Greetings to you and richest blessings on you from your friend, Nadia Egorova.

I was amazed to receive from Petros Diophantus of Athens, the lovely suits and gowns which he did send to me. I had thought with you so newly married, and to such a demanding man! that you would have no time to work out the dress line which you wished to do for us.

I am most pleased with the dresses. Your white lines and black line of Petros are a most charming contrast. I see your hand in the white ones, the delicacy, the modesty, the beauty. I enclose sketches, and will proceed to have these made up here in copies for our market. You are right in assuming that these will go best in the Midwest markets, I plan to send them to a friend in Chicago for selling there.

Will you arrange there for making the blouses and the suits I indicate, in quantities of one dozen each, and have the women of your village to embroider them? They will be charming. If that quantity is too much, arrange as you see fit. I feel sure all can be sold here.

I will show what you have sent to the buyers for the spring line. Then I will inform you what goes best.

However, I think we will have no trouble, not with yours, not with that of Petros Diophantus. I like his work also, I have written to him.

The idea of the scarlet poppy as your trademark is very good. I am arranging for the copyright for you.

If you plan to return to New York City, I offer to you, Iris Patakos, a full-time job in my House. I read between the lines of your letters, and I feel you are not completely happy. Your marriage was very hasty. God forbid I should come between a husband and a wife! However, if you return to me, I shall ask no questions. There is much work to be done, and I have learned in my lifetime that work heals the stricken heart.

If I am wrong about your marriage, forgive my foolish words, and accept my best wishes for a long and joyous married life. Know I think of your good always. You are a sweet good girl, and a hard worker.

Pray consider another line now, and think of a winter group for us. The idea of designing for the Midwest is good, as you know it best, and we can well expand there. However, if something for New York City comes to you, be sure to continue. I look forward to your reply, send some sketches if uncertain how to continue.

> Most sincerely,
> Nadia Egorova

When Iris had read the long letter, and glanced at the pages of sketches enclosed, she looked up, to find several people staring at her.

Charmian was seated across from her. "What does Nadia Egorova say? May I read the letter?"

"No," said Iris flatly. "She does like the white line, and wants to see more sketches."

Charmian's slim ash silver eyebrows raised in an arch.

"Why can't I see your letter? Darling, you are very secretive!" Her blue eyes mocked Iris.

"It is not your concern," Greg answered for her. "But I would talk to you about this, Iris!"

She did not want to quarrel with him before them all. She nodded. "Later on, Greg," she said dully.

"It is good she liked the dresses," said Lydia tactfully. "Petros Diophantus will be most happy. I presume she liked those also?"

"Yes, she does, and has written to Petros directly." Iris gathered her thoughts, glanced at the letter again to refresh her memory. "She wants us to make more blouses and suits, and have the village women start right in to embroider them. She says a dozen of each of those she sketched, or less if they cannot accomplish so many."

Lydia cried out. "A dozen of each—how many, Iris?"

Iris counted the sketches. "Five blouses, two suits, and one dress—no, a second dress. She likes the one that Nike did very much. I think it will take Nike all winter to do those she wants!"

"Oh, that is very good—work for Nike, and for a dozen women all the winter," Kyria Lydia smiled. "Is that not good news, Gregorios?"

"Yes, very good news," he agreed, abstracted. He was watching Iris's face keenly. "The women will be most pleased. Do you wish to go to the village this afternoon, Iris?"

She hesitated, then nodded. She wanted to talk to him anyway, she might as well steel herself and do so today. But how could she supervise the work of the women, and still return to New York? Well, perhaps Melania could take care of that, with the help of Charis.

She must not worry about others! Nobody else did, she thought bitterly. Iris would start to think about Iris, and put her own good first! Why should she worry about strangers, when her own family ignored her!

"Yes, I should like to go, Greg. That is, if you have the time to spare," she said very formally.

"It will be my pleasure," he said, as formally. "In about fifteen minutes, if you will?"

She nodded. They could go, and be back soon after dusk. And in that time she would tell him she was leaving him. She felt cold, but determined, as she went to get her brief jacket and scarf, for the ride returning after dark.

At the last moment, she put Nadia Egorova's letter in her large white pocketbook, it would help to have the sketches with her.

They were both silent as they rode. Greg glanced from side to side keenly, and she wondered if he watched for enemies. They had taken the Land Rover, and he had curtly refused Charmian's tentative offer to come with them.

Near the village, he said, "I must pick up some supplies at the store and the port. Shall I leave you somewhere—and pick you up at the home of Nike?"

"That would be fine," she accepted.

Iris indicated the house of the two women who did their best embroidery, and he helped her down when they arrived. The women came out, bowing and smiling.

Iris talked to them, showed them the sketches. They agreed happily to do more work. "Do not rush with it," she warned them. "I do not wish to spoil the beauty of the embroidery with rushing. Work at your usual pace. You will be well paid," and she named the sums, which made them gasp and nudge each other.

She asked them if more women would be willing to do some embroidery.

"Yes, yes, my cousin, and another cousin's wife's sister, and they know another woman who will do good work—"

Everybody knew everybody, and the talents were known also, and an evaluation of the work. Iris asked about lacework. Yes, they knew who could do good lacework. She wrote down the names, Melania and Kyria Lydia would help here.

She ended with Nike, who was immensely pleased about the work. "You mean they wish more—enough to work all winter?" she asked, her face radiant with relief. "Oh, then I can hire someone to dig the garden, and I will rent out the boat of my late father. How happy I am! I can do the work I enjoy, and be paid for it!"

"That is a great joy, is it not?" agreed Iris, smiling. "I find it is the greatest pleasure in the world, to do work that I enjoy doing, and have it appreciated."

"Yes, yes, that is true," Nike agreed. Her slim talented fingers pointed to some drawings in a pad. "I have been sketching ideas, do you wish to see?"

They put their heads together on the work, it was very clever and pleasing. Some designs were for children's clothes, some for adult. That gave Iris more ideas.

"I am sure there would be a market for these in children's clothes! I wonder if I could design for small children!"

Nike was flatteringly positive. "I am sure that you can! You are very talented!"

Gregorios came for them before they had finished talking. Nike brought fresh hot tea, and some sweet cakes. He was more pleased with the cakes than the tea, but praised both.

He looked over the sketches she had made. "I am not versed in this, but they look excellent to me. Can they be used, Iris?"

"I am sure of it," she said eagerly. "Look at this design, the cunning puppets and dolls. And I like these, the clowns and balls, the little performing dogs and baby elephants. Oh, they are very sweet."

417

Janet Louise Roberts

Iris promised to bring two dresses to Nike soon, and to forward her ideas for children's designs to Nadia. "If she does not work them out, she may know of someone who will be glad to have the idea," Iris said.

"You are very good. Mother blesses you daily in her prayers, and so do I," Nike added shyly. She indicated the silent woman on her bed of pain in the other room.

Impulsively, Iris went in to the woman, who smiled faintly up at her. "Thank you for your blessed prayers," said Iris. "I am sure they ascend up to God and the Virgin. Blessings on you."

The woman's twisted mouth moved slowly. "I am—truly—blessed—daughter—Nike—" she managed to say in a guttural whisper.

Iris laid her hand softly on the gnarled twisted hand. "She is one of the truly good," she murmured. "You taught her well. She is a credit to you."

The mouth managed a smile, the black eyes shone in the wrinkled face. "God—bless—your—pretty—face—"

Iris had tears in her eyes when she returned to the cluttered living room. Nike pretended not to notice. "Pray take the sketches with you, I have copies," she urged. "I think the cotton and linen mixture blouse would be best for the blouses. And about the dress—I can do that on silk, but it looks better on the butcher linen. The fabric holds the embroidery better."

They discussed that a few minutes, then Greg and Iris left.

"What courage," said Iris, in the Land Rover.

"Nike is very attractive, I had forgotten how pretty she is," said Greg.

Iris hated herself that a strong pang of jealousy shot through her. Could he think of nothing but a woman's beauty of face?

"Yes, she is," she said stiffly.

"I wonder if I should arrange her marriage. She will never

418

leave her mother—there is nobody in the village suitable," he said, half to himself.

Iris half turned to him, a little dangerous in the lurching Land Rover on the slanting uphill track. "Did you ever stop to consider that Nike might not wish to marry?" she cried out. "Perhaps she is perfectly happy there, with no man to worry about!"

Greg's mouth tightened. "I think that is not what makes you angry today," he said outright. "What was in the letter that troubles you?"

Iris drew a deep breath. "Nadia Egorova asked me to return to New York and work full-time with her," she told him bluntly. "She says I do have much talent, she is very pleased with my work. I think it is time I returned home."

Greg went stiff. "This is your home! A wife's home is with her husband!" he said dangerously. "Forget about dressmaking! Your place is at my side! I will inform Madame Egorova she does wrong to interfere in my marriage! I have tolerated this work, only because as a hobby it pleased you. It shall not separate us!"

"I never expected our marriage to last," Iris forced herself to say. "I don't know why you married me—perhaps because I defied you! But you will flit from one woman to another. I do not expect to enjoy that! I would rather not be married than endure the humiliation of a husband who cannot keep his hands off other women!"

"Ah—ha!" said Greg, sounding like the villain of an old-time melodrama. "So that is it! You saw me and Charmian this noon! That is it!"

"So—if I did? I am sure that is not the only time you have held her and kissed her! She is a very attractive woman!" said Iris, trying not to sound wildly jealous.

"I knew it, I knew it. That bitch is a troublemaker. She must have known you were near. I had told her that morning I thought she should make plans to go home and get back to her modeling! She came upstairs to my bedroom, and wept, oh, what an actress! She flung herself in my arms, and begged me to let her stay. I told her I thought it would be well for her to go home. How she cried! I patted her back, and told her to go!''

Iris was silent. It could be true, it could be a plausible lie. If only she could be sure of Greg.

"You believe me!" said Greg fiercely, his voice deep and rough.

"I—don't know—" she hesitated.

He swore, some very wicked words in a dialect Greek. She pretended not to understand. "What a man of patience I am," he concluded fiercely. "Any other man would be stopping the jeep and beating his wife!"

"A model of patience, I am sure," she muttered.

They were silent on the rest of the way home. His jaw was set grimly, her face was troubled. The darkness hid the glory of the land, as the early September covered it with yellowing grasses, some last scarlet poppies and blue iris.

Yet they could smell the fragrance of the fields, the olive trees, the salt of the sea. She would miss it if she left. Was he telling the truth? Was Charmian up to her old and new tricks?

They arrived at the Big House, and dinner was ready for them. Iris washed, did not bother to change. Charmian was slinky and eye-catching in a white gown with a border of gold, the dress slit to her hips. Her golden earrings swung from her small ears, her hair was a swirl of ash silver. Iris felt like a country wife beside her glamorous half-sister.

Iris retired early, then stiffened in the bed as Greg came in. "I don't want you tonight!" she said fiercely.

"Oh, you don't!" he said roughly. "Well, I want you, and you had best make up your mind about being a wife!" And he lay down with her on the bed, and flung the sheet to the floor, and her nightgown of blue cotton soon followed.

He put his hands on her, and they were big rough warm hands. The hands of a man who worked hard, and she loved them. She put her fingers on his, meaning to make him stop, but the touch of them changed her mind. If she left soon— why not make the most of this night?

He stroked his one hand over her naked silky body, and she sighed and turned her face against his hairy chest. He felt the change in her, and softened and slowed his embrace.

"My bad-tempered little wife!" he whispered in her ear, and kissed the lobe, and bit it softly with his strong white teeth. "Why do you fight me all the time?" He curled his free hand under her body, and put his arm all about her, and pulled her close to his hard body. She felt his strength all down her softness, and she pushed herself tighter against him.

Why did she fight him? First, she had not wanted anybody to touch her. Now she felt lost when he did not touch for a time. She loved his touch on her, though not the touch of anybody else. His hand stroked so cleverly, his fingers knew her soft spots, his arm knew how to hold her, his body knew how to curve itself to cuddle her.

Second, she loved him madly, bitterly, wantonly, completely. She could lose herself in his embrace, with a passion that terrified her. When he kissed her, she sank into a sea of madness. She wanted him so furiously, her arms went about him, she moved like an Aphrodite to entice him.

And third, she wanted his child, especially his son, to please him and herself. She could picture his child, his baby, with wildly curling black hair, grave black eyes, a sweet baby face that echoed his father's strength. Oh, how she wanted his baby in her arms! Only then would she feel complete. She felt as primitive as any Greek in some remote island.

Oh, why did she fight him? She could not. And so she

curled into his body, and enticed him silently with her hips pressing to his hard masculine strength. Her hands went to his muscular warm back, and she dug like a kitten into his flesh, with her fingers kneading him. His mouth kissed at her shoulders, her arms, her breasts, furiously, his tongue licking her soft skin, his teeth biting softly.

"Oh, I could eat you up," he murmured.

"I am not a sweet cake with icing," she protested breathlessly.

"No? I thought you were. Here are some sugared rose petals—" and he nibbled at her lips. "Here is some peach marzipan—" and he licked her cheeks. And he went on down her body, saying things that made her blush wildly even in the darkness.

He teased her with his kisses and his hands, until she was wild with her need. She held her hips open, and drew him to herself, and they came together with fury and sweetness mingled. He rested on her, making her hold himself in her, until she was gasping with pleasure. And then he began to move slowly, slowly, making her wait, pressing on her subtly, showing he knew how she felt, how she wanted—

"Oh—Gregorios—oh, my darling—oh—it is so marvelous—"

He groaned his response to her in Greek, and fell on her, and held her closely for a time, and they finally slept.

Sometime in the night, he moved, and got up from the bed. "Where are you going?" she asked sleepily.

"I have to make a long-distance call," he said brusquely.

Iris felt a keen disappointment as he left the warm bed, stumbled into a robe, and left her. She lay alone for almost an hour, and tried to sleep, but could not.

He returned about four o'clock, and mumbled to himself as he took off the robe and lay down again. "Awake, Iris?" he asked.

"Yes. You got your call through?" She tried to sound casual.

"Finally," he said, pleased. "Half a world away, it is a miracle of today! All is well, thank God."

She wondered if a relative was ill. She waited for more confidences, but he drew her to himself, nuzzled against her, sighed twice, and fell asleep, quite relaxed.

Iris lay awake another hour before she could sleep. Men, she thought, how inconsiderate, how difficult, how crazy, and they thought women were irrational!

She finally slept, held closely in his arms.

Chapter Twenty-seven

Iris brooded. Should she believe Greg and remain with him? Or should she admit to herself that he probably lied to her, that he was a womanizer, he would go from one woman to another, and she might as well get out while she could? If she once had his child, she might find it impossible to leave him. He would love his son!

She found it difficult to concentrate on work. She sighed, and went out in midmorning to take a short walk, with sketch pad in hand. She returned with the pad empty, and her brain seething with worry.

Greg eyed her keenly, but said nothing. He seemed on hot bricks, pacing from the telephones to the terrace, and back again. Lydia watched him meditatively.

Charmian rose about noon, as usual, and came down in a rose pink cotton dress with white sandals on her narrow feet, her hair piled high in a sleek silver chignon. There was such a complacent look on her well-manicured face that Iris could have slapped her.

Iris was ashamed—and how ashamed for her the good nuns would have been! To atone, she offered to make a herb tea for Charmian, one of her favorite drinks.

Alex was at the telephone when she returned, writing down something rapidly, and acting very excited. Melania stared over his shoulder, bending to the desk.

Iris set the tea down beside Charmian, to receive a lazy cat-smile and her thanks. "You are a darling to wait on me like this!" said Charmian.

Alex sprang up, waving the pad of paper. "Charmian— what news! A telegram for you," and he limped over to hand it to her.

Charmian began to read, then shot up in her chair, her face registering shock. "What is this? It cannot be—"

"What is it, Charmian? Good news—or very bad? It isn't one of your friends," asked Iris. "Not—your mother?"

Much as she disliked Shelley, she did not wish her ill.

"No—no, it is from Victor Paxinou! But I never met him—how could he know—"

"We are all waiting for your news, Charmian," said Greg smoothly. Iris eyed him from under her lashes suspiciously. She knew that tone. He was up to something. "What is it? Bad news or good?"

"Good news," breathed Charmian, going quite pale under her makeup. "It says—I cannot believe it—he wishes me to come to Hollywood at once—there is a part for me in his new movie—oh, the chance of a lifetime—Victor Paxinou!"

Greg came over and took the pad from her limp hand, and read the message closely. He seemed to be thinking deeply.

Iris asked, "Who is Victor Paxinou? Does he have a good reputation?"

"Oh, marvelous! His film *A Woman's Desires* was terribly

426

popular, and so beautifully made! The photography was exquisite—you remember, I tried to get you to see it!'' Charmian was all aglow now. She snatched the pad back from Greg. ''Oh, he wants me to come at once—I must leave!''

''Let me see,'' said Greg, glancing at the clock. ''We could get you to Athens tomorrow—then on to the United States—or, I have to go to Paris anyway. I could change my plans, go a little early, and see you off in Paris for New York. Yes, I think that would do.''

''Oh, Greg!'' Charmian hugged his arm, beaming up at him with eyelashes fluttering madly. ''You could show me Paris! How divine!''

Had he planned this? Iris was so furious she could now have hit them both!

''Well, if you don't mind risking losing this job,'' said Greg mildly. ''I know Paxinou slightly—isn't he a bit of a dictator? He says right away, not next week. What do you want to do?''

Charmian hesitated, then sighed. ''I must go right off to Hollywood,'' she admitted. ''I cannot take the chance of losing this! Oh, I must get in touch with my agent! He must come with me, for the contracts—he is very clever—I wonder if he knows about this—'' She gave Greg a rather suspicious look.

''It is about four in the morning in New York. If you want to waken him—''

Charmian gave a theatrical shudder. ''Never! No, I'll wait till—when will it be noon in New York, dearest Greg?''

''About eight tonight. You can be packed and ready, and tell him what you want him to do. Would he drop everything and go to Hollywood with you?''

''He will insist on it!'' said Charmian gaily.

And so it proved. Her agent had also heard from Paxinou, and urged Charmian to be at Kennedy Airport as soon as possible. Greg figured she could get a plane in Paris that would be in Kennedy by late evening, with the time difference. He himself would see that she made the plane in Paris.

Charmian had had Charis packing for her all afternoon. She had four suitcases, a huge cosmetic case, and a large pocketbook, and wailed about the charges for overweight.

"I'll take care of all that, Charmian, don't fret," said Greg kindly.

At dinner, Charmian was full of her plans, nobody had a chance to get a word in edgewise. Iris was silent, except for directing the servants quietly. She felt a little strange. She was glad for Charmian's opportunity to act, but . . . for Greg to be accompanying her to Paris!

Iris went up to her bedroom soberly that night, but stopped wide-eyed in the doorway. Charis was packing her suitcases! The maid gave her a mischievous look.

"Gregorios Venizelos gave me directions, Kyria!" said the maid. "He said to pack for you three suitcases, of formal dresses and informal, for the weather in France! I do so, see?"

"But—I am not going!" gasped Iris. "I mean—he didn't say a word—"

Greg popped his head in the paneled door to his room. "Why do you think I would go to France without my wife?" he demanded, with a grin, and a heavy wink at her. "I told you I would show you Paris!"

Only Lydia was not surprised when Iris came down dressed to travel. Charmian cried out, "You're not going!" at her sister.

"Why, yes, Charmian," said Iris, managing to look coolly amazed at her. "Of course!"

Charmian was silent all the way to the landing strip. She accepted Greg's help into her seat and with fastening the seat belt. But she was cool to Iris all the way to Athens, and on to Paris.

At the immense Charles de Gaulle airport outside Paris, Iris was caught up in excitement. The wings out to the planes, and the long sloping rubber mats like escalators that led to the far tips where they would get the airplanes looked like *Star Wars* to Iris. All the long white walls, the struts and huge windows, the glimpses of mammoth planes, were amazing, like going off into space.

"Are we in a science fiction movie?" she murmured to Greg, as he held her hand on the moving rubber mats.

"I'm afraid so, we are going off to the stars," he said solemnly in her ear. "I wonder what kind of food they have on Jupiter?"

She giggled, the question was just like him! He flashed a smile down at her, and Charmian was temporarily forgotten.

Greg got his sister-in-law efficiently through customs and passport desks, and they saw her to her exit station. They waited for the plane, and saw her disappear into the tunnel leading to the plane.

Then they watched at a window, to see the huge white plane take off into the darkening night sky, with all the immense de Gaulle airport lit up like a space station.

Afterward, Greg tucked Iris under his arm, and they started back to the long passageways leading to the entrance to the airport. She was sure she would have been lost a dozen times, but he managed efficiently.

A silver Rolls-Royce met them there, and Iris slid into the luxurious velvet seat with a sigh of relief. The chauffeur, Henri, a brisk man in his forties, drove them into the city past country scenes, then the distinctive streets of Paris, with its ancient buildings accented by flashing neon signs for bars and cafés. Smartly dressed people sat at sidewalk tables, talking, laughing, drinking.

"Paris," said Greg. "I think you will enjoy it! We shall be here several days, my darling, then on to one of my hotels in the Loire Valley."

"Really?" Iris had something else on her mind. "Greg? Do you know Victor Paxinou well?"

He slanted a mischievous look at her, and nodded. "Very well, love. We went through school together. We were apart in college years, but later I met him when he was just starting out as a producer. He needed funds to make a little movie he wished to do. I gave him the money, on condition nobody knew about it! I didn't want to be chased down by other hopeful movie producers."

"And the movie did well, and made a million dollars," said Iris. "I might have known!"

"No, it failed," said Greg. "He was humiliated. I told him it was a good job, even if the public didn't like it, and said I would back another. About a year later, he found a script he liked, and asked me about funding. It was a big job, I helped, and found several other men to fund it with me. You would faint if I told you how much money went into it!" He chuckled.

"And did that one succeed?"

"Yes, it did, and made a fortune for Paxinou. He was very grateful. Since then, we have worked together several times, and he is doing well, I knew he could do it, he has the talent, the ambition, the drive, and the patience."

"And he owed you favors," said Iris thoughtfully.

"Yes, indeed. And when I begged him to put Charmian in a film, and take her off my neck for at least six months, he agreed like a shot. He will be pleasantly surprised if she can act."

Iris began to laugh at his complacent one, and he reached out, grabbed her, and kissed her soundly. The chauffeur eyed them in the mirror and smiled with them, not understanding a word of Greek.

"Paris is for lovers!" said Henri happily.

Iris was quite surprised when the Rolls turned in to what looked like an alley or a back street, and came to a halt. The building looked dark and very old, the entrance hall was downright tiny.

Greg smiled at her bewilderment, as they got out of the car. "The Ritz is a very old hotel, and the porter is at this entrance," he told her with a twinkle in his eyes.

"The—Ritz Hotel?" This was the Ritz, this very old quiet place?

She looked about dubiously, as they were greeted and taken up to their rooms in a small creaky elevator. Compared to some modern glass and steel hotels, this was very strange.

They were taken up a few stairs, down a few stairs, along a narrow hallway lined with old-fashioned prints and carpeted with soft rugs. Then the porter opened a door with a large brass key.

Inside was a huge bedroom, with a massive plump bed covered with a down flower-printed spread. The drapes had been drawn, their suitcases had been unpacked, their clothes were in the two massive wardrobes. A vase of beautiful autumn flowers was on the small antique writing desk. Greg gave a critical look around, then nodded, tipped the porter and sent him away.

After a comfortable night in the old-fashioned flowery room, Iris opened the drapes the next moring— and gasped.

"Oh—Greg, look!"

He came to her side, still knotting his silvery tie. He gave an appreciative look at the view. Below them was a courtyard filled with small green trees and pots of red filled with scarlet geraniums. A gardener was spraying the flowers with water. On a wall beyond their room was a vine covered with brilliant purple flowers. And straight out from them was Paris—rooftops of mansard windows in little peaks, chimneys with hats on them, and a gray cat on one roof washing its face.

"Paris," Iris breathed. "It looks just like I dreamed!"

"And where would you like to go today? A fashion show—the Louvre—the Champs-Elysées—the Ile Saint-Louis—" Greg teased, smiling at her wide eyes.

"All of them!" she cried, and he gave a mock groan.

In the next few days, she managed to get to most of the places she desired, though the more she saw the more she wanted to see. They rose early in the morning, to start out walking along the nearby Champs-Elysées, to peer in the shop windows at the world-famous perfumes, dresses, scarves, hats displayed for them.

When the museums opened, Iris and Greg were in the first lines, to explore the wonders of the Louvre; the Jeu de Paume with its marvelous Impressionist paintings; a tapestry museum, and many others.

They walked until their feet gave out, to Notre Dame, and the exquisite Sainte-Chapelle with the breathtaking stained-glass windows from floor to ceiling, along the Left Bank to many churches and cafés and art shops. They crammed as much as possible into the days, stopping only at dark when they ate early and fell into bed.

Iris frankly did not want to waste time with nightclubs when there were so many other wonders to see. "Another time," said Greg, quite satisfied to skip them.

They drove down to Versailles, with Henri at the wheel to show them sights on the way. They explored the huge palace rooms, but Iris enjoyed even more the marvelous flower gardens.

Greg finally said, "I am sorry, Iris, but we must move on, I have to see one of my hotels!"

"Oh, I knew we must leave—but there is so much to see!" And they had gone to only one fashion show!

"We shall come again."

They packed up, and with regret left the luxurious quiet Ritz Hotel. Henri drove them to the south, and soon they began to see the rolling hills, the poplar trees, and châteaus on the hilltops.

"They look like fairy castles," breathed Iris, as she gazed from the road up into the blue distance where a white stone château perched seemingly in the midst of green trees. The trees were just beginning to turn golden and scarlet, and a soft misty yellow green. "I expect to see the Sleeping Beauty at any minute!"

"There is one château where it is said that Charles Perrault gazed on it, and had his idea for the story," said Greg unexpectedly. "What is it? Henri—" he broke into French and asked the chauffeur.

"*Oui, oui*," the man agreed. "It is the château of Ussé. Ussé—in the forest of Chinon. It has the round pepper-pot roofs, massive towers, and lovely gardens. But we have beautiful pepper pots, also, madame! And most lovely gardens!"

Iris looked at Greg in question, he nodded. "We have borrowed Henri from the Château Foucher. That is where we are going today."

She saw more enchanting vistas as they went farther south into the Loire Valley. Small pretty villages, with red roofs and blue on the little cottages, and gray slate on the chapels and churches. Lovely old oak trees, and maples, and golden poplars along slim streams winding into the meadows. Scenes that were like those in a medieval book of hours, with blue-frocked workmen slashing yellow wheat with scythes, and castles on the hills.

Henri was a most knowledgeable guide, and he was proud

of his part of France. "These châteaus were built by noblemen in the days of the early kings, madame. All were supposed to be close enough to attend the court in Paris. However, they wished to have homes in the country, to entertain guests, to hunt the animals in the forests, to relax from the strain of being always formal, you comprehend? So they were given lands by their king within a day or two ride from Paris, all clustered about Paris, you comprehend? And they built grand houses, to rival each other, and invited the king to come, and he came and he stayed and he stayed, you comprehend?"

About midafternoon, after a luncheon at a lovely country inn, they arrived at Château Foucher, at the end of a long pleasant lane in the midst of a light grove of trees. They saw it with the afternoon sunshine on the large rectangular windows, and the blue pepper-pot towers on the blue gray slate roof, and flowers of yellow and crimson and blue in the gardens set out primly with dividers of green clipped hedges.

"A typical French garden," murmured Greg. "Mother says they are like the French mind, all set and formalized, and brilliant, and predictable!"

Iris had to chuckle with him. "What about English gardens?"

"A pleasant clutter, with unexpected touches, and some bushes all tangly, and roses next to garden pinks!"

"Why do you say that?"

"The English are not afraid to be eccentric. They are so sure of themselves, they can afford to be different! Americans used to fear being different, some still dread it. Greeks—now they think only the classical times were good, everything in the past two thousand years was a comedown!"

She was still laughing when they drew up at the entrance to the château. Madame Foucher came out to greet them, a pleasant smile on her face, a worried look in her eyes.

She bowed to them formally, and showed them into the lovely hallway of the château. "We are still full of tourists from the summer, Monsieur Venizelos," she told Greg. "I hope you will enjoy your room."

She did not exactly apologize for it, but Iris thought she had probably been afraid of their reactions, for the room was rather small and there was no sitting room with it. However, the bath was large, well kept, with hot towels on the warming racks. And the bedroom was beautiful, with flowery drapes, and a view of the sunset in the west.

Greg left Iris to unpack and rest, while he went prowling about the château. At dinner that evening, Iris met Monsieur André Foucher, a pleasant man in his thirties, more calm than his wife, and sure he could satisfy Greg.

The dinner was excellent, so well cooked and served that it was a feast in itself for eyes and for taste. The Fouchers made their own goose paté, they served it with a dark brown bread with a glass of crisp white wine, and some celery and lettuce form their own gardens.

This was followed by broiled white fish, so tender it fell from the fork, and small new potatoes and peas barely cooked. The next course was roast beef, sliced thin, with horseradish dressing, a type of squash mashed with butter and herbs, and a lovely wine.

The dessert was a puff pastry so light it was filled with air as well as a caramel custard and marshmallows. This was served with hot black thick *café filtre*, and followed by a coffee liqueur as delicately sweet as the dessert.

Madame came round with the dessert to make sure they were pleased, anxiety lines around her eyes. Iris assured her they were very happy with the room and the meal. Greg said little.

Later in their room, Iris asked, "Is something wrong here, Greg? Or would you rather not tell me?"

"Um. I've had a couple complaints, so I decided to come.

Don't worry, Iris, I'm sure it isn't serious,'' and he said no more.

Breakfast was served in their rooms, hot chocolate and warm sweet pastries, chunks of sweet cheese, and glasses of orange juice.

''The juice is a concession to foreign tourists, such as Americans,'' Greg told Iris. ''We are all more nutrition conscious these days, perhaps it is just as well. What do you wish to do today?''

''Sketch in that beautiful garden,'' she told him promptly.

He nodded. ''I'll ask Madame to show you around. That will keep her off my back while I tour about with her husband,'' he said bluntly. ''She is inclined to worry and fuss.''

''Happy to be useful!'' said Iris, with a smile. He ruffled her hair so much she had to brush it again, and smooth it back into a chignon.

She wore her lilac suit with the black braid, and her black sandals. It was a little formal for the country, but she thought the French were more formal. In Greece she often wore slacks or even shorts in the morning, but not here, she thought.

She found Madame in a flowered dress covered with a crisp little white apron with lace about it. Madame Jeanne Foucher was a beautiful woman, with a haunting oval face, large brown eyes, a slightly plump figure that men gazed at with appreciation. She had two children, and produced their pictures quickly from her desk when Iris happened to ask how old they were.

''Eight and six, madame, and good as gold! They are in school today, you will see them this afternoon,'' and she beamed fondly.

Iris carried her sketch pad with her, but had little chance that day to pause and sketch. Madame Foucher trotted from one task to another, and Iris followed her about, on her invitation, showing her interest.

They went from the flower gardens, where Madame Foucher issued her orders to the gardeners, to the vegetable gardens, where Madame looked critically at the peas, and decided there would be enough to be picked for dinner.

"Luncheon will be a country soup, Madame Venizelos," she told Iris. "We do not have menus, we serve all alike, from a limited menu, what we can do ourselves easily; we use our own meats, our own chickens, our own vegetables, until the autumn frosts kill them. We have even our own berry bushes," and she showed them proudly.

Iris had luncheon with Madame Foucher, the men had disappeared to look at the roads nearby, said Madame, with a worried frown. "There are some holes, and the state has not fixed them. There are complaints about them, for the tires, you comprehend?"

The vegetable soup was thick and rich with beef broth, and was served with their own French bread, butter, cheese, cold meats. For dessert there were bowls of apples and oranges.

After luncheon Iris followed Madame to the kitchens, on her hostess's invitation, and observed with interest the process of preparing the evening dinner.

They sat at the table of butcher block, and compared recipes. Madame Foucher became more relaxed and calm as they talked about food and regional differences in France, and the different cheeses and desserts, and life in a château with difficult plumbing.

The cooks worked around them, giving them curious interested looks, and frankly listening to them. Presently, about midafternoon, the two men came in.

"Ah, here they are, I might have known it," said Greg, with a smile. "My wife is also a very good cook!"

"So you are a most fortunate man, as I am myself," said

André Foucher comfortably. He put his hand on his wife's shoulder soothingly. "All goes well, eh?"

"*Oui*, André, very well, I believe. You will choose the wines for dinner?"

"At once, *chérie*," he agreed, and went to the wine cellar with Greg, to look over the wines, and discuss what they would buy next.

The next day, Henri drove Iris and Greg about in the countryside, he said he had some men to see. Greg would stop Henri at some spot, get out and go inside a building, and come out looking thoughtful or satisfied.

Iris was puzzled, but did not ask questions. She enjoyed the ride immensely. The French countryside was so lovely in its autumn haze, with the golden-glowing trees, crimson flowers dotting the hedges, the last roses flaunting their pink petals, a vivid blue sky arching over it all. And always on each hillside, it seemed, there would be yet another misty château or castle, with towers and turrets and pepper-pot towers, looking unreal and storybookish.

She recognized the names of the rivers, the Loire, the Cher, the Indre, and the Vienne. Each was lovely and winding, silvery under the sun, with green banks and creamy sands. Henri showed her his maps, with the names all spelled out in antique lettering. She realized it was his pride and joy, the work of his hands, and praised it. He too was an artist. He beamed when she said so.

"I have always liked the old lettering, madame," he explained. "I study the road signs, the inn signs, the old names. At nights, I practice them. The old ways are not so bad, eh?"

"Some are not so bad," she agreed.

They were back at the château after dusk, with just time to wash and change for dinner. Greg had bought a pile of flowers at a roadside stand, and sent them to Madame. When they went down to dinner, there was a small vase at their table, with some of the flowers in it, roses and blue lupins, and in the hallway two more vases full of the flowers.

Another delicious meal, clams stuffed with herbal dressing, veal steaks and fresh vegetables, chocolate *mousse* and lady-fingers. Madame came by with the coffee, looking worried.

"All is well, monsieur and madame?"

"Very well, madame. I would like to see you and your good husband after dinner, perhaps in your parlor?"

"But of course, monsieur!" Deeper worry lines, she filled their cups, and went to tell her husband.

In their parlor, with the children sent to bed, Greg and Iris sat down with the young couple. André drew on his pipe, Jeanne fidgeted with a bit of embroidery.

"Well, I think I have solved the problem," said Greg, with a pleasant smile. "Madame, I regret that you are very pretty."

They both looked stunned and shocked, he grinned at them.

"You see," he continued, "it seems that the superintendent in charge of the road crew came to see you last summer, and made a—we call it—an advance at you? Eh? And you rebuffed him. So, he is a spiteful man, and he deliberately slows down the work on the roads. Also, he sent two friends here to make trouble about some meals, and they wrote complaints to the Venizelos office. I decided to check on this myself. Of course, the meals are excellent as usual. The roads? Well, I went over the man's head, explained what had happened, and we confirmed it with other men who had been here at that time."

"Good heavens!" cried Jeanne Foucher, wringing her hands. "What is a poor female to do! I never thought another thing about it—what must I do? Dress in drab clothing, and

439

put my mouth down like this?'' And she curled her mouth down in a weepy pout.

Iris and the two men laughed, André patted his wife's shoulder. ''So, so, you have solved it, eh, Monsieur Venizelos! I am most grateful! But what will be done about the roads? I will take care of my wife!''

''The department will transfer the man who made trouble. The roads will be mended within the next week,'' said Greg calmly. ''I said if they were not, I would have them mended, and send the bill to them! So—they will be done, eh? Let me know, send word to the office in London.''

''Gladly,'' said André. ''And I thank you so much for your kindly assistance,'' and he got up, and shook Greg's hand solemnly.

Greg and Iris remained another day. She sketched in the flower gardens, and did a sketch of Madame in the kitchen, and gave that one to André. The men discussed wines and the price of meat, whether to close the château at Christmas (they decided to do so), and whether to raise the prices next year (decision delayed).

Then, on the following day, Iris and Greg departed for the airport in Paris, where they got the Venizelos jet back to Athens, to a hot sunny day.

Chapter Twenty-eight

"I have some business in Athens, we will remain for a few days," said Greg on the way to the apartment. "I expect you will wish to visit with your associate, Petros Diophantus! However, I hope you will not begin another line with him."

Iris compressed her mouth. She said, very quietly, "I wish to continue the work, Greg," and she felt very unhappy to quarrel with him after such a beautiful vacation.

"I do not mind if you sketch for a hobby," he told her impatiently, a frown beginning between his black eyebrows. "However, you know I do not want you to work so much. It is not necessary at all!"

She did not try to answer that. She gazed from the window, scarcely seeing the active Athens streets, with cars whizzing about, and sidewalks full of café tables, tourists pausing to finger the worry beads that dangled from many shop stands.

It was all very well to depend on one's husband. But she had early resolved never to trust nor to depend on a man.

They let one down! If he discarded her, or she could not endure his affairs, she would have to leave him, and make her own way. She would never live on alimony, it offended her sense of dignity and her pride and independence.

At the apartment, she went to her bedroom with a sigh of relief. It had been a long hot journey today from France to Greece. Greg stood at the table in the large living room, sorting through some mail that an office clerk had brought up to them.

Iris showered, and lay down for a time. She must have slept, for when she wakened a violet dusk covered the city, and golden lights shone on the Acropolis. She lay looking at it for a time, its beauty soothing her feelings.

She dressed in a light robe, she hoped it would not be necessary to go out tonight. She peered out, heard nothing, and padded downstairs to the main rooms in her slippers and robe.

Greg was lounging on the couch near the huge windows, gazing out over Athens, for once idle. He too wore robe and slippers, evidently he had been resting, she was glad of it. He held out his hand to her with a smile, and she came and sat beside him.

"Is it not lovely, my city?" he murmured.

"Yes, so beautiful."

"I enjoy traveling, but when I return my heart sings. I am home, I am home. It is good to have a place where one belongs. I hope you feel that you belong in Greece, Iris."

Iris hesitated. There was no place in the world that was truly home to her, only temporary residences where she would make a nest for herself, to be discarded when she must move on. She brooded, wondering when she must move on. Or was she being too pessimistic?

He sighed when she did not answer. "There are letters for you, Iris. They are on the desk. I asked for dinner to be served for us up here about ten, you have some time. Would you like a drink?''

''Yes, fruit juice, please. I'll find a maid—'' She got up and went to the kitchen area, where the woman who cooked their meals and served them was working on an enticing platter of salads.

She obtained her juice, and went to the desk, to sit down and read in comfort. One letter was from Nadia Egorova, one from one of the nuns, and one from her father. She was really surprised by the latter.

She read Nadia's letter first, it was full of enthusiasm about Iris's white line, and her ideas for the children's clothes. She thought there would be a good market for them, especially for children ages two to five. She liked Nike's sketches very much. She also had several suggestions for a winter line, and enclosed some sample fabric bits.

The nun wrote of the death of one of the elderly sisters, of other news of the convent, who had come and who had been transferred. They all wished Iris well, and included her in their prayers. Childishly curious, the nun asked, ''Are you pregnant yet? I know you will be a motherly woman, fond of your children,'' and that gave Iris a pang.

She finished her juice, then picked up her father's letter. It was not thick, she fingered the letter. Somehow she knew the news inside would be bad, she had that feeling.

It was. Iris read the letter grimly, shaking her head. Greg came over to her as she laid it down. ''What is it? Your father is not well?''

''He has decided to divorce Maria Ardeth,'' said Iris colorlessly. She handed Greg the letter. ''She has given him no sons, only trouble. I wonder what he gave to her?''

It upset her, this fickleness. Her father had chosen Maria Ardeth freely, the marriage had not been arranged. What excuse did he have for putting her aside now?

"You liked the woman?" asked Greg, puzzled at her reaction. He read the letter. "This makes sense to me," he added. "She is a greedy woman, she is expensive, she is barren. And he has met another woman he likes better—"

"I am sure of it," said Iris, rising. "He always finds another woman he likes better! I wish him joy!"

"Iris." Greg caught her arm, detaining her, he gazed down into her face. "You are upset by this. Your father confided in me. He has loved no woman since your mother died. He hopes only for a son. Do not condemn him for this."

"I do not condemn," said Iris. "I wish him happiness, I really do. But when one goes looking for happiness, it usually evades one, the nuns said this. We are not in this world to be happy, but to work for the love of God and our fellowmen. In work well done, we find satisfaction. In love we find our joy and happiness."

"You are an idealist, my darling, I thank God for it," Greg said gently. "You must realize also, I am sure the nuns would say it, that there are some people in the world who take, take, take. They think the world owes them everything, in the way of possessions, idleness, pleasure. Maria Ardeth was one of them, it is no wonder he is unhappy with her."

Iris sighed. "Yes, I realize that. But he thinks nothing of the sanctity of marriage, my father. Three wives, and he thinks to take another! I wonder how long she will last!"

"Do not be cynical, love. Wish him joy. Perhaps he will be lucky. Maybe she will be one of those in the world who give, and give again."

They ate dinner together, looking out over Athens and its golden lights, and the soft gleam of the moon. Iris was thinking of Greg's words.

There are some who take and take in this world. That was Charmian, and Shelley, and Maria Ardeth.

There are others who give and give, unselfishly, taking joy

in giving. They were the nuns, who took nothing, but always gave whatever they had. They were the Kyria Lydias, the Melanias, the sweet and gentle persons, the strong and kind persons, the givers, with open hands.

Those who took and took thought the world owed them more and more. They were never satisfied. Receiving gave them no joy.

But the givers always received joy in return for their gifts, she thought. Or they should! Perhaps that was not always true. Perhaps they were hurt in their giving, perhaps the ungrateful did not thank them, or express any pleasure in the gifts.

"What are you thinking?" asked Greg, as they drank their coffee, stretched out on the lounges before the huge windows.

"Those who give and those who take," said Iris somberly.

"Ah, yes. Speaking of that—" Greg hesitated, then set down his cup. "I have news for you from home. Alex telephoned. He is engaged to Melania, and asked our blessings. He seems very happy."

Iris was silent, astonished. She had expected that, someday, but it was too soon. Only a couple of weeks ago. Alex had been under the spell of Charmian. Now he had turned back to Melania. Was it because he loved her truly, or was it because there was nobody else around who was young and pretty and spellbound by his charm?

"You do not approve," he said softly, taking her hand. Iris shook her head.

"Alex—is a taker," she said, with difficulty. "Melania is a giver. It is not fair to her—it is not fair!"

"She has always loved him. And I hope that with marriage he will mature, and gentle into a loving man. He has changed since his blindness, I believe."

"I hope they will be happy." Iris left her hand passively in his. He squeezed it encouragingly. "But do you think Alex will truly change his nature? Do you think a man in his twenties will change and become unselfish and giving?''

"I hope so," said Greg. "I will protect Melania as I can. Alex is dependent on the House of Venizelos for his work and his money. That is some control. He shall not stray far!''

"How far will you allow him to stray?" Iris lashed out, in pain, thinking of her own marriage and her husband who had straying eyes. "Just to have a brief affair now and then? Or a faithful mistress kept carefully hidden from Melania? Or jaunts to London, Paris, and New York to have flings out of her sight? She will be sure to hear of them, and be hurt.''

"Is that what you think of Alex?" Greg asked her.

"Yes.''

At the flat word, Greg gazed at her thoughtfully. "And of me also, Iris? Is that why you are so cool and suspicious?''

She gasped, "I cannot help it! You have the same reputation!''

"That was before my marriage to you," said Greg. "Since our engagement, I have been loyal only to you. Do you think me a taker only?''

She bent her head, finally whispered, "No, you have been kind and giving. You give much—to me, to your family, to everyone. I have been—impressed—by your attitude toward the people you employ. They think the world of you, because you are so considerate, and have always been.''

"Then why do you not trust me, Iris?" he asked sadly. "I have tried to show you I love you, I will be good to you, you have nothing to fear from me—''

"You—love me?" she asked doubtfully. He had never said this before. "You—do—love me?''

He drew her into his arms. "Yes, my stubborn little wife! I was going to wait until you told me yourself, but I must give in and say it first! I love you, I have since we met. And when are you going to love me? Eh?''

She pressed her cheek against his rough one, and rubbed it

softly. "I love you—I have for such a time! Oh, Greg, I am a very foolish wife. I doubted you, and myself—"

He turned her, and kissed her mouth passionately. In the dusk-filled room, they kissed and murmured. Her heart was full of joy that he did love her, and she might express her love to him in words.

"I love you—" she said. "I love you so very much. It hurt—when I saw Charmian with you—"

"She is a wicked tease, I am glad to be rid of her," he said. "I had to send her away, to make you feel secure. No matter how we were together at night, when daytime came you withdrew, you looked at me with doubt in your eyes. Such lovely sapphire eyes, and so full of sadness at times." He touched each eyelid with his lips. He ran his fingers through her loosened hair, tied back with only a ribbon at her neck.

They went to his bedroom presently, and lay together in such ecstasy and joy that tears came to her eyes. Long after he had finished, and lay on her breast, sleeping, she lay awake, and stroked his head gently, and thought how happy she should be.

Yes, Greg was a giver, not just a taker. He demanded love and he was possessive, but in return he gave generously. But for how long, oh, Lord, how long? Would it last a lifetime?

She wished so much that hers would be one of those rare marriages when wife and husband were truly one. In heart and mind and body, giving and receiving happily. In their home, children would be happy and blessed, sheltered from the hate and turmoil and violence of the world outside. In trouble they would support each other. In pain, they would hold to each other. In peace, they would grow in love of God and help their fellowmen.

Such rare marriages, how good they were, and how infrequent. She thought Lydia's had been one like that. Perhaps all people sought for it, without knowing how to find it.

Oh, if only her own marriage might be like that—could they both make it come true? She would give and give—only he must not stab her to the heart with unfaithfulness. She knew if he did she would crumple up, and become twisted and bitter.

She thought of her father, and prayed for him, that he might one day find happiness. She had little hope of it, but it might happen.

And poor Melania—was she going to be sacrificed to make Alex temporarily happy? Iris resolved to find out how Melania felt about the marriage, and if she should go through with it. Melania was only seventeen, the marriage could be postponed. Perhaps Iris might take her to New York for a while, to see how others lived.

In the early morning, Iris wakened to find Greg softly kissing her cheeks, her lips, her throat; she turned sleepily to him.

"Ah, how pretty you are in the dawn light," he whispered. He stroked his hand down over her body, then up to cup a breast, and to tease a taut nipple. His black eyes sparkled as he saw her response to his caresses. "Did you think when we first met, how soon we would be in bed together?"

"Never! you were such a bully, I thought I would best avoid you," said Iris demurely.

He flung back his black head and laughed aloud. And you were so stiff and cold, I wondered what was wrong with you! I thought you might be frigid! And I wondered what Alex saw in you—that he would have an affair with you! I soon learned you were not Charmian, eh? Instead, you were mine to waken and rouse." And he bent and touched his lips to her breast, and licked around the silky flesh of it.

He was rousing her, and knew it, his sideways looks at her

told her so. Deliberately he held back, until she was moving restlessly on the bed, and clinging to him with her damp hands, refusing to beg him in words, but nevertheless imploring him with hands and lips and touches of her lips to his.

A sunbeam roamed into the room, and lit the golden body of her lover as he leaned over her. She saw the blaze of the sun glowing behind him and around him like an aura, and he was glorious as a pagan god, naked and shining.

Iris opened her hips, and he slid down between them, and came to her, easily, silently, and they were one body and one mindless ecstasy. He plunged in her again and again, and she held him to her with slipping fingers, and her moans smothered against his shoulder. She opened her mouth, and tasted the cool salty sweat of his flesh, and the warmth of his lips as he sought hers. She could not get close enough, she could not get enough of him, and one slim hand slid to his taut hips and pressed.

"More?" he whispered, and she groaned, "Yes, yes." He came in more deeply, and moved about slowly, carefully. He held against her, in the place that would give her most pleasure, and she moved against him, jerkily, madly needing him. He held himself still then, and let her find her pleasure blindly against his hard masculine body, and when the thrills shot through her he knew it. She writhed and twisted under him, clasping him furiously to herself.

And when she was finished, he was moving and plunging again, and bringing her to another climax, and he came with her this time, and it was mind-bending, and glorious in that early sunshine, to cling and feel life flowing through them both.

They slept several more hours, and wakened to find it noon, and the sun high in the sky. Greg smiled sheepishly at the clock, and shook his head.

"How sweet to be a married man," he said, and stretched

and rose lazily. He went to take a shower, singing unharmoniously, but nonetheless it was sweet to her. She went to her own bath, and soaked in bubble bath of a lilac fragrance.

She put on a blue linen dress with matching jacket trimmed with white embroidery of seashell motif. Nike had done it for her as an experiment, and she liked it very much. With it she put on white sandals, and put her compact and notes in a small white handbag.

She went down to luncheon to find Greg ready before her, rereading her father's letter. He put it down when she came.

"Do you wish to go home to Texas, to visit him?" Greg asked, as they drank orange juice and ate hot crisp rolls.

"Visit father—in Texas? Oh, no, I have never been there, I don't want to go," she said quickly.

"So. Well, if you change your mind, let me know. We could go. I have the feeling he may need us."

"He has never needed me," said Iris curtly.

Greg studied her face. "Perhaps he did, and did not know it."

Iris was uncomfortable with that thought, and shrugged it away. Later they went out together. Greg left her with a bodyguard at the House of Diophantus, and he went on to the Venizelos office to do some work.

Petros greeted Iris with outstretched arms. "How are you? You look marvelous. Where have you been, eh? I tried to telephone you on the island, but Alexander said you were not there."

"I went to France with Gregorios," she said, and turned to Marta, who waited discreetly. "I have heard from Nadia Egorova, she has some ideas we may like."

Petros's face lit up like a cherubic child, his hair stood on black curly ends, as he ran his fingers through his locks. "Good, good, good! She writes to me also, but says little of

450

the future. Come in my office, eh? You will have some coffee? Marta, come and talk with us, eh?''

Iris was glad to sit down with them and discuss matters. She told them of Nike's designs, and showed them some.

"Madame Egorova likes the idea of some children's clothes, especially two to five years of age. Do you like the idea of doing something for children?''

He put his finger to his lips in concentration. "I never have, except for some mother and daughter outfits. Marta?''

"We have had requests at times,'' said Marta, gazing at the sketches. "Madame Venizelos makes designs of some simplicity. They would translate into matching outfits for a small girl or boy. For example—her linen dress and matching jacket, with seashells—we could make a small girl's outfit just the same, with the same embroidery. It would be enchanting.''

They stared at her, up and down, nodding and smiling. They talked about designs for small boys, long pants and little sailor jackets, with matching pantsuits for their smart mothers, and anchors on the sleeves. There could be other clothes for little ones, with Nike's charming embroidery of clowns and balls, sailboats and kittens.

Then they turned to thoughts of a winter line. That took even more thought. She told them about winters in Chicago, when the temperatures could go below zero, and it was difficult to look smart and stay warm. They discussed warm pantsuits, with matching slim yet woolen-warm jackets, to be worn under thick long coats to the boots. For women who liked skirts, there could be long skirts to the boots, four inches below the knees, of thick wool and matching sweaters, in pullovers and cardigans.

Iris began sketching out some of the ideas they discussed, her pen working rapidly on the pad. Petros leaned to look at them, nodding. "How I love your talent," he beamed admiringly, then he sobered. "Times are difficult just now, only the most wealthy buy much. But you say our lines will sell well to the middle classes, eh? And if they are practical enough, the clothes sturdy enough to last for years, then many will buy our clothes, eh? That is very good. With our talents combined, and your contacts in New York City, we will work together very well for years!"

"Do not plan on taking the time of my wife for years!" The deep gravelly voice made them all jump. Greg had entered in time to hear this last. Marta jumped up. Petros rose to his feet awkwardly.

"She has such good ideas," Petros said hopefully. "Look what she has done just today, all these sketches!" He waved his hand at the fluttering papers on the table, the lengths of cloth they had been examining.

"But she is my wife, I will decide her future," Greg frowned at them.

"Is it late?" Iris interrupted. She glanced at the tiny Swiss watch Greg had given her in Paris, golden with little diamonds circling the face. "Almost six o'clock! I had not meant to talk so long!"

"You may return tomorrow?" asked Petros hopefully. "I will think about these ideas, Marta and I will discuss them. More fabrics have come in—"

He followed them to the door, Greg had Iris clutched tightly in one arm, drawing her quickly with him.

"Not tomorrow! We have other plans!"

"But there is much work to do!" wailed Petros, like a small boy, clutching his head. He stood on the steps calling after them, "The next day, if you will? She can work part-time, Kyrios? I need her, Kyrios Venizelos! We work well together! I beg you—"

Iris called back at him, "The next day, Kyrios! I will come back. Have some fabrics ready for me to see!"

Greg held the door for her to enter the car. His face was dark red with anger. In the car, he slammed the door, and directed the chauffeur.

"He takes too much for granted," Greg growled.

"I wish to work at least part-time with him, Greg," Iris pleaded, putting her hand on his fist. "Please! I have worked all my life for this—"

"But I am your husband, and you do not ask my permission first! You go ahead, and make plans with him! How do you think I feel about this, eh?"

She looked into his troubled face, and sank back in the car seat. Greg disliked her career ambitions intensely, she knew it. But she could not give up her dress designing, she could not. She had worked so long for this.

And she was talented, she knew it now. Petros said so, Nadia Egorova said so. On the verge of success, she could not stop! And what if Gregorios turned to some other woman? He did not seem shocked at her father's wish for yet another divorce! He took it calmly enough!

"Well, well," said Greg, more quietly. "You can go back in two days, and make some few plans. But I wish you would consult with me before you plunge into any more work! I want you to travel with me before—I mean, while events work out that we may go to Italy, to America, and so on."

Before—what? What had he been starting to say? Iris supplied the words. Travel with Greg before—before she became pregnant, and had to stay home, as she had one child after another for him. While he ran about on his own!

Yes, she did long for children, the thought made her heart ache with longing. She wished to be a wife and a mother, and to feel his child growing under her heart.

Yet something in her rebelled at letting him plan all her future for her. That way would lead to grief! She would stay home and have his children, and care for them. And Greg would then feel free to travel and have his adventures, as her father did.

Greg was very popular with women, and he was wealthy. Iris stared ahead, and saw, instead of Athens, the future with Greg, as her father's had been with his women. And the picture was not pretty to her. It was ugly and humiliating, and horrible.

Chapter Twenty-nine

Iris and Greg returned to the island, and she began more work on her next sketches. She was troubled about Melania.

The girl had a beautiful engagement ring of a huge diamond with smaller diamond points clustered about it. The ring was heavy on her small hand, and the weight of her coming wedding seemed heavier.

Iris said to Greg, "I think the wedding should be postponed. After all, Melania is not yet eighteen."

"And you think something will happen to stop it completely," he sighed. "I want Alex settled!"

"Even if Melania must be sacrificed?" she asked, with her hand pleadingly on his arm.

He shook his head slowly. When he told Alex the wedding was not to be for another six months, Alex was surprised. Iris, watching keenly, thought he was relieved.

"But why not?"

"You are not yet completely healed, and ready for a

full-time job in one of the hotels,'' said Greg easily. ''And Iris wants to plan Melania's trousseau.''

Melania agreed readily to the delay. She seemed even quieter these days. Iris worried over her, but could not get beyond the girl's simple statement, ''I love Alex, I have always loved Alex.''

Iris went out to sketch one morning, out in the fields that were turning golden, ready for the harvest. When the men thrash the wheat, their sharp blades will also slash the scarlet poppies, she thought. They would soon be gone.

But they would spring up again next year. Nature had her ways of renewal and rebirth. people came and went, the earth remained.

She was absorbed in sketching, so deeply absorbed in capturing the shape of the fields and the flowers that the Land Rover did not disturb her concentration.

Then she smelled something, and turned about—too late— a huge man had crept up behind her, and he snatched her up in his arms!

Iris cried out, it was the nightmare repeated. He struck her on her head, and she descended into darkness.

When she began to come to, with aching head and dizziness, it was to find herself bundled into the backseat of a Land Rover, tied hand and foot, and gagged. She bounced around on the seat as the jeep hurtled down the side of a winding road. She could just see the wide shoulders and black curly hair of the man at the wheel—Orestes Sicilianos.

She ached all over, but that was nothing compared to the cold hear in her heart. Captured—by the feudal enemy—a man of little intelligence, and no mercy. A beast, a bully, someone who thought little and hated much.

Where was he taking her? She did not recognize the road, nor the valley into which they were descending. The Land Rover bounced over a series of gravelly ruts, and she had to hold herself back with an intense, aching effort, to keep from being sent to the floor of the vehicle.

The Land Rover jerked to a halt, and she twisted about, eyes wide with fear. Orestes lurched out of the vehicle, and came around, to grin down at her triumphantly.

"We arrive here," he announced. "Now we see how proud you are, with your nose in the air!"

"Orestes!" said a sharp masculine voice. "What is this?"

Iris half hoped it would be Nikolaos, he might be sensible, and help her get home again, unharmed. But instead the tall man who came to the vehicle was a gray-haired older man, with a reddened sunburned face and sad eyes, with wrinkled face, stooped shoulders. He stared at her.

"Who is she?" he breathed.

"This is the Kyria Venizelos!" announced Orestes, beaming, and nodding his shaggy black head. "I want her, papa!"

"Blessed Virgin Mary and all the saints of heaven!" breathed the older man. "Orestes, you have done evil!"

Orestes looked puzzled. "But she is our enemy! She is the wife of our enemy Gregorios Venizelos! He will be very angry, it is our revenge! I take her, keep her. Is she not pretty, papa?" And he reached out his big dirty hand and fingered a long lock of black hair that had come loose from her chignon.

Iris felt her blood run cold, and a chill on her spine made her shudder.

"Oh, Orestes," groaned the older man. "Come—let me untie her—we must discuss this!"

Orestes picked up Iris, and set her on the ground. He began to untie the knots carefully, puzzling over them. He had evidently tied them tight, and could not unknot them. His father took out a knife. Orestes shook his head.

"Do not waste the cord, papa!" He had a high whining childlike voice today, Iris wondered if he was mentally retarded—or worse, insane!

The man watched in silence, his brow furrowed, as Orestes carefully unpicked his knots, and loosened the cords around Iris. When they fell away, she was so stiff, she swayed. Orestes tried to pick her up in his arms, she shrank from him. All her fear and loathing of being touched had returned, she could not conceal her hatred of him.

Her blue eyes blazed at them. The older man—his name was Timotheos, she recalled—took the gag from her mouth, shook his head at the white marks around her cheeks.

"I am most sorry, Kyria," he said formally. "Permit me to introduce myself. Timotheos Sicilianos, at your service."

"I am Kyria Venizelos, sir. I wish to be returned to my husband, at once!" She tried to keep her voice even and calm, though she seethed inside.

He rubbed his rough unshaven cheeks, looking troubled. "That is not easy. He may kill us on sight, Kyria," he said simply.

That was true enough.

"The feud has gone on too long, Kyrios," she said urgently. "I wish you and my husband would speak together, and settle the matter. It is too bad, the things that have happened."

The sad eyes turned hard and fiery. "I have tried to speak with Kyrios Venizelos! He insulted me, he turned me away!"

"Yes, there is wrong on both sides," said Iris diplomatically. "May I sit down?"

"Of course—of course—" Timotheos looked about, and for the first time she noted the cottage behind them. It was a small hut, half hidden against a cut red-mud bank of earth. No wonder Greg and his men had not found them, here in this remote valley! She looked up, saw mountains all about them, not high, but sufficient to hide the valley, and this small brown hut that blended with the reddish brown earth.

"You will come into our poor house?" asked Timotheos, with a courteous gesture.

She had no wish to be trapped inside. "The air is so clear and pure, and the sun so good on my face," she replied diplomatically. "May we not sit outside and talk?"

"Of course, of course. Orestes, bring a chair for the lady and one for me!"

"But she is mine!" protested Orestes, hovering, shuffling from one foot to the other, his dirty bare feet in sandals, his torn pants showing his trunklike brown legs.

"You captured her," agreed his father. Iris thought he was skilled by a lifetime of evading Orestes's demands. She hoped he was today, for his thin body would be no match for Orestes's brute strength.

Orestes brought out two chairs, holding the two heavy wooden objects easily in his fingers. He set them down, in the open, with a view out to the mountains.

"And bring tea for us," said Timotheos easily.

Orestes grunted, and frowned, but shuffled back into the cottage.

"I ask for peace," said Iris quickly, taking advantage of the absence of the younger man. "This—difficulty—has gone on far too long. When did it begin—yesterday? No, it was almost forty years ago!"

"It began in 1944," sighed Timotheos. "During the war with the Germans. Horrible people, them. Not Greeks!"

"No, of course not, not Greek at all," Iris agreed soberly. She was beginning to realize that Timotheos, while not as stupid as Orestes, was not overly endowed with brains. "But this has been allowed to blacken all the years between, when we could have been friends."

"Yes, yes, friends," he agreed.

"It is too bad. It has hurt you, it has hurt the Venizelos."

"Are they hurt badly?" he asked eagerly, smiling.

"Alex Venizelos was hurt badly. Thank god and the Blessed Virgin Mary, he has begun to recover his sight."

"Oh, truly? He is no longer blind?" The man seemed disappointed, and Iris had to repress a sharp remark.

"No, I thank the Virgin Mary," she repeated. "We pray often for him in the chapel."

"Ah." The religious touch evidently reached him, he crossed himself, and took out a rosary, which he began to fondle as worry beads. "Yes, yes, we must pray for peace between us."

"It would be good. After all, we are cousins."

"Many cousins fight much."

"But we are all Greeks," she persisted. "How well we fought when the Germans tried to take us over!"

His face lit up. "Yes, yes, we had some good fights then! I was in the mountains, I was with the guerrillas! How we tossed the rocks down on their heads!" And he began to laugh, his eyes sparkling.

"That must have been a good fight," said Iris, restraining her shudder. It was true, then, that some men enjoyed war! She had heard an older friend of her father say to him that his happiest years had been in the Second World War! He had fought as a Marine. And his life since then had seemed so tame!

"Yes, yes, many a good fight," said Timotheos happily. "We Greeks like a good fight!"

"But it is sad for the women when word comes that their men are dead," said Iris softly. "How they must pray for peace! Women do not like wars."

"No, no, you are right, women don't like wars. My woman died, she was very sad about it all. She gave me two sons, then she died," and he sighed.

"That was hard for you. A woman makes life a little softer and sweeter for her man," said Iris.

"Yes, yes, and the boys missed their sweet mama," said Timotheos. He rubbed his hands over his unshaven cheeks. "Ah, ay, ay, ay, how sad those times were!"

"Sad, indeed. I am sorry for it."

"You were here during the wars?" he asked, with childish eagerness, not seeming to consider her young years.

"No, no, I was not born yet."

"That is true, that is true. I am getting old!"

Orestes brought out the tea. To Iris's relief, it was drinkable. And there was something very civilized about drinking tea together. Even Orestes folded up his bulk on the earth, and drank tea from a huge china mug.

When the tea was finished, Iris tried again, in a calm even voice. "I wish you would speak to my good man," she said. "Between you, you could settle this terrible feud. No more blood should be shed between us. We are cousins, after all."

Timotheos looked interested, he nodded his gray head. But Orestes shot up from his place. "No, no, we must fight! It is good to fight! Shed blood, indeed! Shed blood!"

Iris swallowed her fear, and kept her face calm by an intense effort. "The Blessed Virgin does not like that," she said quietly. "The women pray for peace to the Blessed Virgin."

"That is true," said Timotheos, fingering his rosary again. His old fingers touched one bead, held it, then held the next. "My woman prayed for peace, but she died before it came."

In the mountains before Iris, she saw a small dust cloud rising, a reddish brown cloud that moved down the mountain road. Was it rescue? Could someone be coming for her? Her heart leaped up to choke her.

She reached slowly into her hip pocket, where she kept a small sketch pad. "Do you have a pencil?" she asked. "Let me show you what work I do!"

Timetheos frowned. "A woman's work is in the house," he said. "And sometimes in the fields, helping her man."

"Yes, yes, that is good," she agreed hurriedly. He handed her a stub of pencil, and she began to sketch a flower. A scarlet poppy, the petals and the heart of it. "You see, this is from the fields, the scarlet poppy. This is how I sketch. I make these lines, so—"

Both men came closer to watch what she did. She worked slowly, drawing each line carefully. "You see—" Timotheos said to Orestes. "She draws a flower!"

She finished that one, turned over the page, and began an iris. "And this is my name flower, the iris," she announced. "I draw it like this..." And slowly she drew in the lines. She could hear the Land Rover now, approaching, coming down the hill, but she still held their attention. "This is the iris, my name is Kyria Iris—"

The roar of the engine was close now. Orestes stood erect, and stared, then gave a roar of rage. "They come!" he yelled, and ran inside the cottage, to emerge with a rifle.

Iris screamed. Timotheos yelled at his son, "Put that down! I order you to put that down—"

From the Land Rover a man fired a rifle, and Orestes fell. Iris heard him yelling curses, and rolling in the red dust in his anguish. A red stain slowly welled into his shirt fabic, he clutched at his shoulder.

Greg leaped from the Land Rover and ran to Iris, grabbed her and held her tight. Nikolaos slid down from the backseat of the vehicle and came to her also, his face taut with worry. And Vanessa was there also, sitting huddled in the backseat. Another man drove, another held a rifle trained on Orestes.

Then another Land Rover appeared, driven at speed down the hill, to pull up in a whirl of red dust, four more men in that one.

Greg was demanding urgently, "Are you all right? Have they harmed you?"

Iris managed to shake her head. "We were—talking," she said faintly. She clutched at his arms with her small hands.

He folded her against himself, as though he would surround her with protection. He was shaking badly, Greg, the sturdy, the tough.

Greg buried his face against her hair, and held her for a little time, until the shudders slowly ceased. "God," he whispered. "I thought I might not be—in time—that monster—"

Timotheos stood with his head hanging, Nik had gone over to Orestes, and was examining the wound. Orestes moaned and howled, "I want her, I want her! You cannot take her away!"

Greg lifted his head, his black eyes flashed at Iris. "Does he say—"

She nodded. "I think he is a very—simple man, like Caliban, Greg. You know—in *The Tempest*—Shakespeare— he has simple wants, he goes and takes. Timotheos tries to control him, but it is not easy—"

"God Almighty and the Virgin Herself," breathed Greg. "And I did not guard you with my life!"

Nik came over to them. "He needs a doctor." His handsome face was anxious, he looked at her straight. "He is my brother, I must help him," he told her.

"Yes, of course," said Iris. "Bind up his wounds, we will get him to the doctor in the village." Greg seemed incapable of his usual forceful direction.

Nik nodded gratefully. Timotheos came to them. "I am— most sorry, Kyrios," he said dejectedly. "My son—will he go to prison, eh?"

"He would die in that blackness, not seeing the land and the sea, and the mountains," Nik objected harshly. "I pray you—do not do this! We will take him away—somewhere safe—"

Greg interrupted. "That will be done. Timotheos, we have quarreled too long. I almost lost my most precious wife. We must settle this matter at once."

"Yes, yes, Kyrios Venizelos. We will settle it. You wish us to leave Greece?" His face was pathetic.

"Nay, that would be to die, for you," said Greg gently. His arms were still tightly about Iris. "I think there are other ways of settling this—"

Vanessa had left the Land Rover, and made her unsteady way to them. Her black hair hung loose, her face was worried and her gaze went right to Nik. "I had to tell him where you were, Nik," she whispered. "It was the life of his Iris. I could not deny him."

"No, of course not." His handsome face gentled toward her.

Iris said, "I think the feud could be settled very simply, Greg. Marriage between the cousins. If Nikolaos is willing, and if Vanessa agrees, would this marriage not settle the matter?" She held her breath.

Vanessa looked at Nik, then hung her head, blushing. He beamed down at her, his face glowing. "I am agreeable to this!" he cried happily. "I love this woman!"

"And I love Nikolaos," said Vanessa softly. Her face shone with joy, as she reached out her hand to his. They clasped hands, as Timotheos watched in growing relief.

Timotheos turned to Greg. "There is the problem—he has no work—if you have some job for him—"

"Yes, of course," said Greg quickly. "It will solve a serious problem for me, also. I intended to give Vanessa Michaelides, my cousin, a dowry. If Nikolaos wishes a farm—" he looked questioningly at Nik.

"A farm—for a dowry! Oh, I would like to work a farm! It

is my dream! I like all animals," said Nik simply. His hand clasped Vanessa's more tightly.

"There is a farm on an island some fifty kilometers across the sea. It has been in the family a long time. Just now it is worked by an elderly couple, but they are old now, and unable to carry on the labor. The farm would be the dowry of Vanessa Michaelides. Her husband would work the farm, there are some five hundred sheep, some milk cows, chickens, of course, and ducks—" He watched their faces.

Nik looked bewildered, and turned to his father. "So big! Father, what a big dowry. Is this true?"

Timotheos was beaming. "We will go and look at the farm, my son. If it is true, I think we will accept, eh? You like this woman, eh? It will be a match?" he sounded as though he could not quite convince himself of the glorious truth.

"Sheep, cows, chickens, ducks!" repeated Nik happily. "Oh, what a heaven! And land, much land, eh?"

"Yes," said Gregorios. "I think it is some four square miles now. And a large house, some twelve rooms. Two barns, many other buildings on the property. A large job, Nikolaos! You had best look over the land well!"

Vanessa was beaming up at him. "He can do it!" she cried. "He loves the land! He will be a fine farmer! And I shall help him with all my strength!"

"A good woman!" muttered Timotheos approvingly, looking with kindly eyes on this woman with such a huge dowry.

"I would ask that you allow the old people to remain for a year or two, with you," said Greg. "They have lived there all their lives. They can show you around, help you meet everybody in the nearby village, which is really a good-sized town—many shops, a rather smart restaurant—" He was eyeing Vanessa with a sideways look, which made Iris chuckle inside.

Vanessa would love to shop at some smart shops, and even more to show off her handsome husband at a smart restaurant to all the locals!

"I will take Orestes to the doctor, then I will come to your house," said Timotheos, suddenly in command of his family. His chest was swelled up. He was going to have a rich son, and his line would go on! "We shall talk of these matters, eh, Kyrios?"

"Yes, yes. And in a couple days, we must fly or take a boat to the other island, to view the farm. Then we can have our lawyers draw up papers, for the wedding and settlement, eh, if all is in order, and you approve!"

Timotheos's chest swelled so much, Iris was afraid he would burst. His shabby torn shirt could scarcely hold him.

Greg saw off the blustering Orestes, his proud father, and several men to drive and guard them. He put Iris into the other Land Rover, with Nik and Vanessa holding hands in the backseat, and they started back to the Big House.

Nik and Vanessa were talking in the backseat. "You have forgiven me," she said, in a low flirtatious tone, "for revealing where you were to Gregorios? He was worried about his wife, and she is a virtuous woman!"

"I was very angry when you came," he admitted. "However, *then* your first loyalty was to your relatives. When we are married, then your first loyalty will be to me! You understand?"

"Oh, yes, yes, Nik, I understand and will obey!" said the proud Vanessa joyously. "Do you—really wish to marry me?"

"I shall be the happiest man in the world!" he assured her gravely. "To have such a fine intelligent wife who went to college! And to have a fine dowry, a big farm and sheep and cows and chickens and ducks—"

She accepted this happily. Greg was shaking, Iris tried to

hold her laughter inside. Vanessa would never forgive them! Iris concentrated on the mountains they were driving through, the scarlet and yellow of the autumn leaves, the deep green of the evergreens, the pines and olive trees.

Then she stopped laughing. She was glad for them. Each would bring something important to the marriage. He would work hard for her and for their children, proud of her dowry and farm. Vanessa would bring the farm, and her intelligence, and her hard work, and her love, to him. And they would probably make a good marriage of it.

And, Iris thought, Nik would be faithful to Vanessa, even if tempted to stray, for the dowry would be hers if anything happened to the marriage. If he left or divorced her, she would get the farm, and he would have nothing! That was the Greek way, not so foolish, she thought. It provided for the woman for all her life.

They came back to the Big House, to find Lydia and Melania anxiously waiting for them. Their faces showed deep relief as the Land Rover pulled up.

Lydia came out to greet them, Melania hung back shyly. "You are all right, oh, my daughter!" said Lydia fervently.

"Yes, and she has settled the feud," smiled Greg. "Vanessa and Nikolaos are to marry! Please greet your future cousin!"

Lydia turned to Nikolaos, and solemnly took both his big hands in her slim ones. "I welcome you. May you both be truly happy. And I rejoice that the feud will be over at last. How my husband would have loved to see this day!"

Vanessa and Nik went to tell Xanthe the news.

Lydia turned back to Iris, and drew her tenderly into her arms. "So, you have settled it, my dear daughter! How happy I am. Gregorios, this woman of yours is loyal to our family, she is virtuous, worthy of the highest honors. The scarlet poppy is rightly the symbol of her as well as of Greece!"

Iris knew she blushed brightly at this lavish praise from the woman she loved and respected. "Thank you, mother," she said. "You honor me too much."

"Never too much," said Lydia. "Now come inside, and tell me all that has happened!"

Chapter Thirty

Nik and Vanessa, Xanthe and the children came over for the late luncheon. Xanthe looked bewildered at this sudden turn of events. Was she to be deserted, now that good fortune had come to Vanessa?

Through the luncheon, Vanessa bubbled over with her plans.

"Perhaps you will assist me with my wedding gown, Kyria Iris!" She turned to Iris, her black eyes were afraid of a possible rebuff.

"I should be delighted, Vanessa," said Iris. "And we must plan some trousseau dresses. What colors does Nikolaos like for you?"

Vanessa glanced at her fiancé. To their surprise, he said promptly, "Red and yellow. I like those colors best. I have often thought how handsome she would be in a red dress!"

"Lovely," said Iris. "Yes, with her complexion, red would be good, and set off her lovely dark hair. And yellows—yes, a sunny yellow, and a cream suit with yellow blouse . . ." Her fingers itched to start sketching.

Vanessa preened at all the attention. "Yes, yes, but it must be soon! Nikolaos and I thought we would be married in a month—that is, if the farm is suitable," she hastily added.

"I hope you will like it," said Greg, with suitable gravity. "Of course, it is very large, and will mean a great deal of work."

"I am not afraid of hard work," said Nik, and Iris thought he was not. He was big and tough, as well as very handsome.

"But what will happen to me?" Xanthe blurted out at last. Her voice broke on the words. "We have always lived together! Must I return to Crete—with my two girls—never to see my sister again?"

Iris bit her lips at the blatant plea. Greg looked at Nik, leaving it to him.

Nik cried out at once, generously. "But you must come with us, Xanthe! God forbid I should separate you from your sister! Vanessa, pray tell your sister she is welcome in our household, and the young girls also!"

"Of course she is," said Vanessa promptly. "And my sister is an excellent secretary and bookkeeper, she has held important positions in this! She will help us with the accounts, and the letters and all!"

Xanthe swallowed hard, and nodded eagerly. "Yes, yes, I will help, I will earn my keep! I am a good bookkeeper and I type well, everybody knows it." Anxiously she looked from Nik to Greg. "You know, I am a good worker, Gregorios!"

"Well, well, I know little about books," said Nik cheerfully. "That is woman's work, after all, in the house! You and my good wife"—he smiled affectionately at Vanessa—"will keep the books, and I will take care of everything else! We shall do well, eh?"

"Yes, you will do well," Greg agreed soberly. "Xanthe

and Vanessa will do the women's work, the books, and the letters, and the accounts. You will wish to keep on some men to work for you, also. Is Orestes a good worker?''

There was a little silence, Nik's face was a study. "He goes not to prison?" he faltered, with relief. "I love my brother, I know him, he would die in the darkness.''

"I think he would do well on a farm," said Greg easily. "Let us say, he will be in your care, and you will see to his work; he seems very strong.''

"Oh, he is very strong! And he works well with cattle! He will learn the sheep also! I promise it! And my father, though he is graying, he works hard. You should see him haul logs! And he handles the boat by himself when we fish!''

Greg looked at Vanessa. "We shall all be happy together," she said loyally. "Your father and brother would be most welcome. And my sister and her children also. Is there a good school, Kyrios?'' she asked Greg with more respect than usual. Iris saw her now as a matron, strong and proud and hard working.

"There is a school in the town, I know that," said Greg. "We must inspect it when we go there in a couple days. I believe the town is about four kilometers from your house.''

Greta piped up boldly, "What about us? Where do we live, then? With mama? Will you be our papa?''

Nik held out his arm, and she slid down from her chair, and ran to him, her face glowing. Nora followed slowly, and came to his other arm. His handsome face smiled down at them, naturally, with no mockery. he was a very primitive man, thought Iris. He was strong, sturdy, with masculine emotions, and would be a proud husband and father, a farmer and good citizen.

"I will be your Uncle Nik," he said slowly, so they would understand. "I am going to marry your Aunt Vanessa. And you and your mama will live with us, and we shall have many little lambs to see, and little chick-chicks to play with.''

The town children stared blankly. ''Chick-chicks?'' echoed Nora.

He cupped his hand to show them. ''Little chickens, that can sit in your little hand. Little yellow chick-chicks, to touch very carefully and put back with their mama hen. And little fluffy duck-ducks, who will learn to swim on the pond.''

''And you will be there?'' whispered Nora, her arm going timidly about his burly neck.

''I will be there always, your Uncle Nik,'' he reassured her. ''And you will one day go to school, and learn much, like your Aunt Vanessa. And you will have many friends at school, and in town. And we shall ride the horses—'' He paused, looked at Greg. ''Are there horses?'' he asked eagerly.

''I believe several farm horses. There may be a riding horse or two,'' said Greg. ''It may be necessary to buy more, when the girls are old enough to ride.''

Iris said severely to Greg later, ''You are bribing them shamelessly!'' Her eyes brimmed with laughter.

He grinned down at her, as they strolled slowly in the evening air beyond the terrace. ''Wouldn't you? Just think, we are settling them all at once! Vanessa and Xanthe and the two girls, Nikolaos and Orestes and Timotheos!''

''To say nothing of your two elderly cousins who are such a problem!'' she mocked gently.

''Oh, them. I telephoned them at once, and they will stay on for a year, and help out. But they are anxious to move to Athens, to be with their elder daughter. So all will be well,'' he said, satisfied.

''And you could have sold the farm, or put someone else there,'' she teased him, loving the way he settled things with no hurt to anyone's pride.

''I could have. But it is worth it, to settle the feud, and

have it all peaceful again. I could not endure it, to have the threat of Orestes hanging over us! If anything had happened to you, my love, I should have gone mad, I think," he said, half under his breath, and his arm closed about her tightly.

"I knew you would come for me," said Iris, knowing that was why she had not felt more panicky that morning. "I thought if I kept talking to Timotheos, all would be well. You would come. I love you—very much, Greg." And she lifted her face for his kiss.

He bent his head, and touched her lips, gently, reverently. "My own darling wife," he breathed. "I am so happy, surely the gods will be angry with me! We must make sacrifices to them, especially little Selene, and her lover!"

She blushed, remembering that night. "It is more important to pray in the chapel," she murmured. "Oh, Greg, can it last? Can our marriage last, and our happiness?"

"I know your fears," he said soberly. "You see your father, and think I will not be faithful to you. How can I convince you? All I can do is take one day at a time, and love you more each day."

A Land Rover rattled up just then, and they turned back to the terrace. Timotheos got out. He had shaved, and bathed, and put on a black suit and white shirt. He looked very handsome and even distinguished. The men shook hands gravely. Greg introduced him to Kyria Lydia, and to Melania and Alex.

Nik came out from the Cottage, and greeted his father. The women and girls came also, and they talked for a time on the terrace.

When Timotheos learned that his son invited him to live with them, and Orestes also, he was overcome. "Both of us, you will do this for both of us?" he cried. "It is a miracle! What a good son you are! And we are most grateful to Kyrios Venizelos for the fine dowry! I must thank God and the

Blessed Virgin for this miracle! Orestes will be overcome. He growls like a bear, there in the clinic, thinking he will go to prison! Now he will learn he is forgiven, and will live on a farm, with animals and all to take care of! What joy!''

"Chick-chicks," said Nora, on cue, and Timotheos beamed at the little blond girl, and took her up on his knee. "And duck-ducks, in my little hand!" she said, and beamed up at him.

"Yes, yes, chicks, and ducks, and little lambs," said Timotheos, patting her head. "And what is your name, tiny one? You are so pretty, and so is your sister!"

Nora and Greta thrived on all this masculine attention. They were so good they were allowed to remain up for the predinner drinks and appetizers, before Xanthe took them off to bed at nine-thirty.

After dinner, Timotheos and Nik, Xanthe and Vanessa strolled in the moonlight, talking of their future. Light laughter came from them, from time to time, and Nik had Vanessa's hand tightly in his.

"I think it will work out," said Lydia thoughtfully, from her seat on the terrace. Melania and Alex had gone for a stroll also. "I wish I could be as sure of Melania."

"You have the doubts of Iris," frowned Greg. "Shall we put off the marriage yet longer?"

"Leave it to them, but I am not sorry they will wait six months," said Lydia. "Let us see if Alex settles down."

"Melania does not want an engagement party," said Iris abruptly.

"Well, well, we shall not, then," agreed Greg. "Now, you were thinking about Nadia Egorova's letter? She asked about the name you wished to use for your line."

Iris held her breath. She had shown him the latest letter from Nadia, urging her to work out a name that would be distinctive, and let her know about the line of winter clothes.

"Iris is to continue to design clothes?" asked Lydia, picking up her coffee cup, and glancing at Greg over it.

"Yes," he said. "At least part-time. I want some of her time for myself," and he reached out and caught her hand in his. "Iris is first my wife, and later a mother. But I think she craves the sketching and dress designing she has worked so hard on. Eh? So she will have some time for this!"

"Oh, thank you, Greg," said Iris, from her heart. She squeezed his hand. "Thank you for understanding me!"

He smiled at her, his face gentled in the moonlight. "I hope so, darling," he murmured.

"And the name?" said Lydia, musing. "She liked the scarlet poppies design as your trademark. What name would go with that?"

Greg said, "Scarlet poppy dresses—no—"

Iris said, "Poppies—or Iris Poppea—"

They sat and thought, watching the others strolling in the moonlight.

"Poppea, I like that," said Greg.

"Scarlet Poppies—" murmured Lydia. "Symbol of Greece. Poppies of Greece—"

Greg said suddenly, "Poppea of Greece! Poppea of Greece! There, how do you like that? It is different, distinctive—"

"Oh, yes, I like that!" cried Iris. "Poppea of Greece! That is me!" And she laughed aloud with pleasure. "Poppea of Greece!"

They all smiled at one another. Iris was so happy that Greg seemed to be more reconciled to her continuing her career. That would make her happy—if anything happened to her marriage.

But why did she think that way? Greg loved her, he said so, he showed it. She must have faith that he would keep his word to her, that he would be faithful to her. After all, any marriage must be built on faith, or it would not last.

She loved him very much, very deeply. She admired the way he worked with people, was considerate of them. He had been very good to his extended family, to his employees, and it was his nature to be thoughtful.

Surely such a man would be good to his wife and children! She must put away all doubts, and treat him with the trust that he gave her.

That night, they retired about midnight. Greg disappeared into his masculine bedroom, and Iris undressed, and put on her little cotton nightdress of blue, and the negligee that matched.

She smiled sheepishly at herself in the mirror. She was not dressing up for her own amusement! She turned out the lights, then tapped lightly on the panel between their rooms.

A moment of silence, then the panel slid open, and Greg stared down at her. He was in his pajama bottoms, nothing else, and his brown chest glowed golden in the lamplight.

"You tapped on the panel?" he asked.

She nodded her head slowly, the black curly hair sliding over her shoulders. "Yes. May I—come in?"

He reached out and touched her, and drew her inside his room, and shut the panel after her. "It is the first time you have come to me," he said softly. "This means something very dear to me, Iris."

"To me also," she responded. "I love you—very much, Gregorios. You have been very good and patient with me, and I thank you for it. It took me a long time—"

"To learn to trust me," he finished, and smiled with his large generous mouth and his shining eyes. "Sooo—now you trust me, eh? And love me?"

"Yes, so very much." She went into his arms, and he folded her against himself. "Greg—when I talked today to Timotheos, I thought to myself, what a simple man. A man who thinks in black and white. Why have I complicated our lives so much? The good things we have in our marriage are the most important to me. What other marriages involve does not matter to us. We are ourselves, we will make what we will of our lives.''

Greg was listening intently. He said, ''Yes, that is true. You have seen bad marriages, and that made you wary. But you are learning to trust, and to give in love. And when our children come, they will be nurtured in that love, and will be the most fortunate of children.''

''Yes. And Greg—I am not sure,'' she hesitated. ''But I think—perhaps—it may be before very long.'' Her face glowed as she gazed up at him.

''You mean—a child?'' he gasped. ''You are sure?''

She shook her head, and pressed her face against his chest. ''No—I just think the past couple weeks were—well, I'm very late,'' she said shyly. ''In another couple weeks, I should know—I'll see the doctor then—''

He folded her close to himself, and she felt the warm chest under her cheek, and the heavy beating of his heart. Such a sure steady heart, how could she have doubted him?

''We will be very careful of you, then,'' he whispered. ''I wonder—may I take you to bed with me anyway?''

''That is why I came in!'' she said, and giggled brazenly, her face flushed.

''Oh, you—darling!'' And he picked her up and carried her to his large bed, and laid her down in it. He was chuckling a little. ''I remember a very timid girl I tried to take to bed with me some months ago, you recall? On that island? After the crash? Little did I think how she would come to me—''

She smiled, and waited for him to shed his one garment, and come to the bed. He drew off the negligee, and then her nightdress, and in the light of the single lamp, he lay down, and put his hand on her slim body.

''How lovely are thy breasts,'' he murmured, and bent to

kiss them tenderly. His words were very beautiful to her, in English and then in Greek, as his passion grew.

Her arms twined about his strong neck, and she drew him down to her, so she might stroke over his back and twine her fingers in his black curly hair. His kisses were warm on her body, as he trailed caresses from her throat to her thighs, and up again. His hand moved slowly over her belly, and she knew he was thinking of the child growing in there. Perhaps his son! Though she knew him well now, and knew he would welcome a small daughter just as much.

She had been designing some mother and daughter outfits, and in the back of her mind she had thought to make some for herself! And some maternity dresses as well! She would think of something smart and pretty as well, something she would enjoy wearing, and then make a line of them too!

And as her life went on, she would change her lines with it, and her own experiences would supply ideas for her designs. Designs for life, she thought. Poppea of Greece! Her destiny lay here.

And she lay back happily, when her husband bent over her. His body glowed golden, her hand caressed his hair, he gave her little hot kisses on the shoulders and cheeks, before settling on her.

She felt his hard masculine flesh touching her softness, and she relaxed and lay passive as he come closer to her. Her hands moved over his broad back, and then began to clutch him as he pressed gently inside her.

Oh, how sweet he was, how good, and understanding. How fortunate she was . . .

And then the thoughts slid away from her, and she could only feel and move and gasp, in growing excitement. Her mind went blank, she moaned in pleasure, and pressed her thighs to his as he came deeper into her. He thrust more and more, and the pressure made the pleasure build in her, until he moved again, sharply, again, and the ecstatic thrills zipped through her body, from head to heels, and centered on her belly.

"Gregorios—Gregorios—I love you so—ohhh, it is so beautiful—" She moaned in his arms, and he responded with passion, making his thrusts longer and deeper.

"My love, my life—my love, my life," he whispered, in a deep voice, and came to her, and responded, and they soared in ecstasy to the heights of mutual desire.

Especially For You from WARNER

___**FORGET-ME-NOT**   (D30-715, $3.50, U.S.A.)
by Jane Louise Roberts   (D30-716, $4.50, Canada)
Unhappy in the civilized cities, Laurel Winfield was born to bloom in the
Alaskan wilds of the wide tundras, along the free-flowing rivers. She was
as beautiful as the land when she met the Koenig brothers and lost her
heart to the strong-willed, green-eyed Thor. But in Alaska violence and
greed underlie the awesome beauty, and Laurel would find danger here as
well as love.

___**GOLDEN LOTUS**
by Janet Louise Roberts   (D81-997, $2.50)
She was reared with delicacy in a Japanese-American family. He was
tough, competitive, direct. Could she love him when he made her feel
more like a prized possession than the woman he needed? Could he ever
make her understand the depth of his love? Their marriage is a passionate
struggle that will revolve itself in either ecstatic triumph or rejection.

To order, use the coupon below. If you prefer to use your
own stationery, please include complete title as well as
book number and price. Allow 4 weeks for delivery.

WARNER BOOKS
P.O. Box 690
New York, N.Y. 10019

Please send me the books I have checked. I enclose a
check or money order (not cash), plus 50¢ per order
and 50¢ per copy to cover postage and handling.*

_____ Please send me your free mail order catalog. (If ordering only the catalog,
include a large self-addressed, stamped
envelope.)

Name _____

Address _____

City _____

State _____ Zip _____

*N.Y. State and California residents add applicable sales tax